THE
TEMPLE
SCROLL

The Old Covenant Meets
the New World Order
in Modern Jerusalem.
Danger and Intrigue Follow
When an Ancient Text
Reveals Plans to Rebuild
the City of God.

THE TEMPLE SCROLL

The Old Covenant Meets
the New World Order
in Modern Jerusalem.
Danger and Intrigue Follow
When an Ancient Text
Reveals Plans to Rebuild
the City of God.

STEPHEN P. ADAMS

MOODY PRESS
CHICAGO

Special thanks are owed to
Howard Stewart and Laurie Mitchell for research assistance,
to Jim and Barb Piwonka, Pastor Jim and Betsy Clevenger,
and Larry and Dawn McNamee for their ongoing help and support,
and to Daniel Adams for technical aid.

All Scripture quotations, unless indicated, are taken from the *New American Standard Bible,* © 1960, 1962, 1963, 1968, 1971, 1972, 1973, 1975, 1977, and 1994 by The Lockman Foundation, La Habra, Calif. Used by permission.

Quotations from the Dead Sea Scrolls appearing at the beginning of each chapter are from *The Dead Sea Scrolls in English,* by G. Vermes (Penguin Books 1962, Third Edition 1987). Copyright © G. Vermes, 1962, 1965, 1968, 1975, 1987. Reproduced by permission of Penguin Books, Ltd.

ISBN: 0-8024-3207-8

1 3 5 7 9 10 8 6 4 2
Printed in the United States of America

But in the mysteries of His understanding, and in His glorious wisdom, God has ordained an end for falsehood, and at the time of the visitation He will destroy it forever. Then truth, which has wallowed in the ways of wickedness during the dominion of falsehood until the appointed time of judgment, shall arise in the world forever.
—The Community Rule, Col. IV

1

Time becomes an excruciating thing when it's measured out in the ticks of an antique clock upon a marble mantel in a strange house. Alien sounds flit across the threshold of hearing— a wooden creak, an electric hum, a chattering pipe, a muffled cough—and set the nerves on edge, teasing the imagination.

Where are these people? When will they come for me? How do I get out?

I was beginning to detest Dorothea Benson Cray, and I hadn't even had the pleasure yet.

It was a matter of common courtesy. If *I* had asked a biblical scholar from rural western Pennsylvania to fly halfway across the country to confer with me at *my* mansion in Dallas, I would have had more consideration than to leave him cooling his heels in the drawing room for an hour and a half with nothing to do but study the grim-faced portraits of my ancestors and wonder why in the world he had agreed to come here.

But that's what Dorothea Benson Cray had done.

Ordinarily, I didn't pack up and fly to faraway cities just because a woman picked up the phone and called. But when she's phenomenally wealthy and paying the tab—well, I could be flexible. And in this case, her operative—a man named Swanson—

happened to say the magic words "Dead Sea Scrolls." That always got my attention.

Mrs. Cray, he'd said, needed a troubleshooter, and my name had come up. Trouble, as someone once said, is my business.

This, I soon discovered, was *the* Dorothea Benson Cray, a major benefactor to Qumran Scrolls research and heiress of the Benson spark plug fortune. At least, that's what they called it. I understood that most of the family fortune actually was made in the defense industry, manufacturing ignition systems.

That's why I was there. But finally I could stand the waiting no longer. I stuck my head out the door, looking for the little Mexican senorita who had left me in this room to waste more precious remnants of my youth. No Mexicans. There weren't even any short Texans.

So I stole off down the long hall and stopped at the first open door. Inside sat a stern-looking old lady behind a desk the size of a tennis court, speaking into a white Victorian telephone.

This looked like the place. I stepped inside and approached the desk at a respectful distance.

Dorothea Benson Cray was wearing a dark jade dress with a bright green scarf and a gold choker ring. Apart from her stylish attire, she could have passed for Methuselah's maiden aunt. Her blue hair was in tight ringlets like a Greek statue in the art museum, and her glasses were on a pearl chain around her wattled neck. They were the kind of half-glasses that made the wearer peer up at you in a disapproving, raised-eyebrow way.

In fact, that was exactly how Dorothea Benson Cray regarded me just then—as if a dreadful bug had flown into the room.

Just as she was hanging up the phone, a man hurried in behind me and immediately began apologizing.

"I'm sorry, Dr. Harper," he began, "but Mrs. Cray—"

The old lady cut him off. "Never mind, Swanson. I'm finished. You may go."

This apparently was the man who had called me in Pennsylvania earlier in the week. He looked like a young man who had been ridden too hard. He opened his mouth as if to say something else, but Mrs. Cray gestured toward the door, and he skedaddled.

"Now, young man," she said, fastening her lasers upon me. "Just who are you, and what are you doing here?"

I cleared my throat. This was not quite what I'd expected.

"I'm James Harper. Your man Swanson—"

"Never mind him," she snapped. "Just what is it you want?"

"Dead Sea Scrolls," I blurted, groping for the right buttons. "You—"

She was incredulous. "You want *Dead Sea Scrolls?* Young man, I collect Hepplewhite. I collect Hummel. I collect Spoons of the World. I collect tropical butterflies. I collect vintage wines, nineteenth-century cookbooks, American impressionist paintings, and player pianos. But I can assure you I have no Dead Sea Scrolls."

"Please listen, Mrs. Cray—this time without interrupting," I said and watched her stiffen. "I'm C. James Harper from Williamson College in Bellville, Pennsylvania. I am something of an expert in biblical languages, and I had an appointment to see you an hour and forty-five minutes ago."

"Well, then, it's about time," she said tartly. "Why didn't you say so in the first place? These employees of mine are getting more and more forgetful. Have a seat."

I could see she was a hard case. Rather than prolong the farce, I sat mutely in a straight-backed brocade chair facing her desk.

"C. James Harper," she murmured. "What does the 'C' stand for?"

"Charles. But I go by James, Mrs. Cray."

"Oh?" she said rather suspiciously.

"I just never liked being called Chuck," I explained, "especially at the age of thirty-two."

"My late husband was named Charles," she said vaguely. Mrs. Cray straightened. "Well, young man, this is 1996."

I nodded authoritatively. So far, so good.

"That's why I called you here. Do you know what next year is?"

I knew there had to be a trick question. "1997?"

7

She scowled. "The golden anniversary of the Dead Sea Scrolls. Think of it—fifty years since the first ones were found in the caves of Qumran. Already, publishers are coming out with new books. Cities like Stockholm, Vienna, and Rome are planning to host international conferences and symposiums. And television networks are lining up the leading scholars for interviews on upcoming specials."

"They haven't contacted me," I sniffed.

"But *I* have," she said. "And do you know why?"

I was hoping she'd get to that. "No, ma'am. Why?"

"Well, think. What's the one thing that's missing in all of this?"

"I don't know," I admitted.

Mrs. Cray snorted. "A big event. Something new and really big. You follow me?"

I nodded. "Big. Really big."

"Listen. Nigh onto fifty years, and we still don't think we have all the scrolls. I don't mind telling you that I've spent close to the gross national product of some small nations to help underwrite scrolls research in Jerusalem, and nobody's really doing anything to find those other scrolls. Yet everybody seems to think they exist. And the CIA and the so-called intelligence community—well, never mind that. Don't you think somebody ought to do something?"

"They certainly should," I agreed. "But where do I fit into all of this?"

"Listen, Chuck," she said, as I cringed, "I think *you're* the one who should do something about it."

I should have seen it coming, but I didn't, and it hit me like a torpedo amidships.

"Me?" I yelped. "Surely you have the wrong man." I was just a washed-up pastor who'd sought refuge from the hurly-burly of the real world in the ivory tower of academia and biblical scholarship. "My name's not Chuck. It's Jim."

The old lady just looked at me for a moment with those steely eyes, then sighed. She reached into a desk drawer and pulled out a manila file folder.

"Are you the Reverend Dr. C. James Harper who wrote

these?" she said, spreading out half a dozen articles on the desk.

I recognized them. They were some of my articles from various magazines and professional publications, such as the *Journal of Ancient Literature, Trowel & Tel,* and *Judaica Journal.* Although I had published a number of articles in various areas of biblical archaeology, philology, and paleography, these particular monographs all were concerned with my favorite topic—the Scrolls.

"Sure," I said. "I was addressing some pretty obvious misreadings. Anyone who understands the Hebrew and Aramaic from the Late Second Temple period can see how these radical scholars have attempted to twist the meaning of the texts."

"That may be so," said Mrs. Cray, apparently unconvinced. "All I know is what I'm told. But what about your work regarding the book of Esther?"

"Oh. Someone had to speak out. Just because Esther is the only book not found among the Qumran Scrolls doesn't mean it shouldn't be part of Scripture. That's an argument from silence and quite disturbing—especially coming from a member of the Editorial Committee itself. That's Dr. Freemantle, of course. I'm concerned that if one part of the holy canon can be discredited, it casts a cloud upon all of Scripture. I feel I have to defend Esther. If that makes me a craven apologist—well, I'm sorry."

Mrs. Cray was shaking her silvery-blue coiffure. "No, no, young man. Your work is very much appreciated in certain quarters. For the kind of job I'm looking to be done, you seem to be on everybody's short list. You may not be first on the list, but you're acceptable to just about everybody, and I thought you might be available."

"That's where I don't follow you, Mrs. Cray," I objected. "If the job is finding missing scrolls, wouldn't you be better off hiring an adventurer or a private investigator?"

At this, she pulled another manila file folder from a desk drawer. "Is this your CV, Chuck?"

Baffled, I looked at the glorified résumé that academicians call a *curriculum vitae.* Then I understood what she must have had in mind. Working for my Uncle Steve's investigative agency in Detroit for those five years had paid a lot of college bills.

"Those were just summer jobs, Mrs. Cray—a lot of gofer work for a college kid."

"Oh, fiddle-dee-dee," Mrs. Cray groused, rooting through her lap drawer until she found a note. "Ah, here it is. Do you consider the Bobby Bingham case 'gofer work'?"

That shut me up. This lady might look ancient, but she was sharp. At least she had gone to the trouble of having someone dig up that old missing person case, one that the police and the FBI had all but forgotten. But I'd refused to give up and finally tracked down the kid in Panama City. I hadn't realized until much later just how much risk I was taking by pursuing sources in the drug community. At the time, I was just focused on the thrill of my first overseas adventure.

"I had a couple of good breaks," I conceded.

"Young man," the old lady continued, "you really must stop selling yourself short. So—then you decided to become a minister?"

I nodded. "I'd really wanted to become a foreign missionary. I always had a gift for languages. But I washed out in my home service. Both churches where I pastored had internal dissension that cost me my job—the usual kinds of disputes over music and money. I suppose there were things I could have done—if I'd been more attentive—to ease the situation. But . . . well . . . I wasn't willing to go through a third round of agony. So I went back to school."

"I understand a great many congregations dine on roast pastor these days," she observed. "Do you see yourself as a quitter?"

I shook my head. "I just realized pastoring probably wasn't my gift. I may not be the kind of people person a pastor has to be."

"But I presume you have found yourself in your current scholarly occupation?"

"It has its moments."

"And you're a bachelor?"

"That's right. So there'd be no awkwardness about a widow and orphans if the assignment turned ugly."

Mrs. Cray ignored that remark and started gathering up her folders. "All right. I believe you'll do."

"Excuse me," I said. "But I'd have to clear this with the college. They kind of frown on professors not showing up for class."

Mrs. Cray made a dismissive wave. "That's a detail. I shall speak to your superiors."

It dawned on me that she probably underwrote part of the Williamson College endowment too.

"But still," I added, "I would need more information. The Middle East is a big place to go looking for ancient scrolls."

She was staring daggers over her glasses again.

"If we knew where they were," she said slowly, as to a child, "we wouldn't have to go looking for them, now would we?" Mrs. Cray decided to cut to the bottom line. "I am prepared to be most generous, young man."

Without reference to a single piece of paper, she proceeded to outline a series of terms—expenses, stipend, finder's bonus, publishing rights, fringes—that proved irresistible. The most enticing fringe benefit wasn't a sure thing, but if all worked out, she had reason to believe that the *Journal of Ancient Literature* might be open to a contributing editorship.

"Let me guess," I said. "You're a major benefactor for them too."

Mrs. Cray almost smiled. Instead, she proposed to have me credentialed forthwith as a writer for the *JAL* through her friend Sheldon Hirsch, its flamboyant editor. Along with some letters of introduction from Mrs. Cray herself, that should open most of the doors that needed opening. Beyond that, I would be fairly on my own.

Naturally, I didn't tell her that when it came to a chance to work on a Dead Sea Scrolls project, I'd probably work for free—maybe even pay *her*. I simply agreed to all of the terms and conditions, including signing a paper to release her from any legal liability for my death, dismemberment, and incidental paper cuts.

"Very good, very good," she said, as if she'd just pulled a fast one. "You won't be sorry. Now, other details. You will shortly receive a checkbook for an account in your name at the Tel Aviv branch of UniBank. Here's my card with my phone numbers. Dealers, of course, will expect earnest money. You have my prior authorization to make such disbursements up to ten thousand dollars. Beyond that, call me. All right?"

I nodded.

"When you get to Jerusalem, contact Miss Miriam Boynton. She's administrative assistant to Merrick Starlander, editor-in-chief of the Scrolls Editorial Team. She's a very nice young lady, and I believe you'll find her to be very helpful. Who knows? Maybe you'll even hit it off."

I hoped she hadn't seen me blush.

I will remember you, O Zion, for a blessing; with all my might I love you; your memory is to be blessed forever. Your hope is great, O Zion; peace and your awaited salvation will come. Generation after generation shall dwell in you, and generations of the pious shall be your ornament.
—Apostrophe to Zion (11QPs)

2

Not much had changed in Jerusalem in the three and a half years since I was last there. It did smell better. This, I soon realized, was due to the absence of burning tires that I had associated with the city. But still, that did not mean all was well.

My cab driver, Moishe, who picked me up at Ben Gurion Airport, gave me an earful as soon as he learned I was going to the Old City. Despite the formal peace process, Jewish and Arab mothers continued to bury their sons from internecine violence. In an accent suggesting a Russian heritage, Moishe blamed religion generically.

"Have you heard about the new quarrel over the Temple Mount?" he asked.

I pleaded ignorance.

"There have been some clashes," Moishe continued, "at the Western Wall with Arabs accusing the Hasidim of poking around on the Mount. Somebody, they said, was digging between the Dome of the Rock and the Al Aksa Mosque."

I recalled that several years ago an ultraorthodox group attempted to lay a cornerstone for a new temple on the Mount and had been rebuffed by Israeli authorities, fearful of sparking a larger conflict. And several years before that, a number of Arabs had died in fighting with police over the same group's attempt to pray on the Mount.

We fell silent as we entered the Arab Quarter. The majestic golden orb of the famous Dome of the Rock loomed in the distance to the southeast. I was trying to picture in its place the grandeur of the biblical temple—of Solomon and then Herod—when Moishe spoke again.

"Are you a Christian?"

"Yes."

"If I were a Christian . . ." Moishe began, then faltered.

"Yes?"

"I would look into the inscriptions inside the Dome of the Rock."

"Oh? Why is that? What do they say?"

He shrugged noncommittally. "I have heard things—not good things."

That was the last I ever saw of Moishe. I gave him a good tip and a copy of the gospel of John in Hebrew.

He had given me words to ponder.

From my hotel—the elegant, if slightly frayed-at-the-edges Belvoir—it was only a ten-minute walk to the Rockefeller Museum on Suleiman Street. Although I had never been inside, I recognized the sprawling museum complex by its dun-colored limestone walls, arched porticoes, and octagonal tower.

Here was the "Scrollery," the nerve center of Dead Sea Scrolls research. Here was the site of the world's largest—and oldest—jigsaw puzzle. Hundreds of ancient scraps of Late Second Temple Hebrew writing lay pieced together under glass. Here I would find the walking legends of Scrolls research—and that helpful young lady Miriam Boynton.

I gave my name to the uniformed attendant at the front desk. It appeared that I was expected. I was directed upstairs to the administrative assistant's office, where I had just enough time to get comfortable with the *Jerusalem Post* before my name was called.

In retrospect, it would be accurate to say I was a bit unprepared for this moment. When it came to Miriam Boynton, it was like Solomon's wealth and wisdom—the half had not been told. She had it all—looks, poise, intelligence, nice clothes. From her perfect teeth to her auburn-brown page boy to her bright blue eyes, the effect was breathtaking.

Not that I was really affected by that sort of thing. My voice often cracks like a fourteen-year-old boy's. And it's not unusual for me to nearly forget my own name. It's just more embarrassing to do so when you have a "Th.D." after it.

But I coughed and shook my head and made a reasonable recovery. She knew who I was anyway. I told myself to cool it. She was probably like all the others—either already spoken for or non-Christian. It seemed as if refusing to be unequally yoked was destined to keep me single forever.

"So welcome to the Rockefeller, Dr. Harper," the young woman purred in a rural American accent, turning away from her computer screen. "What can I do for you?"

"Dead Sea Scrolls," I blurted with my tangled tongue. For a moment it was as if I were back in Mrs. Cray's office, fumbling for words.

"Yes," she said smoothly. "You've come to the right place. Would you like those for here, or shall I wrap them to go?"

I stopped dead in disbelief. Then we were both laughing.

"I don't know what Mrs. Cray may have told you," I said, "but I need to see about making some appointments with members of the Editorial Committee for some brief interviews."

"Yes, we were told you were coming but nothing about the nature of your business."

"Well," I said, weighing my words, "I'm here officially for a fiftieth-anniversary story for the *Journal of Ancient Literature* on the state of the entire Scrolls project."

Miriam Boynton raised her shapely eyebrows. "Officially?"

"You don't miss much," I said, glancing at my watch. "Uh . . . look . . . what are you doing for lunch?"

"It's a little early . . ." she began uncertainly.

Then I saw her expression cloud over as her eyes focused on something behind me.

Her voice dropped to little more than a whisper. "Don't look now, but here comes Zeev Nahat."

I recognized the name as a member of the Editorial Team, second generation. "What's wrong with that?"

"He's like glue. You can't get rid of him."

I felt like a conspirator. "You *want* to get rid of him? Let me take care of that."

Apprehension flitted across her face as I stood up. She probably wondered if I intended some rough stuff.

But I didn't. I simply nodded at the tall, wiry Israeli in passing and headed for the lobby. Finding a public phone, I punched in the number that I had found on Miriam Boynton's business card.

"Miriam Boynton," said a sweet voice after one ring.

"Hi, Miriam. This is Jim Harper, out in the lobby. But you can pretend I'm someone else—your boyfriend, your boss, whatever it takes to shake this Zeev guy. This is a rescue call."

There was only a moment's pause. "Oh. Yes, sir. You'll have it right away, Dr. Starlander. No problem. Good-bye."

I secretly rejoiced that she had invoked her boss rather than a boyfriend. Maybe she *wasn't* spoken for. I waited until I saw the Israeli leaving before I went back inside.

She looked at me with amusement and something else I couldn't quite read. "My hero."

"Does that merit lunch?"

She laughed. "You don't know the half of it. That merits lunch, dinner, a movie—you name it. Come on, let's get out of here before he comes back."

She suggested a little French place only a few blocks away, off the Jericho Road. It had all the charm it needed—right across the table from me. I guess the food was fine, but I hardly noticed. My mind was elsewhere, hanging on Miriam Boynton's every word and just trying to keep my lunch out of my lap.

"If your official reason for being here is the anniversary story," she said, picking up right where she'd left off, "what is your unofficial reason?"

I had few qualms about answering her question. To Miriam Boynton, I might have confessed state secrets, if I had any. But I also instinctively trusted her—and knew that she would probably figure it out sooner or later anyway.

"The so-called missing scrolls. I'm supposed to find them—or at least go look for them."

A cryptic expression visited her face briefly.

"You are either very brave or very naive," she said grimly.

"I've never been accused of being brave. Let's talk about naive. Is there something you know that I don't?"

She looked away. She had stopped eating.

Finally she spoke. "Let's just say you're not the first person to try such a thing—and leave it there."

I didn't like the sound of that. But as much as I wanted to know what had happened to these others before me, something told me not to press her. She seemed to be withdrawing. I filed it away for future reference and decided to change the subject to something lighter.

"Where are you from, and how did you end up here?"

Her expression brightened.

"Well, I'm from Fort Worth originally, but my family moved to Oregon when I was in fourth grade, and I pretty much grew up there. I graduated from Seattle Pacific University with a major in business administration, intending to go on for an M.B.A. But in my senior year I ended up doing an internship here at the museum. It turned out that my predecessor was retiring, and on a whim I applied. Amazingly, they held the job for me until I graduated. I've been here five years. I love the institution and the city and the country, and I'll probably stay here to collect my gold watch—or whatever they give retiring old maids."

I smiled. "Your turn. Ask me something."

I was still digesting the information I had just received. It explained the faint Lone Star brogue I had detected in her speech. Her background also suggested she was a believer. And again, no mention of an attachment. This was getting better all the time.

"Are you married or attached to anyone?" she asked with a mischievous expression.

It took me a second to get my breath back. She was certainly direct. "I don't think so," I managed.

She laughed lightly. "You get used to bluntness around here. Is this your first visit to Jerusalem?"

"Third. Both were very brief tourist visits while I was in the neighborhood for a couple of six-week stints at archaeological digs."

She brightened again. "Oh? Which ones?"

"Hazor and Petra."

"Wow. That's covering the territory—from Dan to Beersheba. Didn't they film one of the Indiana Jones movies at Petra?"

My heart began to pound as I sensed an opportunity. "That's right. The third one, I believe. Speaking of movies—"

In the hope of initiating something, I was about to remind her of her remark about lunch, dinner, and a movie, when her head snapped around and I lost her attention. Then I saw why.

A familiar figure cruised into sight across the room. He was a tall, wiry fellow, with an almost military bearing—clean shaven, with close-cropped, prematurely gray hair. Or maybe he was older than he looked.

Zeev Nahat.

"Oh, no," Miriam said under her breath as he moved our way.

"He certainly seems to have your number," I observed. "What's his problem?"

"I don't want to know. Maybe he needs a girlfriend, and I wish he would find one."

Nahat approached our table wearing an expression of surprise. "Well, well, Miriam. Imagine running into you here. Mind if I join you, or would I be intruding?"

Miriam gathered her purse and gave him a cool look. "I'm afraid we were just leaving."

"That's too bad," said Nahat, glancing my way.

We both stood up. I was chafing from my spoiled opportunity but curious nonetheless.

Grudgingly, Miriam began to introduce us. "Colonel Nahat, this is Dr. C. James Harper—"

"Oh, yes," he interrupted, taking my hand. "Is this the fellow from the *Journal of Ancient Literature*?"

18

"That's right," I said. "Call me Jim."

I had the feeling that Miriam was itching to leave.

"I was planning to call you," she said. "Dr. Harper wants to interview team members. If you're free tomorrow morning . . ."

"Absolutely. I'll be free all morning. No need to make an appointment. Just stop by whenever you're ready."

We left the restaurant in silence.

Once outside and comfortably away from Zeev Nahat, Miriam seemed to cheer up. "Your appointment with Dr. Starlander is not until three," she said. "Would you like to see a movie?"

Trying not to appear too eager, I agreed, silently exulting in my male prowess.

The movie was a documentary about the Dead Sea Scrolls. It was playing at the Shrine of the Book at the Israel Museum on West Jerusalem's Givat Ram. I went there alone and feeling silly. Miriam Boynton hadn't been suggesting a date. She was just being helpful, while I was pole-vaulting to conclusions.

So much for male prowess.

First, I paid homage to the Scrolls. There were the famous Isaiah Scroll and the granddaddy of them all, the twenty-seven-foot-long Temple Scroll, sequestered behind glass in their hermetically maintained, temperature-controlled, low-humidity environment, where the lights were turned on for only fifty seconds at a time.

There was a fragile precision about this graceful, mystical script, yet something very human. Closer inspection revealed occasional corrections and insertions in neat emendations between the lines and up the margins.

The movie was predictable. Some Oxford-sounding chap narrated in a deep, rumbling voice.

"Here, along the wind-swept, marly cliffs of Wadi Qumran, one can almost hear the echoes of the words of God as written by the desert prophets of old. This was the Judean wilderness, where some say Jesus Christ was tempted by the devil and where inhabitants of Jerusalem from time to time sought refuge in its myriad caves—from King David on the run from Absalom to the

19

Maccabean Jews fleeing imperial Rome on the rampage."

The camera panned back around, looking down on the skeletal stone ruins of Khirbet Qumran from a majestic aerial vantage. Off in the distance, across the Great Rift Valley, appeared the lowest spot on earth, the briny waters of the Dead Sea, 1,300 feet below sea level and another 1,000 feet to the bottom.

"Was this a military fortress or a pleasure villa for wealthy travelers along a trade route, as some suggest? Or, as the majority believe, was this a kind of monastery for the Essenes, those mysterious sectarians who are said to have penned the documents that the world now knows as the Dead Sea Scrolls?"

A new angle inadvertently revealed the ground-racing shadow and whirling rotor of the cinematographer's helicopter. So much for *cinema verité*. Then came the talking heads.

One told the story of the Bedouin shepherd's 1947 search for a lost goat that led to the discovery of the caves that held terra cotta jars containing biblical manuscripts older than any other biblical texts by almost a thousand years. Then came the familiar story of the penny-ante intrigues as money and scrolls repeatedly changed hands, followed by the endless speculations about who those Essene scribes really were.

Another talker explained the complex process of modern dating and preservation techniques. I suppressed a yawn.

And finally, the narrator hinted almost rhetorically that perhaps the last ancient scroll had not been found. More scrolls in hidden chambers could await discovery, he suggested, through modern high-tech electromagnetic scanning and imaging techniques. This was something I intended to check out.

And then I sat up straight. Here was, for a change, something new: In recent years, said the talking head, two men had met their deaths in tragic falls from the Qumran cliffs while attempting to probe the caves for additional scrolls. I didn't know why that fact clung to me, nagging like an old wound. I was not particularly apprehensive that this could happen to me.

I sat there for long moments after the lights of the little theater came back up and the place began to empty. I wondered what this impression was. There seemed to be a connection I had failed to make. It was maddening. The harder I tried to put my finger on it, the more elusive it became.

But now it was almost 2:30, and I had an appointment back at the Rockefeller with Dr. Starlander at 3:00. I would have to hustle.

Clay and dust that I am, what can I devise unless Thou wish it, and what contrive unless Thou desire it? What strength shall I have unless Thou keep me upright, and how shall I understand unless by (the spirit) which Thou hast shaped for me?
—Thanksgiving Hymn, 1QH x, 5–7

3

Dr. Merrick Starlander looked older and frailer than his pictures. He also seemed a tad frowsy in the manner of the aged British pundit in rumpled tweeds who has transcended his generation—or thinks he has. Behind his dark-framed glasses lurked eyes that were red-rimmed and world-weary. I had to remind myself that, as a member of the original Editorial Team, Starlander had to be in his seventies.

The slack hand he offered was about as warm and inviting as road kill. He was also a shade less charming than one might have expected under the circumstances.

"So," he said in a voice like a smirk after withdrawing his hand, "you are the Dr. Harper of Esther fame, I presume?"

"If you want to put it that way," I confessed.

"I am somewhat familiar with your . . . uh . . . work. And so now you're here in some capacity for Sheldon Hirsch's . . . uh . . . publication?"

I gathered that the *Journal of Ancient Literature* did not quite measure up to his standards.

I smiled. "Why, yes. It's about the Dead Sea Scrolls."

"Then, do I take it that Mr. Hirsch is planning another exposé of the academic scandal of the century?"

"Not exactly, Dr. Starlander. This is for a curtain-raiser kind of story looking forward to next year's golden anniversary. Besides, the *JAL* has become supportive, if not outright congratulatory, about the final publication schedule and the forthcoming release of the full record."

Starlander snorted. "The *Israeli* publication schedule, you should say. But, of course, we shall do our level best. Now, what is it exactly that you want from me, Dr. Harper? I am afraid I have nothing to offer regarding your . . . uh . . . gospel of Esther."

He was still trying to get under my skin, but I was not about to give him the pleasure. I placed my pint-sized tape recorder on his desk.

"As I explained to Miss Boynton, the *JAL* wants to give its readers the big picture of what's happened in nearly fifty years of Scrolls research. Why is it relevant to people living on the edge of the twenty-first century? What new things have been learned, and what are the implications for Judaism and Christianity? Is that fair enough?"

Starlander sighed, glanced at his watch, and nodded.

I hit the button on my machine and sat back. "Now, Dr. Starlander, why don't we start by addressing the so-called deception controversy up front?"

"By which you mean . . ."

"By which certain critics, radical scholars, and some writers mean the decades of delay in the release of the full record of the Qumran Scrolls for public view. In other words, has there been a deliberate attempt—even a conspiracy—to suppress certain texts in order to protect one interest or another, such as—"

"Yes, yes. Such as Judaism, Christianity, the Catholic Church. All that rot. My good man, do we have to dignify these things all over again?"

I was ready for that. "Your very silence has led many people to think that maybe there's something to these allegations; otherwise, they'd be refuted instantly. Isn't it your position, for example, that the entire record of the Scrolls *is* available for public inspection?"

Starlander pursed his lips and rubbed his hands nervously. "Yes. Has been for several years. We didn't plan it that way, but after those bootlegged editions were fabricated from the concordances, and the repositories decided to let any and all scholars view the photographic plates, there was no way to put the genie back in the bottle. Anyone can go view them—even you."

"Is that bad?"

"Well," he said somewhat reproachfully, "just look at what's come of it! We have academic four-flushers making their own translations, twisting the texts to suggest that the Essenes were the original Christians and that Jesus, Peter, and Paul were Larry, Curly, and Moe in some kind of convoluted rigmarole to trick Rome. Now, really! You actually think we're better off now?"

His righteous indignation was impressive, but I had a problem with his logic. "Wasn't this sort of thing bound to happen sooner or later anyway, once the texts became available?"

Starlander's eyes flashed. "That's exactly where you're wrong. If an orderly process had been followed, the correct interpretations and commentaries would have come out first, and then these fraudulent versions would have had no leg upon which to stand."

"But doesn't that get back to the extended delays in publication by the Committee itself? Naturally, people would begin to complain of suppression. Is it reasonable to have to wait four or five *decades* to find out what the world's arguably most significant documents say?"

Starlander sat up straighter in his chair. "But don't you see? Their importance is all the more reason to proceed with caution and deliberation. Some of these men—certainly the original members of the Committee—have invested a lifetime in this work. Should the rug just be pulled out from under them by turning their life's work over to others?"

I could have questioned his priorities, but I decided to move on. "Then, you're saying there are no texts being suppressed that would be harmful to the church if released?"

Starlander smiled faintly. "It's all hanging out there for all to see—anyone who can read the original language. I would submit, just looking at the Committee scholars themselves, that the charges are false on the face of it."

"What do you mean?"

He waved an impatient hand. "We're not all of the same mind at all. Far from it. Take your friend Elliot Freemantle. He's gone off in all kinds of directions that give some of us dyspepsia. I believe he's actively *looking* for things to challenge the fundamental doctrines of Judaism and Christianity. But you ought to talk to him about that, once he returns from the West Bank."

There he went again. Freemantle was the chief scholar promoting the idea that Esther—the only Old Testament book not found at Qumran—was a skeleton in the closet of biblical inerrancy. Starlander certainly seemed to enjoy baiting me.

"OK," I said agreeably. "Moving from the conspiracy theories, what have we learned from the Scrolls?"

Starlander's eyes grew distant. "We now have proof that the Old Testament books have come down to us with incredible reliability. It's a strong testimony to the rigorous discipline of the scribal system. The variances in words and phrases are hardly worth discussing—they're often nothing more than differences in spelling. At the same time, no evidence has been found to support some of the notions of the radical schools of criticism."

"Such as . . ."

"Well, such as the idea that originally there was a first, second, and third Isaiah, written centuries apart, that were later sewn together into the quilt we now call the book of Isaiah. Isaiah was one of the books found at Qumran in its entirety, and guess what? Isaiah today is virtually identical to the Isaiah of two thousand years ago. The higher critics are going to have to keep looking for some other nonmiraculous way to account for things like the prophet's amazing prediction of the coming King Cyrus of Persia by name."

"What else have we learned? What about the nonbiblical texts?"

Starlander scowled. "Virtually all of those have raised more questions than answers. That's what most of the debate is about—bits and pieces that lead people to speculate all sorts of things, even to the point of a different Jesus than we have in the gospels. Unfortunately, I'm certain that all the average person ever hears will be whatever sensational twaddle the media choose to report."

"So you don't have much faith in the so-called free market-place of ideas?"

"How free can it be when only the bizarre and sensational is reported? I prefer that people would pay careful attention to the Committee's final, official commentaries when they are issued. All of the redactors are under a deadline to complete their work by the end of 1997."

"What about the charges of anti-Semitism that have been made from time to time? Is that a media creation?"

"Poppycock!" he sputtered. "That's what it is. Why don't you ask Zeev Nahat and Benjamin Dalitz and their colleagues?"

"That's another frequent complaint. Considering whose sacred documents these were, why has it taken so long to open up the project to participation by Jewish scholars?"

"You have to remember how this all started. These scrolls were found in what was Jordanian-controlled territory. This very institution used to be the Palestine Archaeological Museum, under the authority of the Jordanian Department of Antiquities. When the Jordanians looked for scholarly assistance, they turned to the archaeological schools of the British, French, Germans, and Americans. The Jews were specifically excluded. Then those Western scholars naturally tended to bring only their own students and protégés aboard. You might call that a monopoly, but the fact remains that we have come a long way since those times."

"But prior to the crackdown by the Israel Antiquities Authority, you—"

"Yes, yes. I recognize that I'm the chief target of those charges. But there's a world of difference between anti-Semitism and simply asserting your belief, as I have, that God's promises to Israel have passed to the church because of Israel's apostasy."

"Are you talking about the doctrine of supersessionism?"

"I most certainly am. That's exactly it—the church, which accepted her Messiah, has superseded Israel."

I'd been waiting for this. "Well, Dr. Starlander, there's one thing I'd like to know about this supersessionism business. If we're to transfer all of God's blessings for Israel to the church, what do we do with the curses?"

I wished I had a camera instead of just a tape recorder. Starlander looked thunderstruck.

"Do you have any further questions?" he said testily. "I have a great deal of work to do today to maintain this scholarly monopoly."

I didn't really think he would have an answer. "Yes, Dr. Starlander, one last thing. There has been recent speculation that modern technology may soon reveal previously unknown hiding places for ancient Jewish manuscripts. Do you think there are more Dead Sea Scrolls yet to be found?"

Starlander pushed his chair back and looked as if he was done talking. "Who knows? If you've been getting ideas listening to those rumors about the Temple Scroll, I'd just caution you to watch your step. Those cliffs are pretty treacherous. A couple of treasure hunters found out the hard way, as Miriam Boynton could tell you."

I wanted to pursue that but thought better of it. There were other fish in the sea besides this crawdad.

Starlander was now standing, pushing buttons on his telephone as if I were already gone. Then he was frowning at my tape recorder, forgotten on his desk. "Would you like to turn that thing off, old chap?"

I killed the tape and walked out of the office with a gnawing in my gut. That feeling I had had in the little theater at the Shrine of the Book was back.

But I was also bubbling with more questions than Mrs. Cray had Porsches. Was it just a coincidence that *two* so-called treasure hunters had taken fatal falls from the cliffs of Qumran? Why had Dr. Starlander brought up the Temple Scroll in reference to rumors about undiscovered scrolls? Speaking of the temple, what were Moishe's "inscriptions" inside the Dome of the Rock? And why were supposed Christians such as Dorothea Benson Cray and Dr. Starlander such disagreeable people?

Then there was the most important question of all: What was Miriam Boynton doing tonight?

The answer was right around the corner, literally. A good thing too, because it gave me no time to start thinking about things and possibly chicken out.

At her desk, Miriam turned from her paperwork with that radiant smile. "Everything go well with Dr. Starlander?"

I basked in her expression. "Oh, fine. It was productive and all that, if not entirely cordial. We probably won't be exchanging Christmas cards."

There was that giggle again.

"And the movie over at the Israel Museum was fine too," I added more seriously. "Miriam, I was wondering . . ."

Her eyes were inquisitive. "Yes?"

I took a breath. "What are you doing tonight?"

Her expression turned partly cloudy. "Sorry, Dr. Harper—Jim—but I'm sort of busy tonight."

"OK," I said lightly, puzzled by the deadened tone of her voice and more disappointed than I cared to show. "That's all right. I guess I didn't ask if *you* had attachments."

"Oh, it's not that, it's—maybe some other time, OK?"

"OK," I sighed, trying to look neither too crushed nor too blasé.

It was her turn to look puzzled as I pulled out a notepad and began writing. After a minute I tore off the small page and handed it to her.

"Rain Check," it said at the top. And then there were some choices with little ballot boxes to be ticked off—Breakfast, Lunch, Dinner, Movie, Walk in the Park, Et Cetera.

The sunshine returned to her face. She tucked the paper into her desk drawer.

"Thanks," she said. "I think I'll hang onto this. The 'Et Cetera' sounds particularly interesting."

As I left, she flashed me a grin that gave me goose bumps. I felt as if I were falling off a Qumran cliff. There was no way of telling what might be at the bottom.

If I wasn't going out with a beautiful woman, there was only one thing to do. I shook the dust off my shoes, struck out down the street, and waved my arm at the first cab I saw. I was a desperate man in need of desperate measures.

The cabby, a hard-bitten, middle-aged Arab with a taxi that smelled like a bad cigar, gave me a strange look when I told him my destination—the municipal library. It was the look of a Wild West bartender who's just been asked for a sarsaparilla. But then with a shrug, off he drove.

I sat in the back, watching late-afternoon Jerusalem skid by in deepening shadows, bemused over Miriam Boynton and all other people of the female persuasion.

I wasn't too thrilled with myself either. If it hadn't been for Miriam, I wouldn't have known what I was missing. I would have been perfectly content to muddle on in my normal monklike fashion. Maybe I would have walked the streets, visited a museum, even taken in a concert, without the slightest twinge of loneliness, with no particular awareness of being a lone ranger, an orphan, an irrelevance.

But now it was no good. I was getting in touch with the bad stuff. I was painfully aware of being a lone ranger, an orphan, an irrelevance. I knew what I didn't have, and there was no use pretending. Miriam Boynton had done this to me.

Now there was no going back to a lonely hotel room and reading technical manuals or learned commentaries on ancient manuscripts. I would have to kick out the jambs, stir things up a little. Otherwise, the bad stuff might get in touch with me.

The public library was a modern affair, as were many of the more serviceable public buildings in Jerusalem. I headed for the basement and the newspaper room. I don't know why they always put a pay phone outside these places, but they do. Maybe it has something to do with the transient types who tend to hang out in newspaper rooms.

I consulted the *Jerusalem Post* business card I kept in my wallet and punched in the number. After a minor runaround, I was connected with Jerry Simon. He was a national desk reporter, originally from Brooklyn, who had called me several times in the States for information about American involvement in some of the ancient digs and for a layman's explanation of the research. I couldn't remember how or why he had been put onto me, but we seemed to have rapport. Maybe it was because he was single too.

"Dr. Harper!" chimed the familiar voice with its dense Hudson River twang. "How in the world are you?"

"Just fine, I—"

"Hey, where are you calling from? You're not in Jerusalem, are you?"

"Well, yes, as a matter of fact—"

"Great! Can I take you out to lunch? I owe you one, Doc."

"That's kind of what I'm calling about. I need a favor."

"Sure. You name it."

I related the incidents about the two men who had fallen to their deaths from the Qumran cliffs and asked if he would check the files—aptly called the *morgue*—for the dates. He returned a couple of minutes later and started to read me the stories.

I interrupted. "You don't have to read them. All I need is the dates."

He gave them to me—one in 1993 and the other in 1994—and said he would send the clips to my hotel.

"These guys had to be nuts, climbing around those cliffs like that," he added. "What's got you interested?"

I told him about my fiftieth-anniversary article for the *JAL*, in which I planned to explore the belief that there were more scrolls waiting to be found. I didn't mention my deeper reason—that I just might want to become a little "nuts" myself.

"Anyway," I said, "I'll be here a few weeks on that story. So there will be plenty of time for lunch."

Simon seemed mollified. He told me to stay in touch.

"Oh, by the way," he added quickly. "Did you know Randy Plunkett's in town?"

My stomach quavered. "No, I didn't. Isn't that a violation of some international law?"

"Should be, Sport."

That was a bit of trouble. Plunkett, a cocky freelance writer, was just the kind of sensationalist that Dr. Starlander had been talking about.

"What's he up to?"

Simon sighed. "I'm not sure I want to know. Just ran into him at the post office. Thought you might know something about it."

"No, but thanks for the warning."

*The sons of righteousness shall shine
over all the ends of the earth; they shall
go on shining until all the seasons of
darkness are consumed and, at the season appointed by God, His exalted
greatness shall shine eternally to the
peace, blessing, glory, joy, and long life
of all the sons of light.*
—The War Rule, 1QM

4

We hung up, and I headed for the microfilm room. I looked
up the dates and soon found what I needed. The first victim was an Austrian, the second a Swiss. Both were in their mid-
thirties. I hadn't expected that. My mental profile would have
pegged them as young hotshot Americans who didn't know anything about rocks and cliffs.

I didn't bother to make a photocopy of the stories since
Jerry Simon was sending me a packet of them. I exited the basement three steps at a time and breezed out the formidable brass
doors and onto the rush-hour street. I'm sure I must have had a
plan, but it didn't stay in my head long.

I froze in my tracks as something halfway between a rumble
and a tingle began in my feet and ended in the hair on the back of
my neck. There was an ominous flash of light. Then in shocking
slow motion I saw the building next to the library burst at the
seams. Windows turned opaque, their fractured panes blowing
out like buckshot. With a roar, the shock wave hit me broadside,
and I went down.

I woke up on the sidewalk, coughing. I didn't think I had
been out more than a moment. My head seemed OK, except for a
spinning sensation and a ringing in my ears. But that was swal-

lowed up in the growing warble of the siren of an approaching emergency vehicle. So I must have been unconscious for a good minute or two.

Somewhat unsteadily, I climbed to my feet through an acrid fog that smelled like fire and nitrates. Now that the silence had been broken by the siren, several voices began shouting things in Hebrew.

I feared for any living thing that might have been inside that building. As I drew closer, I saw a warped sign, indicating that it had been some kind of courthouse, possibly municipal. That part of the sign was now illegible. It suddenly registered that I had just witnessed—up close and personally—my first terrorist bombing. Death to Israel and all that. A few seconds later, and it might have been death to Harper.

The first ambulance pulled up at the curb, its revolving light creating an eerie strobe effect on the blackened building through the swirling fog. The smoke was thickest at the main entrance. There had to be a working fire inside. I considered making a dash inside to see if there were any live victims to bring out but quickly scrapped that idea. If I wasn't overcome by smoke, I'd probably be incinerated in a secondary explosion.

Then, incredibly, a figure appeared in the twisted frame of the main doors.

I raced up the steps toward the brave man who had dared precisely what I had feared to do. He carried in his arms something that he was struggling to get through the wrecked doorway. I moved closer.

"Here," he called, spying me. "I have the mother too."

Before I quite knew what was happening, the substantial bundle was transferred into my arms, and he was gone, back into the place of death. I was holding a little girl no older than seven or eight. She was semiconscious, sniffling with a bloody nose.

Quite a crowd had gathered by now. Sirens swelled to a chorus in the distance as more emergency vehicles approached, including the heartier bellow of a fire truck. A camera flash went off half a dozen times as I descended the steps.

I looked at the girl in my arms. Her brownish hair was largely burned away, and her clothes were in tatters. But she was alive. There were no obvious major injuries, but there'd no doubt be some burns. I prayed for her under my breath as paramedics passed me on their way up.

Didn't anybody want the little girl? I carried her to a big white ambulance, where another paramedic eased her onto a stretcher and began shining a light into her eyes. I turned and headed back up the steps.

By the time I got to the top, the big man who'd rescued the girl was struggling out the door again, this time with a full-grown woman slung across his back in the fireman's carry. He eased her off his back into the waiting grasp of the paramedics, then turned to go back inside.

This time I was right behind him. There might be more people, still alive.

A firm hand on my arm pulled me back, and an authoritative voice told me in Hebrew to back off and leave the scene.

My friend the rescuer shook off the paramedic who tried to stop him and plunged into the building. But the rest of the paramedics charged in after him and in another moment had him back out the door.

And then there was a resounding concussion and a belch of smoke from the blown-out windows. I fell off the step I was on and barely recovered my balance on the stair below. I hoped this wasn't a gas explosion, or this blast might not be the end of it.

Initially I'd been outraged at the paramedics for wrestling with the big guy rather than going in to rescue more people. But now—after the twin explosions—it was not likely that there could be any more alive.

I next became aware that the place was crawling with security forces. In Jerusalem I never knew who was police and who was military. I hoped they knew.

Two officers started marching my friend down the steps. It looked for all the world like an arrest. One of them said something in Hebrew about a "filthy Arab."

Without thinking, I blocked their path. In their moment of confusion I gave it my best shot.

"Officers," I said firmly but politely, "my friend Kamlo was helping me get people out of this building before help arrived. I will vouch for this man. He is with me."

It was a straight-up bluff. And I didn't know how the name "Kamlo" came out of my mouth. It must have been something from a book or a movie. But if my friend had any sense, he would play along with it. We could always claim it was a nickname.

"And who are you?" said the older looking of the officers. They both appeared young and just a little anxious.

Now I had to do something I really hated—throw my weight around.

"I'm an American—Dr. C. James Harper. I'm a biblical scholar and researcher working with the Israel Antiquities Authority for the *Journal of Ancient Literature*."

Coolly I whipped out my wallet and flashed my ID to the officer, who squinted briefly at it. This appeared to be working.

"Please unhand my friend," I said. "We will leave."

The officer nodded, and both men let go of "my friend's" arms.

The two of us, walking closely together, beat it out of there. I noticed as we descended the steps that a young woman, probably a reporter, had been writing down every word. I also noticed with a shudder as I put away my wallet that the ID I had flashed was my Williamson College library card. But it is a pretty impressive card.

"This way," said the big man. "I have a car."

I followed him down the street and around the corner to a battered blue Toyota. We got in, and I finally started breathing more easily.

Outside, I had judged this fellow to be about six feet four. Inside the compact car, he looked even bigger. He had a light olive complexion with prominent ears and nose and a mustache. It was a big man's face with craggy forehead and bushy brow, but at the same time it was a kindly face. I guessed it was the relaxed, friendly mouth. I didn't even know him, but I instinctively liked him. These instincts had never steered me wrong.

"I want to thank you for getting me out of that difficulty," he said, after turning the key in the ignition. "Who knows what they might have done with me? I could have been blamed for the bombing if they had no other suspect. When Israeli justice demands payment, woe to the Palestinian bystander!"

He had a look of utter sincerity in his big brown eyes. His English was pretty good.

"Forget it," I said. "You saved the lives of a couple of people. You could have been killed. In fact, you probably would have been if the paramedics hadn't pulled you out."

The man shrugged and put the car into gear.

"And the two you rescued were probably Jews," I added.

"Those things mean nothing to me," the man said, pulling out onto the street. "All flesh is grass, no matter. Where to?"

I gave him directions to the Belvoir.

"What's your name?" I asked after a minute. I was tiring as the adrenaline began to wear off. My head probably wasn't 100 percent yet.

He looked puzzled. "Kamlo, as you said. Kamlo Mattar."

Now it was my turn to be puzzled. The man half turned to me and with one hand tugged at his khaki shirt, the kind worn by gas station attendants, where a word was embroidered with navy blue thread: *Kamlo*.

It's funny how the mind works. I could only guess that I'd seen the name on his shirt during the uproar of the bombing, but it hadn't consciously registered. Only when I needed to pull a rabbit out of my hat did this name suddenly spill out, seemingly from nowhere.

"What do you do in life, Kamlo?" I asked, intrigued by this man. Something told me this might be more than just a chance encounter.

The big man was silent for a moment. "I am unemployed. Every time there is a bombing, the Arabs are put out of work until the city returns to normal. And it will be so again this time."

"But what did you do before you lost your job?"

"I am a security guard. It is good work and bad. Good, because you can work for an agency or, if you choose, be a private contractor and move about on your own. Bad, because either way it is only the Arab merchants who will hire you."

"What are your plans?"

He shrugged again. "I have been thinking about moving to

Jericho and applying for a job with the new Palestinian security forces. After tonight's bombing, it will be bad here again for a while."

"You don't sound too thrilled about this. Is moving what you really want to do?"

"No," he said softly. "You see, Dr. Harper, I am a Druse. That makes me neither fish nor fowl. My heart is with neither side in this Arab-Jew madness."

I tried to recall something about the Druse. "Please excuse my ignorance, but what do the Druse believe?"

Kamlo became visibly uncomfortable. "Please, Dr. Harper, do not think me impolite, but these are things that must not be spoken of. It is not our way."

That, in fact, was precisely what I had forgotten. "That's perfectly all right. I did not mean to intrude."

We fell into an amiable silence as we approached the hotel. I decided to answer an idea that had been knocking at the door.

"Kamlo, how would you like to go to work for me?"

We stopped at the curb somewhat abruptly.

"I? What would you have me to do?"

"I am in search of valuable documents that are missing. The search may involve physical hardships, treacherous heights, and other dangers that I can't even contemplate."

Kamlo was smiling for the first time. It dramatically transformed his face from homely to winsome. "OK. You have told me the benefits. What is the downside?"

"I'm serious, Kamlo. Having seen you in action, I know you're the right man for the job. It's more than I have a right to ask of anybody. And yet I am. Will you work for me?"

The big man's smile faded into utter sobriety. "Work for you? Dr. Harper, after what you did back at the courthouse, I would crawl through hell for you."

I nodded mutely, overwhelmed. Something told me I wouldn't be sorry.

The next morning I tried to get past Miriam Boynton without a lot of chitchat. I had work to do, and I wanted to get on with it. There was a new tape in my machine, just waiting for Zeev

36

Nahat's interview. Besides, I didn't really want to answer questions about the little flesh-colored pressure dressing on my head.

I was not to be so fortunate.

"Good morning, Dr. Harper," she said ever so sweetly. "What's wrong with your forehead?"

My forward motion faltered. She was so pretty, it almost hurt. I touched the small bandage as if wondering how it had gotten there. I was actually stalling.

"Oh, it's nothing—just a little scratch."

I started to walk away, but her eyes held me fast. "How did you do it?"

"I . . . you know, just had a little . . . uh . . . fall."

In fact, it was a kind of nasty cut for its size. But it hadn't been until I got back to my hotel room that I'd even noticed it. One look in the mirror, and I saw the blood. Then it finally started hurting.

Miriam wasn't smiling, but her eyes appeared to dance with secret amusement. "I guess it's not easy being an American hero, huh?"

"What?" Now I knew something was up.

She reached somewhere under her desk, pulled out a newspaper, and unfurled it before my eyes. There I was, pictured on page one of *Ha-Aretz*, one of Israel's leading dailies. I was carrying a little girl out of a burning building. There was a cut on my forehead and a grim expression of selfless courage on my face.

"An American Hero," said the cutline.

I wanted to retch. It identified me precisely as I had identified myself to the cop on the courthouse steps—Dr. C. James Harper, biblical scholar and researcher working with the Israel Antiquities Authority for the *Journal of Ancient Literature*. There was no mention whatever of the Palestinian Druse named Kamlo who had actually risked his neck to save these people. I was certain that was no coincidence. It made me want to call one of the Arab papers and give them the real story.

Miriam's expression was full of mischief.

"Let's see," she said abstractly. "There was Lawrence of Arabia. What should we call you—James of Israel? Nah. Doesn't sound right. How about Jim of Pennsylvania?"

"Oh, stop." I groaned. "Give me a break. This whole thing is just—"

"Just what?"

"Well . . . silly."

"I hardly think that little girl considers it silly. She's alive because of you."

"Look, Miriam. If you haven't heard this before, write it down: 'Don't believe everything you read in the newspaper.' Some day I'll tell you what really happened."

Her long, dark eyelashes were batting at me in a most unsettling manner. "What's wrong with now?"

I decided to get even. "OK. If you must know, it's like this. The whole thing was your fault."

Her eyes grew very wide. "*Moi?*"

"*Oui, vous.* You wouldn't go out with me last night, remember?"

"What's that got to do with it?"

"Well, I was pretty upset, despondent even."

She looked skeptical.

"Yes, I was. So I decided to end it all by throwing myself into a burning building."

I could tell she was laughing, but she tried to make her mouth not show it.

"Uh-huh," she said with a fairly straight face. "So what about the girl?"

"Hey. It wasn't easy, but I finally managed to get a date."

"Oh!" she said with mock outrage. "You're bad."

"See what you're missing?"

Now she was giggling. I liked it when she did that.

"Hold on," she said, rummaging in a desk drawer. She finally found a piece of paper, made a mark on it, and handed it to me.

I recognized it as the facetious checklist I had given her the day before. The box marked "Lunch" had been checked. A cold tingle raced up my spine, followed by a warm rush of joy.

Miriam's merry eyes held me in a long moment of captivity until we both remembered what we were about and got to it.

Whenever Israel rules, there shall not fail to be a descendant of David upon the throne. For the ruler's staff is the Covenant of kingship, and the clans of Israel are the feet, until the Messiah of Righteousness comes, the Branch of David. For to him and to his seed was granted the Covenant of kingship over his people for everlasting generations . . .
—The Blessings of Jacob, 4QPBless

5

I sat in the spartan office of Zeev Nahat, waiting for a few more minutes while he finished some sort of information search on his computer terminal. It gave me time to look around and absorb character clues. An office can reveal much about its tenant.

Merrick Starlander's chamber had been untidy and cluttered, befitting his quirky and disorganized relational style. And that leadership, in turn, was reflected in the meager output of an editorial committee that was roundly criticized for its failure to deliver.

In Zeev Nahat's case, there was nothing in excess—no books, files, or papers out of place, no desktop overflowing with memos, reports, or scholarly journals. There was an almost military order and precision from the carefully arranged pottery shards and other artifacts on bookshelves to the four pieces of hanging artwork on the walls—three of them maps of key archaeological sites.

It fit. The registry that Miriam had given me in the press kit identified him as Col. Zeev Nahat, Retd. But the books and artifacts here suggested that Nahat was not a linguist or philologist or paleographer as were most of the team members. And a closer look at the fourth picture, the one almost behind his door, suggested archaeology. There was, in fact, a sort of tradition of ex-soldiers in Israel exchanging army uniforms and weapons for the khakis and trowel.

The picture was a black-and-white photo portrait of a vaguely familiar bald man with a mustache. The little brass plate at the bottom identified him: the late Yigael Yadin, war hero, deputy prime minister, and Israel's most renowned biblical archaeologist. Yadin had already been dead nearly ten years when I worked briefly at the Hazor dig. But I'd heard plenty about him.

The older Israelis at Hazor liked to talk about Yadin's military exploits. He had headed *Haganah*, Israel's underground army, during the 1948 War of Independence and then was Chief of Staff for Israel Defense Forces afterward. Yadin's military strategies, they said, were based on his knowledge of biblical battles. Once, he led Israeli troops along a two-thousand-year-old road buried under sand dunes to capture a large Egyptian force.

At last Zeev Nahat was ready for me. He apologized for the wait and pumped my hand firmly. His English was flawless with only the slightest accent. I judged him to be about fifty, possibly a very fit fifty-five. He had a rough-hewn face that looked more the part of the football coach or captain of industry than a researcher. It had something to do with the stern mouth and strong nose but especially the fearless, unflinching eyes that seemed to say they could watch you die if they had to.

"How may I help you?" he asked, gesturing toward the seat before his desk. "Even to half the kingdom it shall be done."

Maybe he meant it innocently or facetiously, but I felt myself reddening. The Esther quote was too reminiscent of Starlander's calculated digs.

"If I have found favor in your sight," I rejoined, "I would like to get your observations, as Miriam may have mentioned, for a fiftieth-anniversary prospective in the *Journal of Ancient Literature*. This has nothing to do with Esther, I assure you."

Nahat smiled perfunctorily. "Good. I am afraid I am with Freemantle on the matter of Esther, but for a different reason. I have to go with the record, and there is no evidence that the

40

Essenes observed Purim, though they outdid everyone else when it came to festivals."

I shook my head. "An argument from silence, Colonel Nahat?"

He kept his smile. "Sometimes arguments from silence can be loud. Some things are most conspicuous by their absence."

I let it go. The last thing I wanted to do was to feed into this Esther business.

He had no objection to being tape-recorded, so off we went. It turned out that Nahat's primary focus was the Qumran question and the identity of the mysterious Essenes. I told him I was also interested in the Scroll scholars and their controversial interpretations of the mysterious texts.

"In the beginning," he said, "there were seven members of the work committee—three Catholic priests, three Protestant scholars, and one agnostic—all Gentiles. Today, we have nearly seventy scholars."

I hadn't heard that high a number before. "Seventy?"

"Yes, including only a handful who work here at the Rockefeller. The rest work from photographic plates and reprints in their own offices and institutions wherever they are. But it is a total of seventy scholars from eight nations, including nine women and eleven Israelis, one of whom is an archaeologist. I speak of myself, of course. Perhaps our own diversity is beginning to reflect our subject matter."

"Please explain."

"You ask the significance of the scrolls. One major thing we have learned is that Judaism was less monolithic—more diverse and mystical and messianic—than was previously thought."

"Because of what you have learned about the Essenes or from the writings themselves?"

Nahat folded his hands and looked thoughtful. "Both, actually. Take the Essenes. Partisans for years have been trying to stretch the evidence to connect them with the Sadducees or Pharisees or Zealots or some other known quantity. But some of us are coming around to another idea. Suppose the Essenes were just an ultrapious sect of their day?"

"Like the Hasidic today."

41

"Exactly. In fact, the Aramaic term is *Hasayya,* which may account for the name *Essaioi,* or 'Essene.'"

"And from their writings?"

"We see ultralegalism, especially in the Sabbath, ritual purity, and festivals. Where the books of Moses—the Torah—provide for a few festivals such as First Fruits, the Essenes go on to add many more—like New Wine and New Oil. That's in the Temple Scroll. It is interesting to see how fluid the Hebrew canon was until the Christians came along."

"The Christians?"

"Surely. Once Christianity became a force, there was a great desire among the Jews, especially the priests, to close the canon and call an end to revelation. The Hebrew religion had become too diverse. In fact, the Pharisees closed the book by the end of the first century at the Council of Jamnia. They abandoned a number of writings, including the Apocrypha, that would have been lost entirely except for the Christians who preserved them."

This was enough serious stuff for the article. It was time for my more immediate concerns.

"Do you believe there are more scrolls yet to be found?"

Nahat pursed his lips and appeared to be sizing me up. "You have heard something, perhaps?"

I noted the evasion and responded obliquely. "There have been stories. Dr. Starlander referred to 'Temple Scroll rumors.' What does that mean?"

"Why don't you ask him?"

"I may have overstayed my welcome with Dr. Starlander. That's why I'm asking you. I saw the Temple Scroll yesterday at the Museum. It's been here in Jerusalem for decades. What does that have to do with undiscovered texts?"

Nahat looked askance. "So the readers of *JAL* are now interested in rumors? Interesting. Perhaps you should talk to someone who traffics in those things, like Elliot Freemantle."

"It keeps coming back to Freemantle," I retorted. "So where is he?"

Nahat shrugged. "They say he is doing some exploration in the Judean wilderness. Exactly what, I cannot tell you."

Connections were begging to be made.

"Treasure hunting?" I guessed. "Looking for missing scrolls?"

The colonel, having already given his answer, sat unmoved and unmoving.

I tried again. "Dr. Starlander warned me about the treacherous cliffs of Qumran. He said a couple of treasure hunters had found out the hard way, as Miriam Boynton could tell me. What's that mean?"

Nahat formed a thin smile. "Again, why don't you ask her?"

"It doesn't seem to be something she likes to discuss."

"But you have read the stories about the treasure hunters— the Austrian and the Swiss."

I didn't like the direction this was taking. "What makes you say that?"

The smile put on some weight. "A lucky guess. So you know that the Austrian and the Swiss fell to their deaths while searching for undiscovered scrolls."

I nodded. But I didn't believe his lucky guess. It sounded more like a lucky source. I thought immediately of Jerry Simon. My good friend Jerry. I hoped I was just being paranoid.

But Nahat was speaking again. "Apparently you do not know that Miriam Boynton was engaged to be married to the Swiss?"

I managed to shake my head. Something had kicked me in the gut, hard. I tried to remember how to breathe. Things were getting complicated.

Nahat seemed almost amused by my reaction. "Archaeology teaches that it is essential to have every bit of available information. I find that is helpful in life as well."

I was not amused. I could see how he got on Miriam's nerves. I determined to get this back onto some reasonable footing.

"You never answered me about the Temple Scroll, Colonel Nahat. You can't tell me about that, or you don't want to?"

Nahat surprised me with a change of tune. "Think when the first scrolls were found."

"Nineteen forty-seven?"

"Correct. Immediately prior to Israeli statehood. The Jews naturally would want nothing to do with anything that could alienate their main friend, the Christian nation of America, at a time like that. It was an environment fertile with rumors and stories of almost messianic proportions."

"How is that?"

"Think of it. The first scrolls were obtained for Israel by Yigael Yadin's father, Professor E. L. Sukenik. The Isaiah Scroll, a commentary on Habakkuk, and a sectarian Manual of Discipline. This happened on an otherwise insignificant day, twenty-four hours before the United Nations voted into existence the state of Israel."

My skin bumped up like the Sea of Galilee on a windy day. "It was not until twenty years later," he continued, "that Israel acquired the Temple Scroll. But it was under similarly dramatic circumstances. On June 7, 1967, during the Six-Day War, Israel Defense Forces captured the Old City. On June 8—the day Israeli forces united East and West Jerusalem—Yigael Yadin, military adviser to the prime minister, held the Temple Scroll in his hands. Intriguing?"

I nodded mutely.

Nahat held up a finger. "But this time there was a difference. This national treasure was actually recovered from the home of a Syrian cobbler who'd kept it hidden in a shoe box under some floor tiles in his home in Bethlehem. It was supposedly found in Cave Eleven at Qumran, but there have been some natural questions about its actual pedigree. That's one story. In any case, that's the last scroll ever recovered. No doubt that has something to do with the strong-arm tactics used on the Arab cobbler. Since then the antiquities market for ancient documents has been as dry as a Judean wadi."

I was intrigued by a nuance in Nahat's account. "You said 'one story.' Is there another?"

Nahat frowned.

I sensed he was done talking.

"Yadin has written all about this," he said tersely. "Check it out for yourself."

"I shall," I declared, getting up to leave. "Care to give me a clue?"

The colonel appeared to soften. "Let me just say that there may be reason to believe there *could* be a more ancient document more properly deserving of the name 'Temple Scroll' that has yet to be found. But whatever you do, remember Dr. Starlander's advice. Those cliffs can be deadly."

I gave him a wink before leaving his office. "I'll leave the worrying to Dr. Starlander," I said. "As for me, if I perish, I perish."

Back in the outer sanctum, Miriam looked at me with those eyes. "Can you stand one more interview before lunch?"

I looked at my watch. It was barely ten o'clock. "Why not? You have another live one?"

She nodded. "Are you familiar with Mme Catherine Lacuneau?"

"Are you kidding? *The* Catherine Lacuneau? As in 'the Gospel According to St. Catherine'?"

"Be nice," Miriam chided good-humoredly. "She may be batty, but she's the hottest interview we've got. Everybody wants to talk to Mme Catherine. For your information, Dr. Harper, Catherine Lacuneau was part of that last wave brought in to expedite the work. But if you don't want to talk to her—"

"Uh—how soon can she see me?"

"How does eleven o'clock sound?"

"What's wrong with right now?"

Miriam gave me a professional smile. "Well, we didn't originally expect her at the Rockefeller today. Right now she's doing another . . . uh . . . interview."

"With whom?"

"A gentleman by the name of Randall Plunkett for *Ground Zero* magazine."

My stomach did a triple gainer. "Tabloid Randy! Oh, that's terrific. What is this for—the secret lives of consenting scroll redactors?"

"Well, since you mention it, there's something else you probably should know."

45

"What's that?"

She hesitated just slightly. "Mme Catherine and Elliot Freemantle are sort of an item these days."

I thought that one over a moment. "Hmm. That would fit, come to think of it. Maybe she knows how I can reach Freemantle."

"If she does, she's the only one. People are starting to get a little concerned."

That caught my attention. "Why? Has he been out in the field too long?"

"He's missed some appointments—hasn't called in or anything. No one knows how to reach him. It's not like him at all."

"I see. Maybe that has something to do with Mme Catherine's being here today."

Miriam nodded. "Do you have something you can do between now and eleven?"

"Let's see. What would Jim of Pennsylvania do? Leap a tall building in a single bound? No, I did that last night. I think I'll go bend some steel with my bare hands."

Actually I went into the men's lounge and took a nap on the couch. The strategic catnap is one of the secret weapons in my arsenal.

I will dwell with them forever and ever and will sanctify my sanctuary by my glory. I will cause my glory to rest on it until the day of creation on which I shall create my sanctuary, establishing it for myself for all the time according to the covenant which I have made with Jacob in Bethel.
—The Temple Scroll (11QT), XXIX

6

I had never met Randall Plunkett, nor had I ever had any such desire. I knew as much as I needed to know.

Tabloid Randy had cut his teeth as a freelance *papparazzo* of the written word for several of the more lurid British rags that pandered to appetites for sex, violence, and the domestic contretemps of the royal family. From there he became somewhat of a media celebrity, eventually doing daytime talk shows on radio and TV.

Several years ago Plunkett published a book called *The Qumran Cover-Up*, promoting various conspiracy theories behind the alleged suppression of the unpublished Qumran texts. One chapter was devoted to the Allegro theory, named after an early member of the international Scrolls team who actually asserted that Jesus was a mythical character and that the visions of the prophets were largely due to their ingestion of a psychedelic drug. That was bad enough. But I stopped reading when I got to the chapter that dealt with the theory of Qumran's being an ancient landing site for truth-imparting aliens.

I think that was the only book I've ever thrown in the trash—an option unavailable in the case of trashy authors themselves.

I was not a reader of *Ground Zero* magazine, but I knew of

its reputation as a chic glossy with pretensions to biting social commentary from a countercultural perspective. Considering the new Scrolls controversies that had emerged in just the past two or three years, I shuddered at the thought of what Tabloid Randy could do with those.

It turned out that Plunkett's interview with Mme Catherine had run over a bit, and I was forced to cool my heels for a few minutes in the hall outside.

At last, the conference room door opened.

But then I had to wait while a photographer buzzed through a roll of shots of Plunkett and Lacuneau in candid repose. I felt somewhat chastened. Where was *my* photographer for capturing these historic moments with Mme Catherine?

From the doorway, Catherine Lacuneau did not look like a woman consumed with worry over her lover. She looked every bit the brilliant and beautiful academician that she was reputed to be. She had such a stratospheric IQ that she wrote a monthly column in some major magazine on how to be smarter, like herself. She was handsome in an over-forty way, with upswept gray-streaked black hair, keen blue eyes, China doll complexion, and magnetic smile.

All I could remember about her work was that she was in the business of debunking the international team's consensus view about the Qumranians and their scrolls and was posing counter-explanations. Exactly what, I wasn't sure. I had long given up on the conspiracy theorists—ever since Plunkett's ill-conceived book. But it appeared her appointment to the Editorial Committee had been politically motivated to appease the international clamor for full disclosure.

When the picture taking was done, Plunkett met me in the hall, looking as if he thought he knew me. Randy Plunkett was a lanky-boned fellow with longish, dishwater-blond hair, tortoise-shell aviator glasses, and possibly the most self-confident expression I had ever seen.

"Jim Harper," I said with the obligatory handshake.

"Of course," Plunkett said, as if he'd known all along. "The Esther chappie. Awfully nice and all that. Well, I've got the old girl all warmed up for you. It should be interesting."

"Interesting?" I asked.

"Well, you know, to compare the different approaches. My story, of course, will deal with the more radical new developments, while yours, I must assume, will attempt to support the traditional establishment view."

I was irritated just enough to say, "What did you say your name was?"

He gave me a deadly look and grumbled, "Randall Plunkett, chappie. See you around."

And then he was gone.

Mme Catherine was much more civil. There was even a pot of tea for us at the conference table.

I was a bit more gracious myself. I didn't hit her up immediately on Freemantle. I explained my ostensible mission for *JAL*, set up the tape recorder, and asked her to give me the scoop on the anticonsensus view.

She had the kind of elegance that shone through drab garb, a plain brown dress almost like an institutional uniform, with no jewelry or makeup. Her eyes glimmered as she warmed to her subject.

"I like to think of this approach as the Radio Free Europe version of Scroll scholarship," she asserted, "as opposed to the prevailing Kremlin-style imposed orthodoxy."

I didn't want her unloading a canned spiel on me, so I stopped her. "Then, do you see yourself as a sort of Joan of Arc of academic freedom here?"

Mme Catherine smiled demurely. "Not at all. I am certainly not the first dissident. I merely stand on the shoulders of giants who have risked academic disrepute to challenge the religious establishment."

"And where has all this original thinking brought us?"

"We are better able to understand the genesis of the early church and its relationship to the Essenes."

"Didn't the early dissenters think they had found something like the true origin of a mythical Jesus Christ?"

"Yes. They saw striking messianic resemblances in the leader of the Qumran community—the Teacher of Righteousness.

49

And so they came to see Jesus Christ as just a romantic embellishment of an earlier tradition."

"What kind of resemblances?" I pressed.

"Well, there were obvious parallels. The Teacher preached righteousness and humility. He opposed the teachers of the law and the corrupt temple practices. And he was persecuted by the Gentiles at the instigation of a wicked priest."

"OK," I countered, "but one could argue that the differences are even more obvious. The Essenes were ultralegalists; Jesus was called a lawbreaker. The Essenes were a closed society of ascetics and celibates, shunning women. Jesus sought out sinners, outcasts, lepers. Some of His closest followers were women. And the list goes on."

"That may be," Mme Catherine conceded. "The point is that the dissenters eventually abandoned that view in light of better arguments."

Now it was coming back to me. "Oh, do you mean where Jesus and Paul become the enemies of the Essenes—the Man of Lies and the Wicked Priest?"

Mme Catherine flinched. Put that bluntly, it was not so easy a position to endorse.

"It is much more than that," she sniffed. "There is good evidence of a schism between the followers of Jesus and those of John the Baptist, who may have been the actual Teacher of Righteousness."

"John, as leader of the Essenes? What kind of evidence is there for a schism?"

"According to a symbolic reading of the gospels, the tearing open of the heavens at Jesus' baptism indicates a split between the factions of the Essenes and the Christians."

"But a *plain* reading of the gospels," I objected, "says John rejoiced as if he were the best man and Christ were the bridegroom. How do you justify a symbolic reading?"

She was still unruffled. "Much of Scripture contains two levels of meaning—a literal meaning for the masses and an allegorical meaning, which can be discovered by certain techniques."

"I've read a little about this approach," I volunteered. "I get the impression that it's reserved for passages involving anything

50

miraculous or supernatural. Almost as a way of debunking the Bible. Would that be fair to say?"

Mme Catherine was beginning to look uneasy. "Not quite. But, yes, it does help to explain some of these miraculous things that were never intended to be taken literally."

"Well, then, how do you explain the problem with the radiocarbon and paleographic dating? The physical evidence indicates that much of the Qumran material was not written during Christ's lifetime but a century or two before."

She started to say something about the unreliability of those procedures, then faltered. She excused herself, got up from the table, and walked to the window, facing away from me. When Mme Catherine returned a long minute later, her eyes were red-rimmed. The savoir faire was gone. She asked me to turn off the tape recorder.

"You must excuse me, Dr. Harper," she said at last. "I am not myself today. When it comes to physical evidence, that is not my field. Normally, I would suggest you speak to Dr. Freemantle, but—"

She seemed incapable of continuing, so I finished it for her. "But nobody seems to know where he is?"

Mme Catherine nodded. "He kept talking as if he were on the verge of some breakthrough that he said would revolutionize Qumran studies. Then I . . . lost touch with him. It was very sudden. I am—I am quite concerned about him."

"When was the last time you talked to him?"

"Wednesday the fourteenth, eight days ago."

"How unusual is that? How often do you usually talk?"

Her voice was unsteady, and her eyes dropped when she spoke. "Every day."

"I see. Have you talked to the police?"

"Yes. They say they will look into it, but I am not sure how hard."

Then another thought struck me. "Did you discuss any of this with Randy Plunkett?"

Doubt and uncertainty crossed her face, now so transparent without the smiling mask. "Some. Does it matter?"

"I'm not sure," I admitted. "How much did you discuss it?"

"Quite a bit. He asked many questions."

"What did you tell him?"

"No more than I told you."

"Enough to know that Elliot Freemantle is missing and that he might be on the verge of a major discovery?"

She nodded miserably. "Did I do the wrong thing?"

"Not if you wanted to carpet the globe with reports that Dr. Freemantle had been abducted by aliens along with the amazing secrets of the Dead Sea Scrolls."

She cringed. "But I did not give him the papers."

"What papers?"

"Elliot's work papers. Mr. Plunkett has asked both me and Dr. Starlander to see them, and we have refused."

Now that was something. "What might be in these papers? Have you seen them?"

Mme Catherine shook her head. "I have access to them because we have worked together, but I have not read them."

"Then I suggest it's time you do so. We need to have all the facts."

"'We'?" she echoed, catching the nuance. "Will you help me?"

I nodded. "If I can."

"Do you want to read the work papers?"

I was starting to have trouble keeping up. "Why don't you read them first and then let me see them? You don't have a problem with giving them to me?"

She shook her head. "No. You, I trust. Why, I am not certain. You are a minister, are you not?"

I got up from the table. "I once was, if that's of comfort to you. Then may I give you some pastoral advice?"

She looked at me with question-mark eyes, then nodded.

"This would be a good time for you to start believing in miracles."

I left Mme Catherine, one sizable hunch forming in the back of my mind. I didn't believe Elliot Freemantle's disappearance had anything to do with radical new theories. I believed it had something to do with the fabled missing scrolls.

We went to lunch at that little French place off the Jericho Road. This time I concentrated on keeping my wits in the same room with me. The last time, it had seemed more as if my brain had gone to lunch.

"How come you didn't tell me about Tabloid Randy?" I asked with my usual tact.

"Who?" said Miriam, in between tentative nibbles at her steaming soup spoon.

"Randall Plunkett. You know, the *Ground Zero* chappie who interviewed Catherine Lacuneau."

Miriam looked guarded. "Well, it developed kind of suddenly. But why *should* I tell you? Would you want me telling other writers about your appointments?"

"You consider Tabloid Randy a writer?"

Miriam looked slightly amused. "That's not for me to judge. We've had enough trouble with allegations of stonewalling. But somehow I don't think that's what's really bothering you. What is it?"

I was going to have to stop underestimating this young woman's perceptions. "Miriam, I understand now why you don't want to talk about searching for missing scrolls."

Her spoon stopped dead, and her eyes grew round. She said nothing, but I certainly had her undivided attention.

"I'm an investigator and researcher," I reminded her. "Information is my business. I've been doing some homework. I have read the stories about Kurt Alzner and Hans Borger and their untimely deaths. I understand that you and Hans were engaged, and I'm very sorry, Miriam. I know it had to be very painful for you."

I held my breath. It was a calculated risk. Maybe she would freak out or withdraw even further. But it was something we had to face.

When she didn't freak, I pressed on. "I think it would be good if we talked about it."

She made a weak little shrug, her eyes distant and full of sadness. "It's still very painful."

"Sure. It was only two years ago. That's not long. Tell me about Hans."

Whatever inner struggle this caused was over quickly. I knew the pattern—initial resistance until the dam is finally breached, and then the deluge.

"All right," Miriam said at last. "You asked for it."

She finished her soup, dabbed at her mouth with her napkin, and looked up at me with haunted eyes.

"Hans was a skier and a gadget freak," she began. "He was tall and blond and very smooth. He also turned out to be an adventurer and treasure hunter at heart. I met him on a ski trip to Switzerland. He was my instructor, and I fell very quickly in love with him. When he found out what I did for a living, he quit his job and moved here. He spent a lot of time climbing around the cliffs of Qumran with his strange gadgets. I began to realize that I wasn't much more to him than just another gadget. Toward the end, we drifted apart. I was disenchanted, and he didn't seem to notice or care. I was on the verge of breaking off the engagement when he . . . died."

I patted her hand across the table. "I'm sure it doesn't hurt any less for that. In fact, I'd guess you'd almost have to have some self-recriminations."

She nodded, eyes lowered. "I know it's silly, but I've felt guilty, as if I had something to do with his death. I know that's not the case, but I can't help it."

"That's natural, but totally false of course. So Hans was looking for scrolls?"

Miriam nodded again. "It was all he could talk about. He said that whole section to the west of the Jordan Valley and the Dead Sea was like a big piece of Swiss cheese, honeycombed with caves and recesses. He said previous explorations had only scratched the surface of possible hiding places."

"Did he have any connection with the Austrian, Kurt Alzner?"

She shook her head. "None. Alzner apparently was just a climber and explorer. I guess it's just a case of lightning striking twice in the same place."

"You don't have any suspicions about the incident?"

Miriam looked somewhat alarmed. "Nothing beyond the unlikely nature of the coincidence. Should I?"

I shrugged. "I don't know yet. What kind of gadgets did Hans use?"

"I was afraid you were going to ask that. All I remember is they were some kind of acoustic and electromagnetic probing devices. He said they showed up empty pockets in the rock that could not be seen from the surface."

"How long did he do this?"

"Oh, for several weeks."

Things were starting to take shape on the radar screen. "And did he find anything?"

She looked puzzled, as if the thought had never occurred to her. "No. At least, I don't have any reason to think he did. I didn't actually see him much during that period. He didn't want me around."

"You mean you don't know."

Her eyes shifted back and forth, then stopped. "Well, no. I guess I just assumed he didn't find anything or I would have heard otherwise. It never occurred to me that—do you think he did find something?"

"I'm not saying he did. Sometimes it's just a good idea to question basic assumptions. What kind of inquest was held?"

"Inquest?"

"Yeah. You know, where the authorities hold a hearing to determine whether the cause of death was natural, accidental, or the result of foul play."

"There was no inquest. As far as I know, it was an open-and-shut accidental death ruling by somebody. I don't know quite how they do those things here."

"You weren't questioned at all?"

"No. Why should I be? Just what are you suggesting, anyway?"

"I'm just curious, Miriam, because of my own interest in undiscovered scrolls. What about Hans's personal effects? Were all those shipped back to Switzerland?"

"There really wasn't anything to forward to his family. I have his climbing gear and other stuff in a box in my apartment."

"Did he rappel?"

"Yes, he did."

"Do you have his line?"

"Yes, I believe I still have the actual line he was using at the time. It was cut. That's apparently how he fell."

My radar screen was now full of enemy planes. "Cut?"

"Well, frayed . . ." Her eyes were big. "Are you saying somebody *cut* it?"

I hesitated. "These lines are designed not to fray. It might be good if I could take a look at it."

"You want to . . . look at it?"

"Sure. If you don't want to lug it in to the Rockefeller, I could stop over after work."

"You could, eh?" Miriam got a mischievous look. "Well, I happen to have a firm policy about letting strange men into my apartment."

I couldn't help myself. "Pro or con?"

"You better run, mister."

And God observed their deeds, that they sought Him with a whole heart, and He raised for them a Teacher of Righteousness to guide them in the way of His heart. This was the time of which it was written. . . . Like a stubborn heifer thus was Israel stubborn, when the Scoffer arose who shed over Israel the waters of lies.
—The Damascus Rule I

7

M iriam's apartment was one of those town house units that could have been straight out of the hills of suburban Pittsburgh. The place was so neat that a guy should check the bottoms of his shoes to make sure he wasn't tracking anything in. It was furnished in a cross between Early American and Late College Sorority, from the homey camel-backed couch and maple end tables in the front room to the poster-size reproductions of Picasso's *Guernica*, Dürer's *Four Horsemen of the Apocalypse*, and other equally cheery prints on the walls.

She must have noticed my absorption. "Are you into art?"

"Very casually. I just would have expected something a little lighter than visions of death and doom."

"Just because I'm a young female doesn't mean I have to be into *Blue Boy* or *Pink Lady!*"

I marveled that, with this mind of hers, somebody hadn't pushed this woman into law school.

After putting on some coffee, Miriam disappeared down a hallway. I took that opportunity to pull down her copy of Janson's *History of Art* and refresh my memory.

Before I could get very far, she was back, toting an orange

crate containing a large coil of something visible through the slats. She saw me return the book to the shelf.

"OK," I said lightly. "Pop quiz. What was the significance of Guernica?" I didn't really expect her to know.

Miriam set the box on the coffee table and headed for the kitchen. "Saturation bombing," she said over her shoulder.

"I beg your pardon?"

She returned with two steaming mugs.

"Saturation bombing," she repeated. "During the Spanish Civil War, the Basque capital of Guernica was the first place to experience the new technique of saturation bombing that was later used so effectively during World War Two."

"Not bad for a business major," I admitted, truly impressed. Next thing, I expected to find out that she played first-chair clarinet for the Israeli Philharmonic.

She smiled one of those scary smiles. "What can I say? I'm just a Renaissance woman."

We were sitting on the couch now, mere inches from each other. "I'm awfully glad the Renaissance agreed to share you with us."

She began to blush and quickly changed the subject. "You may examine the rope, Dr. Harper."

"The what?"

"The rope. In the box."

"Oh, yeah. The rappelling line." I fished in the crate and came up with an end. "You see, rope is only one part of it."

"What do you mean?"

I held it up for her to see. It looked just the way I suspected it would.

"The core of the line here is natural rope fiber—garden variety cotton, probably. It's nice and light, strong, and loose, not like stiff, bristly hemp. The problem is, it's too soft to stand up to much abuse from sharp objects."

"OK," she said, sounding tentative.

I pointed to the dark-green outer layer. "So it's encased in a protective nylon sheathing that's almost as flexible but is much more resistant to abrasion. Normally, you wouldn't see a cross section like this because the end would be sealed. Do you notice anything interesting about this end?"

Miriam touched the clean edge of the squared-off end. "Well, it's a very straight cut."

"Very good. Now, is that what you would expect if this line had been severed by scraping back and forth, say, against a sharp rock?"

She frowned. "No. I would expect something more ragged."

"Exactly. This outer nylon sheathing, especially, would be frayed. But it's not. It's severed as neatly as you please. I could do this with bolt cutters or a very sharp knife, but that's about all. No rock would do it like that."

Miriam was very quiet, so quiet that I could hear the passing of a car outside and a little burp from the coffee maker in the kitchen.

"I see," she said at last, very softly. "But who would want to kill Hans?"

"Did he have any—"

"No enemies, no friends. He didn't *know* anybody but me!" she snapped, then softened. "Sorry."

Her coffee mug appeared to have the shakes. She set it down.

"No problem," I said. "It might not have been personal. Maybe somebody wanted something he had. Maybe I'm just overly suspicious and needlessly upsetting you. You know the saying about the man with only a hammer—everything looks to him like a nail."

Miriam smiled wanly. "No. I think you speak with wisdom beyond your years."

"What can I say? Maybe I'm just a Renaissance man."

"Well, I thank the Renaissance for sharing you with me."

I finished my coffee and made some excuse about needing to go. I really wanted to quit while I was ahead.

That night I curled up with the collected writings of archaeologist-soldier-statesman Yigael Yadin, which Miriam had arranged for me to borrow from the Rockefeller library. Besides having genuine interest in the material, I figured it would be a surefire way to induce sleep. Instead, it inspired just the opposite. Before I knew it, I was sucked into an intellectual roller-coaster ride that had me alternating between disbelief and wonder.

Here was a man who was unafraid to advance bold theories and risk being wrong—without promoting a specific agenda. And for a Jewish scholar, he appeared equally at home in the New Testament, where he professed to see Essene influences. The apostle Paul's references to the sons of darkness and the sons of light, for example, were taken straight from the Essenes, according to Yadin. And in the Sermon on the Mount, it was allegedly the Essenes that Jesus was quoting when He said, "You have heard that it was said . . . 'hate your enemy.'" That was, in fact, how they regarded Gentiles, the sons of darkness, and the temple priests.

Jesus, according to Yadin, was just as opposed to the Essenes as He was to the hypocritical legalism of the Pharisees. Yadin argued that the Herodians were the Essenes.

There followed an interpretation of the feeding of the five thousand and the feeding of the four thousand such as I had never heard from a Christian minister, commentator, or seminary professor.

I had always been baffled by Jesus' question about how many baskets were left over in each case—and why He considered that significant. Twelve baskets were left from the feeding of the five thousand, seven from the feeding of the four thousand, the disciples answered, according to Mark 8.

"Do you not yet understand?" Jesus asked.

I certainly didn't, but Yadin thought he did. The twelve baskets, he said, represented the Pharisees, who controlled the Jerusalem temple, where each week the priests ate the twelve loaves of the bread of the presence. And the seven baskets stood for the seven loaves that the Essenes used in their annual ceremony for the ordination of priests.

I wondered if Yadin had fully appreciated what he was saying: In this interpretation, Jesus would be pronouncing an end to the earthly priesthoods of the Pharisees and the Essenes, who had to present recurring gifts and sacrifices on behalf of their people and themselves. Jesus was demonstrating that His priesthood superseded theirs.

I thought of the book of Hebrews calling Jesus the new great high priest from the order of Melchizedek. And I thought of chapter 8, which referred to the earthly tabernacle as merely a "copy and shadow of the heavenly things." I marveled that a non-Christian had made this kind of connection.

But what I really wanted to find in Yadin's writings was the material on the Temple Scroll that Zeev Nahat had mentioned. It had something to do with a document more deserving of the name *Temple Scroll* . . .

But then the phone rang. I wondered who would be calling me at this hour, and then I saw that it was only 9:45.

"How are you this evening, Dr. Harper?" inquired a pleasantly growly voice. "This is Kamlo. I hope I am not disturbing you."

At once I had guilt pangs. I flashed on the "American Hero" picture of myself and the little girl in the newspaper. Maybe my embarrassment had kept me from calling him.

"You're not disturbing me at all. How are you?"

"I am OK, mostly."

"Nothing wrong, I hope?"

"Oh, no, Dr. Harper. I am just tired of being idle. I long for those challenging physical hardships and treacherous heights we talked about."

"Sorry, Kamlo. I should have called you sooner, but I haven't figured out quite what I'm doing when."

"That is OK. I can call you tomorrow or the next day."

His long-suffering was starting to get to me. "Look, let's get together tomorrow. Can you drive me down to Qumran? We might as well start by scouting out the territory."

He sounded delighted in a gruff sort of way. "I can be at the Belvoir by six and meet you for breakfast, OK?"

I chuckled at his eagerness. "No, no. I will have some . . . things to take care of first thing in the morning. Why don't you meet me at the Rockefeller Museum around ten?"

"Sure, Boss. I will be there with a full tank of gas."

"Great. Just ask for Miriam Boynton's office at the front desk."

He bade me good night, sounding as if I had made his day. I was just glad he hadn't mentioned that American Hero newspaper picture.

I got back to Yigael Yadin. He had written plenty on the Temple Scroll—including a three-volume opus. All I had here were a few articles and excerpts. The Temple Scroll, according to him, was the Essene Second Torah, a holy book on a par with the Torah of Moses, which became the first five books of our Bible.

Like the book of Deuteronomy, it incorporated and restated much of other Scripture but with stricter interpretation of the law, especially in the area of ritual purity. It also contained a detailed description of plans for the construction of the temple, which had prompted Yadin to name it the "Temple Scroll."

And then the phone rang again.

"Dr. Harper?" said another familiar voice, this time female.

"Yes?"

"This is Catherine Lacuneau. If you are not retiring immediately, I would like to stop by. I have something for you."

"Oh, no," I assured her. "American heroes never sleep."

"What?"

"Nothing. Just a dumb joke. I'll be up, whenever you want to stop by. If it's not too much bother."

"No bother at all. I will be over in fifteen or twenty minutes."

Respecting decorum and Mme Catherine's sensibilities, I suggested that she meet me in the restaurant off the hotel lobby.

She agreed and rang off.

I grabbed up my papers, stuffed them into a file folder, and headed downstairs. On the elevator I glanced at my watch and saw that it was going on 10:30. This was promising to be a long night.

The restaurant was open till midnight, but the only customers at this hour were sitting at the bar. Ignoring the glare of the waitress, I chose a booth away from the traffic flow. All I wanted was coffee, and I didn't particularly care if the service wasn't five-star so long as I had a table.

While I waited for my coffee and for Mme Catherine, I dug into the file and picked up where I had left off. With one turn of the page, some information I had sought was staring me in the face. It was a section regarding *Megillat Beth Ha-Mikdash*—which was a bona fide "temple scroll" transmitted, according to rabbinic tradition, to David through Moses, Joshua, and the prophets.

Whereas the furnishing of the tabernacle was described in the book of Exodus down to the smallest utensil, Yadin asserted that no such detail could be found in the Torah for the construction of the temple. And yet, he noted, the twenty-eighth chapter of 1 Chronicles said David passed on to Solomon exact details for building the temple—including its vestibule, houses, treasuries, upper rooms, inner chambers, and most holy place—in the form of "writing from the hand of the Lord."

Yadin said he was not claiming that the Temple Scroll found at Qumran was *Megillat Beth Ha-Mikdash*, but he did believe its author may have been writing with knowledge of the genuine article.

Entirely engrossed, I pushed my cup forward for a refill. My mind raced. Did this mean there could be a "real" Temple Scroll out there—a *Megillat Beth Ha-Mikdash?* To think that there was the remotest chance of a scroll from the time of Moses waiting to be found was staggering. That would make even Dorothea Benson Cray crack a smile.

Someone cleared her throat and snapped me back to the present. I looked up to discover that the woman standing by my table was not the waitress but Catherine Lacuneau.

"Forgive me, Dr. Lacuneau," I said, rising and gesturing to the seat across from me. "Please have a seat. I was somewhere else just now. Yigael Yadin had me in his thrall."

Mme Catherine looked more pale and gaunt than the last time I had seen her. Her eyes appeared more deadened. She was showing all the telltale signs of worry-sick.

"This is the material," she said woodenly, setting down a bread-box-sized parcel. "If you make any copies, please destroy them when you are done."

"Certainly," I agreed.

She sat down and slid the package toward me. I peered inside the cardboard box and saw a half dozen or so file folders bound together with a large red rubber band.

While I did so, Mme Catherine murmured something to the waitress. Then she turned back to me. "If Elliot is still alive, I know he will not be too keen on people rummaging through his work."

There was something about the way she said it that raised a red flag in my mind. "You say 'people'—plural. Are there other rummagers besides me?"

The waitress appeared with a white wine for Mme Catherine, who gathered herself around it as though it were a fire in winter. Her face looked drawn with fatigue. She took a sip from her glass, then a larger swallow.

She shrugged. "Apparently. His papers all seemed to be in order, but his computer files appear to have been tampered with."

The planes were back on the radar screen. "What do you mean?"

"Our computer network has a security system that detected it. A startling message appeared, notifying us that some files had been illegally accessed. Nothing appears to be missing, but there is reason to believe that the files have been—what you call 'hacked,' I think."

I nodded. "Without special precautions, academic and research networks are often easy picking for computer hackers. When did this occur?"

"I found out about it this afternoon. Our systems person said it may have occurred sometime last night. Miriam may be able to tell you more about it tomorrow."

"OK. What kind of material was in Dr. Freemantle's computer files, versus these work papers here?"

"Oh," she said, sounding surprised, "you have it all. One of the folders is marked 'Printouts.' That includes anything significant from the computer files, mostly articles for publication—some already published, others in draft form."

I resisted the temptation to start pulling out folders to satisfy my hyperactive curiosity. That would have to wait until I got back upstairs.

"You've been through it all, as we discussed?"

She nodded, apparently too stressed to pick up her cues. There was also the wine that she was making disappear.

I continued playing dentist. "Why don't you give me an overview?"

"What . . . what would you like to know?"

It was my turn to shrug. "Anything at all that strikes you as significant."

This thinking apparently was a thirsty business for her, but when she saw the waitress coming for her empty glass, Mme Catherine finally found her tongue.

"Oh, there is much that is significant. I think Elliot was preparing to make himself even more unpopular with the religious establishment."

I was tempted to go after her on this "religious establishment" thing but resisted for the sake of the task at hand. "How was he fixing to do that?"

Mme Catherine wetted her whistle afresh. "He has been cataloging the instances where the Judeo-Christian tradition has borrowed from other religions and passed off these things as original."

"Such as . . ."

"Such as the Genesis Flood myth that was borrowed from the Chaldeans, the story of Moses in the bulrushes that was taken from the Akkadians, the commandments from Jehovah on Mount Sinai that were lifted from Hammurabi and the Amorites."

"What's that got to do with the Scrolls?"

For the first time Mme Catherine showed the trace of a smile. "This is where the prudent biblical archaeologist fears to tread. It has to do with Jesus."

On that score my confidence was unshakable, I thought. "What about Jesus?"

"If Elliot published some of these things, he would be a very unpopular man. They throw things into question."

I was losing patience. "What things?"

Mme Catherine looked uncomfortable. "Things like the virgin birth. Like raising the dead and the resurrection."

"Hmm. Not exactly peripheral issues. I wasn't aware the Dead Sea Scrolls addressed any of those things."

"By implication they do. But it is all in there—in Elliot's papers."

Her eyes danced over the parcel before me as if it were a bomb. I wondered why she now appeared uneasy discussing controversies that not so long ago were part of her own stock and trade. I wondered if this owed more to her nerves or to a change in attitude.

Suddenly I found my left hand seized in a surprisingly strong grip from across the table. On the other side were the haunted eyes of Mme Catherine Lacuneau.

"I have made a vow to God," she confessed.

"Regarding Dr. Freemantle and his safety?"

She nodded self-consciously. "I must be going mad."

"No," I reassured her. "From God's viewpoint, you may be coming to your senses."

For a long moment she seemed to consider what I had said, and I pondered what kind of vow she may have made. I felt the grip relax.

"Please find Elliot," Mme Catherine whispered fiercely. "Please."

And then she got up and withdrew into the Jerusalem night.

"I'll try," I told her empty glass. "I'll certainly try."

And when these become members of the Community in Israel according to all these rules, they shall separate from the habitation of ungodly men and shall go into the wilderness to prepare the way of Him; as it is written, Prepare in the wilderness the way of . . . (YHWH), make straight in the desert a path for our God.
—Community Rule, 8:13–15

8

It was some time after 3:00 in the morning before I fell asleep on the floor of my hotel room, surrounded by Freemantle's papers. I had only been resting my eyes for a moment, of course. Now it was nearly 7:00.

I pried myself off the floor, stumbled to the phone, and ordered a high-sodium, high-cholesterol breakfast from room service. I was sure Mrs. Cray would have approved under the circumstances. I needed to get used to spreading her money around like a Dallas tycoon rather than a Pennsylvania theologian.

I would think about all the things I had read during the night, eat breakfast, shower and shave, and then take care of a little business at the Rockefeller before meeting Kamlo for that field trip to Qumran. Right now I felt like something half alive that had washed up on the shore of the Dead Sea. This was going to require liberal amounts of coffee, steak, eggs, and toast.

There was something else too. It started coming back to me as I bent to the task of picking papers off the floor, reassembling them into their appropriate files, and setting them in a neat stack on the little kitchenette table where I would tackle breakfast. It was a feeling, a tone, a disquieting sense of something being dreadfully wrong, like a misremembered bad dream.

I backed off, knowing how these things slip away like eels. They can't be caught; they have to come to you. I went into the bathroom and scooped cold water onto my face, trying to ignore my bedraggled image in the mirror.

I was stalling, hoping that fading memory would sneak back up on me.

I migrated to the curtained picture window and pulled the drapes, flooding the room with light. I looked down and out across the ancient stone structures gleaming in the morning light in the Old City. On this glorious sunny morning, it really did look like the pictures in those travel books.

I was engrossed in the high-relief contrasts of minarets, domes, arches, and humble, boxy structures with windows like eye sockets when the memory sneaked up again and tapped me on the shoulder. But just as quickly it was put to flight by an insistent rapping on the door.

It was room service. The stirring of my stomach made it a bit easier to forgive the old man with the steaming tray who had just burst my bubble.

Shoveling in the food with one hand, I flipped back through the files with the other. Most of the papers were half-legible, handwritten notes on yellow legal pads. They dealt with intriguing subjects, most of which were laid out more intelligibly in the computer printouts from the tampered files. Freemantle apparently had been working toward a book-length manuscript, not specifically about the Dead Sea Scrolls but using them as ammunition where they suited his purpose.

Mme Catherine was right. This was not stuff designed to advance the cause of Christ or Moses. Freemantle argued that the bulk of the Old Testament would never have existed without the Jewish captivity in Babylon, where most of it was written, he claimed, under heavy pagan influence and reimported by Ezra the scribe.

Some of the allegations threw me. I had no idea how to account for the Babylonian figure whom the god Ea commanded to build an ark as a floating zoo before a flood was sent to wipe out evil men. Like Noah's vessel, this ship eventually went aground on a mountaintop, and a dove was released to search for land. Freemantle claimed the Babylonian story was first.

Nor could I account for the tale of the infant Sargon of the Akkadians, whose mother launched him upon the River Euphrates in a pitch-covered basket. After being rescued by a canal builder, Sargon grew up to become a mighty king of Mesopotamia for half a century. All of this occurred nearly a millennium before Moses.

But it got worse. Freemantle took a swipe at the Messiah concept, which he traced to the Egyptians and their mysterious notion of the long journey of the afterlife. Accordingly, the pharaoh's lot was to die, descend to the underworld, and undergo judgment before rising again to save the souls of his people.

Even the virgin birth did not escape attack. Freemantle accused the gospel writers of misquoting Isaiah 7:14—"a virgin will be with child and bear a son"—as New Testament fulfillment of a messianic prophecy. He argued that the correct translation should be "maiden" or "young woman," as it is today in the Hebrew Bible, not "virgin."

Freemantle also challenged Christ's own claim to be the Anointed One on the basis of Isaiah 61:1, restated in Matthew and Luke as preaching the gospel to the poor, releasing captives, restoring sight to the blind, raising the dead, and freeing the downtrodden. The problem, he noted, was that Isaiah said nothing about healing people or raising the dead. I double-checked in my own Bible, and he was right.

Freemantle concluded that either the Jesus of the New Testament was pumping air into His product or the real Messiah was actually an Essene, perhaps the Teacher of Righteousness. He cited a Dead Sea Scroll fragment from Cave Four, which referred to a Messiah who would be put to death but who would also release captives, make the blind see, raise up the downtrodden, heal the sick, resurrect the dead, and announce glad tidings to the poor.

How *did* things like that get into the caves of Qumran?

I was done eating breakfast, but now things were eating me. My faith endured better with tornadoes that threatened to flatten the structure than with termites that undermined the foundation.

Freemantle had sown questions in fertile corners of my

mind that threatened to grow into actual doubts. I had always believed the doctrines of literal interpretation of Scripture and absolute biblical inerrancy. But was this *really* the whole story? Just because Freemantle was somewhat inept and ham-handed in his approach didn't necessarily mean he was all wrong. I'd have to have better answers than that.

The breakfast that had seemed like such a good idea a half hour ago now lay heavily in my stomach, souring like the little scroll that John had to eat in the book of Revelation. Here I had patronized Mme Catherine, leading her to believe that I would be her hero, and now I couldn't even refute obvious error in front of my face.

Just then the bird flew back in the window. The misremembered bad dream was back. I could see again that eerie twilight between sleep and waking, as words of Scripture echoed strangely in my head . . . something to do with a voice crying in the wilderness.

Sure. Now I remembered. I had been reading Isaiah 40, which Freemantle claimed had been misquoted concerning John the Baptist. I had discovered to my surprise that he was not far wrong. It wasn't the *voice* that was in the wilderness. There was an entirely different emphasis in Isaiah 40:3: "A voice is calling, 'Clear the way for the Lord in the wilderness; make smooth in the desert a highway for our God.'"

And as I pondered, I'd found myself transported to that shadow world between the idea and the reality. It was called falling asleep on the carpet. But in this state the words had taken on a certain life of their own.

In my dream I had gone to the desert—and, oddly, I was meeting Kamlo today to do just that. What I might have done there, I could not recall. All I could remember was that something was there for me.

Now, I realized, I probably needed to get back on the carpet before I did anything else. But this time it would be on my knees.

I was in a guardedly better frame of mind by the time I got to the Rockefeller. Time on one's knees can do that. It also didn't hurt that, while putting things away, I discovered some material in a file that I had overlooked the night before. It appeared to be a kind of inventory of Qumran caves in reverse, focusing especially on caves where no scrolls had been found and on additional documents that remained to be found.

Freemantle's prejudices were reflected in the fact that his list of undiscovered manuscripts did not include the book of Esther. But it did include *Megillat Beth Ha-Mikdash*—the "real" Temple Scroll.

Even better, this material was all handwritten; no computer hacker would have had access to it. And it encouraged me to believe that I might have a pretty good idea what Elliot Freemantle was really up to.

It was nearly 9:30, and Miriam did a major double take when I walked in the door. She rattled off several hurried syllables, hung up the phone, and wheeled around to greet me with a magnetic smile and incandescent eyes. I wasn't quite prepared for this.

"Good morning, Jim," she said with feeling. "It's good to see you."

The expression and the tone were almost reverential. Maybe my insistence on candor the day before had been the right medicine. Still, it made me feel entirely undeserving, as with Mme Catherine's trust.

"Please remain seated," I said in my four-star general voice, adjusting the knot in my tie with dignity and a magisterial gaze. "You may call me Dr. Harper."

Sometimes my timing is pretty good. This was one of those. Hilarity exploded in her face, culminating in a piercing giggle that turned heads out in the hallway. It took her a moment to recover. I couldn't help thinking it wasn't *that* funny.

"Stop," she said, regaining her composure. Then her face turned serious. "Do you always deflect genuine warmth and affection with humor?"

That stopped me cold. This young woman had a frightening way of seeing right through me. But it was also an intriguing choice of words.

"Maybe," I acknowledged. "Does that mean we're going to

be having genuine warmth and affection from now on?"

Miriam suddenly looked a little less self-assured. "Sure. I mean, we'll see."

"Great."

"Well, do you have any more of those little sheets?"

I smiled. "You mean with the ballot boxes for lunch, dinner, and movie?"

"Yeah, that one. I could use the one for dinner tonight."

It was silly, but my heart was pounding. "Pick you up at six?"

"If you remember how to get there."

"Sure do."

"On second thought, better make it six-thirty. I'd like to wear something nice."

"You always look nice."

She began to glow. "Thanks. But enough about me. How about Mme Catherine? Did she manage to get to you yesterday?"

"Yes. Late last night. I don't know if you're supposed to know this, but she's sharing Dr. Freemantle's work papers with me."

She nodded. "That's her business. I understand she also wants you to find him."

"Yeah. Trouble. That's *my* business. Speaking of which, I understand there's been a security breach with Dr. Freemantle's computer files."

"Yes." Miriam flipped open a folder and let her eyes roam the contents. "The systems operator was running a morning routine virus scan and file integrity check when the computer's security system alerted us that there had been multiple log-in attempts from some outside source and some files had been accessed illegally. Do you have any idea who would do something like that?"

I shook my head. "We'll probably never know. Could have been Tabloid Randy looking for goodies. Or it could have been just a hacker committing random cyber-vandalism. The possibilities are almost endless."

"At least, it appears that nothing has been damaged or destroyed."

"That's what Mme Catherine indicated."

"She should know." Miriam gave me a direct look. "So, how do you plan to help Mme Catherine find Dr. Freemantle? Do you have a plan?"

I glanced around and then spoke in a lowered voice. "Hans Borger may not have been the last man to catch the scent of buried treasure."

"You think Dr. Freemantle may have fallen off a cliff?"

I shrugged. "I have reason to believe that he was at least curious. There's really only one way to find out."

Miriam's face fell. "You mean you're . . . going out there?"

I nodded and glanced at my watch. "In fact, there's a guy by the name of Kamlo who's supposed to stop by here in a few minutes and pick me up."

Miriam nodded, reacquiring her professional poise. "I'll let them know at the front desk."

I imagined an emotional tug-of-war behind those eyes. She was probably wondering why she kept getting involved with cliff-climbing fools.

"Thanks," I said. "Are we still on for tonight?"

She smiled weakly and nodded. "Yeah, I guess. Should I get out the black dress?"

"No, but we might want to make it seven o'clock instead of six-thirty—just in case."

"We can make it some other time," she offered.

"No, no. I'll be there."

She nodded. "Just do me one favor."

"Sure."

"Please don't be late. Every minute past seven will be about a year off my life."

Something in her eyes said she meant that.

Everybody was glad to see me today. At the sound of my footsteps by the front desk in the lobby, a seated figure lowered his newspaper to check me out. It was Kamlo, with a cheesy grin.

"Hi, Boss," he said, deploying to his full six feet and then some. "Are you ready to spin?"

I shook his hand and assented, assuming he meant "go for a

spin." Many a foreigner has foundered in his attempts to master the American idiom, a language deceptively, but only superficially, like English.

We headed for the back parking lot and soon were spinning down the road in the battered blue Toyota. I couldn't help thinking this was the model most often used for car bombs. But it was a great day for a spin, sunny and warm. Except for my slight headache, it almost made up for missing half a night's sleep.

I remembered that it was less than an hour's drive down to Qumran from Jerusalem, but the scenery was like that of two different worlds. We left the city and skirted the Mount of Olives, the mountainside from which Jesus and His disciples had considered the stones of the temple that would all be scattered. It was here that He taught them about the signs of the end—wars and rumors of war, nation rising against nation, earthquakes, and famines—that now seemed right off the front page.

We came to the little mountain town of Bethany, only a few kilometers outside Jerusalem, where Jesus visited His friends Mary, Martha, and Lazarus. From there Route 1 became a long downhill stretch toward Jericho. Palm trees appeared. I thought of the palm branches spread before Jesus as He entered Jerusalem at the outset of the first Holy Week.

Kamlo stopped the Toyota momentarily by a plaque at the side of the road. It informed us that we had reached sea level. Soon we would be at the lowest spot on earth.

Approaching Jericho, we intersected Route 90 and turned south toward the Dead Sea. We were still high enough to catch sight of this huge azure body shimmering on the horizon. Now we were entering Bedouin country. Kamlo pointed out the little knots of black leather tents belonging to individual clans. We began to spot the ubiquitous camel.

Suddenly we rounded a bend, and he had to hit the brakes. Otherwise, we would have plowed into a small herd of camels crossing the road. They kicked up their heels and made ghastly noises. The camels weren't so bad, but right behind them came a gnarled old camel driver, who looked as ancient as the parched landscape and as angry as a mother bear.

He presented quite a spectacle in his long, ragged garb,

shaking a wooden staff at us, like Moses challenging the magicians of Egypt.

Maybe I should have resisted the temptation, but I wanted a picture. So I got out my camera and took it.

That only further incited him.

"What's he saying?" I asked Kamlo.

Kamlo looked a little sheepish. "Uh . . . some of it you do not want to know. But he says we have upset his camels. And besides, he says he does not give free pictures to American tourists."

Then I got it. "I see."

I reached into my wallet and counted out two hundred shekels. Baksheesh—the monetary lubricant that makes things run in this part of the world.

"Here," I said, handing the money to Kamlo. "Tell him one hundred shekels is for the picture and the other hundred is to compensate him for any egg losses."

Kamlo looked bewildered.

"In case we scared any of his female camels so that they stopped laying."

He looked at me as if I were crazy, but I kept a straight face.

"Uh . . . Dr. Harper, camels don't—"

"Just tell him."

"OK, Boss. It's your money."

Actually, it was Mrs. Cray's, but I wasn't going to get into that.

Kamlo got out of the car and offered the money to the camel driver. I could see the Bedouin roll his eyes, and his stony face began to crack up. Then I was seeing a mouthful of bad teeth as he burst into laughter. He was convulsed with it as Kamlo started to get back into the car.

"Now," I instructed a very confused Kamlo, "you can tell him we're just kidding. But ask him if he has any cousins near Qumran. Tell him we're looking for an Englishman named Freemantle, and we need help."

There was another brief animated huddle before Kamlo returned to the car a second time.

"Hold on," he said, reaching across to the glove compartment and extracting a note pad.

He took it back to the Bedouin and jotted a few notes while the older man spoke. Then Kamlo returned to the car a third time, and we were off.

The last I saw of the camel driver, he was grinning and waving after us, clutching his money. Another satisfied customer.

"How did it go?" I asked.

Kamlo smiled. "His name is Ishtak. Everybody in the land of caves is Ishtak's cousin, nephew, or something. We have many names. Though I am not sure I understand what we just did." Then, after a pause, "Uh . . . Dr. Harper?"

"Yes?"

"Do you mind if I tell you that you are a strange man?"

"Strange?" I queried. "I would just point out, Kamlo, that *I* have never been seen in the desert—or anywhere else, for that matter—offering a camel herder a hundred shekels in compensation for camel egg losses."

That gave Kamlo something to think about. He drove on silently, shaking his head and chuckling.

The Angel of Darkness leads all the children of righteousness astray, and until his end, all their sin, iniquities, wickedness, and all their unlawful deeds are caused by his dominion in accordance with the mysteries of God.
—The Community Rule (1QS), III

9

The landscape reminded me of the *Voyager* pictures from Mars—endless pebbled plains littered with myriad brown-colored boulders and rust-hued rock, flanked by imposing, gnarled yellow cliffs like something from the wilds of Utah or the Badlands of South Dakota. Here, the adjective *rugged* would not be a cliché.

At this point, still north of Qumran, we could well be in the very stretch of Judean desert where Christ had met the Tempter head on, where the fasting Savior who called Himself the Bread of Life had pictured the rocks as loaves of bread. I could picture that too.

I was also impressed by the fact that Kamlo had conspicuously not pressed me for the details of this mission, apparently respecting my discretion. This seemed a good time to begin clueing him in.

"Kamlo, do you have any questions?"

The Judean wilderness glided past in a long moment of silence.

"I believed you would tell me when the time was right," he said at last. "But, yes, I would like to know who is this Dr. Freemantle, and why are we looking for him out here?"

"Have you heard of the Dead Sea Scrolls?"

He nodded. "Of course. Ancient Hebrew writings from the time of Christ. Found by Bedouin right around here almost fifty years ago. Probably fathers of Ishtak's kinsmen."

"Well, Dr. Freemantle is one of the scholars on the Scrolls project. However, he is not what we could call a Bible-believer. In fact, he is a skeptic who has been writing things designed to undermine major tenets of both Judaism and Christianity."

"What do you intend to do with him after you find him?"

I chuckled. "No, Kamlo, I have not hired you for any rough stuff. I just want to find him, period. Because he's a human being—same as you and me and the people we carried out of that bombed building."

"Is that all?" He sounded unconvinced.

"No. I came here originally in the belief that not all of the ancient scrolls have been recovered. If there are more to be found, it is my job to do so."

"I see. So where does Dr. Freemantle fit in?"

"I have reason to believe that he has been pursuing the same objective."

"You think there are more scrolls in the caves?" Kamlo voiced the same skeptical tone.

"That's a distinct possibility."

"Then why have not the Bedouin found them? They know these cliffs and caves like nobody else, and they have made much money finding these scrolls."

"But the Bedouin do not have high-tech radar and acoustic probes that can see beneath the rock."

"You think there are more scrolls buried underground?"

"I would not be surprised, for a couple of reasons—including a well-documented earthquake in the first century B.C. that some believe may have buried many other scrolls."

"Is that how you intend to search—with these high-tech devices?"

He had me on that one. "I don't know yet. If necessary. But first I want to explore the possibility that some of these documents have already been recovered."

"Why do you think that?"

"The last two people who came here for that purpose died in mysterious accidents around the cliffs."

"And it is possible that Dr. Freemantle may have been a third?"

"It is possible," I agreed. "Especially if he found something."

"And if he did not?"

"Then perhaps we will find him somewhere—alive."

After another long moment of silence, Kamlo asked, "Was this Dr. Freemantle exploring alone?"

"Yes, as far as we know."

"That, I do not think, was such a good idea."

At last we came to the escarpment that bore the stony skeleton of Khirbet Qumran, the ruins of the purported Essene community. We blew on past the turnoff, which was OK; I had seen it all before. I had read the competing alternative theories for its function—as a fortress or winter resort rather than an Essene monastery—but I preferred the plain vanilla, noncontroversial explanation.

The existence of a scriptorium—a writing room for scribes and scrolls—complete with stone tables and ancient ink wells, as well as the settlement's proximity to the caves where the Scrolls were found, were compelling to my mind. The alternative theories struck me the same as the theories that someone else had written Shakespeare's plays: intriguing but not very convincing.

I was gazing far out across the eastern horizon at the beautiful, glittering azure ribbon of *Yam Hamelach*—the Salt Sea—when I spotted opportunity.

"Over there, Kamlo," I said poking at the window to his left.

Kamlo immediately spotted them too—tents and donkeys—and pulled off the road at an expedient juncture. He then proceeded to terrorize me by barging full tilt across the axle-busting landscape. This jalopy was far from an all-terrain vehicle, and I had figured we would park it and then hike to the Bedouin camp. Instead, we bounced and careened toward them in a teeth-rattling, vertebrae-busting charge.

"N-n-next t-t-time," I stuttered, "let's rent a J-j-jeep!"

Blessedly, he pulled it up short of a boulder-strewn stretch that was perilously impassable and cut the engine.

"This is the end of the string, Boss," he announced, then opened his door.

I thought about that. "I think you mean 'end of the line,' Kamlo."

We began closing the distance on foot, a hundred feet below the terrace of Qumran and the higher marl cliffs beyond. I felt as if we were still descending, though more slowly, toward the bowels of the earth. At least, it was the kind of almost effortlessly brisk pace that told me we were on a slightly downhill course.

The sun was a dominating presence. Yet it was an intensity without ferocity. This, I knew, owed to the low humidity, a deceptively benign phenomenon that could cost the ignorant desert traveler his life through dehydration. Then I noticed that Kamlo had remembered to strap on the backpack containing our water bottles.

For a while it seemed as though we were making no progress toward the little tribal settlement. But by the time we were perhaps halfway to the first cluster of black tents, a donkey and rider began moving in our direction. We had been spotted. I consciously relaxed. This was only one man and one donkey. Besides, the Bedouin were known as peaceable sorts, most of the time.

This one was a young man with an inquisitive expression and an anemic attempt at a beard. Still, he had that elegantly tattered look of the Arab nomad, whose chief possessions are the sun and the wind, a curved knife, a woolen cloak, and a serviceable pair of sandals.

I could understand none of the many words that passed between Kamlo and the young Bedouin save one—"Ishtak." But that, early in their exchange, appeared to open the floodgate. I marveled again how long a simple conversation can appear to take to the outsider who does not speak the language.

And then I was startled to see the young Bedouin turn tail and set his donkey to a trot back from where he'd come.

"He will return," Kamlo said before I could ask.

We resumed our trek toward the tents.

"Did you ask him about Freemantle?"

"Not by name. But I described what we're interested in to him, and he says maybe he has something to show us."

"What?"

He gave me a strange look and shrugged, as if it was absurd to suppose that anyone would volunteer that kind of information or that another would ask for it.

We walked on, my imagination working overtime, suggesting everything from a dehydrated, vulture-picked body to a new cave full of ancient Hebrew scrolls.

The young Bedouin met us with two more donkeys and led us down the desolate Wadi Qumran through passes that reminded me of serpents, bandits, birds of prey, and voices crying in the wilderness.

I knew my way around horses well enough at low speeds, but I wasn't so sure about the donkey. It turned out to be much like riding a pony, however, but for the treacherous footing that made the experience feel like a rodeo ride. We had gone far enough to need the water bottles when the young man said something to Kamlo.

"He says it is up ahead," Kamlo said, taking pity on me.

It was indeed up ahead—as a drunken crow would fly. I was beginning to grow weary, if not irritated, by the laconic Bedouin and the winding, desiccated ancient riverbed. Improbably, the words of the nursery rhyme came to me about a crooked man with a crooked wife and a crooked house.

We were close enough to the Dead Sea now for me to imagine I was feeling a moister breeze and smelling a saltier tang in the air.

Then I saw that both Kamlo and the Bedouin were looking ahead at something. A football field away, in the lee of a pile of boulders that might have been the ruins of some young giant's game of blocks, was an abandoned vehicle.

We closed the distance.

It turned out to be a late-model Range Rover that had been picked clean of battery, radio, tires, and anything else remotely usable. The keys were still in the ignition. I didn't like that.

81

And I particularly didn't like the fact that the key case was imprinted with the initials *ERF.* The first thing I wanted to learn when I got back to Jerusalem was Elliot Freemantle's middle name.

Miriam Boynton, behind her desk, looked at me as if I were a ghost. She shook her watch and held it up to her ear.

"Dumb thing must have stopped," she said. "Or else you're almost three hours early."

This time I wasn't kidding around. "Look, Miriam, something has come up. Is Catherine Lacuneau in?"

She gave me a searching look and nodded. "She was. You need her now?"

I nodded.

She picked up the phone. "Let me check."

A moment later Miriam was nodding again as someone on the other end of the line confirmed that Mme Catherine was indeed in.

"Wait," I said, stopping myself. "Do you have Elliot Freemantle's middle name?"

She looked curious but didn't pry. "Not committed to memory. But I can look it up."

She tapped a bit on her terminal keyboard, then waited and tapped a bit more. Finally she looked up and said, "Yes. It's 'Ridley.' Is that something significant?"

I winced. "Yeah, could be."

"Jim, has something bad happened?"

"It doesn't look real good. But I'll tell you all about it tonight."

Catherine Lacuneau looked as if she were reading my mind. Her eyes regarded me the way a prisoner's might greet the padre prior to execution.

"I've been knocking around Qumran today," I began.

"But you did not find Elliot?"

I shook my head. "Does he drive a Range Rover?"

She stiffened. "Yes. Why?"

I steeled myself and plunged ahead. "We found an abandoned Range Rover out in the Judean wilderness. The keys were still in the ignition. Do you recognize these?"

I placed them on the table between us.

Mme Catherine's eyes widened. She didn't have to answer me with words. Her aggrieved expression and then her fingers said it all as she tentatively touched, then seized and caressed this token reminder of her dear Elliot. Silence enfolded us as twin tears welled up and overflowed.

"Was there any sign of a—" Her voice shook and then cracked.

"A struggle?" I filled in for her. "No, Dr. Lacuneau. Nothing like that at all. I would caution against jumping to any conclusions. In fact, I plan to continue searching on the assumption that Dr. Freemantle is alive and well, until I hear otherwise."

Mme Catherine considered that and nodded thoughtfully.

"But I don't want to raise unrealistic hopes either," I continued.

"Is there—is there anything I can do?"

"I would urge you to get back to the police with this information. Maybe they will take his disappearance more seriously now."

I slid a piece of paper across the table to her.

"What is this?" she asked.

"The vehicle identification number. It's the language police speak. Tell them any Bedouin in the land of the caves can take them to it."

Mme Catherine lapsed into silence, and I decided that was my cue to leave her with her deep and personal thoughts. She didn't even look up as I left her office. She was just turning the key case in her hands, over and over, then over and over again.

It was almost 7:30 before I pulled up outside Miriam's apartment house, feeling like a heel. It was embarrassing to admit that I had fallen asleep in the car I had just rented. I had parked it behind the Belvoir, intending to go up to my room to clean up and change. I'd paused to just "rest my eyes"—not realizing how weary I was. This 1996 Buick Regal had lots of options, but the wake-up call wasn't one of them.

At least, I had managed to reach Miriam by phone before 7:00—and before she was scheduled to start worrying. She had taken the phone call in stride. I just hoped that my fatigue wouldn't interfere with our time this evening. I didn't want to give her the wrong impression.

But when she came to the door, Miriam certainly gave *me* an impression. She had said she wanted to get into something nice, and she wasn't kidding. I didn't know what the Rockefeller paid her, but in this dress she looked more like Fort Knox than the proverbial million bucks. It was kelly green with features only a fashion designer could adequately describe—velvety brocade body material with billowy gossamer sleeves that set off her fair skin and deep blue eyes. It hardly seemed possible that this creature would have time for the likes of me.

"You look great," I managed to say and offered her my arm.

"Thanks. You look OK too for a busy American hero short on sleep. Are you going to tell me about your expedition?"

I promised I would, once we found the restaurant she'd suggested. It was a place called Ehud's in a newer part of downtown.

Miriam was enthusiastic about several selections, and I ordered one that she recommended. It was some kind of lamb with an exotic sauce and some half-cooked vegetables that didn't do much for me. Like a hypnotist's subject, I simply complied with her every suggestion—anything to keep gazing into those enchanting blue eyes.

She wanted to hear about my "expedition," so I told her everything—even about Ishtak and the camel eggs. When I was done, she continued munching thoughtfully with a slight frown of concentration. Then she cut to the heart of the matter.

"How do you explain the fact that this Range Rover of Dr. Freemantle's was picked clean, while the keys were still in the ignition?"

I was impressed all over again with her insight. "You mean, why didn't somebody just steal the whole thing?"

She nodded.

"The same question occurred to us. Then we noticed something was unusual about the front end of the vehicle. Its grill

84

was kind of mangled. We looked under the hood, and it appeared that the engine had been raked with automatic weapons fire. Kamlo found that the radiator was drained, which would have caused the engine to overheat very quickly and seize up."

Her frown deepened. "And since the keys were still in the ignition, Dr. Freemantle—or whoever was driving it—could have been trying to escape from someone when it overheated and died."

"Correct. Of course, somebody could have used it for target practice after it had been abandoned. But that would still leave us with the question about the keys left in the ignition."

"There's no question it was Freemantle's vehicle?"

I shook my head. "Only the police can tell us if the identification number matches, but it's the same model. And the clincher is that Mme Catherine identified the keys."

"Was there something distinctive about them?"

"Yeah. Initials on the case."

Miriam's eyes grew wide. "So that's why you wanted to know his middle name."

I nodded. "ERF—Elliot Ridley Freemantle."

Silence fell as we both digested much more than our Mediterranean entrées. I felt a heaviness that wasn't just brisket of lamb.

"This Freemantle must have the gift of grief. Causing it, that is," I began.

Miriam's perfect eyebrows went up. "What do you mean?"

I hesitated. "Well, it's not just Mme Catherine who has suffered things on this man's account."

"Who else?"

"There's also a young woman named Esther and a young man named Jim."

I filled her in about our professional disagreement over the book of Esther and then the major swipes at other Scriptures in Freemantle's work papers. And the attacks on pillars of the faith—Noah, Moses, Christ. I told her about the Flood story, the "messianic" pharaohs, and the idols of Babylon. And I confessed that at this point I had no good answers for any of it.

"So," Miriam concluded, "what do you plan to do? If

you're thinking of converting, there are plenty of good mosques in town that could be recommended."

I sighed deeply. "No, Miriam. I'm going to defend the faith. I'm going to get back on that horse and ride it to the very end of the trail. Not that I'm looking forward to it. I know it's not going to be easy. But I sometimes wonder, why me?"

Miriam's eyes danced. "Isn't that what American heroes do?"

I shook my head. "This would be far more a case of God's strength being made perfect in weakness."

"Jim, what do you *think* are the answers to Freemantle's tough questions?"

"You're asking me what I *think?* I'm not sure what I think matters much, but I almost have to believe that the Babylonians and Akkadians and Egyptians all got their stories from an earlier source, from which God's chosen people handed down the true version. But I don't *think* it's anything anyone at the end of the twentieth century can prove."

"Prove. So where does faith come into the picture?"

"OK," I conceded. "Maybe this is all part of walking by faith, not by sight."

Miriam smiled patiently. "Well, then. At least you have something that makes sense for you without putting your own faith under a cloud. Right?"

When she said it like that and looked at me with those eyes, everything seemed right with the world. I actually felt lighter, as if a burden had been lifted.

"Yeah, I guess so. Maybe I don't have to be a lone voice crying in the wilderness."

I told her about the two different versions of the Isaiah verse and my dream of being drawn to something in the Judean wilderness.

She looked intrigued. "Then you think it was Dr. Freemantle's Range Rover that you were supposed to find?"

I shook my head. "Not exactly. Maybe the man himself."

"You mean, you think Dr. Freemantle is still alive?"

I nodded. "Don't ask me why. But I can almost hear him

breathing in the next room. Something tells me I'm going to meet this man someday soon."

"Male intuition?"

I shrugged. "Hey, why not?"

Her eyes held a mischievous glint. "What else does your intuition tell you?"

"About what?"

"Like about us—about you and me, for example."

I couldn't tell if she was putting me on. "I've got half an idea, but I wouldn't call it intuition."

"No? What, then?"

"'Fantasy' might be more like it."

I thought Miriam would have been amused, but her face paled, and her eyes lost their sparkle. She nervously dabbed at her mouth with her napkin as her attention appeared drawn to something over my left shoulder. I realized then that it wasn't anything I had said.

I turned to see for myself and was struck by a wave of déjà vu in the form of Zeev Nahat. I blinked and wasn't sure, blinked again, and believed it couldn't be anyone else. It was the same lank frame, the same nubby gray hair, the same military bearing. He was moving toward the front of the establishment, as if just leaving.

I eyeballed his probable vector and retraced it to a booth along the wall behind our table. From there I imagined he could have invisibly eavesdropped on our conversation. Certainly he could have done so with electronic assistance, the kind of eavesdropping device used by military intelligence. Or was I getting paranoid?

That first supposed chance encounter with Nahat a few days ago had seemed just a benign coincidence. This time, I found myself plainly annoyed. These coincidences were wearing thin.

And Miriam did not look amused.

"Excuse me just a minute," I murmured to her.

I got up and, as discreetly as I could, gave pursuit to my bogeyman, who was already out of sight. I didn't know what I intended to do when I caught him, but I couldn't let him evaporate into an allegation, like a UFO or an Elvis sighting.

"Where did he go?" I asked an older woman behind the front counter, examining a register tape.

She looked up blankly, and I realized she was probably a non-English speaker.

"*Ayayh halach hu?*" I tried again in Hebrew, which I read much better than I spoke.

"*Mee?*" she answered with a baffled expression.

"Colonel Nahat," I began, then stopped. "Sorry. Maybe he left without paying."

With that, I ducked out the front door to take a look down the street.

The woman was out the door behind me. She was now as intent on finding this man as I was. She gestured that I go one way while she went the other.

I saw only a halting old man and a young laughing couple on the sidewalk—no one resembling Zeev Nahat.

Starting to feel a little foolish, I turned tail and went back inside. I wondered what Miriam was thinking. I decided, for her sake, to lay aside my own annoyance and lighten things up a bit.

Back at our table, Miriam had ordered coffee. She greeted me with questioning eyes and a smile that looked a little forced.

I dusted my hands in exaggerated fashion. "Well, he won't do that again for a while."

"Oh? What happened out there?"

"Old Nahat has gone to meet his maker."

"His maker?"

"Yeah, Mattel."

It was so dumb, she had to laugh a little. "Mattel? I thought it was Fisher-Price."

At least, she was smiling. Which was more than I was doing on the inside.

My eyes have gazed on that which is eternal, on wisdom concealed from men, on knowledge and wise design (hidden) from the sons of men; on a fountain of righteousness and on a storehouse of power, on a spring of glory (hidden) from the assembly of flesh.
—The Community Rule (1QS)

10

It was going on 11:00 when I returned to the Belvoir. I was really rattled now. Halfway to the hotel, it seemed I had acquired a tail. I took some detours just to test the theory. The car never left me, nor did it ever approach close enough for me to make visual identification. It obviously wasn't this driver's first time around the block, so to speak.

I considered taking another spin out into the desert, trying to give this guy the shake. But I quickly dismissed the idea. If I were in any danger, I'd be in worse straits away from civilization. And if I wasn't, then why not just go on about my normal business and see what developed? Maybe I could still make a visual ID.

A few minutes later I pulled into the back lot of the Belvoir. I cut the engine, but my heart was still cranking some high RPMs. Another car followed right on my heels, its headlights bouncing in my rearview mirror as it crested the driveway apron. I might have cranked the Buick back up and pulled out of there, except that this car had me boxed in.

And then I got a good look at the vehicle—a battered blue Toyota.

"Kamlo!" I said, getting out. "You gave me quite a start."

89

"Hi, Boss," said Kamlo, shutting his door. "Did you know there was someone making tail on you?"

"Yeah, very funny, you big—" I began, then stopped as his words sank in. "Wait. Do you mean that wasn't you following me?"

"I was following the one who was following you. He turned off the other way on Jaffa Road. I think he knew I was following him."

"I must have missed that, and then you showed up in my rearview mirror. Could you see who it was?"

Kamlo shook his head. "I could not see a face, but I wrote the license number on a paper."

"Excellent. Let me have the number, and I'll get it checked out."

"Right, Boss."

He fetched the slip of paper from his front seat and handed it over.

"Kamlo," I said, curious. "Why were you following me in the first place?"

He looked a little self-conscious. "I have a worry for your safety—and I have something to tell you."

I was intrigued. "Do you want to go inside, up to my room, and talk about it?"

He shook his head. "No. I will come by here at eight in the morning, and I will take you to a man. Can you be ready then?"

"Sure. But what man? Who is this?"

"He is the Old Man. Maybe he can tell you something."

"The 'Old Man.' What's this all about?"

But Kamlo was already going back to his car. "He is just the Old Man, who knows things. See you at eight, Boss. Good night."

I saw the headlights bounce one more time, leaving the parking lot, and listened until I heard the last of the Toyota's engine putter away. It sounded as though it would be needing a muffler soon. I felt in need of sleep, much, much sooner.

Eight o'clock came a lot earlier than usual the next morning. I was still trying to figure out which leg to stick first into my trousers when the front desk informed me that my visitor was awaiting me in the lobby.

"Please tell him to fetch some strong coffee, and I'll be along presently," I told the desk man.

It bought me almost enough time. By the time I was down in the lobby, Kamlo was just returning with two large, white polystyrene coffees and a relaxed smile that advertised his inveterate morning exuberance.

"Good morning, Boss," he enthused, handing me one of the coffees.

"That's an oxymoron," I grumped.

He gave me a wary look, and I felt instantly convicted. "Sorry, Kamlo. It's probably a wonderful morning. Where did you say we were going?"

"Bethlehem."

That, he had not said. I hadn't forgotten our conversation the night before. I wanted him to say more about this mysterious "Old Man." But I was having a hard enough time just matching his hurry-up stride out the door to the parking lot.

It *was* a beautiful morning. We took the Hebron Road out of Jerusalem, and I remembered having been there several years before. Bethlehem was just four miles south, but it was a different world in one important respect. Though this was still Israel, it was the heart of the West Bank and all that entailed with young firebrand Palestinians and Intifadah violence. Here, the Westerner's best defense was a low profile.

Just as Route 60 approached the town, Kamlo broke his silence. "You are probably wondering who is this man we are going to see."

"Kamlo, you must be psychic."

He ignored my sarcasm. "He is Adar Al Malik, the barber."

"Big Al the Barber. I don't need a barber. I need information."

"Barbers know everyone and hear everything. Al Malik is said to be about ninety years old. And there is another reason even greater."

"What's that?"

We were now entering residential streets of a most modest stripe. One gray Palestinian grandmother was hanging out the wash on lines drooping between two dingy stone dwellings.

"He is the younger brother of Jafar Al Malik, the old trader who was the go-between for many of the old scrolls found by the Bedouin."

Suddenly Kamlo had my full attention. I recognized the name of the elder Al Malik from accounts of the early days of Dead Sea Scrolls discoveries. Those were the days when the scrolls were being treated like hot radios on the back of a flatbed.

"Jafar Al Malik—he's not still alive, is he?"

Kamlo shook his head. "No. He has been dead a few years. That is why we are going to talk to Adar. I know one of his grandsons. He has promised that the Old Man will talk to us."

Now it did seem to be a beautiful morning. The coffee had done its work, and I was feeling like a man who was finally caught up on his sleep. I was glad I had remembered my tape recorder. This trip to Bethlehem could be worth it for the magazine interview value alone.

A few more winding streets with dangerous-looking potholes, and we were there. Kamlo angled his jalopy into the drive of a particularly decrepit stone house, scattering a half dozen squawking chickens. A curtain at the front window moved slightly askew as someone inside apparently checked us out.

As we were getting out of the car, the front door opened, and out came a thin man with a goatee who looked to be in his thirties, attired in jeans, Reeboks, and a traditional Arab kaffiyeh headdress. I gathered that this was the grandson.

We did not shake hands. The man's hawkish eyes merely flitted over me once as he and Kamlo exchanged words in Arabic. There was no change in his expression when he abruptly turned on his heel, gestured over his shoulder for us to follow, and led us inside.

It took my eyes a minute to adjust, but my nose was working fine. I smelled coffee, tobacco smoke, a dog in need of a bath, and more than one herb used in Middle East cooking.

Kamlo and I were left to stand in the living room, a shabby affair with threadbare couch and folding wooden chairs, straining our ears to pick out the sounds of the house. There were men's voices in a room down the hall. From the opposite direction came the muted strains of some distant Arab music, the hypnotic drone of one of those reedy instruments sounding like an oboe in the hands of a hashish smoker. The effect was disquieting to the spirit.

Unaccountably, my thoughts turned to Dallas and the drawing room of Dorothea Benson Cray, where visitors left too long with the ticking clock on the mantel and the grim-faced ancestors on the walls might eventually crack and admit to unsolved crimes just to be taken away from there. I wondered how Mrs. Cray was doing and if she was wondering how her money and I were doing over in the Middle East.

My inquiring mind was just beginning to wonder about Sheldon Hirsch and whether he was getting anxious for a story for the *Journal of Ancient Literature* when the grandson reappeared in the living room doorway. Again he beckoned for us to follow.

He took us into a bedroom that was clearly the source of the tobacco smell. In a corner of the surprisingly spacious room, across from a sagging bed covered with a coarse gray comforter, sat a wizened old fellow with slumped shoulders in a tattered brown cardigan sweater. He was motionless in a rocker, except for smoking a cigarette held with knobby, arthritic fingers. By the look of the fulsome ashtray, he had been at it for some time. By the look of his emaciated face and carriage, he had been at it for most of his ninety years.

Grandson with a gesture bade us sit down. Kamlo deposited himself on the creaky bed while I took the one other seat in the room, a folding wooden chair like the ones in the living room.

Grandson gave Kamlo a nod and left.

Before anyone could say anything, a dark-haired preadolescent girl, who could have been Grandson's daughter, entered the room with black coffee in two chipped cups.

I was considering taking a pass when Kamlo whispered, "Drink it." It no doubt had something to do with Arab hospitality.

I was seated toward the end of the bed, farther from the Old Man. I tried a sip from my cup and found it as strong as Turkish coffee and as thick as transmission fluid. Much of this too quickly and I'd probably start picking up radio signals.

Kamlo began addressing Adar Al Malik in that serpentine tongue that eluded me for the most part. It was another reminder

93

that I needed to add Arabic to my linguistic repertoire.

Several times the Old Man grunted something that appeared to cause Kamlo to back up and repeat himself. The first time he did it, the Old Man pointed to an ear, as if hard of hearing. Considering his condition, I didn't doubt it, although selective deafness has been known to happen at times like this. I did hear "Freemantle" a time or two.

Finally the Old Man waved dismissively at Kamlo as if he'd heard enough and proceeded to extinguish his cigarette among all the others in the green glass ashtray on the table beside him.

Kamlo turned tiredly toward me. "He says he does not understand anything I am telling him."

"Doesn't understand or doesn't hear?"

Kamlo shrugged. "'Will not' may be more like it."

I understood the situation entirely. "I believe his understanding may be capable of improvement, Kamlo."

Kamlo looked blank.

"Remember Ishtak and the camel eggs?"

He nodded and smiled faintly. "Baksheesh."

I pulled out my wallet and peeled off a few of Mrs. Cray's bills. "Please tell the Old Man I'm doing an article for a big American magazine about the Dead Sea Scrolls and the rumor that there may be more scrolls. I don't think Elliot Freemantle means anything to him. Tell him we want to pay for his time as a consultant on the story—or whatever pretense he needs to fleece us politely."

Kamlo took the bills and looked at them for a moment, apparently collecting his thoughts.

The Old Man lit another cigarette.

Then Kamlo began explaining things once again, climaxing with The Fork, which Al Malik accepted with greedy fingers.

The Old Man's eyes gained new life, and his thin lips parted in a grin that revealed what ninety years without flossing will do.

"See, Kamlo," I said. "He likes that. Tell him there's much more where that came from if we actually find something, based on his information."

Kamlo began translating that promise, and I wondered what the Old Man would do with the money. Move to a better

94

neighborhood? Doubtful. He'd probably buy a few more chickens and a truckload of Camels—cigarettes, that is.

Now the Old Man was nodding.

Kamlo turned to me. "He wants to know if there are any documents in particular that you are trying to find."

"Tell him if we find Elliot Freemantle, we may find the documents."

Kamlo translated once again, but this time the Old Man frowned at his cigarette and shook his head sadly.

Kamlo shook his head too. "No dimes."

"That's 'dice,' Kamlo. 'No dice.' All right. Tell him we're also looking for *any* unrecovered scroll that may be out there on the black market or wherever. Tell him there is a wealthy American who is willing to pay big money. And tell him that these scrolls could be additional copies of things already discovered. But we're most particularly looking for things that have not been seen here before—like the book of Esther and a more ancient version of the Temple Scroll."

Kamlo returned to the drawing board. I heard "Esther" and then a second name I didn't recognize that had to be "Temple Scroll."

At that, the Old Man visibly started, recoiling in a reaction very much like horror. The next thing I knew, he was halfway out of his seat, waving his arms and talking animatedly in a loud voice. I heard "Selmar" several times, but that sounded like anything but a happy subject. Al Malik's voice continued to rise.

Kamlo said something, and the Old Man responded heatedly. That kind of exchange happened twice more before the Old Man went off into a coughing spasm that set him back down in his rocker.

Grandson reappeared in the doorway with a look of concern.

I took a last sip of my battery acid while Kamlo explained what was going on.

The little girl reappeared, eyes downcast, to collect our cups, and I understood that the audience was over. It appeared that Big Al the barber had given us something of a clipping. But I wanted to hear Kamlo's account of the conversation before judging.

95

We wasted no time retracing our steps out of the house to find a bright Bethlehem morning—and a few more chickens—waiting for us. But the sunny day did little for my outlook. I was beginning to worry all over again about all the people who were depending on me: Mrs. Cray, Mr. Hirsch, Dr. Freemantle, Mme Catherine. I reckoned it wouldn't look too good if I spread tens of thousands of dollars around the Holy Land for characters such as Big Al, only to come home empty-handed.

Kamlo seemed a bit more sanguine as he got behind the wheel and I piled in beside him. He was whistling softly as if, instead of this blue beater and me, he had a car like Mrs. Cray's and a girl like Miriam. That might be a good sign.

But I was confused. "Is the Old Man better off than he looks?" I asked.

Kamlo appeared puzzled as he began backing the car out of the drive. "If you mean financially, I do not think so. Why do you ask?"

"Oh, as greedily as he gobbled up the money we gave him, I'm surprised he's not more interested in earning more. Maybe at his age he doesn't think about future pleasure."

We were working our way out of the neighborhood now.

Kamlo gave me a funny look. "I would not say that, Boss. What you saw was fear. The information was there, however, if we can make use of it."

Now I was as curious as a moth circling the flame. "But what was the Old Man afraid of?"

"Some of this he would say; some he would not. When I asked about the Temple Scroll, he became upset, but he would not say why. That is when he would start talking about Selmar."

There was that name I'd heard. "Who or what is Selmar?"

Kamlo furrowed his brow. "That is the key. All I know is he is a Jordanian, very rich, and he has something to do with the black market. Maybe something high up. There are whispers. Usually I do not listen much to such things. Now I will start listening."

"What about the Old Man? What's his beef with this Selmar?"

"Beef?"

"You know, what gets him so worked up? What was he saying about this Selmar, and what does it have to do with the Dead Sea Scrolls?"

"He was saying with much insistence that he knows nothing about such things—that all of that was years ago. He does not deny that there are more treasures from the caves, but he says only Selmar knows about this."

"Did he say anything about our missing friend Dr. Freemantle?"

"No. Each time I pressed him, he would make it come back to Selmar, as if no one would want anything to do with *that*."

"So in his mind Selmar is someone to be feared?"

"Very much so."

"Did he say why?"

"No. That was the thing he would not discuss."

"But in his mind the missing scrolls and our missing friend are linked, and that link would appear to be this Selmar."

Kamlo thought about that for a moment and then nodded. "It would appear so."

We were back on Route 60 now, northbound to Jerusalem. I was reminded of the trip into the city from Ben Gurion Airport, when Moishe the cabby remarked about disturbing inscriptions in the Dome of the Rock. We passed a Greek Orthodox monastery and the burned-out ruins of a kibbutz that had been shelled during the Six-Day War.

"Where to now, Boss?" asked Kamlo as the city loomed before us.

On impulse I said, "Let's take a look at the Dome of the Rock. Then we'll tackle the mystery of this Selmar character."

He gave me another quizzical look. But he was probably getting used to my unpredictable ways. He shrugged and began whistling again softly.

This time I recognized what it was—the theme song to *Hogan's Heroes*. And they say America's influence is on the wane.

Next stop was the Temple Mount—*Haram esh-Sharif*, "Noble Sanctuary," to the Muslims and *Har Habbayit*, "Mountain of the House," to the Jews. Kamlo assured me that I would have no trouble gaining admittance to the Dome of the Rock, as long as we showed up at the time of a public tour and we left our shoes outside.

It turned out that we were in between tours. So we did the usual tourist thing for such eventualities—got gasoline and drove around. We took a windshield tour, as the cabbies and travel agents call it.

First was *Ha-Kotel Ha-Ma'aravi*—the Western, or Wailing, Wall, the last vestige of the Second Temple of Herod. Not only was it no part of the original temple of Solomon, it was not even part of the temple proper. It was merely the retaining wall for the Temple Mount on which the edifice had been built.

And yet, what power even this shadow exerted over the hearts of the Chosen People. If I were mayor of Jerusalem, I would post a sign inscribed with Job 26:14: "Behold, these are the fringes of His ways; and how faint a word we hear of Him!"

It was a staggering thought that it was in my own lifetime—while I was yet in diapers—that the Jews were finally able to reclaim this piece of religious real estate after centuries of estrangement.

We parked and walked up to the *Azarah*, the great open plaza before the section of the Wall where the wailing occurred. This day was not unlike all the rest throughout the past thirty years. Men in jeans and T-shirts, sport coats and ties, long coats and sidelocks, prayed, implored, wept, and stuffed prayers written on little pieces of paper between the stones.

I bowed my head and prayed for the peace of Jerusalem, as it says in the Psalms. I prayed for Elliot Freemantle and his health. I prayed for myself, for wisdom on this mission and in my relationship with Miriam. And I prayed for Kamlo, standing beside me with his own head bowed, whose spiritual condition was a mystery to me—that he would come to know the one true God.

We got back into the car and moved on.

Around a bend, I felt as if we had suddenly stumbled through a time warp. We came upon an open-air sheep market in progress. The place was crawling with shaggy, bleating critters and ancient-looking shepherds with flowing cloaks and headdresses like Ishtak's Bedouin cousins' in the land of the caves.

Kamlo stepped on the gas and gave the area a wide berth.

"Careful you don't scare any mother sheep, Kamlo," I warned.

He laughed. "Sheep do not lay eggs either, Boss."

Farther along, in the middle of the sawtoothed, crenelated Eastern Wall, was a sight that was as moving as the first time I saw it several years ago. The Western Wall might have the press clips, but for me this was the main attraction. Here was the site of the Eastern Gate, also known as the Golden Gate.

"What is the big deal, Boss?" asked Kamlo, pulling off the road at my request for a longer look. "Is this not just a wall?"

We got out of the car and strolled closer.

"Do you notice anything about the gate?" I asked.

He shook his head. "Just that it is blocked up."

"Are you familiar with the Christian tradition of Palm Sunday?"

Kamlo thought a moment and then brightened.

"Yes," he said, waving his arms like palm fronds. "'Hosanna!' The Druse honor both Christian and Islamic traditions."

I nodded and pointed at the structure. "This is the gate through which Jesus entered the Holy City on a donkey—at last allowing Himself to be proclaimed Messiah and heir to David's throne. 'Hosanna to the Son of David.' It's the same gate through which the Messiah is prophesied to come again to claim that throne."

"These prophecies you speak of are in the Old Testament?"

"That one's in Ezekiel. Muslims in the Middle Ages sealed up the Golden Gate—unknowingly fulfilling Ezekiel's prophecy that said the gate facing east would be shut up because the Lord God of Israel had entered through it. But Ezekiel also prophesied it would be entered again one day by the Prince."

"The Prince . . ."

"Messiah. Isaiah the prophet called Him the Prince of Peace."

Kamlo looked simultaneously intrigued and puzzled. "You speak like a minister."

My ears weren't burning, but they began to tingle. "I used to be one—before I got into the academic research racket."

"Sorry, Reverend Boss. No offense. I did not know."

"No problem. And you can call me Jim."

"OK. If you are sure. Jim?"

"Yes?"

"I have another question."

"OK."

"Do you really believe the Messiah will return here?"

"Yes, I do."

"Uh . . . how will He get through the solid block?"

I chuckled. "I don't know. Solid walls have been no problem for Him in the past. But who knows? They say the actual gate from the Second Temple period is below ground level. Perhaps it will be excavated some day."

"What will He do when He comes here?"

"He will rule the nations as King of kings and Lord of lords."

Kamlo thought that one over.

We walked back to the car, more slowly this time. It was time to be heading for the Dome of the Rock.

"Jim?" he said softly, his hand resting on the key in the ignition.

"Yes?"

"Tell me more about this Messiah. My heart is—stirring."

I told him about the narrow way and the Savior who is the Way, the Truth, and the Life. I told him that no one comes to the Father but by Him. And I told him about the key to heaven—trusting in Christ alone for salvation.

Before we moved on, the Lord turned the key in Kamlo's heart. I prayed with him as he crossed over from death to life.

I realized with amazement that, before the hour was out, the God of Israel had already answered one of my prayers at Ha-Kotel Ha-Ma'aravi. It was staggering to think what might happen next.

Afterwards they shall damn Satan and all his guilty lot. They shall answer and say, Cursed be Satan in his hostile design, and damned in his guilty dominion. Cursed be all the spirits of his lot in their wicked design, and damned in their thoughts of unclean impurity. For they are the lot of darkness and their visitation is for eternal destruction. Amen, amen.

—Curses of Satan and His Lot (4Q286–7)

11

If the Lord was doing a work in Kamlo's heart, He was at least reviewing the blueprints for mine. Something most strange and subtle occurred as we stood in line to enter the Dome of the Rock. In one timeless moment I felt transported above the fray and glimpsed in my mind's eye a larger scheme of things, if not my own place in it.

As if from far above Har Habbayit, I could picture the entire sweep—the Garden of Gethsemane, the Mount of Olives, the Wailing Wall, the Golden Gate, the raised platform of the Temple Mount itself with the silver-domed Mosque of El-Aksa at the foot, and then the jewel in the crown, the golden Dome of the Rock itself. It was as if they were all part of me because I was their epicenter, standing on the front porch of eternity.

And then we were going inside the octagonal structure. The years peeled away until we were back in the seventh century A.D., when the Roman Empire was in ruins, the Dark Ages had fallen in Europe, the Jews were scattered throughout the Gentile lands, and the followers of an Arabian prophet named Muhammad were claiming the Holy Land as their own.

Kamlo and I shuffled in lockstep alongside a score of other

tourists in stocking feet through the structure's concentric colonnades.

The special, silent rapture I had experienced outside continued. This time symbols and images fell into place like concentric circles. Some suggested themselves in triplicate: Africa, Asia, Europe—Christendom, Judaism, Islam—Temple, Mosque, Church—Garden, Hill, Wall—Sea, Mountain, Valley—Earth, Wind, Fire. There was a sense of unity, wholeness, completion—*shalom*. Yet there was also a disquieting feel of something akin to sorrow or loss.

The experience was beyond explanation.

As we approached the enshrined rock that gave the place its name, I was faced with another triplicate: the three legends attached to it.

The oldest account had it as the altar of Mount Moriah, where Abraham's hand was raised to sacrifice his son, Isaac, until the Lord Himself provided a ram for the offering. Then, it was said to occupy the innermost sanctum of the Jewish temple until it was twice destroyed, by the Babylonians and the Romans, leaving not one stone upon another. And last, it was the fabled spot where Muhammad made his giant leap on horseback from earth to heaven.

I thought of the pundits who predicted that this Kubbat es-Sakhra was fated to destruction because it was a roadblock to the rebuilding of a Third Temple. Some said that the Third Temple would arise either to the north or the south, without requiring removal of the ancient mosque. Others said the Antichrist would gather some of his power and influence by solving this thorny real estate conflict.

Although these alternative theories were intriguing, my own study had led me to the traditional conclusion: the site of Solomon's temple and Kubbat es-Sakhra were one and the same.

I tended to favor the wild-card factor of divine intervention. Earthquakes had a way of moving things around over the centuries. Both the Dome of the Rock and the Mosque of El-Aksa had been heavily damaged several times and required major reconstruction.

But then I forgot everything else when I caught sight of the cupola from the inside. I became absorbed in the ceiling of the dome, lavishly adorned in gold and mosaics and encircled by sixteen stained glass windows. They were intensely stylized patterns, radiating outward in progressively larger flourishes, in obedience to the injunction against images of created beings.

It was the kind of hypnotic design, bordered by Arabic inscriptions in dancing characters that resembled crossed swords and scimitars, for which the word *arabesque* had been coined. And within this swarming device I could see the repeated symbol of the crescent moon, so prominent in Islamic themes. I was reminded of the myth of the pre-Islamic moon god Al-Illah, which some believed to be the origin of Allah.

Stealing a glance at Kamlo, I found my associate scribbling in a small notepad. Then I remembered what we had come for—the inscriptions. I had originally suggested using my tape recorder, but we feared mosque security would never allow that.

At this point, two official-looking men behind us asked for our attention and began reciting, in English and Arabic, some vital statistics about Kubbat es-Sakhra. There were various dates of construction, renovation, and other significant events, plus trivia such as square footage and quantities of building materials.

And then just as abruptly, it was over. The two men invited us to come back again some other time. Kamlo and I repeated our stocking-foot shuffle back out the door.

Outside, the uncanny sense of history, destiny, and *shalom* persisted. Blinking in the intense sunlight, we receded from this Byzantine shore of eternity and struck a course toward the battered blue Toyota. I was consumed with curiosity about the words that Moishe the cabby had regarded as so disturbing.

In the car, Kamlo said he'd been inside Kubbat es-Sakhra several times, but this was the first time he'd paid serious attention to the inscriptions.

And the first time, I thought, *that he'd read them through the eyes of salvation.*

"Yes," he said, flipping through his notepad. "Here it is. These are all from the Koran: 'The Messiah, Jesus, son of Mary, is but a messenger of Allah and His word which He cast upon Mary, and a spirit from Him. . . . Allah is only one God. Far be it from

His glory that He should have a son . . . . It is not for Allah to take for Himself any offspring, glory be to Him. . . . Praise be to God, who has not taken unto Himself a son and who has no partner in sovereignty, nor has He any protector on account of weakness.'"

I was floored. "Do you understand what this means?"

"I am not so sure, Boss. But it sounds to me like saying Jesus is not God."

"That's exactly what it's saying. It's an express denial of God the Son. We would call it blasphemy."

I had to ask myself why this shrine of Islam in the Holy City—this latter-day substitute for God's temple—should be dedicated to a monumental desecration of the name of the Lord. It was like finding a worm in the apple at the core of the universe. I felt slightly ill.

As we drove off, I felt as though I were experiencing the prophet Elisha's vision in reverse: Instead of having my eyes opened to chariots of fire and legions of angels at the ready, I sensed myself in a place surrounded by demon hordes perched for destruction.

Kamlo drove me to the Rockefeller just outside the north wall of the Old City. I gave him one of my gospels of John in Arabic, and he agreed to begin reading the chapters I suggested. He also said he would work his grapevine until he found out more about this Selmar character.

I had some business of my own to attend to. I wanted to find out about the license number of the car that had tailed me. I wanted to confront Zeev Nahat about his clandestine behavior. And most of all, I wanted to see Miriam.

As so often happens, however, life had other plans. I knew something was up when Miriam forgot her professional smile as she looked up from her desk at me.

"Why so long faced?" I asked.

"It appears you were right about Randall Plunkett," she said dryly.

"What do you mean?"

"Well, it's—why don't you see for yourself? They're in Dr. Starlander's office."

104

"Who are?"

"Everybody. Just go on in. I think they might like to talk to you."

She was right. Besides Merrick Starlander, there were Catherine Lacuneau, Zeev Nahat, and two other staffers I knew by sight but not by name. Starlander was talking to someone on the phone while the others pored over a document on his study table. Barely a head turned upon my entry.

Mme Catherine was saying in a low voice to no one in particular, "But that's *not* what I said!"

Upside down and sideways I tried to read the words. All I could make out was the publication name across the top, *Ground Zero.*

Just then, a secretary came in with a stack of papers. "Here they are," she said, offering them around.

Nahat looked at me, nodded, then handed me one.

It was a photocopy of a magazine article. I shuddered as soon as the headline came into focus: "Maverick Scrolls Scholar Silenced by Religious Establishment." A smaller deck below that declared: "Missing Archaeologist Believed on Verge of Damaging Revelations." The byline was Randall Plunkett's.

I didn't even have to read the story to know what it said. I have a terrific imagination, especially when it comes to impending disaster. But I was morbidly curious about his sources and what they said. Or, to be more precise, what Tabloid Randy *said* they said.

Before I could get very far into the story, Starlander was calling to me. "Dr. Harper! Dr. Harper, would you come to the telephone, please."

I gave him a quizzical look and took the phone.

Starlander said nothing. He wasn't going to make it too easy for me.

"Harper here."

"Dr. Harper," said a man in a firm, authoritative voice I had not heard before. "Sheldon Hirsch. Have you seen the story in *Ground Zero* by this Randall Plunkett?"

"Well, I just—"

"What do you think of it?"

Here was a man who didn't believe in standing on ceremony, let alone introductions or complete sentences. And he was ostensibly my editor—my adoptive boss.

"I haven't read it yet to know what it says," I asserted.

"Then I'll tell you. It says Elliot Freemantle was the victim of academic discrimination by some of his no-talent colleagues, who were motivated by jealousy and a desire to preserve the religious status quo. It says these other scholars have been desperately trying to hush up things found in the ancient record that would bring both Judaism and Christianity crashing down like Humpty Dumpty. And that Elliot Freemantle, of course, was the man who has figured out all of these dirty little secrets, and now he turns up missing with all kinds of insinuations of foul play. *Now* what do you think?"

"It's a bunch of unadulterated bunk."

"Of course, it's a bunch of bunk. My question is, what are you going to *do* about it?"

He sounded like Mrs. Cray. *"Do* about it?" I asked.

"Is there an echo in here? I'll spell it out for you. The *Journal of Ancient Literature* needs that story from you, and we need it right away. Just when do you plan to grace us with this piece?"

I recognized the character type—much bark, little bite. Not a bad guy but anxiety-ridden enough to need others around him either to share his anxiety or to shake him out of it. I decided upon the latter course.

"It's not going to be right away," I began calmly. "Is it your idea that my story can somehow be used to erase the damage done by Randy Plunkett's?"

I could tell he hadn't expected this. "Well, of course not," he grumped. "But how do you plan to explain to Mrs. Cray that Randall Plunkett can deliver his drivel and you can't?"

I was glad he couldn't see me smiling. "First, I don't deal in drivel. If you want facts, the truth takes a little longer because you can't make it up like Tabloid Randy. Second, since you bring up Mrs. Cray, how do you think Mrs. Cray would view the kind of story you apparently have in mind?"

"Well, I—"

"I think she'd say, 'Sheldon Hirsch, what do you mean by publishing defensive denials of wild allegations? All you're doing is convincing everybody that maybe there *is* some kind of conspiracy to protect the so-called religious status quo.' I'll tell you what I plan to tell Mrs. Cray next time I speak to her."

"And what is that?"

"I plan to tell her that the best response to all of this is not to *tell* the world that people like Tabloid Randy are wrong, but to *show* it."

"And how do you plan to do that?"

"By finding Elliot Freemantle and the missing scrolls."

There was a gasp of disbelief. "What? You've found Freemantle and the scrolls? Now, that's a—"

"No, no. I haven't found them yet, but I'm on the trail."

"Well, Jim, may I give you a piece of advice?"

"OK."

"Don't promise more than you can deliver, because it will come back to haunt you. And I don't think Mrs. Cray will be amused."

"Thanks, Mr. Hirsch. I'll keep that in mind."

"Listen, Jim. You have to do things the right way. I respect that. Just let us know as soon as you know something for sure. Miriam has my number, and she's very good at a lot of things. You'll find her very helpful to you."

"Yes, indeed. You have my word."

"Oh, and one more thing."

"Yes?"

"I'm not really trying to give you a hard time. It's just that American heroes have to live up to very high standards."

I was floored. "American hero? Where did you hear that?"

"Why, in the article, of course. I suggest you read it."

We hung up, and I took his suggestion. The article was just as he described it, only worse. I was sickened, angered, and embarrassed all at the same time.

Sickened, to see the way the public was being misled by untruths, half-truths, and total fabrications, especially when I knew that the average reader's only source of information would be this sort of mass-media sensationalism.

Angered, to see Mme Catherine's confidence exploited in so shameless a fashion and Elliot Freemantle presented as a tragic, persecuted figure to fit this preconceived story line.

Embarrassed, to see myself portrayed as the last great hope of the so-called religious establishment.

Of course, Tabloid Randy presented it all as posturing and prostitution. There was a reprint of that newspaper picture of me carrying the little girl out of the burning building, suggesting that I had exploited the situation for publicity purposes.

Interestingly, his article indicated that I was a paid apologist on the payroll of some rich American benefactor, whom he neglected to name. I wondered why. Perhaps he didn't know her identity, but I had little doubt he could find out. Perhaps without a name it would sound more sinister. Or maybe even Tabloid Randy feared the power and influence of someone such as Dorothea Benson Cray and her New York lawyers.

Starlander stood before me, looking solemn. "Dr. Harper, do I understand that you think you can find Elliot Freemantle? If so, this committee would be most indebted to you. This kind of publicity is terribly damaging to the very important work we have to do, as I am sure you can appreciate."

I was struck by his humility, despite the verbosity. "No promises, Dr. Starlander, but we are not without some resources, I assure you."

He nodded appreciatively. "Anything at all we can do—it's all yours."

Since he was offering, I didn't want to pass up the opportunity. "Miriam Boynton has been most helpful. If you can spare her, I'd—"

"It's done," said Starlander with a wave of his hand. "I'll arrange some other support services and assign her full-time to you."

I glanced over at Mme Catherine, who was looking pale and drawn. "If there's any chance at all," I vowed, "we'll give it our very best shot."

She nodded, biting her lower lip.

Just then, Miriam bustled into the room with a handful of pink memos. She handed several to Starlander and several to me.

"They're all from the same people," she said. "Associated Press, UPI, Reuter, CNN. And Dr. Harper, you also have one from the *Jerusalem Post,* a guy named Simon. They're all asking for comment on the *Ground Zero* story."

"OK," I said, taking the pink slips. "We're giving you a battlefield promotion, Miriam, to media spokesman. You and I need to construct a three-sentence no-comment statement aimed at shaming any news organization that traffics in this kind of report. Is that office of Dr. Freemantle's available?"

Miriam and Starlander exchanged glances.

He nodded, waved authoritatively, and said, "Go to it. It's yours."

I led Miriam down the hall at a brisk pace until she called out, "Last one on your left."

I turned the handle and entered an office much like Zeev Nahat's but with more contemporary art on the walls. Someone—Mme Catherine, I hoped—had been going through Freemantle's files, leaving drawers open and a few folders lying about. It looked untidy and unprofessional.

"Can you get somebody to take care of this?" I suggested.

Miriam looked at me questioningly. "I'm now your new administrative assistant?"

I nodded. "Temporarily. That article by Tabloid Randy has shaken everybody up. You think it will be OK for you, working with me?"

She didn't smile, but I detected a slight twinkle in her eyes. "I think so. Aunt Dot predicted we'd probably hit it off."

The words sound hauntingly familiar. "Who's Aunt Dot?"

I could see in her face that she'd thought I knew what she was talking about and suddenly realized I didn't. "Why, your benefactor and my great-aunt—Dorothea Benson Cray."

I gulped. "You mean you're Mrs. Cray's niece?"

She nodded, smiling this time. "*Favorite* niece, I might add. Of course, that had absolutely nothing to do with my getting this job."

"Naturally," I agreed, shaking my head in amazement.

This was getting complicated. I hoped Miriam didn't think I was interested in her because of her family connections or money, but she seemed to accept the fact that I'd known nothing about them. I wondered how this new information would affect our relationship. But then, it was probably premature to think in those terms.

Getting back to business, I handed Miriam one of the pink slips. "Jerry Simon at the *Jerusalem Post*. Let's get him on the horn right now."

*Violent men have sought after my life
because I have clung to Thy Covenant.
For they, an assembly of deceit and a
horde of Satan, know not that my stand
is maintained by Thee and that in Thy
mercy Thou wilt save my soul since my
steps proceed from Thee.*
—Thanksgiving Hymns 2 (1QH)

12

It only took a minute to get through to Jerry. I told Miriam to put him on the speakerphone and take notes. We would use the best of it for our official response to the other media.

"Hey!" said the familiar voice. "Is this *the* Reverend Doctor C. James Harper, American hero?"

"Don't be funny, Jerry," I said with some weariness. "Tabloid Randy is no laughing matter. We've just had a job done on us."

"I know, I know. Plunkett is a scavenger. Why don't you tell me all about it? I promise I'll do right by you. You know me."

"Listen, Jerry. Let me give you the official response to Plunkett's story, for the record. Then I'll talk off the record. Mr. Plunkett's story in *Ground Zero* is nothing more than fabricated sensationalism at its worst. It should not be regarded as responsible, objective journalism, which respects the truth, including both sides of a story. Therefore we will have no further comment until the facts are known regarding Dr. Freemantle and the scrolls. End of statement."

"Uh . . . who is this 'we'?"

"That would be the staff of the Rockefeller and myself. So

111

what I'm telling you goes for Dr. Starlander too, since you also called him."

"Well, your official statement is a little underwhelming. Not much to hang a hat on. You say you have something to tell me off the record?"

I took a deep breath. "Yes. And I need to ask you for another favor, but I promise to deal exclusively with you on this story after we put out this official statement."

"Thanks. So what's this secret off-the-record stuff?"

"Just that Plunkett's story is so off base, I expect him to have to eat it."

"What do you mean?" There was a note of doubt in his voice.

"All I can tell you is that his characterization of Freemantle is incorrect in virtually every respect."

There was a moment of silence while he thought that over. "Including the allegations of foul play?"

I had to put the brakes to this. "Perhaps, Jerry, but I'm not going to play 'Twenty Questions.' All I can say is that, the Lord willing, I intend to get to the bottom of it, and when I do, you'll be the first to know. I promise."

"I appreciate that. Now, what's that favor you wanted to ask?"

"Oh, not a real big deal. Can you run down an auto license number for me?"

"Sure. Give it to me."

"And can you do it without trying to use the information you think it might reveal?"

There was a chuckle at the other end. "Man, you spoil all the fun. All right."

I gave him the license number of the car that had followed me the night before.

"Have it for you within the hour," Jerry said. "Now, about that lunch—"

"Sorry, Jerry, but I'll have to take a rain check again. I'm going to be in and out a lot—mostly out—for the foreseeable future."

"Oh? And where might that be? The land of the caves?"

"Nice try, Jerry, but no dimes."

"No dimes?"

"Just a local expression."

"With all due respect, Dr. C. James Harper—"

"Yes?"

"This better be good."

"Oh, I think it's safe to say it will be well worth the wait."

"OK. I'll call you back with that plate. And anything else I can do, just let me know."

"I most certainly will. And if I'm not here for any reason, please give the information to Miriam Boynton, who is our . . . uh . . . public information officer here."

I shot Miriam a glance as we hung up, and she looked as though she could barely believe her ears.

"'Public information officer'?" she said incredulously. "You make this stuff up as you go along, don't you?"

I smiled at her. She was not only pleasant to work with, but she was beautiful too.

"Isn't that what American heroes are supposed to do—improvise?" I asked. "Yankee ingenuity and all that."

"There are some other words for it, but I don't use them."

"Seriously, folks, I may be making it up as I go, but it's also very much for real. Dr. Starlander is temporarily reassigning you to me, and I'm designating you as administrative assistant and public information officer."

"That's easy for you to say."

"Well, you probably ought to get a raise, but I have no authority to do that. That's between you and Dr. Starlander. And you don't have to accept this assignment."

"What? And miss my chance to become rich and famous, working alongside a genuine American hero?"

"More like your chance to end up in one of Tabloid Randy's smears."

"I'll take my chances. I'm a big girl."

"OK. In that case, please read back my on-the-record remarks to Jerry Simon."

I weighed the words as she read them back and was satisfied that it was close enough.

"Just change 'fabricated sensationalism' to 'baseless sensationalism,'" I said. "No need for overkill. Then call or fax the statement to the other news organizations who called. If we do it right away, that will stop others from calling."

Miriam looked skeptical. "How will it do that?"

"Once it goes out on the wire services, all the other news organizations will see it and know there's no point in calling."

"Makes sense. But how did you know that?"

"My brother had a paper route once."

"But I thought you didn't *have* a brother."

"No. I just made that up. And he didn't have a paper route either."

"You nut."

"I love it when you talk like that," I said, glancing at my watch. "Listen, if anybody's looking for me, tell them I'll be back in a few minutes."

"Where are you going?"

I had to tell her. "I'll be with Colonel Nahat. Please interrupt me if Jerry Simon calls back."

Zeev Nahat was looking his usual steely-eyed self. He gave the appearance of not minding my intrusion, but then he always looked that way. I imagined he'd look the same way if I were about to jump off a bridge.

"How may I help you?" he offered.

"Well, you said to come back when I had some more intelligent questions."

This time, the colonel looked mildly surprised. "Are you sure that is what I said?"

"In so many words. At any rate, I have a couple of questions that I think at least graduated from high school."

Now he was looking slightly amused in his own poker-faced way. "Very well."

"First, does the name *Selmar* mean anything to you?"

For the first time, I thought I saw Nahat flinch, but it could have been my imagination.

"Selmar? No, should it?"

"I don't know. It's just a stab in the dark."

"Is this someone who may know something about extracorporeal texts?"

That was a fancy way of saying unrecovered scrolls.

"Could be," I agreed. "That's what I'm trying to find out."

"So you are still pursuing the conspiracy theories?"

"If you want to call it that. Sometimes that term is used to cover a multitude of sins."

He shrugged. "I believe in conspiracies sometimes."

When he didn't amplify, I had to ask, "Such as . . ."

"Oh, there is one conspiracy theory to which I subscribe. It involves Har Habbayit, the Temple Mount."

"In what way?"

"The Arabs. It would not be to their advantage to turn over any ancient texts that might confirm the precise location of the ancient temple. And it certainly would not do to have it documented that their precious Kubbat es-Sakhra is occupying that place. Such a document would be highly inflammatory."

"Are you referring to the Temple Scroll?"

He gave me a penetrating look. "We already have the Temple Scroll. It is in the Shrine of the Book."

"I'm talking about a more ancient archetype. A thousand years more ancient—from the time of David."

Nahat's eyebrows arched slightly, but he said nothing.

I added, "I told you I've been doing my homework. Is there more to this conspiracy of yours?"

There was that shrug again. "Not really. Just that it also would not be to the advantage of the Israeli government for such information to become public."

That took me a moment to understand. "In terms of domestic tranquility."

He nodded. "Already it is not good. Could you imagine the conflict that could be ignited if the lid comes off and the zealots on both sides begin trying to push each other off Har Habbayit?"

"I've got a pretty good imagination. I could see that kind of conflict spreading like a grass fire in August."

Nahat just stared back through narrowed eyes. Then he glanced at his watch. "What was the other question?"

"I'd like to know where you were last night."

"I beg your pardon."

Just then, his phone rang.

"Nahat," he said, picking it up. Then he looked up. "It's for you."

I took the receiver from him.

"Listen," Miriam said quickly. "Jerry Simon called back. Said it was a strange deal about that license number. Said he hit a brick wall. It came back as an unregistered government number. What's that all about?"

"Tell you later," I said. "Thanks."

I gave the phone back to Nahat and sat down again.

There was no discernible curiosity in his eyes. "Why do you want to know where I was last night?" he asked.

"Because Miriam and I were eating at Ehud's, and we thought we spotted you. Again."

He smiled smoothly. "I eat in the New City a great deal. Ehud's is one of my favorite places. Yes, I was there. What of it?"

"Don't you think it strange that you keep popping up at the same restaurants where Miriam and I go?"

He shrugged again. "Maybe it is you who keep popping up where *I* go. Maybe we both have the same good taste. Maybe there is such a thing as coincidence. How often has this happened? Twice?"

"And then I'm followed back to my hotel by a strange car with unregistered government plates. What's your license number, Colonel Nahat?"

He frowned. "How do you know you were being followed?"

I wasn't falling for that. "Let's just say I do. I have ways."

"Maybe your ways involve too much imagination."

"I don't think so. What's your license number? If you won't tell me, I can check it out."

Nahat waved a hand dismissively. "Go right ahead. So there are lots of government cars. What does that prove? Will that be all? I have things to do."

"That's fine. Thank you very much, Colonel Nahat."

I walked out stiffly, wondering if I had done the right thing. If Nahat really was shadowing me, I had no illusions that he'd stop just because I gave him a hard time. He'd probably just be

116

more careful about it, which would certainly be no advantage to me. Or maybe I'd just made an enemy needlessly. Still, even that would be better than my worst suspicions.

I returned to Freemantle's office and was struck for the first time by the full irony of my situation—to be occupying the digs of the man I was supposed to be rescuing. This American hero stuff was wearing thin. I felt more like a virus living off the body of its host.

I told myself to relax. I was neither hero nor villain. I was what I'd always been, a sinner saved by grace.

"Any messages?" I asked Miriam.

She handed me one pink slip. "Kamlo. No number to call. He's on his way here to talk to you about something."

That could be a good sign. Maybe he was finding out things.

The hour was getting late when the front desk announced Kamlo's arrival. This time I had him sent in.

"Hi, Boss," he said, looking somewhat somber but relaxed. He glanced around the office. "Are you taking over the place?"

"Infesting it, maybe."

"I beg your pardon."

"Never mind. What have you found out?"

He made an uncharacteristic scowl. "This Selmar. He is big trouble. Everybody says stay away from him. He is one bad . . . um . . ."

"Egg?"

Kamlo gave me a look as if I was pulling his leg again. "No. Dude. Bad dude. His name is Selmar Hajabeel. People do not want to be heard criticizing him."

"So what do they say about this Selmar Hajabeel?"

"They say he is a Jordanian merchandiser, a very wealthy man who has his own organization."

"OK. Let me see if I can translate: This Selmar fellow is a Palestinian black marketer who runs a gang of thieves and puts a big hurt on people who talk too freely about his business."

Kamlo was nodding. "I think you have it, Boss."

"Where does our man Selmar hang out?"

"They say he lives on top of a mountain near Jericho. They say it is like a fortress."

"Hmm. That would be a good place for a kidnapping, wouldn't it?"

Kamlo looked puzzled. "What do you mean, Boss?" Then his eyes brightened. "Do you think that is where Dr. Freemantle may be?"

The idea alarmed me, jarring me into a new appreciation of the gravity of the situation. "It's way too soon to say, but it's a start. But listen, Kamlo, it is extremely important that you not breathe a word of this to anyone."

His jaw squared itself. "I am not afraid of thieves and bandits."

"That's not my point. We just can't afford to tip off anyone, if we hope to have any success. I wouldn't even ask any more questions that might give anybody ideas."

He nodded, his big brown eyes burning dully. "I say we go right to the man himself and make him answer the question."

"I applaud your courage and determination, Kamlo, but I hear it's not that easy to ask questions with a cut throat."

Both of us fell silent.

I was bombarded with various thoughts revolving around the providence of circumstances. Even a couple of hours ago I wouldn't have particularly thought about political factors in this equation. But Zeev Nahat had changed all that with his observations about the Arab-Israeli conflict over Har Habbayit. If something like the archetypal Temple Scroll even existed, would the enemies of Israel ever allow it to see the light of day? I could imagine its getting the Adolf Eichmann treatment—cremation with burial at sea.

But the picture changed dramatically when I considered this Jordanian pirate named Selmar Hajabeel. I flat out could not imagine a character like that intentionally destroying something worth so many thousands of dollars.

Then something clicked, and I was forcefully reminded of God's sovereignty, particularly in adverse circumstances. A major Christian revival occurred in China partly as a result of atheistic communism, which had effectively swept away long-entrenched pagan beliefs. Longer ago, Joseph's captivity in Egypt resulted in saving the Chosen People from famine. In the book of Esther—which was becoming so closely identified with myself—evil Haman ended up hanging from the gallows that he had constructed for Mordecai the Jew.

And then I thought of one more instance. The unrecorded disaster that drove the Essenes from Qumran prompted them to stash their library in ceramic pottery in the arid land of the caves, thus depositing them in the perfect environment to preserve God's Word intact for two millennia.

Looking at it that way, it was not so hard to see Selmar Hajabeel as somehow an instrument of divine providence, intending for evil what God intended for good. And then, with fear and trembling, I dared to think of myself as another latter-day actor in the divine drama of the scrolls' ultimate recovery.

I thought of Tabloid Randy's story and suddenly realized what I'd been missing.

"Kamlo!" I nearly shouted, startling the poor man in his chair. "You're absolutely right. You're a virtual prophet."

He blinked in confusion. "I am?"

"Yes. We go right to the man and confront him."

I told him all about Randy Plunkett's article and the furor it was creating.

Kamlo's eyes widened, and he shook his head in amazement.

"So," I concluded, "we have to be at least as bold as the enemy. Fact is, I'm a journalist for the *Journal of Ancient Literature*. If we can get a phone number for this Selmar character, we'll call him. If not, we'll track him down."

He looked unconvinced. "There will not be a phone number! You mean go to his place?"

"Sure."

"That is great. But what about those cutthroats you were worried about?"

"Hey, we'll just take trench coats and cameras and notebooks. There's a story out there in the news that Selmar needs asked about. Reporters almost never get fed to sharks."

"'*Almost*' never?"

"What's the matter? I thought you were the one who wanted to take no prisoners."

He grinned. "I was only wondering where your courage was coming from all of a sudden."

It was a fair question. "From God, Kamlo. I believe these circumstances are providential and that the man on God's mission has a divine enabling. There was a queen in the Old Testament named Esther who had to risk her life by pleading for her people to the king. She was afraid, but her uncle encouraged her by saying, 'Who knows whether you have not attained royalty for such a time as this?'"

"So did she do it?"

"Yes, she did. She said, 'If I perish, I perish.'"

Kamlo's eyes lit up. "That's me, Boss. If I perish, I perish. Even more so now that I know for sure that I go with God."

"OK, Kamlo. Let's go for it."

The torrents of Satan shall break into Abaddon, and the deeps of the Abyss shall groan amid the roar of heaving mud. The land shall cry out because of the calamity fallen upon the world, and all its deeps shall howl. And all those upon it shall rave and shall perish amid the great misfortune.
—Thanksgiving Hymns 5 (1QH)

13

Kamlo was right; Selmar Hajabeel was not going to be found just by looking in the Yellow Pages or calling the Chamber of Commerce.

And a "mountaintop near Jericho" was not exactly a specific location. This land had more mountains, albeit small ones, than Tabloid Randy had molehills.

I debated calling Jerry Simon again. I could not forget, though, what had happened when I'd asked him for old clips on a couple of dead mountain climbers. Maybe I was just being paranoid, but Zeev Nahat had seemed to know all about that request. I had to admit that I really didn't know Jerry Simon well, and there was too much at stake here to risk a security leak. Accordingly, I shelved the idea.

So it was back to the library.

I asked Kamlo to float outside just in case he could spot any surveillance. That made me think of how far a cry this modus operandi was from the back alleys and mean streets of the more traditional, pavement-pounding private investigator whose stock in trade was the fast draw, the quick wit, and first-name relationships with stoolies and cops.

The word to the wise in the waning days of the twentieth

century was *data,* as in databases. The high-tech information explosion meant that if a Jordanian merchandiser named Hajabeel had ever attracted the attention of the business press through fancy trading, or the attention of the authorities through too-fancy footwork, my chances were good of turning it up in some data bank.

Unfortunately, I immediately started turning up blanks everywhere I looked for Selmar Hajabeel. I checked the newspaper indexes. I checked the periodicals indexes. I checked the computerized indexes. Nothing. *Nada. Nichts.*

So much for the direct approach. I tried them all over again through the back door—subjects such as black marketeering, Jericho, Jordanians, smuggling. This approach was much more time-consuming, however. In the local press there were scores of stories any given year mentioning Jericho alone. But I plugged on, in the hope that each next straw in the haystack would be the needle.

Finally there was a modest payoff for all of this persistence. Under "smugglers" I found a 1985 obituary for a Muhammad Hajabeel, a Palestinian refugee who had made a fortune in the art and antiquities trade but who died while serving time in Israel on a variety of charges involving smuggling, immigration, and, of course, taxes. The kicker was an oblique reference to Hajabeel's estate, a former monastery east of Jerusalem.

This wasn't the whole bagel, but it was a good first bite. I guessed that this Muhammad Hajabeel, who died at the age of seventy-one, might be the father or other elder kinsman of Selmar Hajabeel. And if this former monastery was on a mountaintop near Jericho, then we had our boy.

I made a photocopy of the obit and tallied all my other dead ends. With a mixture of satisfaction and frustration, I acknowledged that I had exhausted this trail. It was back to the back alleys and mean streets.

When I found Kamlo outside, he said there had been no sign of anything or anyone untoward. I asked him to get us back to the Rockefeller. I needed to find an expert in old Judean monasteries, and I bet someone back at the ranch would have a clue at least as to where to begin.

Miriam had spruced up Freemantle's old office. All the clutter was gone. File folders were off the floor and file drawers shut. In fact, the filing cabinets themselves had been squeezed to the far corner to make room for another desk—a smaller version of Freemantle's—which looked to be Miriam's new work station. There were real cut flowers on both desks and a small framed picture on hers.

This I had to see. Who in Miriam's life was sufficiently dear to her heart to merit this place of honor? I leaned over for a look—and almost fell over.

It was myself and the little girl I'd carried out of the burning building—the "American hero" picture. But there was one big difference. The picture in the newspaper had been black-and-white. This was full color.

Miriam laughed when she saw my face. I guessed she'd been waiting for this moment.

"How—how did you get the color?" I sputtered, nonplussed.

"Computer colorization. You'd be surprised how easy it is. Even I can do it."

I thought about that. I knew someone had to scan in the original image, and someone probably had to set it up on the computer. This had either occupied several people for a short time or one person for quite a while.

"Look, Miriam. If you don't have enough to do—"

"No, Dr. Harper, it didn't take that long. Besides, it's your fault anyway."

"How's that?"

"Your new public information officer *didn't* have much to do. Just like you said, that news release stopped everybody cold. There were no more calls. But you're sounding as bad as Dr. Starlander."

"Who, me?"

"Yes. What happened to the sense of humor?"

I looked at the photo again and started to smile. "Sorry. There for a moment I thought you were making fun of me. American heroes do not invite ridicule."

Miriam rolled her eyes. "Of course not. Wouldn't *dream* of it."

"Listen, Miriam. I have a serious question. Does anyone in this institution know any experts in Judean monasteries?"

She looked as if I'd asked for a spaceship to fly to Neptune. *"Monasteries?* I'm sure nobody here would even know anybody in a monastery."

"Not living in a monastery but knowing all about them. That kind of expert."

"Oh. What kind of monasteries?"

I shrugged. "Any kind, so long as they're east of Jerusalem and on a mountain. Say Byzantine, Greek Orthodox . . ."

"You think you've found something?" Excitement and expectation tinged her voice.

"Not so fast, my dear. This is still in the development stage. So keep it under your yarmulke. It might be nothing."

"Well, OK, but how do you ask around without saying what it is?"

"I'll take care of that part. You have someone specific in mind?"

"Yes, Sally Glatt—Dr. Sarah Glatt. She knows all about that sort of thing."

"She someone I should know?"

Miriam shrugged. "She's on staff here. I'm sure you've seen her. You'll probably recognize her."

I did recognize Dr. Glatt as one of the nameless individuals I'd seen occasionally around the copy machine and the water cooler. With her middle-aged strong-woman face and big hair, Sally Glatt reminded me more of a manicurist in a dish-soap commercial than what she really was, an architectural historian.

"You would be very surprised, I am sure, just how many places there are that match your description," Dr. Glatt told me up front, as a secretary began pulling reference files.

"How many?"

She looked as if she hadn't actually expected me to ask. "Well, that depends. I can give you the range. By the time of Muhammad, there were more than one hundred and thirty Orthodox retreats in the wilderness east of Jerusalem."

I gulped.

"But today only a handful of those sites are still actually functional."

"Like seven or eight? That would be easy enough to narrow down."

Glatt shook her head. "Unfortunately, the field extends to two or three dozen if you include other structures that are marginal or have been converted to other purposes."

"Oh," I said, deflating. "And that's our situation, I'm afraid. This one has been converted to private use as a residence and possibly a commercial enterprise."

"Then that is not so bad. Of those two or three dozen, most are along the Jordan River—"

"Which we can eliminate because this one is on a mountaintop."

Glatt stared at me over her half-glasses, reminding me for all the world of Mrs. Cray. "You should have said that before. That changes things. Let me see what the computer might do with those variables."

She pecked around on the keyboard for a couple of minutes, muttering under her breath and making odd faces at the screen as she scanned the results. After a moment, she hit a couple more keys and looked up.

"That should do it," she said as a printer at the end of the table launched into a high-tech rap song.

It didn't take long to spit out copy. When Sally Glatt handed over the printout, I saw why. There were only four names on the list, none of which I recognized. But I liked the percentages. This was even better than the seven or eight that it might have been. With these, I had a fifty-fifty chance of hitting it on the second try.

Sally Glatt gave in to her curiosity. "Miriam didn't tell me what you needed the information for."

"Good," I said. "She's not supposed to."

When her eyes widened, I added, "All I can tell you is that it has something to do with an article for the *Journal of Ancient Literature.*"

That seemed to satisfy her.

I thanked Dr. Glatt for her help and left her office with my veritable buried-treasure map.

I should have known better. Just when you start getting cocky is when the wheels come off. Always.

"Any luck?" Kamlo asked when I showed up at his blue Toyota in the back parking lot.

I waved the paper at him as I climbed into the passenger side. "Yessiree, Kamlo. We are truly privileged to live in the information age. Look. We've already narrowed the field to four possible locations."

He didn't look impressed. "Do we have to go to all of those places until we find the right one?"

"No way, José. All we have to do is go to the records in the tax office and see who owns these parcels. We should be able to figure it out from there. I say let's hit it."

"Do you mean right now?"

"Right now."

He shrugged and gunned it out of the parking lot. "OK. Where to, Boss?"

"Oh, the courthouse or tax office or whatever administrative services building that keeps that kind of tax records."

Kamlo scratched his head, frowned, and muttered something under his breath as Sally Glatt had done. It wasn't like him.

I was beginning to get a bad feeling. "What's the matter?"

His voice was soft and almost apologetic. "Uh . . . do you remember how we first met?"

"How could I ever forget?" Then it began to register. "You don't mean—"

"Yes, Boss. I think that is the building that was blown up."

My heart sank. "Oh, great. How sure are you?"

He shrugged again. "Just a feeling."

Somehow I had that feeling too. "Let's stop at the first pay phone we see."

We found a convenience store, and I called Miriam.

"Hello, Jim. Let me guess. You've found Dr. Freemantle."

I suppressed some initial irritation. "Not quite. In fact, we've just lost something we needed."

126

"What's that?"

"A whole building. Look, Miriam. I need you to do two things."

"OK."

"First, please call and make an appointment for us to get a car phone installed so we can stay in close contact and work right out of the car."

"All right."

"Second, while we're getting that done, will you please find out where property tax records are being kept these days, if they haven't been lost or destroyed. They may have been moved. If they will give ownership information over the phone, ask them about the four properties that are on our list from Sally Glatt."

I read her the list. Then I gave her the pay phone number to call us back.

I told Kamlo to keep an eye peeled while I went into the convenience store and picked up a copy of the *Jerusalem Post*. Then I went back out and stood by the phone booth with my paper unfurled. After a minute of flipping pages, I found the story: It was a three-paragraph short, reporting that a story by *Ground Zero* magazine, alleging a conspiracy to silence dissenting Dead Sea Scrolls scholars, was being condemned as fabricated sensationalism.

Perfect. I knew by the word choice that it was the work of Jerry Simon. This was far preferable to what could have been. Just a "no comment" would have been enough to encourage a much longer story, taking the allegations far more seriously.

Leaning against the phone booth, I paged randomly through the rest of the paper while a few dozen cars scooted by and the wind tried to flip the pages back on me. The phone rang. I jumped, even though I had been waiting for it to do that.

Miriam spoke in a low, conspiratorial voice. "Purple Parrot and the Fat Man sleep with the fishes."

Either my ear or my brain didn't get it. "What?"

She repeated it. "Isn't that the kind of thing they say in the movies when they do this cloak-and-dagger stuff? I don't know what it's supposed to mean."

"Yeah. Well, in this case I almost hope the line is tapped. It would serve them right to have to try to figure that out."

She giggled and then told me where to take the car for a phone implant. It was only a few blocks away, and they would take us now. It would give me a chance to get a cup of coffee and finish the paper.

I tried out the new car phone, courtesy of Mrs. Cray's expense account, by calling Miriam. This time she wasn't kidding around about purple parrots and fat men and fishes.

"Bad news," she said, sounding downright glum.

"Uh-oh," I responded. "What's the score?"

"Kamlo was right. All of those records—what's left of them—have been moved to other facilities. Anyone needing to access them must apply in writing. Please allow two weeks for processing requests."

"Two *weeks?*"

"And that's assuming the records still exist."

"OK. How long will it take if they don't?"

"Ask your brother."

"The only child?"

"Yes. The one who doesn't have a paper route."

"OK. What do you suggest we do, Miriam?"

"I don't know, American Hero. But you could ask Sheldon Hirsch. They say he knows everything."

"Sorry. We don't have time for that."

"Well, the good news is that he's here right now."

I didn't need this. "Why is that good news?"

"You may not know, but he's a big fan of yours. Says he's read all your stuff and respects the way you work. I don't know if he'd say that to your face, but he told me. He wants to see you."

"Probably wants to turn up the heat on me some more."

"I don't think so, Jim. He's here for a conference. Says he just wants to touch base and offer any help he can."

With the number of options I had, I didn't have to think too long. "OK. We'll be in shortly."

Sheldon Hirsch was waiting for me in Freemantle's office. He was a large man, tall and big-boned, with a large head and a high, receding, reddish brown hairline. In his tailored gray pin-stripe suit, he couldn't help looking as if he owned the place. He smiled and skipped the handshake and went straight to the bear hug. Maybe Miriam was right. As usual.

"Great work on the Randy Plunkett controversy," he said enthusiastically. "His story had all the credibility in the mainstream media as an Elvis sighting."

I had to smile. "That's about all it was worth."

"Yes," he agreed, his expression turning serious, "but it could have been a lot worse. Nor do I expect this to be the last of it. The best defense, as they say, is going to be a good offense."

I got the point. "We're doing the best we can, under the circumstances. You'll get your story."

Hirsch looked stricken. "No, no. That's not why I'm here. I just wanted to meet you while I'm in town and see if I could be of any assistance. You say 'under the circumstances.' Are there problems?"

"You might say." I couldn't help a chuckle. "The building with the records we needed has been blown up."

Hirsch's eyebrows shot up. "Any connection?"

"No, it was that terrorist bombing the other day."

"Aren't there duplicate records somewhere?"

"Maybe, but it will take us two weeks to access them. It will be quicker to go around knocking on doors and try to get the information ourselves."

Hirsch looked at his watch. "Just what are you trying to find? I have a few sources and connections."

I pulled out my list of Judean monasteries and handed it over. "One of these has a private owner in the . . . uh . . . import-export business, you might say."

Hirsch took the paper and got out a pair of reading glasses. "OK. Let me make a quick phone call and see what happens."

He deposited himself at Miriam's desk and began punching numbers with the paper before him. He had a few words with someone, and he wrote something down. It was over so quickly, I assumed he had failed to connect with his source.

He looked at his watch again and handed the paper back to

me. "I have to leave now. But you'll find your ownership information there. Just do me a favor."

This quick, large man was setting my head to spinning. "Sure," I said.

"Whatever you do, stay away from that last one on the list—Dayr Al Nimrun."

"Uh . . . why do you say that?"

"That's Selmar Hajabeel's place. He's poison." Hirsch stopped en route to the door and turned back to me. "Remember Desert Storm and the Persian Gulf War?"

My head was still spinning. "Yes."

"A bunch of Western journalists wanted to enter Iraq to investigate charges of human rights abuses. Saddam Hussein said, 'There are no human rights abuses. And any journalist who comes in here and says otherwise will have his legs cut off!'"

"So," I said to Hirsch's departing form, "if I get my legs cut off, don't come running to you?"

"Something like that," he agreed.

And then he was gone.

For God shall sound His mighty voice, and His holy abode shall thunder with the truth of His glory. The heavenly hosts shall cry out and the world's foundations shall stagger and sway. The war of the heavenly warriors shall scourge the earth; and it shall not end before the appointed destruction, which shall be forever and without compare.
—Thanksgiving Hymns 5 (1QH)

14

I wondered once again why I never felt quite so brave the next morning as I did the night before. Yesterday evening I had been ready to storm the mountaintop. Now, in the cold light of day, all I wanted was to stay in my cozy hotel room and make plans by telephone and tap keys on a word processor. Or, if I felt adventurous, go over to the Rockefeller and cast aspersions at Zeev Nahat and make eyes at Miriam Boynton.

Anything. Just let some other hero chase vicious criminals and get shot at—or his legs cut off.

Maybe this was all a big fuss over nothing. Maybe Elliot Freemantle was actually OK, holed up in Amman, sipping cocktails and reading *Ground Zero* magazine.

The idea grabbed me. What if Freemantle had wanted to stage his own death or disappearance? Say he had raked his own Range Rover with automatic weapons fire to make everyone think he'd been knocked off or abducted. This kind of thing had been done before. Maybe he was in cahoots with Tabloid Randy. Maybe he wanted so badly to discredit the religious establishment that he'd do so by deception if he couldn't do it legitimately. Or maybe he just wanted out of a bad relationship with Catherine Lacuneau. That wouldn't be a first, either.

But then I snapped out of it. That wasn't what I really believed. I was grasping at straws. My flesh might shrink from the prospect of walking deliberately into the lion's den, but it was not by the flesh that I was supposed to be led—not by might, not by power, but by His Spirit. I just had to claim the promise of His enabling.

Besides, what would I say to Kamlo? Suddenly I was overcome with a wave of affection for the big guy with the soft heart. Here was a man who had been a stranger and alien in his own land and yet had not turned to bitterness and violence. He had been responsive to the light he was given, and he deserved more light. I'd started this by leading him to Christ, and now I was responsible to see him established in the truth. The last thing he needed was disappointment in his spiritual mentor.

I had no sooner hit my knees beside the hotel bed than I heard a soft knock at the door. I got up and went over, pausing for a heartbeat before peering out through the peephole.

"Boss?" came a familiar voice.

I saw Kamlo, smiling vaguely like a hippo munching happily in the paddy. Here was a man who would never have ulcers.

"Come in, come in," I said eagerly, swinging the door open. I gave him a hug.

"Are you OK, Boss?" he said with a hint of concern in his voice.

"Yes, yes, Kamlo. I was just about to pray for our mission. Would you join me?"

Hesitantly, he knelt beside me and followed my lead. I prayed for forgiveness and cleansing and enabling. Kamlo asked for wisdom and understanding and, oddly, courage. I was touched. If he thought I had gone over the edge, he was more than willing to go there with me.

By the time we were done praying for Freemantle and for ourselves, I felt like Teddy Roosevelt, ready once more to charge up the mountain. And I thought of something an old saint had once told me about prayer: We're not telling God something He doesn't already know. But by asking we are getting ourselves into the proper relationship with the Master of the Universe in which He can use us as He sees fit.

I handed Kamlo a cup of coffee and a question. "Did you bring the maps?"

He nodded and shrugged out of his backpack. "And the camera too."

"Yeah, the camera. That's right."

While he emptied his backpack, I fetched my own trusty 35mm with the electronic-everything for idiots. Kamlo had gone me one better—his was an old Leica two-and-a-quarter with manual settings for shutter speed and f-stops.

"That's a nice old camera," I noted.

"Photography was my hobby when I was a boy. This was my father's."

I gave him my camera too. With his brown aviator jacket, two cameras slung over his shoulder, and his usual imperturbable expression on his generous face, Kamlo would look the part. Maybe he'd even get to take some pictures.

I gathered up trench coat, tape recorder, and notebook and hoped that I would be half as convincing as a journalist. Our lives might depend on it.

I found Kamlo back at the table over an outspread map, working down his coffee.

"Dayr Al Nimrun," he muttered to himself, then turned to me. "I think it is about here."

He pointed to a spot on the map sort of northwest of Jericho, getting on toward Bethel.

The problem was, I couldn't see any main roads in the vicinity. "Are you sure?"

"No," he confessed. "But I think it is close."

I picked up the phone and dialed Miriam. It was probably early enough to catch her before she left for work.

It was. After the pleasantries—an apt term in this case—I asked if she would get maps from Sally Glatt for the four sites we'd discussed yesterday.

"Why all four?" she asked. "You still haven't narrowed it down?"

"We've narrowed it down."

There was a pause while that sank in. "Oh. You don't want anyone else narrowing it down."

"That's a big ten-four, good buddy."

"Gotcha. OK. I'm leaving now, and I know Sally Glatt comes in early. By the time you get here, we should have them ready for you."

"Thanks, sweetheart."

There was another pause. "Uh . . . what did you call me?"

"Sweetheart. Is that too forward?"

"No. I guess I just wanted to hear it again."

"I'll have to keep that in mind."

I must have daydreamed for a moment or two after we hung up, because suddenly I found myself wondering what Kamlo was doing in my hotel room, pacing by the door. When I got Miriam into my head, she tended to crowd everything else out.

"Come on, Boss," he said, looking at his watch. "We need to get a moving on."

Elliot Freemantle. Selmar Hajabeel. Dayr Al Nimrun. Teddy Roosevelt.

When I thought of the battered blue Toyota bouncing around Qumran like a Tijuana jumping bean, it occurred to me what they ought to call us—Jim and Kamlo, the Rough Riders.

It began to rain before we got to the Rockefeller, which was more than a bit unusual this time of year. Kamlo dropped me off at the front entrance and waited with the engine running while I ducked into the building, dashing between the raindrops.

Once inside the lobby, I had to downshift. Miriam was waiting for me right there with a manila envelope and a kiss.

Yes, a kiss. She looked both ways before taking the plunge, grabbing the lapels of my trench coat, which caught me totally by surprise. It was no little peck, but a real smacker. Brief but downright serious. Heartfelt. It was a wrecking ball hitting broadside, and I crumbled.

I opened my mouth to say something appropriate if not clever, but nothing came out. My heart was demolished, and my brain was on the condemned list. It was a good thing there was no wind, or I might have blown away.

In words that echoed through the corridors of my mind, I

134

heard Miriam say, "Take real good care of yourself, Jim."

I'd never heard a sweeter voice. And from the sound of it, this was no idle wish.

So there I was, standing in the foyer of the Rockefeller Museum, rain dripping off my coattails, my ears ringing, my mouth working like a goldfish's, and all I could manage to say was, "Yeah, thanks."

From two steps back I could see a telltale glint in her eyes, an extra aqueous magnification that made them look half again their normal size. And they were fastened on me. She handed me the manila envelope as if it contained her heart.

"Promise me you'll come back in one piece," she murmured, then bit her lip. "Never mind. I know you can't promise that."

I looked at the envelope with uncomprehending eyes. She turned on her heel and disappeared down the hall. I stuffed the envelope inside my coat and went out into the rain.

The windshield wipers were flapping, and Kamlo was sitting at the wheel, chewing gum and humming along with some Middle Eastern music on the radio that sounded like a combination of Yoko Ono and fighting hamsters. He shut the Bible he'd been reading, gave me a glance as I piled in, and then shoved the car into gear.

"Did you get the maps, Boss?"

I drew a blank. "What?"

"Did Miss Boynton give you the maps?"

"Oh, yeah." I was still wondering how anybody could hum to a hamster fight. "Right here, I think."

He gave me a funny look as we pulled out of the Rockefeller.

I took out the envelope and looked inside. There they were. I pulled them out and found them to be black-and-white photocopies of the kind of maps printed in books but with route numbers and other details added in a different typeface as if a computer had had a part in this. One map even had a cut-off column of text along the left margin.

"Great," I exclaimed, finding the one for Dayr Al Nimrun.

135

"We might have a fighting chance to find this place."

"How does it say to get there?"

"Well, I would take Route 1 east toward Jericho rather than go down to Qumran and double back. Then go north on Route 458—"

"Into the higher country. Yes, of course. But after that?"

I realized I had just gone over the same ground he had pointed out in my hotel room. "Well, there are some turnoffs onto some smaller roads with Arabic names that go on for a ways. You'll just have to look at it. It's a little complicated."

"OK, Boss. We will stop for petrol soon."

Jerusalem in the rain became a fuzzy pastiche of stone mosques and synagogues, open-air markets and lurching buses, black umbrellas and yellow slickers peeling past our windshield like a full-motion diorama. In such a moment it was easy to imagine the city with a life and soul of its own. My eyes were drawn to the Arabic Bible reposing on the dashboard.

"I see you've bought a Bible, Kamlo. You've been reading the gospels?"

"Yes, I have been. As a matter of fact, I have a question."

"OK."

"Do you ever feel . . . like, drawn to a particular verse that seems like it almost jumps off the page at you?"

"Yeah, sometimes. God's Word is living. I gather you had one of those experiences?"

He nodded, his eyes focused on the traffic ahead. "I read the gospels, and then when it quotes the Old Testament, I try to go back and find that. I go back and forth."

"Yes?"

"I have been reading about Jesus healing people—lepers and the lame, but especially the deaf and blind. And there are all these mentions of the prophet Isaias."

"Isaiah."

"Yes. The one that jumped off the page was in chapter twenty-nine. Wait a minute. Here we are."

We pulled into a gas station and rolled up to a pump. Before getting out, Kamlo grabbed his Bible and flipped it open to a marker.

"Verse eighteen. Saying it in English, it says, 'In that day the deaf shall hear the words of a scroll, and out of gloom and darkness the blind shall see.'"

That got me a few goose bumps. "What does that mean to you?"

With his hand on the driver's door, he looked across into my eyes. "I know it is about the Messiah, but it also reminds me of our day, with the discovery of ancient scrolls. I felt like it was almost a promise for us too. Do you think that is possible?"

Now the goose bumps were running riot. "Kamlo, that is one of the ways God speaks to us today—He makes us think of certain things. Perhaps He is doing that with you now. You could talk to Him about that."

He opened the door and stopped. "But what scroll could this mean?"

"Maybe that is for us to find out."

The weather began to break as we left the city. The sun was even coming out. I'd pumped the gas while Kamlo pored over the map and got his bearings. Now he believed he could drive right up to the place. Almost.

I continued pondering his Isaiah experience. There was something about this that felt like God at work, though part of me worried about taking liberties as with Mme Catherine's symbolic analysis. But it was also eerily reminiscent of my own odd experience with Isaiah and the "voice in the wilderness."

Just for something to do, I got out my traveling Bible and read aloud from Isaiah 32 and 35 the more familiar verses about streams in the desert, the shadow of a mighty rock in a thirsty land, the opening of eyes and ears, the healing of the deaf and blind, and the redeemed of the Lord returning to Zion with singing and everlasting joy as sorrow and sighing flee away.

"There it is again," said Kamlo. "The blind seeing and the deaf hearing. When are these things supposed to be?"

I remembered something from Dr. Sawicki's class in seminary. "Theologians see multiple applications, all related to the first and second comings of Christ and the restoration of the nation of Israel."

"Israel?"

"Yes, but ultimately the kingdom of God. Isaiah foresaw the return of Judah after the Babylonian captivity. Then in our own day there's been a rebirth of the state of Israel."

"So these verses can apply to today?"

"Yes. But their ultimate application may be to the Millennium."

"What is *that?*"

Somehow, hurtling down the highway toward the Judean wilderness in pursuit of ancient scrolls seemed an appropriate time to take a little excursion into eschatology.

I reminded my Druse friend of our visit to the Golden Gate. He remembered Ezekiel's prophecy about the shut gate awaiting the Prince's entry. I reminded him of how the Messiah would rule over the nations. The thousand years of peace on earth with the Lord on the throne, I explained, would be the Millennium.

But just how all of that related to the present day was not so easily explained. I just stated as simply as possible my own views on the end times, noting that others had different interpretations of the same events.

Kamlo took it all in without comment. Except for an occasional nod, I couldn't tell if it made any sense to him.

Then he hit me with a question I had not really expected.

"Boss, how did *you* come to believe in Christ?"

That stopped me for a moment.

The story was never easy to tell, and I usually left out the more personal parts. But today, with a long road unwinding before us, the sun breaking through the scattering clouds, and an earnest new believer sincerely asking, I somehow felt greater peace about the telling.

I told him about praying with my father to receive Christ when I was five. I remembered vaguely understanding that Jesus loved me, that He wanted me to go to heaven even if I sometimes did wrong, and that only He could get me there.

At that time my father was still a pastor. A few years later, he was fired by the elders in a traumatic dispute that he never discussed, at least at home. The experience was my first major disappointment with God.

He talked very little about God after that. He became a regular working Joe with a clipboard and a ballpoint pen, selling bungalows, ranches, and colonials in suburban Pittsburgh. He would talk about the Pirates and Steelers, the stock market and the housing market, the weather, death, and taxes, but he had nothing more to say, it seemed, on the subject of religion.

He appeared happier. He didn't bring his work home with him, didn't have to rush off with every phone call to minister to the sick or to counsel marriage partners, didn't have to smooth over controversies among his flock, didn't have to explain himself to a skeptical governing board. He was certainly less stressed.

Yet something went out of him when he left the ministry, something that never returned. I never knew what my dad's relationship was with the Lord after that, although he continued attending church elsewhere, singing the hymns, tithing—all of the motions without any of the life, it seemed.

Perhaps a subconscious desire to vindicate my dad was part of my decision to enter the ministry. I couldn't help being a little disappointed at his lack of excitement over my decision, but my mom assured me that he supported me in my career choice, that he was proud of me.

Dad never got to see me graduate from seminary. An undiagnosed heart condition claimed him suddenly one night while I was off at school. I believed he died of a broken heart, and I cried bitter tears for his abbreviated life of frustration and for the fact that few of his old church friends attended the funeral.

That was my second disappointment with God. In religion classes I had learned the textbook answers for how a just God could allow heartache, but it all had a hollow ring when it came to real-life suffering. When it came to *my* pain, I didn't care much about the Fall and free will and the building of character. Something or somebody took my dad, and God didn't stop it.

I didn't go into detail, but I did indicate to Kamlo that my experience in the pastorate had ended similarly to my father's.

That was my third disappointment with God.

Kamlo broke his silence with a soft remark, so quietly I

almost didn't hear it. "I think I know what you mean, Boss."

"You do?"

"Yes. For me, it is being single. It makes me wonder if there is something wrong with me. It makes me feel—rejected."

The remark struck home like an ax laid to the root. "And I can relate to *that*, Kamlo."

After a moment, he asked delicately, "May I ask you a personal question?"

At this point, I felt like an open book. "Sure."

"Are you and Miss Boynton . . . serious?"

He had me there. "That's a good question. I'm not sure I would dare believe it. And Miriam would probably say I'm never serious. Maybe she's right. Life is easier when you're always just kidding."

A deep silence fell upon us as I sank into my thoughts and Kamlo into his. The landscape was rapidly assuming that wild, windswept look of barren cliffs, crags, scrub brush, stumps, and boulders that suggested jackals, vultures, and desert visions.

It took me a long moment to realize that Kamlo was saying something to me. I was somewhere else. I was back in the wilderness of my desert dream.

This time, the idea and the reality were merging. It was déjà vu in a battered blue Toyota. I was a tumbleweed blowing inexorably down the highway of our God toward the something that was there for me.

15

It wasn't exactly the Emerald City, but it was impressive in its own way. Gleaming in the late-morning sunlight, Dayr Al Nimrun first appeared like a cap of snow on a distant mountain peak.

Except in this case, "mountain" might be a bit of a stretch. These weren't exactly the Rockies here. They were more like the Alleghenies, which get called mountains by upstaters who've never been west of Altoona. Still, I wouldn't like to have to confront them on a bike without an oxygen bottle. And maybe a mobile cardiac cath lab with jumper cables.

At this distance, I could see only that this was a large manmade structure of some light rock like limestone. In fact, what we were seeing was probably just the wall around the place.

"That must be it," Kamlo announced, gazing off in the same direction.

"Anybody ever call you a master of the obvious?"

"What?"

"Never mind. I wonder if they have valet parking there."

Kamlo looked as if he wanted to pull off the road. *"Valet parking?"*

"OK. So I'm a big kidder. It's better than thinking about getting your legs cut off."

He nodded somberly. "That is for true."

Now we were coming to yet another fork in the road. At each previous twist and turn, Kamlo had made his choice without hesitation, apparently having committed the entire route to memory. This time he paused a long moment even though there was no other traffic. And when I looked at our options, I could see why. The left fork, to the west, was as well-paved as the road we'd been on since leaving Jerusalem.

So far, the trek had been like Isaiah's Highway of Holiness —straight and smooth, mountains and valleys straightened out, the rough ground level, and the rugged places a plain. But now it appeared all that was about to change. The right fork, to the north, looked more like the Highway of Holeyness. The whole thing was berm, and pretty rough berm at that. I did not have a good feeling about this.

I was not in the least surprised when Kamlo turned right. Within moments we were heaving and bucking to such a degree I felt in danger of losing the change out of my pockets, the fillings out of my teeth, and my brain out my ear.

Kamlo looked over at me and grinned.

About the time I was wondering if it could get any worse, we came to another fork. It got worse. I didn't at first know just how much worse. I only knew that the road had turned from ugly to hideous.

But then Kamlo said something under his breath in his native tongue and tromped on the brake.

"What's up?" I asked, almost grateful to have stopped.

He said nothing, but I could see his eyes fixed on something across the road.

Then I saw a post driven into the ground with an attached sign inscribed in Arabic. "What's the sign say?"

Kamlo didn't respond. He simply stomped on the accelerator, and off we went again.

Maybe he hadn't heard me. "Uh . . . Kamlo, what did the sign say?"

He flashed me a deadpan look. "What sign?" He chewed his gum and gave me a little wink before switching back to deadpan.

Then I got it. No doubt that Arabic inscription would have said something like "Private Road—No Trespassing." If it had existed.

We had been climbing for some time and had lost sight of Dayr Al Nimrun even before that. The road twisted back and forth like a legless reptile. This place had the baked, treeless appearance of the Judean wilderness along the Jordan Valley, except that the higher altitude seemed to have a moderating effect on the temperature.

Now we were zigzagging up switchbacks that were barely wide enough for one vehicle. I was beginning to wonder if we'd gone up the wrong mountain, when all at once we came upon a small blockhouse of modern vintage, made of cinder blocks with apertures just large enough to sight down the barrel of a gun. It looked as if it was built for a siege. But it told me that we must be approaching something still in service.

Up ahead loomed the stone wall that encircled the compound. Its iron gate stood enticingly open. I held my breath as we cruised slowly past the blockhouse without changing speed. I saw no activity inside or outside. We were past.

I exhaled. That wasn't so bad. In fact, as we approached the open gate, I began to think this was all too easy. Then we crossed the perimeter, and we were inside Dayr Al Nimrun.

Straight ahead was an ancient, formidable-looking structure that had to be the old monastery. With its hunkering two-story stone facade, primitive unadorned design, and corner towers with small oriental domes, the edifice looked less like a religious establishment than a desert citadel.

As old as it appeared, I still couldn't believe that it was sixth-century. It had no doubt been rebuilt at least once since the Middle Ages. And somebody had gone to the trouble of cultivating some greenery here, including a number of stately cedars that clearly had been around for a while.

Some kind of motor roared.

Kamlo cast a worried look in the rearview mirror, and I turned in time to see the iron gate swinging shut, apparently of its own accord. That was not a good sign.

But when I turned back around, I saw an even worse sign. Intercepting us was a motorcycle—a big Harley, with a tough-looking customer driving it. This, I realized, had been the roar we were hearing.

Kamlo put on the brakes.

The cycle stopped in a cloud of dust, inches from our front bumper.

A character as big as Kamlo and twice as ugly got off the hog. In a puce-colored running suit with snakeskin cowboy boots, iridescent blue sunglasses, and gold neck chains, he was one walking mixed metaphor. But that was OK. With a pistol riding on his hip, he was "Sir" to us.

At Kamlo's open window, he placed one beefy hand on the car and the other lightly on the holstered pistol. He growled something in Arabic.

Kamlo sighed, nodded, then cut the engine.

The beefy hand came in the window, and Kamlo put the keys into it.

I wondered if we would ever see them again.

Kamlo looked over at me. "We have been requested to exit the vehicle."

We got out in time to see our custodian hand the keys to a younger, swaggering goon who had appeared seemingly out of nowhere. He patted us down for weapons. Then he got into the Toyota and started it up.

"See," I murmured to Kamlo. "And you thought they wouldn't have valet parking."

Kamlo at first shot me a dark, unappreciative glance. Then he visibly relaxed and smiled, chewing that gum, which drew a dark, unappreciative look from the sheriff of Dayr Al Nimrun.

The man snarled something in his own tongue, but it translated pretty well.

He wanted us to march, and we complied, stepping out in front of him toward the monastery. I could hear the cycle growling behind us like a metallic tiger. I wondered how our friend kept his balance at such low speed, but my curiosity wasn't great enough to risk a look back.

As we closed the distance, I was put in mind of *Tio Piña*

"Uncle Pineapple." What many Panamanians had irreverently called their erstwhile strong man Manuel Noriega, the round-headed man with the pockmarked complexion who so resembled our friend here with pistol and boots. I hoped this man was not so dangerous, but I wasn't overly optimistic. I assumed he was Selmar Hajabeel's aide-de-camp or administrative assistant.

To my surprise, we did not enter the monastery through the front entrance with the stone arch and the gnarly, bullet-shaped double doors. Instead, he directed us to make a sharp right and approach an even larger entrance a few yards farther on—what could have been a service bay with a ceiling-mounted track door.

I was right about this entrance. At some unseen command, the door began clocking upward to reveal a sizable garage area containing a small fleet of luxury cars. Their impeccable wax finishes gleamed in the artificial light. I could make out a black Lincoln, a maroon Jaguar, a candy apple red Rolls Royce, a baby blue Volvo, a gray Porsche, and a 1960s-vintage white Mustang convertible. There were a couple of others farther back, which I couldn't quite identify, but I doubted they were Yugos or Chevettes.

I felt as if I had just walked into somebody's private fantasy. If I was not mistaken, that large structure at the far end was a car wash. Why not? In the middle of the garage were a couple of gas pumps. I tried to imagine tanker trucks making the run up here on the same roads that had almost shaken us to pieces, and my imagination for once was not equal to the task.

Our *Tio Piña* said something, which Kamlo instantly translated. "Wait right here."

I looked around at the sound of an engine approaching from behind us. *Tio Piña* sidekick was pulling Kamlo's battered blue Toyota into an empty slot in this private showroom.

I suppressed a laugh. The sight of the beater sitting proudly among all these high-rolling chariots was too much.

Kamlo was smiling, probably thinking about valet parking.

But *Tio Piña* was not amused. From a workbench he grabbed a propane torch and fired it up. He lit a cigarette with it. He blew a cloud of smoke in our direction. Then he said something.

Kamlo translated again. "He wants to know what's so funny."

"Ask him how much he'll take on a trade-in."

But *Tio Piña* was not waiting for an answer.

"He wants us to empty our pockets on the workbench," Kamlo said.

I began turning mine inside out and placing the contents on the bench, but Kamlo continued to discuss the matter in Arabic. *Tio Piña* apparently did not like Kamlo's choice of words. He stepped toward us with the torch in his hand and a wicked gleam in his eye. He gestured with the other hand at Kamlo, who took his father's camera off his shoulder.

Kamlo calmly aimed the camera at *Tio Piña* and began snapping off some photographs of the man advancing with the torch.

"Kamlo!" I cried. "What are you doing?"

"I told him we were journalists, but he does not believe me. I can handle him. Just watch behind you."

"Kamlo—"

I was starting to warn him that our credibility as journalists depended on not starting any rough stuff, but I was a little late. *Tio Piña* apparently decided to go ahead and take the camera from him.

Kamlo responded with a swift, accurate kick to the man's wrist. The torch went rolling across the floor at my feet, its orange-blue jet revolving like a virulent sprinkler.

Tio Piña stopped Kamlo in his tracks with the simple expediency of drawing his pistol and aiming it at the big man's face. The gum chewing stopped.

Somebody behind me was barking something, and I turned. Kamlo had told me to watch behind me with good reason. There stood *Tio Piña*'s sidekick, gripping a knife big enough to skin alligators and with a ruffian's glee in his simple face. He was gesticulating at the torch.

I guessed he wanted me to pick it up. Apparently I guessed right. He accepted the torch with a grin and then made another gesture in my vicinity along with more words that were no help at all.

"He wants the tape recorder," said Kamlo.

At this point, that was the least of my worries. I handed it over.

Our firebug began applying the torch to it. Its plastic case started to twist and shrivel, then emit toxic-looking, sooty black smoke. I tried to turn away from the foul odor, as sickening as burning rubber.

Meanwhile, *Tío Piña* managed to wrest the Leica at gunpoint from Kamlo. Still holding the pistol in one hand, with the other he put the camera into a bench vise and began turning the handle.

I cringed. There was a crunching, popping sound, and the camera's essentially hollow body commenced crumpling and caving.

It was as sickening as the crumpling of a young boy's heart. I grieved for a son named Kamlo and for his father, and then I was filled with rage. I don't know what I thought I could really do about it, but I couldn't just stand there. Before I knew it, I was across the room—and staring down the barrel of a gun.

We were now faced with a mixed bag. The upside was that I'd distracted *Tío Piña* long enough for Kamlo to go on the offensive. The downside was that the thug behind me had caught up.

Something hard slammed into the back of my head. Everything went dim. But before I zeroed out, I had the very brief satisfaction of seeing *Tío Piña*'s face snapping around like a banner in the wind from the force of Kamlo's fist.

Awaking in another room and seeing *Tío Piña*'s puffy and swollen nose was not a great deal of satisfaction up against my throbbing skull. His nose might be broken, but my whole head felt like something that had been rung by Quasimodo. I touched the back of my head and, feeling the nasty knot, almost wished I hadn't. I must not have been out very long, judging by the fact that the blood was still sticky.

Tío Piña, pacing a few feet away, gave me a silent smirk when he saw that I was awake.

Kamlo was slumped in a chair opposite me, looking bored and bemused. At least we were both alive.

We were in a pretty nice place for an old monastery. We were seated in white wicker patio chairs. There were matching cocktail tables. Under my feet was a Persian throw rug over jade-hued marble. On the walls hung several impressive oil paintings from the West, including one that looked very much like a Chagall. Overhead was a skylight. And all around the room were various vases and urns and statuettes in ceramic, brass, bronze, and stone that virtually cried out wealth and breeding. Or—I remembered Selmar Hajabeel's trade—maybe they were crying out for justice.

I wondered how I got there—if Kamlo had been forced to carry me like a sack of feed and prop me up in this nobleman's sitting room. I had to guess that the same thug who'd hit me over the head also had held a knife or gun on Kamlo until *Tio Piña* could regain control of the situation.

But I wasn't about to get a lot of time for reflection. *Tio Piña* picked up an oyster-colored phone from an end table and stabbed at a button. He uttered a few syllables and fell silent, his eyes flitting across Kamlo. After a couple more snappy syllables, he hung up, barking something that brought Kamlo slowly to his feet.

Kamlo gestured at me to follow him.

My head throbbed much worse when I stood, but I had no choice. We glided down a gilded hallway that made me think of Dorothea Benson Cray. But when we entered the double oak doors at the end of the hall, the resemblance ended—except for the desk. This one was almost big enough to land a Harrier jump jet.

One entire wall was a giant-screen TV, the kind composed of smaller component units, one of which provided alternating views apparently of the grounds of Dayr Al Nimrun through different security cameras. Another wall was made up of sliding glass doors onto an indoor swimming pool where several bathers of the female persuasion were splashing it up. I saw a wet bar in one corner. On a third wall were trophy heads of various beasts. Judging from an elephant's foot serving as an umbrella stand, I wouldn't have been surprised if some of these critters were illegal game.

A man in his early thirties, as darkly handsome as Omar Sharif, with the same impeccable mustache and slick haircut, was sitting with his feet propped up on the oversized desk and smoking a cigar. I hadn't seen a man wearing a cravat outside of the movies, but this one was. He was also wearing designer jeans and a smart-looking navy blue silk blazer over a natty plaid shirt in Arizona tones.

If this was Selmar Hajabeel, he was shattering my stereotypes. I'd expected something a little more Middle Eastern.

Leaning upon an elbow and holding his cigar at ear level, he looked directly at me and smiled like a toothpaste commercial.

"You were expecting maybe Yasir Arafat?" he asked, as if reading my mind.

He hadn't even much of an accent.

"Well," I conceded, "I hadn't expected Burt Reynolds."

The unchanging smile was looking increasingly pasted on. "Oh, I am much younger than that."

"Better looking too," I added.

"Absolutely. Please, have a seat."

We sat stiffly in two of the black leather chairs arranged across from his desk, while *Tio Piña* closed the oak doors and leaned against the wall, his arms folded and his eyes half closed. I noted that the pistol was still riding securely on his hip.

Without warning, the feet came down from the desk, the cigar went into an ashtray, and the smile slid off the face of Selmar Hajabeel.

"Now, gentlemen," he snapped. "Just what are you doing here on my property uninvited?"

Without the phony playboy expression, his face acquired a pronounced sharpness, mostly in the dark, hawklike eyes that looked as if they could penetrate reinforced concrete.

I swallowed the golf ball in my throat and gave it a shot. "My name is Harper—Dr. C. James Harper—a biblical scholar and writer. I'm working on an article for the *Journal of Ancient Literature*, and this is my assistant and photographer, Kamlo."

I waited a couple of heartbeats while our interrogator reinserted his cigar and thought about that.

Then I added, "And you must be Selmar Hajabeel?"

149

He nodded faintly, his eyes acquiring a hooded look. "And what would any of that have to do with me? Even assuming it *was* true."

Kamlo sat up straighter in his chair and challenged, "Why would it *not* be true?"

Selmar nodded faintly again, this time at *Tio Piña*, who came off the wall like a fly on a garbage mission. He came over and glared over his swollen nose at Kamlo while he fished some items out of his pockets and laid them upon the desk. The last item stayed in his hand.

I saw with a shudder that it was Mrs. Cray's checkbook for the bank in Tel Aviv.

Apparently, to *Tio Piña* it was a major deal. He waved it a couple of times while he chattered away in accusatory tones.

"What's he saying?" I asked Kamlo.

Selmar interrupted. "We are discussing the great likelihood that you are Israeli agents."

Kamlo, outraged, was out of his seat this time. "*What?* Israeli agents! Listen—"

Tio Piña's pistol was out in a flash and pointing the way to Kamlo's heart.

"Kamlo, sit down," I whispered fiercely, "before someone gets hurt."

"Yes," Selmar agreed. "We certainly would not want that to happen."

Stiffly, Kamlo sat back down.

Selmar nodded again toward his lieutenant and then the door. *Tio Piña* barked something at Kamlo and then underscored his point by shoving the pistol toward my friend's neck.

Kamlo rose stiffly again from his chair and, without looking back, walked out of the room. The door thudded ominously shut behind them.

"Where's he being taken?" I demanded.

Selmar shrugged as if that was of little moment. "Your photographer friend seems a bit on the aggressive side. We would not want anybody to get hurt, as you say."

I pointed to several mounted heads on the wall. "Wouldn't

hurt a fly, I suppose. Are any of those trophies endangered species, by any chance?"

Selmar blew out a large quantity of smoke. "I did not shoot them. I am a merchant, pure and simple. I buy things. I sell things. That is all."

"Like local law enforcement? Is that something for sale around here too?"

Selmar stopped smoking and glared. "You talk big for someone in a very weak position."

He was right about that. I decided it was time to play a wild card.

"All right. Suppose—just for the sake of argument—suppose we *are* Israeli agents. If you really believed that, my guess is you're too smart to get yourself into that much hurt by molesting us."

Selmar laughed. It started with a modest chuckle and built to a lusty belly laugh.

When he was done, he said, "There seems to be something here you do not understand, my friend."

"Please enlighten me, then."

"Have you heard of Palestinian self-rule? That is where you are now at Dayr Al Nimrun. You are in *our* territory. I can do anything I want, my friend. Do you understand what I am saying? Anything."

To my great chagrin, I was beginning to understand. All too well.

By the hand of Thine anointed, who discerned Thy testimonies, Thou hast revealed to us the [times] of the battles of Thy hands that Thou mayest glorify Thyself in our enemies by leveling the hordes of Satan, the seven nations of vanity . . . by the fullness of Thy marvelous power.
—The War Rule, 1QM XI

16

It was finally getting to me. There was a tightness in my chest, and I could feel sweat on my forehead. I didn't suppose Selmar Hajabeel actually cut people's legs off. But I wasn't at all sure what he *would* do.

He stood up, his eyes still fastened on me with that predatory cunning. Then he appeared to soften. The playboy charm was back. He showed me a solicitous smile as true as simulated wood grain. "You look like you could use a drink."

I shook my head as he ambled over to the bar and sprayed himself something fizzy in a glass. He brought it back to the desk but didn't sit down. He just kept watching. Sipping and watching.

It prompted me to wonder at his apparent unconcern about being alone with me—without his enforcer. Maybe he had a handgun nearby. Maybe we were on a surveillance camera. Maybe *Tio Piña* was not far off.

"What I *could* use," I said, partly to break my own paralysis, "is some paper and a pen."

Selmar lifted his eyebrows, but he wasn't about to lift a finger without further explanation. Nor did he apparently care enough to ask for one.

I managed a businesslike smile. "You see, your torpedo

took my effects, including my pen and notebook, and melted my tape recorder with his cigarette lighter."

Selmar's expression alternated between amusement and confusion. "My *what?*"

"Your executive reptile or whatever you call him—*Tio Piña.*"

He asked what that meant. When I told him "Uncle Pineapple," he began laughing so hard I thought he'd spill his sarsaparilla. Then the fun and games slid off his face again.

"I will ask you just one more time, friend. Just what is this *story* you say you are writing? And why does it bring you here?"

"Oh," I said, "so you might be willing to entertain the idea that I'm telling the truth and I'm not an Israeli agent?"

"Let us just say—for the sake of argument—I want to hear your story."

This time I stood up and began strolling while he sat down. He didn't object. In a minute I had my thoughts assembled. I took a deep breath and plunged in.

"Once upon a time, God spoke through His prophets— men like Isaiah son of Amoz. Some of their words were written down with pen and ink on scrolls of animal hide. Some of these scrolls were deposited in caves near the Dead Sea, waiting a thousand years to startle the eyes of the blind and the ears of the deaf of our generation. And, lo, this week along comes a false prophet named Randall Plunkett, who publishes an article alleging a conspiracy to suppress the contents of the scrolls."

I paused and turned to establish direct eye contact with my host. "And this Randall Plunkett further alleges that the one person who knows these secret contents is a man by the name of Dr. Elliot Freemantle."

My host would probably be a natural at poker. There was no visible change in his expression, eye movement, or respiration.

I kept my mouth shut and left the verbal ball in his court.

When he finally spoke, there was no awkwardness or defensiveness. "Tell me, Dr. Harper, are you searching for scrolls or for this Dr. Freemantle?"

"Both. That's why I have that checkbook. It belongs to a wealthy American benefactor who is willing to spend some big money to recover additional scrolls."

This time I thought I detected a subtle reaction. Maybe there'd been a slight twitch of the eyebrows, a shift of the eyes, or a catch of the breath. The smell of greed seemed to be in the air.

"So how much is this rich Yankee willing to pay?"

I smiled. "That's strictly a matter to be negotiated with the person who has the items in question."

I was treading on dangerous ground here.

Selmar's eyebrows knit into a glare.

I decided to go the rest of the way out on the limb.

"Or has the person in question."

Now Selmar's eyebrows went straight up. "You think this Dr. Freemantle is a captive somewhere?"

I nodded. "I have some reason to believe that."

"All right, Dr. Harper," he said smoothly, yet dangerously. "Let us lay all of our cards on the table, as they say. Are you accusing me of holding this Dr. Freemantle captive?"

Now I was smelling possible success within my reach, if I played it carefully. "Remember, I'm a writer—a researcher, an investigator. Unlike Randall Plunkett, I do not make wild allegations. I ask questions. People say Selmar Hajabeel knows a great deal about ancient documents that are out of circulation. I make it a practice to direct my questions to people who know a great deal about the things I need to know."

Selmar was silent for a long moment before speaking. "Very interesting response, which sidestepped my question entirely. I must conclude, therefore, that you are indeed accusing me of this."

Before I could say anything further, Selmar pushed a button on a small desktop console.

There was a tinny response I couldn't make out from a voice that sounded like *Tio Piña*'s.

Selmar said something in Arabic and shut off the box. He wandered across the room then and leaned against the glass, watching the ladies in the pool.

I didn't know what to think.

And then the oak doors opened, and in came *Tio Piña*—behind a tall man with glasses and the kind of tight, curly hair that women always said made them jealous. There was a gaunt,

154

stressed look about his face and a slight stoop to his shoulders that suggested the weight of the world.

When he looked my way, I remembered where I had seen that face before. It was in that press kit Miriam had given me, along with mug shots of all the other Scrolls scholars.

"Elliot Freemantle," I muttered just above a whisper.

I thought I saw a shock of recognition in his eyes when he spied me, but that may have been my imagination. There was no particular reason for him to know me, except by reputation and a mutual female acquaintance by the name of Esther.

Freemantle looked at my extended hand for a moment as if he didn't know what it was. And then with a faint expression of something like amusement, he took it and shook it firmly.

"Dr. Harper, I presume?" he asked, unprompted, in a thin, reedy voice with a soft British accent that suggested dusty tomes and nothing more physical than a tenure track.

I nodded dumbly, frantically trying to play out this chess game a few moves ahead.

"Yes, yes," Selmar interjected. He then performed the introductions as if he were hosting a cocktail party among fellow marketers and merchandisers.

"Dr. Freemantle here is my consultant in the field of ancient documents. As you can see, he is not a prisoner. He is working for me of his own free will."

I couldn't help but notice that Freemantle was scratching his cheek with two fingers, one crossed over the other, oddly. Then it hit me—the sign of the fib.

But maybe this was just a fluke. I would watch and see if it recurred in any pattern. I did not believe that Freemantle was here of his own volition.

"How did you two happen to meet?" I asked Freemantle.

Selmar answered for him. "You might say I recruited him. I have some materials here—ancient documents in an archaic form of Hebrew—that I needed analyzed. But, of course, one cannot trust Israelis. Fortunately, I believe Dr. Freemantle is trust-worthy."

I seized the opportunity to get Selmar in a box. "Is that right?"

He nodded slowly, warily. "Yes, that is right."

"Well, then, why don't you ask him to vouch for me? Ask him if he thinks I could be some kind of agent for Israel."

Selmar shrugged dismissively, as much as to say that was unnecessary.

It might have died right there. It had been a calculated risk. Considering our professional differences, Freemantle might have called me the worst fraud since cold fusion.

But the man surprised me by speaking up. "Dr. Harper is no Israeli agent. He is an eminent scholar of the first rank, Selmar."

I noticed he was smiling—and scratching his cheek with crossed fingers. He wasn't being nice because he liked me. He was in a jam here, and he needed me.

I decided to try a long shot. "Would you mind if Dr. Freemantle and I conferred? Perhaps I could lend some assistance. Perhaps these ancient documents are something that would interest my client."

The hooded look came over Selmar's eyes. "Confer? Do you mean in private?"

I nodded. "Yes."

Selmar put on his alligator smile. "No. With all due respect, Dr. Harper, I do not distrust you. But in my line of work we have to be careful."

I spread my hands. "Sorry. I just thought you were interested in marketing these . . . materials."

Selmar's expression shifted to one of concern. "Oh, I am. Do you have some objection to discussing the matter with Dr. Freemantle right here in my office in my presence?"

Freemantle was looking like a dog waiting for a crumb to drop from the table. What could I say?

"All right. Let's do it right here."

Selmar grinned and snapped his fingers. "Very good. Nadi!"

So that was *Tio Piña*'s name.

Nadi, the pineapple man, jumped to it and pulled out two chairs at the conference table against the far wall, indicating we should inhabit them.

Just one thing was missing.

"Aren't we going to examine any actual documents?" I asked.

Freemantle shot a glance toward Selmar, who was leaning against the glass wall, frowning.

"Not at this point," Freemantle said carefully. "I shall describe the documents to you, and if there is something you think your client would be interested in purchasing, we shall talk further. Is that acceptable?"

I nodded. "All right. But just so we don't have any misunderstandings, how did these documents come into the possession of Selmar Hajabeel?"

Selmar was off the glass in an instant. "They have been in my family many years," he interjected. "They have been lying in a vault awaiting proper identification and the right buyer. There are some things that would not be for sale to the Jews at any price."

When Selmar asserted they were family heirlooms, Freemantle began scratching his face again.

"Then," I persisted, "why are they just now receiving this attention?"

Selmar found a new cigar and began applying flame to it.

"Very simply," he said, in between puffs, "I need cash. Governmental interference is hurting business."

I presumed this was an oblique reference to the black market, but it didn't really wash. "I thought this was Palestinian self-rule. What happened to doing anything you want, anytime you want?"

Selmar was unperturbed. "If only that were true everywhere we do business. Unfortunately, it is not. We are a country under occupation."

I was certain he was lying, but his story was plausible enough on the surface.

Freemantle resumed his description of the materials. "We have four scrolls, and they are all priceless. Two are in excellent condition. One is what dealers would call very fine. And the fourth would be too, except for missing the first several columns. That's the War Rule Scroll."

I nodded. "OK. What are the other three?"

157

"The two excellent ones are Isaiah and Hezekiah texts, and the one very fine is a Hadassah scroll."

My mind was racing. He was giving me some major clues here, if I could just read between the lines.

"Never mind their condition," I insisted. "There are more than a dozen copies each of the War Rule and Isaiah scrolls. But to my knowledge, the Hezekiah and Hadassah scrolls would be previously undiscovered documents."

Freemantle nodded. "That adds greatly to their value, of course."

"But I cannot see them?"

Freemantle glanced at Selmar, who was watching us, eyes hooded and cigar smoldering.

He shook his head. "No."

I got the feeling that there were invisible strings connecting Freemantle's mouth to Selmar's fingers. But I also had the feeling that he was sending me some unauthorized messages. I needed to press the matter.

"Tell me more about their content—the Hezekiah and Hadassah scrolls, that is."

"I am sorry, Dr. Harper, but that would be a bit premature. I'm in the early stages of translation of the first one, Hezekiah. And it appears to be a supplement to or fulfillment of some reference in the twenty-eighth chapter of First Chronicles."

Several pieces of the puzzle suddenly dovetailed. "Uh . . . would that happen to be, say, maybe verse nineteen?"

Freemantle's eyes grew saucerlike, and I thought I heard a sharp intake of breath. He began scratching his cheek with the crossed fingers.

"Oh, no, Dr. Harper, it wouldn't be anything like that, I assure you. You ought to do your homework a little better than that."

Selmar was getting nervous. He began pacing and puffing and stealing suspicious, sidelong glances at us. I believed I was beginning to catch on to Freemantle's game. If I played my cards right, I could probably force Selmar's hand.

I sighed and placed my hands palms down on the table, thinking about getting up. "There is no way to do business sight unseen. No buyer would hold still for that."

Freemantle looked at Selmar and said wearily, "You see, Selmar? Is that not what I've been saying?"

Selmar looked unimpressed. He crossed his arms, his cigar stuck in his silent mouth.

I stayed in character. "Just how much are you asking for these sight-unseen scrolls?"

Selmar took his cigar out and looked at it as if wondering how it had got there. "A million dollars."

"A million dollars?" I repeated in an awed tone. "For all four?"

"Each," he said, enunciating precisely with his lips drawn back.

"Each?"

Selmar kept it casual. "Of course, you and your client are free to make a counteroffer."

This time I stood up. "Not without at least a scroll fragment to check for authenticity."

Selmar's nervousness was back. "Well, I . . ."

Freemantle rose to the occasion. "Now do you believe me, Selmar?"

A kind of fury seemed to rise in Selmar's eyes. He turned to Nadi, who appeared to be napping by the door. "Take him out of here!" he spat.

In the moment of diversion, Freemantle whispered imploringly, "You don't have to tell anyone I'm here."

The pock-faced henchman strolled across the room and in one swift, violent motion kicked the chair out from under Freemantle. While the latter flailed about to avoid hitting the deck, Nadi grabbed the fleshy part of his upper arm and steered him toward the door, without apparent effort. I got the feeling that anything Nadi might lack in brute strength he more than made up for with sheer meanness and deadly instincts.

As I watched Freemantle being carted unceremoniously out the door, I was reminded how a person's true colors have a way of surfacing. Selmar had just exposed as a lie his claim of Freemantle's voluntary servitude here as a consultant. He might affect the style and grace of a Western-style sophisticate, but the brutality of his subordinates spoke clearly of the sharks just below the surface.

Yet I didn't expect the man to change his tune just because he'd been exposed. And in this part of the world, the power of the lie was not so much in its credibility as in the strength of its assertion. Translation: I don't care if you believe me as long as you play along with my story.

I knew I could accomplish nothing by attacking the lie of Freemantle's voluntary residence, other than maybe ending up a prisoner myself. How long Selmar could continue holding people against their will before he would attract unwanted attention was a good question, complicated by the location of Dayr Al Nimrun in self-governing territory—if that were even true. But I didn't want to find out.

I decided to make my move before untoward events overtook me. I took a step toward the door.

"Listen, Selmar. I want to apologize for intruding here uninvited. I'll tell my client about your items. Perhaps some day when they're ready to be shown, we can do business."

When Selmar, cigar stuck firmly in his mouth, said nothing, I took another tentative step toward the door. I wished I knew where they had taken Kamlo. Right now, his blue beater would look mighty good to me, especially with its engine running and its wheels turning.

Selmar took the cigar out. "Excuse me. Wait here a minute." He left the room in a haze of cigar smoke.

I waited. I didn't start exploring his office or going through his desk. I didn't even breathe very hard. I wanted nothing to stand between me and freedom. I was not ashamed to admit I was getting a little scared.

But I didn't have to worry for long.

In another minute Selmar and Nadi were back.

Selmar handed me something in a plain white no. 10 envelope.

"Let nothing happen to that," he insisted. "I expect it to be returned, regardless."

I tucked the envelope, unopened, into my shirt pocket.

Nadi grabbed my arm with an iron grip and began steering

me toward the double doors, just as he had done with Kamlo.

I heard Selmar following us down the hall.

"And by the way," Selmar said, "next time, please do not bother to come all the way out here. You can do any and all business through my old friend Al Malik."

That was OK by me, but there was something still bothering me. Kamlo.

Now we turned into the marble-floored room with the white wicker chairs. I stopped dead, which appeared to startle Nadi. His talons dug more tightly into my left arm, but he stopped too and looked at Selmar behind us.

"Kamlo," I said, half gasping from the pain in my arm.

"Beg your pardon?" said Selmar.

I half turned to see him relighting his cigar and lounging in the doorway. He looked about as serious as a plutocrat waiting for his last dinner guest to hit the road.

The arm hadn't stopped hurting, but I was getting my breath back. "My friend Kamlo. Where is he?"

Out of the corner of my eye, I noticed someone enter the room from the other end. I looked and saw that it was Nadi's associate, probably the thug who had clobbered me in the garage. The fellow was regarding me the way a marksman views a skeet on the fly. The back of my head began throbbing all over again.

"Well," Selmar drawled, "it is like this. Your associate has decided to stay here and assist Dr. Freemantle. If your client should make an acceptable offer—through Al Malik, as I suggested —Mr. Kamlo may be able to serve as our courier, shall we say?"

The man oozed falsehood. I couldn't let him get away with this.

"That's a lie!" I cried. As much as I wanted out of here, I couldn't let this happen to Kamlo. "I won't leave without him!"

The second thug grabbed my other arm. This time they had to work for it. I twisted around until the pain in my left arm forced me into a position allowing my right to be pinned.

Stumbling about, I caught sight of Selmar, still leaning in the doorway and watching his cigar burn.

"We shall see about that," he said as softly as a purring puma.

Just as I thought I saw Selmar make a subtle nod, I found myself being jerked around in a couple of quick moves that ended with Nadi's securing both my arms behind my back and the other gentleman's squaring off before me.

The next moment my head was spinning and my face smarting from a vicious backhand slap. A combination of anger and desperation welled up in me, fueling a last-ditch struggle to break Nadi's grip on my arms that almost succeeded. It was cut short when a well-placed knee was applied in an unsportsmanlike manner and left me gasping.

My knees were sagging, and I was seeing little spots like fireflies on a July night. The fight had gone out of me, and I was out of there. Kamlo was going to have to fend for himself.

17

Half-conscious, dazed, disoriented, I stumbled down endless darkened corridors, propelled by forces beyond my reckoning. I had forgotten where I was, and I had no idea where I was bound. At least my handlers knew where I needed to go. And while these were no friends of mine, somehow I knew they were taking me to the right place. Wherever that was.

It wasn't until I found myself looking up at large fluorescent shop lights and then down at a black Lincoln and a maroon Jaguar that it began to come back to me. By the time I had put it all back together in my mind, I was being hustled into an extremely modest blue Toyota.

Nadi slapped the keys into my hand and made clear without benefit of a single English word what he meant for me to do with them.

The large bay door was clocking open once more, and I wasted no time getting the engine started and putting the transmission into reverse. I was a little wobbly getting out of there, but, at that point, leaving a little scratch on the red Rolls would be the least of my worries.

Once turned around, I could see the big iron gate ratcheting open to show the way out of Dayr Al Nimrun. I wasted no time exiting and putting some distance between myself and Selmar Hajabeel's fiefdom. It didn't seem right, tooling around in Kamlo's car without him. But there wasn't much that seemed right about any of this.

Just then, getting down the mountain occupied all of my attention. Parts of it looked familiar; others didn't register at all. It didn't much matter. There was only one way down, as long as I kept to the road. Once I was past the blockhouse, I felt I could breathe a little more easily, but I wouldn't really relax until I was at the bottom.

At times I thought I saw movement off to the side, but I didn't dare look away from the road. The apparitions up ahead where I could see were more instructive. Each threatening shape, generally in the vicinity of a cedar or pine, would upon closer inspection resolve into nothing more than a rock or shadow.

It had to have been just my strained nerves and wild imagination. If there had been any serious danger on the road from bandits or brigands, it would have surfaced on the way up here. If Selmar was as big as his reputation, anyone leaving his compound would probably be left alone out of respect for the ayatollah of the mountain.

After what seemed hours of twisting and descending, I finally came to a straightaway that joined another road. Suddenly I recognized where I was. There was the warning sign in Arabic— the one that didn't exist. I pulled over and took a deep breath. Now I was beginning to feel free once more. With the engine still running, I remembered to pray in thanksgiving for my safe exit and in petition for Kamlo's ultimate release. And then I remembered the envelope riding snugly inside my shirt pocket.

I pulled it out and turned it over in my hands. Nothing was written on the outside. It was heavy for its size. I ripped the flap open and peered inside. There was my bank book—or, really, Mrs. Cray's. But there was something else too.

I extracted a piece of white onionskin like a bifold brochure, secured along its edges with cellophane tape. I could tell that there was another note-sized object inside, much darker than the onionskin. I peeled the tape back carefully, so that it could be refastened, and unfolded the paper. It took me a moment to realize—or to believe—what I was seeing inside.

On a thin piece of pumpkin-colored hide about half the size of a business card were several dozen Hebrew characters in an ancient flowing hand. This was my requested scroll fragment! With trembling fingers, I plucked it from the onionskin and savored the moment. This was the first time I had ever held a piece of the Scrolls in my own hands. It was almost too amazing to be true.

Then I quickly put it back, silently rebuking myself for allowing my fingers and body oil to contaminate this delicate treasure. Ordinarily I would use instruments such as forceps—assuming I was fortunate enough to get so close.

I marveled for a moment that Selmar would have let even this fragment out of his possession without a security deposit. But then I remembered, sadly, he had Kamlo for collateral. That was more than deposit enough.

But, suggested the cynic in me, could this be a clever forgery? Considering the source, that was not out of the question. Yet, as I feasted my eyes on the scroll fragment, my gut was telling me that this was the genuine article. There was also enough material here for thorough analysis, including radiocarbon dating. If this was a fake, we would not be fooled for long.

I scanned the words. They appeared to be an entire verse, intact.

As I translated into English, I was thunderstruck. "And in that day the deaf shall hear the words of the scroll, and the eyes of the blind shall see out of their gloom and out of darkness."

This was Isaiah 29:18, the verse that Kamlo had felt divinely given. I knew about coincidences. This wasn't one of them. Things like this didn't just happen.

I prayed again when I pulled into the Rockefeller's parking lot and shut off the engine. I remembered Kamlo's captivity and gave thanks for still having Miriam. Halfway back to town I had called her. I said I had some news, and she said she had some for me. Neither of us wanted to say what on a car phone.

Back inside my office, I was grateful that Miriam spared me the "American hero" treatment. There must have been something about my voice on the phone and then my appearance that evoked the mother in her.

"Did you know you have a black eye?" she asked almost disapprovingly.

Reflexively I touched it, and it was sore all right. That must have been the backhand from Nadi's accomplice.

"Did you get that at Dayr Al Nimrun?"

I nodded and without thinking touched the knot on the back of my head, just to see if it was still there.

"What's that?" she asked suspiciously.

When I tried to shrug it off, she ordered me to sit down. Not up to an argument, I dropped into the chair behind my desk and sighed. I was more than a bit weary.

Miriam began fingering through my hair to find the spot. She was so close behind me that I could feel her body heat and smell her fragrance. It smelled like warm baths and home cooking and clean sheets. I felt like a flower in the spring rain. I could stay here for a while.

"That's not so bad," she murmured after a moment, one warm hand still resting on my shoulder. "Nothing a little peroxide won't fix."

"It won't make me a blond, will it?"

She headed toward the door. "Right now, almost anything would be an improvement."

"Hey, as long as you're up—"

"Yes?"

"Order me a pizza, will you?"

"We'll see."

While she was gone, I looked around for a mirror. I hoped I didn't look too frightful. Then I thought of the men's room next door. I went in and splashed some water on my face. I looked worse than I'd thought. With the shiner and the disheveled hair and the bedraggled look, it was actually a bit pitiful. I combed my hair. It was the only thing I could do anything about.

I went back to my desk and began thinking about what I would do next.

I didn't get too far before Miriam returned. She had a brown bottle of peroxide, a little shrink-wrapped apple pie from

166

the commissary, and a cup of strong black coffee. I hadn't eaten since breakfast, and it was the middle of the afternoon. While she fixed my head, I fixed my stomach. I barely tasted the pie as it went down. The coffee felt like new life growing within.

"All right, mister," she said after a minute. "Fess up how you got these boo-boos—and you don't get 'em both front and back from running into a door."

I had to tell her. I started by describing the debonair Selmar Hajabeel and his henchmen and then broke the news about Kamlo's detention. It was the single development that cast a pall over everything else.

Miriam looked alarmed. "Why don't we just go to the police?"

"No good. Freemantle and Kamlo are Selmar's insurance policy against such eventualities. From what I observed, I don't believe Selmar would be above killing, if it served his purpose. I could be wrong, but I don't want to find out."

Her expression turned to curiosity. "Dr. Freemantle was there."

"Yes."

"You're sure about that?"

"I met him. I spoke with him. He told me about four scrolls they have at Dayr Al Nimrun. I have a fragment for verification. Selmar claims Freemantle is there of his own free will as a consultant on ancient documents, but it's pretty clear to me he's a prisoner."

"What are you going to do about it?"

I frowned. "I'm not sure. I think my only choice is to try to work a deal with Selmar for the scrolls. Then he'll let Freemantle and Kamlo go."

"And then he can be prosecuted."

"I wouldn't be so sure. This may be Palestinian jurisdiction. Selmar claims it's part of the self-governing territory. I wouldn't hold my breath for the authorities to act."

"Then you're going to pretend as if no crime was being committed?"

"Well, that's the other problem. With Freemantle, it's almost as if—"

Words failed me.

Miriam prompted, "As if what?"

I shook my head. "There's something that doesn't quite add up with our Dr. Freemantle."

"What do you mean?"

"I don't know. Just a hunch. For one thing, it seems to me that Dayr Al Nimrun would not be that hard a place to bust out of. That's where time may be on our side. Kamlo might be able to escape if we can't spring him ourselves."

"Are you suggesting that Freemantle might be mixed up with this Selmar in some way?"

"Something like that. Let's just say I'm suspicious. He had also told me before our meeting broke up that I needn't tell anybody where he was. He's a prisoner, but it's almost as if he didn't want out of there."

Miriam was silent. "That's interesting," she murmured at last.

"How so?"

"Remember I said on the car phone I had some news?"

I nodded. "Yeah."

"It would appear that Elliot Freemantle is leading a double life."

"No."

"Yes. There's a Mrs. Freemantle—or, at least, someone who claims to be."

"How do you know that?"

"A Julia Freemantle called today from Exeter, England, after reading the Randy Plunkett story in *Ground Zero*. Needless to say, she was concerned about his alleged disappearance and possible foul play. Since you made me public information officer, I got the call."

"Do you believe her?"

"That's the funny thing. Yes, I do."

I was definitely missing something here. "What kind of alleged marriage did they have? Was this some kind of estrangement—so that she had to learn about her missing hubby by reading a magazine?"

"No. The way she told it, they just had that kind of long-

168

distance relationship. She's a stay-at-home mom who was used to his long, globe-trotting absences. But he would check in with fair regularity."

"And she was alarmed that he hadn't called within his normal routine?"

"Yes. I tried to reassure her that the Randy Plunkett story was highly exaggerated, and that seemed to help."

"You didn't mention Mme Catherine?"

She gave me a shocked look, then softened. "No, of course not. But Mrs. Freemantle said something else a little odd."

"What was that?"

"She said she hoped it wasn't anything serious. That maybe Elly's disappearance—she called him Elly—was nothing more than another little 'fling,' as she called it."

"'Fling.'"

"You know, fooling around. Mrs. Freemantle indicated that he has had a history of little infatuations with younger women that never lasted long. She seemed pretty resigned to the idea, the way some women make allowances for their husbands' occasional drinking binges."

A vague, dark notion was taking shape in my suspicious mind. "Yeah. But Catherine Lacuneau is hardly what you'd consider a sweet young thing."

Miriam feigned shock. "Dr. Harper! What kind of talk is that?"

"I'm serious. She's no spring filly. There are things here that don't add up. I'd like you to have someone run me a log of all of her phone calls for, say, the past three months. You can do that, can't you?"

She looked uneasy. "I . . . I guess so. Of course, I'd have to clear it."

"No. I don't want you to say a word to anybody about Dayr Al Nimrun, Elliot Freemantle, or the scrolls until I can figure out what's going on here. And I don't mean just Zeev Nahat. Don't tell *anybody*. OK?"

"Even Mme Catherine?"

"Especially her. She may not be what she seems."

"But Dr. Starlander—"

"You let me handle Dr. Starlander. If there are any repercussions, the story is that you questioned the idea of snooping on a member of the Editorial Committee, and I ordered you to do it and not tell anybody. You had no choice. I'll take any heat there might be over it. Got it?"

She nodded with a little conspiratorial smile. "OK. But you have to tell me about those scrolls at Dayr Al Nimrun. I can't wait to hear about them."

"Well, let's get Mrs. Cray on the speakerphone, and you can listen in while I tell her."

Dorothea Benson Cray was her old familiar self—crusty as a two-day-old Italian roll. I was having a hard time thinking of her as Aunt Dot. As soon as I explained that both Miriam and I were on the phone, she turned on her unique charm.

"Well, young man, I see you have gotten acquainted with my niece. Is this all fun and games to you, or did you call about business?"

"Aunt Dot—" Miriam began indignantly, but I waved her off.

"With as much of her money as I'm about to spend," I said pointedly, "she may have a perfect right to be difficult."

Mrs. Cray's tone warmed from disdain to mere suspicion. "You're not suggesting that you have found some scrolls, are you?"

"That's exactly what I'm suggesting. Did you really think I wouldn't come through?"

"Well, I don't suppose it matters much what I thought. What have you got?"

I took a deep breath and plunged in. "Mrs. Cray, for security reasons I don't want to say anything over the phone that would possibly identify the location of these items, which involves some very sensitive circumstances. Suffice it to say that we have entrée to four documents in allegedly excellent to very fine condition."

"Do you mean to tell me you haven't seen these items?" Skepticism edged her tone.

"I have a fragment of one of them for analysis—a piece of an Isaiah scroll."

"What are the rest?"

"The War Rule Scroll and two other documents referred to as Hezekiah and Hadassah scrolls."

"I have heard of that first one, but not the other two."

"Those seem to be previously undiscovered documents, which would be substantially more valuable than the Isaiah and War Rule scrolls."

"*If* they're bona fide. Listen, Chuck, how do you know if you haven't seen them?"

"That's 'Jim,' Mrs. Cray. As I said, I'm not at liberty to go into detail, but the circumstances are such that the only way we're going to get a look at those scrolls is to put down some earnest money. Once we validate our Isaiah fragment, of course."

"Has your . . . uh . . . prospect quoted a sale price?"

I cringed. "Yes, ma'am."

"Well, then, young man, are you going to tell me what it is?"

"A million dollars," I said quickly, the way you pull off a bandage attached to your arm hairs.

"*A million dollars?*" The tone was incredulous.

"Yes, ma'am."

"For all four."

I cringed again. "Each."

There was a deafening silence while she got her breath back and maybe reinstalled her upper plate. When she spoke again, her voice was steely and subdued.

"I see. You wouldn't possibly be putting me on, now would you, young man?"

"No, ma'am. I am absolutely serious."

"Well, you must know that nothing like that is in the cards."

"Yes, ma'am. But I also know that there is some flexibility in their position."

"Oh," she said, interest creeping back into her voice. "I see. Then how do you suggest we proceed?"

"I suggest we come up with a reasonable counteroffer—including a substantial earnest payment to get a look at the documents."

"Do you have any idea of their provenance?"

"I have some suspicions about their origin, but nothing I can get into on the phone. Let me just say that it's nothing that detracts from their authenticity."

"I understand."

"I have great confidence that we're dealing with the genuine article."

There was a moment's pause. "Young man, I am prepared to offer three hundred and fifty thousand dollars per scroll—assuming they're genuine—or a million dollars for the lot."

My heart sank. I had hoped for a couple million. But there was no point in arguing. She was the boss, and it was her money. And I realized it was only my job to get the horse to water. What happened after that was out of my hands. Still, I wanted those scrolls at least as much as Mrs. Cray did.

"All right," I said slowly, doing some arithmetic in my head. "In that case, I propose writing a check to this individual for seventeen thousand five hundred dollars as a refundable deposit for examination of the documents, to be applied to any subsequent purchase and first right of refusal."

"Well—"

"But I also have to tell you that the purchase offer is not likely to be received very enthusiastically."

"Well, young man, I originally figured, at best, on the remote prospect of *a* scroll under the most favorable of circumstances. I never imagined that you would luck into a small library."

I flashed Miriam a big grin. "That's skill and providence, Mrs. Cray, if you please. Not luck."

"Well," she sniffed, ignoring my jibe, "I am resigned to the idea that I have to trust your judgment until I am given a reason not to. And by the way, Sheldon tells me you have been most helpful countering that dreadful story in that . . . that magazine—"

"*Ground Zero.*"

"Yes. Although he would certainly prefer having his own story for the pages of *JAL.*"

"Listen, Mrs. Cray. If we pull off this purchase deal, there will be a terrific story for Sheldon Hirsch, believe me."

"And if we don't?"

I shuddered. "I don't think that's something either one of us wants to contemplate."

*For the children have come to the throes
of Death, and she labors in her pains
who bears a man. For amid the throes
of Death she shall bring forth a man-
child, and amid the pains of Hell there
shall spring from her child-bearing cru-
cible a Marvelous Mighty Counselor;
and a man shall be delivered from out
of the throes.*

—11 Thanksgiving Hymns (1QH) 4

18

In the silence of the broken connection, Miriam gave me that raised-eyebrow look.

"Hezekiah and Hadassah? What's that all about?"

"I'm not sure, but I have my suspicions."

"You have a lot of suspicions lately."

"I'm just a suspicious kind of guy, I guess."

Suddenly the latent Texas accent took over. "Look, mister. If you don't stop playing games, you may end up with glass in your grits."

I was dumbfounded. "Glass in my grits?"

"Yes, sir."

"OK, I'll bite. What's that mean?"

"That was the way some Southern belles used to dispose of their philandering husbands years ago—putting ground glass in their grits. Tended to perforate their innards. So stop fooling around. Explain what you mean."

This wasn't entirely kidding on her part. There was too much of an edge to it.

"All right. I'm inclined to believe that this Hezekiah and Hadassah stuff is a sham."

"A sham?"

"Think about it. Who was Hezekiah? He wasn't a prophet who transmitted a book of the Bible. He was a king. And there were no books named after kings."

"Good guy or bad guy? I forget."

"Partly cloudy. The one who prayed to be healed, and God gave him fifteen more years. Isaiah the prophet rebuked him for showing his treasures to the Babylonians, but Hezekiah was only concerned that there be peace in his time."

"But authentic Dead Sea Scrolls aren't necessarily books of the Bible. I may not be directly involved in the research work here, but that doesn't mean I'm not interested and paying attention. I do know that many of these Scrolls were sectarian documents."

"That's right. The War Rule Scroll, for example. Or the so-called Temple Scroll. They're interesting, but they're no more than very interesting apocrypha. It's not like anybody is lobbying to reopen the canon and expand the Bible to include them. So a book of Hezekiah is not impossible, but I wouldn't believe it until I saw it."

"What about Hadassah?"

"Do you remember who Hadassah was?"

Miriam wrinkled her brow and then brightened. "Sure. Esther. Hadassah was her Hebrew name."

"That's right."

"Are you telling me that's not a book of the Bible, either?"

"Not one that's ever been found among the Dead Sea Scrolls. Remember my little scholarly rivalry with Dr. Freemantle over the book of Esther?

She nodded.

"At Dayr Al Nimrun I believed Freemantle was playing some kind of charade to throw off his captors. In fact, I'm convinced that he was trying to tip me off to his charade by using a ruse—Hezekiah and Hadassah—that would be so transparent I couldn't help being tipped off. And tweaking me about Esther would be the most obvious. As Zeev Nahat has managed to do every time we've met."

"Is that all Dr. Freemantle said?"

"Not quite. He also indicated the Hezekiah document was

some kind of parallel to a verse in First Chronicles."

"Which says . . ."

"Where David says he was given full details for construction of the temple in writing from the Lord."

Miriam looked blank. "So?"

"So where are those details?"

"They're not in the Bible?"

"If you want an interesting exercise, try finding the construction details in Scripture for the tabernacle and for the temple, as I did. For the tabernacle, no problem. Much of the latter half of Exodus is nothing but detail upon detail down to the precise dimensions—its components and utensils, the color of yarn, the number of curtain loops, the exact ingredients and proportions for the anointing oil . . ."

"So?"

"So. I dare you to find anything even remotely comparable for the temple. Yet David said he had such plans 'in writing from the hand of the Lord.'"

"OK. I admit that's an interesting omission. But don't Kings and Chronicles refer to other books—like the annals of the kings of Judah—that weren't preserved as books of the Bible? Couldn't those details have been recorded in one of those other lost books?"

I nodded encouragingly. "Exactly my point."

Miriam looked as if the light had suddenly gone on for her. "Oh. And *that's* what you think Selmar may have?"

"I think that's what Freemantle was trying to tell me."

"But how's that different from the Temple Scroll, which we do have?"

"The scroll I'm speaking of would be much older, by almost another thousand years, going back to the founding of the kingdom. Way before most of the prophets. But if one exists today, it may be a later copy. The so-called Temple Scroll that was found in the caves was more of a sectarian document peculiar to the Essenes themselves. Their concept of the Third Temple, for example, was so exaggerated that a structure actually built on that scale would take up half of Jerusalem. But Yigael Yadin believed that the authors had some working knowledge of the writing referred to in First Chronicles. That may be what Selmar has."

Miriam's brightness dimmed. "But why would Freemantle be so coy about it? Why didn't he come right out and tell you?"

"Think where the temple was. Right beside or right atop the Dome of the Rock. If a document came to light fixing its precise location and giving the precise details of its construction, what do you think would be the political ramifications?"

Miriam cringed. "That's a no-brainer. That would be an Arab-Israeli hullabaloo beyond anything we've seen yet."

"Exactly. And Selmar told me himself that there were some things he wouldn't sell if it meant the Jews could get at them. So Freemantle may be playing with fire if he's deceiving the man."

Miriam nodded somberly. "I see. Do you think Aunt Dot's offer is going to be enough to work a deal?"

I shook my head just as somberly. "Not unless there's a lot of movement in Selmar's position—and hers. But the immediate order of business is to get our scroll fragment verified. And that's one big hurdle. Can this be done without alerting anyone within this organization as to the possible existence of new scrolls?"

She thought for a moment. "Are you familiar with accelerator mass spectrometry?"

"Sure. Radiocarbon dating that's all but replaced standard carbon fourteen because it consumes much less precious material. What about it?"

"When the researchers need AMS analysis, we have to send it out to a lab. In this case, we can just make sure that no one else gets the results but ourselves."

"Yeah, but how long does it take to get results back?"

"A week to ten days, I think."

"Yikes. No good. We need it yesterday. Lives may be at stake. Where is the lab located?"

Miriam got a distant look in her eyes and a half-smile on her face. "Hebrew University. Right here in Jerusalem. And I've met the guy who does the work. I'm not so sure I couldn't sweet-talk him into doing us a favor."

"Great. I'll go with you so we can write a check on the spot."

She shook her head and gave me a sly look. "I don't think that will be necessary. And besides, I don't think I'll have nearly so good a chance of sweet-talking him if I have a boyfriend with me." Then she winked at me. "Sweetheart."

I couldn't help grinning like a sap. This was amazing. I could twist myself right around her little finger.

I was somewhere in the land of rapid-eye movement, shallow respiration, and technicolor nightmares of mountaintop bandit enclaves when I began smelling the zesty aroma of coffee. Where I was at the moment, I seemed to be playing Dodgem on foot against a garageful of deranged bumper cars that looked like miniature Porsches and Volvos. I was not disappointed to find that it was all a dream.

"Come on, champ," said the girl of my dreams. "No slacking off now. There's work to be done."

I opened my eyes to see Miriam smiling down at me in my office easy chair, where I had been recharging my batteries. I saw by the cup in her hand that she was the source of the coffee aroma.

"Gimme," I suggested. "Please."

She handed me the cup.

Actually, I felt like a load of flotsam. Maybe jetsam too. I could only hope that the coffee would give me a jump start.

Miriam placed an envelope on my desk and then took a seat at her own, where she began sorting through pink messages and other papers.

Glancing at my watch, I saw with amazement that I'd slept for nearly two hours.

Bones creaking like the House of Usher, I pulled myself wearily out of the easy chair and went to investigate. I picked up the envelope and recognized it as that of the scroll fragment. In fact, the fragment was still tucked inside its onionskin.

"No dice?" I asked, assuming she had failed in her attempt to sweet-talk her technician friend at Hebrew University.

"Look again," she said nonchalantly over her shoulder.

I opened the onionskin, looked again, and saw that, in fact, a whole section across the bottom was missing. It had been cropped right up to the bottom of the Hebrew letters. Then I noticed something written lightly in pencil on the onionskin—"202–107 B.C.E."

B.C.E. Before Common Era. The scholarly equivalent of B.C., especially in Israel, where Christ was hardly the preferred way of benchmarking historical events. I was having that spine-tingling sense of historical import all over again. We obviously had connected with the real thing.

"Just that quick?" I asked, truly impressed.

Miriam turned and smiled confidently. "I don't fool around. My friend Danny just assumed we were revalidating a fragment from the main collection, and I didn't disabuse him."

"So he worked you right in?"

She winked again. "Accelerator mass spectrometry while-u-wait."

"What about the cost? We want to be completely above-board here."

"Wait and see how we're billed and whether Dr. Star-lander's team here gets anything out of it. If we're billed and Aunt Dot gets personal possession of that scroll, you can write a check on her behalf for two hundred and fifty dollars or thereabouts."

"Sure. That would be the right thing to do."

"Also," she said, picking a manila envelope out of her stack, "you may want to see these."

She brought the envelope to my desk.

I put away the scroll fragment and looked at her manila envelope. Inside were printouts of phone calls by date from one particular Rockefeller extension.

"These are Mme Catherine's?"

"That's right."

"Boy. I should take naps more often. Talk about service."

She said nothing in reply but went quietly about her own business while I scanned through the log of the past three months of calls.

After a minute, I thought I had found something. Starting six to eight weeks ago, there was a series of calls to New York and London. Actually, only two were to the same number in New

179

York, but nine or ten were to a London number. The rest were almost all Jerusalem and elsewhere in Israel.

"Oh, Miriam," I called. "I have a couple of international numbers I'd like you to check out."

She half turned in her chair. "The ones in London and New York?"

"Uh . . . yeah."

"I already called them."

I never ceased to be amazed. "Oh? How did you approach them?"

"I just said I was checking some numbers and asked who these parties were. They were both businesses. The one in New York was Murray's Rare Stamps and Coins, and the other in London was the Gilbert West Literary Agency."

Wheels started turning but all separately. "Stamps, coins, and literary agents? What's wrong with this picture?"

Miriam turned all the way around. "Dr. Freemantle was a stamp collector."

"Hmm. A philandering philatelist, eh? But don't say 'was.' Let's not start talking about him in the past tense. And remember, these are just Mme Catherine's phone records. We should pull Freemantle's as well."

"Well, I did. And guess what? The same numbers show up. Whatever Dr. Freemantle and Mme Catherine were doing, they were doing it together."

I should have guessed. "But a literary agent? What do you suppose that's all about?"

She shrugged it off. "I don't know. A book-and-movie deal about a real-life Indiana Jones of the Dead Sea Scrolls?"

Now the gears were starting to mesh in a hurry. "Sweetheart, you are absolutely on a roll."

She looked surprised.

"Think about it. It makes all the pieces fit."

"What pieces?"

"Sure. Turn the picture around and look behind the appearances. It often helps to start with the premise that things may not be what they seem."

She looked dubious. "OK. What kind of things?"

"Like maybe Tabloid Randy's involvement here was inspired by more than just a keen nose for news."

"You mean like maybe Dr. Freemantle or Mme Catherine actually sought that kind of publicity?"

I nodded. "Perhaps Mme Catherine's profession of unhappiness with Randy Plunkett and the *Ground Zero* story should not be taken at face value. It's entirely possible that was no more than posturing."

As always, she caught on quickly. "So they hire a literary agent, who advises that the best way to create a market for a blockbuster book on the Scrolls is to dream up a big publicity splash with the kind of sensationalism that Tabloid Randy traffics in."

"Exactly. As I recall, Gilbert West is a specialist in potboiler authors and screenwriters who do made-for-TV movies. Furthermore, suppose this manuscript that Freemantle has been working on needs some violence, so he heads out into the Judean wilderness to—"

"Create an adventure as a real-life Indiana Jones of the Dead Sea Scrolls?"

"Precisely. Among other things."

"Wait a minute," said Miriam, turning skeptical again. "Are you suggesting that Dr. Freemantle's disappearance was staged? That Mme Catherine's supposed worry and grief—"

I shook my head. "No. That may well be genuine. And I'm not suggesting for a moment that Selmar Hajabeel is part of any such charade."

"Then what are you suggesting?"

"Could be the whole thing just got out of hand. Maybe Freemantle really did find something—maybe the very material your Hans was searching for. Except Freemantle didn't reckon on meeting up with agents of Selmar with automatic weapons."

The haunted look returned to Miriam's eyes. "The same way Hans didn't reckon on someone cutting his rope."

"Right. Talk about not taking things at face value, I didn't for a moment believe Selmar's story about these scrolls being family heirlooms."

"Then Dr. Freemantle's big action adventure didn't come off quite as he'd planned."

"Could well be. Indiana Freemantle didn't have a stunt-man to do the dangerous stuff for him. I'm convinced that this delicate spot he's apparently in is very much for real."

"And where does that leave us?"

I got up and began pacing. "Well, I could put my writer's hat back on and just call up Gilbert West and ask for comment. But this is all just a theory based on nothing more than a phone number."

Miriam nodded. "Undoubtedly, Gilbert West would decline comment and refer questions back to the client—"

"Whom he's already instructed not to comment. More important, he would be sure to alert the client that we're onto them."

"In which case—"

"In which case, it looks like I'd want to speak to Mme Catherine first and give her a chance to come clean."

Miriam shook her head. "She's out of town right now on personal business."

"Do you know for how long?"

"It's supposed to be today and tomorrow, then she's back on Friday."

My priorities were becoming clear. "OK. If she calls in, please tell her I need to speak with her. Get a phone number."

Miriam's expression darkened. "Where are you going to be?"

I stood up. "I need to go see a barber in Bethlehem."

"But you don't need a haircut."

"This is Big Al, the man Selmar insists we must go through for the purchase offer."

Her eyes lit up. "Oh. I think I need to be with you."

"Oh, no, you don't."

"And why not?"

"Well—" it was kind of hard to put my finger on a specific issue, and I didn't want to raise unnecessary fears about safety "—what if Mme Catherine calls?"

She waved dismissively. "My temporary replacement with Dr. Starlander can handle that. No problem. Anything else?"

"Well, it's just not . . . necessary."

Miriam got a triumphant look on her face. "Then tell me something else, Dr. Pennsylvania Jim, sir. Who's going to interpret the Arabic for you?"

She had me. Without Kamlo, I had no way of communicating with the old man. I felt helpless and a little foolish. And there was no one else I dared bring into my confidence on this mission. But then an obvious question struck me.

"Since when did you start speaking Arabic?"

She smiled sweetly. "Ever since I moved here. Jerusalem is my home now, and I've worked hard at both Hebrew and Arabic. I like to think I speak it like a native."

"Well—"

"Well, what?"

I was awash in mixed emotions, loving her company but hating to get her involved in the dirty work. But this time it appeared I had little choice.

"Well, I just want you to know that gloating is not at all becoming to you, Miss Boynton."

"Just let me freshen up a bit, and I'll be right with you."

From between his glorious wheels there is as it were a fiery vision of most holy spirits. About them, the appearance of rivulets of fire in the likeness of gleaming brass, and a work of . . . radiance in many-colored glory, marvelous pigments, clearly mingled.
—Songs for the Holocaust of the Sabbath (4Q405) 20 ii 21–22

19

Somehow I managed to find the correct turn off Route 60 at the House of Bread, *Bayt Lahm,* also known as Bethlehem. I even found the correct back streets with the same familiar potholes and at last pulled up the drive beside the dingy stone house. The same half-dozen squawking chickens greeted us, and the same curtain at the front window moved askew as someone checked us out.

"This is the place," I told Miriam, who smiled as enthusiastically as if I had just given her the keys to the city.

I didn't have Adar Al Malik's phone number, so we were arriving unannounced. And I didn't know if that would be an asset or a liability, but at least we hadn't given them advance opportunity to say no.

In any case, the same goateed grandson came to the door to greet us. His greeting was more like what happens to carryons at the airport before passengers are let through the gate. It was a glare that could overexpose your film.

"Miriam," I muttered out the side of my mouth, "ask him if his grandpa can come out and play. If not, may we come in? We brought money this time."

From the sound of it, she seemed to do a credible job of relaying my request in Arabic.

But the glaring grandson was unmoved. Instead, the scowl deepened, and he looked as if he might close the door on us.

Urgently I told Miriam, "Do something!"

This wasn't just academic research in the balance. I was thinking of Kamlo and Freemantle depending on us for their freedom.

As the door actually began closing, Miriam started over in earnest tones. I had no idea what she was saying, but there was something so compelling about it that the door stopped.

And then, remarkably, it went into reverse. Grandson, with a boyish little smile, held open the door for us, ushered us into the living room, and disappeared quickly toward Grandpa's end of the house.

I stood there, admiring Miriam and beginning to think that having her here was not such a bad idea. I congratulated myself for having had the good sense to let her talk me into it.

"What did you tell him that changed his mind?"

She gave me the knowing smile of a cook who refuses to divulge her recipe. "You just have to understand men. Each one is different, yet they're also all the same."

I thought about that. It made sense, sort of. The results were indisputable. There was Grandson here. There was Danny, the accelerator mass spectrographer. And, of course, there was yours truly. It was a scary thought. I probably didn't stand a chance. And what's more, I didn't really want to.

I became aware of that music again. This time it reminded me more of a cross between bagpipes and a dentist's drill, only not quite so soothing. I thought if I had to listen to it very long, I'd want to rake my fingernails down a chalkboard in self-defense. Maybe I'd just discovered one of the reasons people were so crabby over here.

Then we were being summoned back to the smoke-filled inner sanctum of Adar Al Malik. From the other end of the dark little hall wafted odors of incense and something very disquieting. From my limited experience, I suspected it was either marijuana or hashish, the breakfast of assassins. Fortunately, we didn't have to turn that direction.

We entered the old man's room, and it was as if I'd never left. Big Al sat in the same rocking chair, wearing the same old cardigan. Even the pile of butts in the green glass ashtray looked the same. The same little girl came in with coffee, which I graciously accepted, but Miriam demurred smoothly without apparent offense.

As she began speaking, I laid the checkbook conspicuously on my lap and sipped my coffee. It tasted different this time, as if someone had doctored the formula.

But I paid more attention to the ebb and flow of the conversation and the interpersonal dynamics between Miriam and Big Al. It wasn't easy to read. Big Al seemed to have more patience with Miriam than he'd had with Kamlo and me. In fact, if I wasn't mistaken, there was a certain brightness in his eye—I wouldn't go so far as to call it a twinkle—that I hadn't seen before.

I thought about Danny, and about Grandson, and about myself, and began to imagine that with Miriam's magic there might be some degree of hope for us and Aunt Dot's measly million.

As little more than an idle kibitzer, I had leisure to sip coffee and gaze about the spare room and let the unintelligible dialogue roll in one ear and right out the other. If I turned my head a bit, I could hear the music from the hallway. Somehow it didn't seem quite so bad now. It seemed more in tune with the strange space I was in at the moment.

This was clearly an old man's room. One window with a sad gray shade. An old dark-wood dresser with a pair of gray socks on top. A modest pressboard chiffonier in the corner. A small TV on a card table.

One picture hung on the wall. I didn't specifically remember it from my last visit, but now it sucked me in like a liberal to a federal program. Its arabesques and curlicues reminded me of the ornate inner dome of Kubbat es-Sakhra, except that this time the design seemed to have power to transfix, if not hypnotize. In my

186

attempt to follow the interweavings of its elusive lines, I kept getting lost and forgetting where I was.

After a while of this, I lost track of time too. Now the droning, wailing music was even making sense. In fact, it was part of the picture somehow.

And then something even stranger happened. I imagined that I could understand the conversation that Miriam was having with Big Al. Her words sounded remarkably like English.

"Earth to Dr. Harper," she was saying quite pointedly. "We're talking money now. Would you like to make an offer to our host? He will relay it to Selmar Hajabeel. Jim?"

Like someone awaking in church, I snapped to it with a start. My head was swimming. It was hard to think.

"Uh . . . right," I managed, recalling with some difficulty what I was there for. "Tell him there are two scrolls we're particularly interested in. If they're for real, we'll offer seven hundred thousand dollars for them."

I let Miriam translate that before going on.

Al Malik received the offer impassively.

"And," I continued, "under the same conditions, we're prepared to offer a million dollars for all four."

She translated again.

This time Al Malik had a question.

"Explain these conditions," Miriam relayed.

I waved the checkbook. "Tell him we're prepared to make out a check right now for seventeen thousand five hundred dollars as a refundable deposit and for the right to inspect the four scrolls of Selmar Hajabeel."

Big Al's eyes widened just perceptibly as Miriam reeled off the numbers. He licked his lips and said something.

"He wants to know if there are any other conditions."

I thought a second. "Only that Kamlo and Dr. Freemantle be allowed to leave. If need be, I'll take their place."

Miriam gave me a look of fear mixed with reproach.

"Go on," I insisted.

Reluctantly she relayed my message. Or, at least, she made as if she did. For all I knew, she could have told him they could keep Kamlo and Freemantle.

While she spoke, I made a show of writing out a check for the earnest money. In this case, "earnest" was a complete understatement. "Anxious" might be more like it. Even "desperate."

I passed the check to Miriam, who handed it to Big Al. I sipped some more coffee and tried to shake off the feeling that I was dissolving into the room, the music, the picture. The funny thing was, part of me really wanted to dissolve. Sleep would be OK too. So I drained the cup. Wasn't coffee supposed to wake you up?

Things were a little confused, but Big Al was now on the phone.

Miriam leaned over toward me. "He's calling Selmar," she murmured.

"That's nice," I said, settling down farther in my seat, which was starting to feel mighty comfortable.

The next thing I knew, I was startled into wakefulness by loud talking. Not that I was sleeping, but my eyes had become a bit heavy, and I may have missed a few beats.

The loud talking was Big Al, breaking off his phone conversation, which sounded less than pleasant. He hung up and had a few words, again in a loud voice and with a few gestures, for Miriam. He was looking at me too with something other than fondness and cheer.

"What's he saying?" I asked.

"He claims Selmar is insulted by our offer. Furthermore, he says not to bother coming back until you're ready to be serious."

"Well, tell Big Al that we *are* serious—very serious. And you can tell him that we'll be back very soon."

Miriam translated, and the old man nodded. It looked more like a bare acknowledgment than actual encouragement.

"And you can also tell him," I said, more than a bit irritated, "next time to leave the dope out of the coffee."

"You want me to tell him what?"

"Never mind. Let's just get out of here."

I stood up, a bit unsteadily, and saw Grandson standing just inside the door. The little girl took my cup as if it had been milk and cookies.

188

"Jim?" she said pointedly. "The *check?*"

"Tell him to keep it. We have every intention of bringing this deal home. Maybe tomorrow."

"Are you sure?" she asked dubiously.

I nodded. It seemed a good idea at the time.

Miriam told Al Malik, who shrugged indifferently. He was lighting another cigarette as we exited the room.

To my distorted senses, the corridor seemed much longer and darker than before. It was also darker outside, the twilight of a long day that left me feeling drained and distant. At this point, my only hope was Miriam.

"Catch," I called as we walked to the car.

She turned just in time to see the car keys sailing her way through the air. With a puzzled expression on her face, she reached out and snagged them adroitly.

"You know how to drive a stick?" I asked.

"Sure thing. But how come?"

"It's better this way, believe me."

Miriam, flexible if nothing else, rolled with it. As we got into the car, her only question was, "Where to?"

I thought about that. "How about Ehud's? I'll treat."

She nodded, firing up the blue Toyota. "Sure. They have good coffee."

"No, thanks. I'm switching to cream soda."

Whether it was the midafternoon nap I'd had at the Rockefeller or the aftereffects of the spiked coffee at Big Al's, I had a rough night back at the Belvoir. It probably had a lot to do with my anxieties over Kamlo and Freemantle and my inability to pull things off for them.

Whatever the case, I lay on the fresh, starched sheets of my hotel bed, feeling as comfy cozy as a pig in a tux. Mentally, I was still moving. It was much like the continued sensation of motion while stepping onto solid ground after a long boat ride.

I kept reliving the day, from the rough stuff at Dayr Al Nimrun to the failed negotiations with Adar Al Malik to the quiet dinner at Ehud's, where I'd feasted more on Miriam's company than anything else.

I couldn't remember much of what I'd eaten or what we'd talked about. All I could seem to recall were, improbably, blue diamonds. Maybe the words had just slipped out of my mouth, another casualty of Big Al's controlled-substance coffee. I wouldn't ordinarily say something like that deliberately.

"What?" Miriam had said, befuddled.

"Blue diamonds," I repeated. "That's what your eyes remind me of."

She blinked, and they seemed to turn opaque. "Why not sapphires? Have you ever really seen blue diamonds?"

I shook my head. "Sapphire is not precious enough."

"Oh, brother," she groaned, reaching out to feel my forehead for fever.

This time I had her good. "Do you always use humor to deflect personal affection?"

Her mouth opened in amazement and then shut quickly. "Touché."

I probably should have been more careful, but I was past the point of caring. I was crazy about her. At the same time, telling her left me feeling uncomfortably vulnerable. But that was always the price of love.

Now my head was echoing with all of those things. Sleep and I played tag, chasing after but never catching each other.

At one point it almost happened. I was drifting back into that desert wilderness again. This time I thought I knew what I was there for—or what was there for me.

It was Dayr Al Nimrun. I was going there for the long-lost scrolls. The deaf would hear the words of the scroll, and out of gloom and darkness the blind would see. I was going there for Kamlo and Freemantle. At last, the captives would be set free.

But when I got there, the vision evaporated. The compound was deserted. No Kamlo. No Freemantle. No scrolls. No Selmar Hajabeel. No henchmen. Nothing but the echoes of my own footsteps and the sound of my own breathing, magnified in my ears.

I awoke with heart pounding and a clammy veil of sweat on my brow. I swung out of bed and turned on a light.

Maybe the Lord was trying to tell me something. I recalled hearing an old saint say that times of restlessness were often

God's call to prayer—sometimes even to "wrestling" with Him. I had always found that concept a bit uncomfortable, almost sacrilegious.

I got out my Bible and began reading Genesis 32, where Jacob had his desert encounter with God and was changed forever. I had never fully understood this passage, in which Jacob appeared to wrestle God to a draw and then was given a limp and a new name. Taking the old saint's advice, I began praying, asking God to open my understanding.

No such understanding came. I got back in bed, weary and discouraged. Despairingly I confessed—maybe complained a little—that my burden was beyond me, that I was incapable of delivering anybody or anything from captivity. I wasn't even capable of comprehending a simple passage of Scripture. And yet I was a trained minister, a man who was supposed to be able to explain the Word of God to others. What a sham I was.

I thought of all those who had attached their hopes to me —Kamlo, Freemantle, Mme Catherine, Mrs. Cray, Sheldon Hirsch, Miriam—and felt the collective weight of their pending disappointment in my likely failure. I thought of Mrs. Cray's $17,500, not to mention all of the expenses I had racked up. With my mind unclouded by foreign substances, I now realized that leaving the deposit behind may have been a mistake. What if it all went for naught?

I hadn't given serious consideration to the possibility of failure before. Now it was staring me in the face and grinning. I begged for God's mercy.

Then and only then, when I was in total despair of my own devices, did understanding begin to come. By that time, I was exhausted, no longer able to stay awake if I'd wanted to. But in that brief twilight slide toward sleep, I believed I knew the significance of Jacob's wrestling, and it was deeply satisfying.

I had to tell somebody. I would tell Miriam.

When I got up the next morning, it may have been a little late for me, but it was still nighttime in Dallas. Because of the time difference between Israel and Texas, I couldn't yet call Mrs. Cray and tell her the news about the less-than-enthusiastic reception to her million-dollar offer. On the other hand, that would give me plenty of time to talk to Miriam, which beat biting my nails anytime.

She was already sitting at her desk, shuffling papers when I arrived shortly after nine.

"Come on," I told her. "Have you had breakfast?"

She gave me a quizzical look. "Sure. Toast and grapefruit. What'd you have?"

"Um . . . a pecan waffle with scrambled eggs."

"And you're still hungry?"

"Well, we could just go for a cup of—on second thought, let's go for a walk. Let's get out of here."

"What's with you, anyway?"

We walked in silence through the museum corridors, passing employees with sheafs of papers in their hands and thoughts of work projects in their eyes. Miriam seemed to have her own destination in mind, so I let her lead on. We rounded a corner and took a side door off the concourse into the inner courtyard.

I had not been in this airy plaza yet. Even at this hour, the morning sun was dazzling bright on the white stone surfaces, which formed a long rectangle about a sunken pool. Within, big orange fish like koi or Sumo goldfish teemed, while a couple of large turtles that looked as ancient as Abraham's grandfather cruised lazily.

We sat on a stone bench underneath the glare of a stone lion. I just never tired of looking into those blue diamonds.

"Have you thought what you're going to do?" Miriam asked.

"About what?"

She looked incredulous. "About ransoming our friends Kamlo and Dr. Freemantle."

"Get your Aunt Dot to cough up more money."

"As simple as that?"

I smiled cryptically. "Almost."

She was beginning to look perplexed. "And what did you want to talk to me about?"

"Wrestling with God."

192

I'd never seen those blue diamonds filled with more question marks.

"I had trouble sleeping last night, which turned out to be a good thing. It was as if God invited me to wrestle with Him."

To Miriam, I realized I must be talking in riddles. I began to share with her some of my disappointments with God, going back to my father's life as a pastor. If I could open up to Kamlo with these things, why not to Miriam? For better or worse, she needed to know my heart.

She never took her eyes from mine the whole time. It helped, knowing she cared.

Finally I said, "And so, I've had this wall of resentment as a barrier between me and God, as if He had treated me unfairly, when it was really evil men. I've felt forsaken. Maybe down deep I've thought I deserved not to have to live in a fallen world like everyone else. But I felt God was really speaking to me last night through the story of Jacob."

Miriam pursed her lips. "I'm not sure I've ever really understood the story of Jacob wrestling with God."

"Well, it began to make sense when I started reading in the Hebrew. A few miles north of the Dead Sea, Jacob—name means 'trickster'—crossed the Jabbok River. Then he wrestled—*jabeq*— with a man all night. He'd obtained both his brother's birthright and his father's blessing by tricking them. But all that got him was to become a refugee in a foreign land. His Uncle Laban fooled him into working for him seven years twice—by pulling a bait-and-switch with Rachel and Leah. So the trickster himself got tricked."

Miriam nodded.

"And more. God meant all along to bless Jacob, but now Jacob was going to have to stand up and fight for the blessing, get it legitimately this time. He and this strange man wrestled all night until Jacob realized it was God, and Jacob said he wouldn't let Him go until He blessed him."

She frowned. "But if this *was* God, why couldn't He beat Jacob?"

"The fact that He could give Jacob a limp with just a touch of His finger is a pretty good indication of who really won."

"OK."

"Then God gave Jacob a new name—Israel—which means 'he struggles with God.' Losing to God is not such a bad deal. You know how it's said the best thing that ever happened to Germany and Japan was to lose to the United States in World War Two."

Miriam looked tentative. "Yes . . ."

"The terms of surrender to God are much better than that."

She brightened again and then squeezed my arm. "I like that. You know what?"

"What?"

"Anybody ever tell you that you should have been a preacher?"

It stung a little, but I couldn't help laughing. "Yeah, but they were outvoted by the ones who said I shouldn't."

Thou wilt destroy in Judgment all men of lies, and there shall be no more seers of error; for in Thy works is no folly, no guile in the design of Thy heart. But those who please Thee shall stand before Thee forever; those who walk in the way of Thy heart shall be established for evermore.

—Thanksgiving Hymns (1QH) IV 7

20

Miriam reached into her purse and dug out a small-print Bible.

"The picture of Jacob struggling with God is interesting," she said, riffling through the pages, "because 'Israel' became the name for the entire nation. I love my adopted home here, but it certainly has had its struggles with God. And it's a nation in struggle with all its neighbors. But—here it is. Zechariah chapter twelve:

"'Behold, I am going to make Jerusalem a cup that causes reeling to all the peoples around; and when the siege is against Jerusalem, it will also be against Judah. It will come about in that day that I will make Jerusalem a heavy stone for all the peoples; all who lift it will be severely injured. And all the nations of the earth will be gathered against it.'"

There was something eerie here.

"That's being fulfilled in our day," I said. "Every nation that has attacked Jerusalem—during the War of Independence in 1948, the Six-Day War in 1967, the Yom Kippur War of 1973—every one has had the tables turned on itself. Those nations all ended up losing territory to Israel."

She gave me a pointed look. "Yes, Reverend Harper. But

what's the application for you in all of this wrestling and struggling?"

I was ready for that. "The personal relationship. To seek Him with all my heart. He hates indifference, and He not only honors my struggles with Him, but He'll even bless me if my heart is right. The fact that I suffer in a fallen world doesn't mean God has abandoned me."

Miriam nodded. "And sometimes He removes every other prop so we depend solely on Him."

"Right. God told Abram, 'Go forth from your country, and from your relatives and from your father's house, to the land which I will show you.' Just walking by faith, one day at a time."

"And Abram believed God, and He reckoned it to him as righteousness."

"Exactly. I always want to walk by sight. Instead I need to move out in faith to the place He *will* show me as I obey."

A disturbing conviction began to grow upon me. This was talking a good game, but I needed to apply it to my present circumstances. Still, the idea that began to form was just too wild and crazy.

"Maybe your father's work was not in vain," Miriam was saying.

"What do you mean?"

"Maybe it's bearing fruit right now through you. Because of—because of Hans, this whole search for missing scrolls scares me. But I also sense that God is doing something."

I smiled. "Who knows but that we have to come to this place for such a time as this?"

"What?"

"Oh, nothing. Just a little inside joke between Zeev Nahat and me."

She surprised me again. "Oh. I get it. Esther. Right?"

I nodded, and then I felt a familiar nudging that was impossible to describe but one I had learned to recognize as divine prompting. It was something like the proverbial still, small voice, except that there wasn't a voice or even a whisper.

It was more like an instantaneous file transfer into my personal computer without benefit of wires or electricity. I was seized by the overwhelming conviction that the wild and crazy notion I'd just had was exactly what I should do.

"Come on," I said, standing up. "Let's go."

She stood reluctantly. "Where?"

"To Big Al's. We need to get Kamlo and Freemantle out of that place."

"But," she protested while quickening her pace to catch up with me, "but how?"

"Just come with me," I said over my shoulder. "I'll explain in the car."

Miriam waited until we were on the road again to start peppering me with questions.

"How do you expect to spring our friends with no better offer for the scrolls?"

"Who said I wouldn't make a better offer?"

She paused. "Help me understand this. You're going to kick in some additional money from your college pension fund?"

"No. Remember I said we were going to get Mrs. Cray— Aunt Dot—to cough up some more dough?"

"Yes, but don't you have things backwards? Don't you need to get the money first—or at least the approval—and then talk to Al Malik?"

I shook my head. "Nope. Oh, it would be nice. But we don't have that luxury."

"We don't?"

"Think about it. There's an eight-hour time difference between Israel and Texas. That means it's two in the morning back in Dallas. I don't think your aunt wants to chat with us right now, especially to hit her up for more money."

"Then why not wait till she can talk to us at a decent hour?"

"Do you realize what time that would be here?"

"Uh . . ." Miriam paused, mentally doing the arithmetic. "Oh, say, four or five o'clock."

"In the afternoon. Right. The end of the business day."

"So?"

"So put yourself in Kamlo and Freemantle's place. You're a

hostage. You don't know what these people may do to you. I wouldn't want to spend *one* hour of life like that, let alone another six or seven, just because some little old lady in Dallas might have a fit over the high price of scrolls in Jericho. It's all a matter of perspective."

"Jim, that's not entirely fair—" There was a bit of indignation in her voice.

"You're right. I'm sure Mrs. Cray, if she knew the situation, would want to do the right thing. After exhausting all the other alternatives first. Look, it's a different ball game now. At one time, we thought Freemantle might be in trouble. Now we know he is. Kamlo too."

"What are you going to do if this blows up in your face? What if Selmar accepts your higher offer, and Aunt Dot doesn't go along with it?"

"At that point, I'll just tell her there are lives at stake. I won't be able to say anything more than that over the phone, but I could beg a lot. I'd probably pray a lot too."

She shook her head, apparently unconvinced. "I don't know. I think you're taking an awful gamble."

"Probably," I conceded. "But at least I'll know I tried. If I perish, I perish."

Kamlo's jalopy knew the way to the Al Malik estate in Bayt Lahm by this time. Much more of this and it would be wearing grooves in the pavement.

I don't know why I kept expecting the house to disappear, but I was secretly relieved when we pulled into the driveway to find our chicken friends and the window peeper yet again. It almost seemed like home.

This time I got a distinct impression about the window peeper before the curtain swung back into place. I glimpsed a bit of long dark hair and a pair of eyes about sternum-high. Undoubtedly this was the little coffee girl. I shuddered at the thought.

Grandson once again greeted us at the door, but this time without his standard headgear. He looked somehow less grim and imposing. His aquiline eyes were noticeably less intense, and the rest of his face looked more relaxed. He actually smiled perceptibly and held the door open for Miriam.

I was just along for the ride, I was sure.

We stood in the same spare living room, cooling our heels, except that this time things were a bit different. The room was illuminated from the far end by the shifting lights of a television. The little girl was watching some black-and-white sitcom that I soon recognized as an old *Phil Silvers Show.* I was most relieved not to have to endure that ubiquitous wailing music. I guessed it was too early in the day for hashish-crazed hamster fights and dueling dentist drills.

About the time I was wondering why the little girl wasn't in school, Grandson returned to invite us into the inner sanctum. I glanced at the hypnotic picture on the wall and shuddered again. This place was really beginning to give me the creeps.

Al Malik wasn't exactly jumping for joy to see us. He merely lit one more cigarette. Then he and Miriam exchanged pleasantries. Actually, it didn't sound particularly pleasant. After a minute of that, Miriam turned back to me with a professional smile.

"What's he saying?" I asked softly.

The smile never left her face. "Basically, that this had better be good. I think he means it."

"OK."

"But my advice to you as Mrs. Cray's niece is that it better hadn't be *too* good."

"Thanks. You're a pal. Tell him we'll pay half a million dollars apiece for the two rare scrolls or one million seven hundred fifty thousand for all four."

Miriam gave me a dark look that told me I was really pushing it. Then she started translating.

I took a deep breath and said a quick prayer.

Big Al gave her a dark look that suggested we might be more than a few bricks shy of a full load. Maybe a deal wasn't in the cards today after all. But I would have to reserve judgment until he'd spoken to Selmar.

I didn't have long to find out. Big Al got on the horn to

someone. I hoped it was Selmar Hajabeel. Then, when I heard the unhappy tones, I hoped that it wasn't.

Finally he hung up and looked back and forth at Miriam and me as if we had been caught siphoning gas out of his car. Then he jabbered and gesticulated, making circles of smoke in the air with his cigarette. His tone sounded almost angry, certainly unfriendly.

Miriam sighed. "He says the deal is off. Forget it. Take your filthy Yankee money and go buy your fancy woman a pleasure cruise or a mink coat or a South American plantation. But just go away from here and leave an old man to himself to wait for the undertaker."

My heart began pounding in my ears. "No, wait. Tell him not to take that attitude. Tell him we'll be back this evening with a truly better offer. I promise."

Miriam gave that a shot, but Big Al shook his head as if warding off unwanted words. Then he seemed to become truly angry. He sliced the air with a hand while he gave her a piece of his mind that he appeared ill prepared to lose.

"What's he saying?"

"He says Selmar is no longer dealing—at any price—with liars. Just go away and don't come back. Salaam. Au revoir——"

"OK, OK. I get the idea."

Just then the little girl came in with her coffee tray.

That did it. Big Al got out of his rocker again and began hollering things that didn't need translating.

The little girl froze, her eyes widening in fright.

Grandson reappeared, this time with his customary headgear and a new piece of equipment—a long gun. It didn't appear to be an automatic weapon, but I guessed it could make nasty holes nonetheless.

I stood up. "Uh . . . tell Big Al we were just leaving. Ask him nicely for Mrs. Cray's check, please."

As soon as Miriam translated the request, I realized the visit was over. It wasn't hard to figure out. Grandson leveled the gun at my chest and chambered a round. It was a chilling sound.

"Jim," Miriam pleaded, clutching my arm, "let's go. *Now.*"

She didn't have to ask twice.

200

Outside in the car, I sat for a minute in a numb cloud before I summoned the will to turn the key and begin backing out of the driveway. Somehow I felt certain it was for the last time.

Miriam was so quiet I almost forgot she was there. She had more sensitivity than to say, "I told you so." She didn't have to.

I was mentally kicking myself all the way to Jerusalem. Maybe if I had waited, as she had advised, until Aunt Dot's generosity had the opportunity to rise to the occasion, none of this would have happened. Maybe Mrs. Cray would have come through with the financial offer to save the day if I'd been forthright and let her know up front just how much was at stake. Instead, I had to play hero and do it my way.

Now the fat was really in the fire. The deal had collapsed, and there clearly would be no third chance. I'd effectively burned that bridge. In trying to singlehandedly work a miracle for Kamlo and Freemantle, had I instead sealed their doom? What could I do next?

Halfway back to the city, I started at the unexpected sound of Miriam's voice. "How do you feel about what happened back there?"

"In a word? Bummed," I conceded.

"You're not doubting the leading you sensed from God, are you?"

"I—well, I don't know. Maybe I was getting a little carried away with these 'leadings.' Why? What are you getting at?"

"Don't let the enemy get you questioning yourself. Remember who's in charge. If God's in this, He won't let you go far wrong."

I truly appreciated her compassion and encouragement, but I sensed she had something else on her mind.

"OK," I prompted. "You don't think that was all a big mistake back there then?"

"We just may not have the entire picture. What, for example, do you suppose Al Malik—or Selmar—meant by saying he would have no dealings with liars?"

I hadn't especially thought about that before, but now the idea began to raise multiple red flags.

"I don't know, Miriam, but I don't like the sound of it. I don't trust Selmar even a little bit."

What I didn't tell her was my fear that Selmar had discovered Freemantle's charade. If he thought Freemantle was covering up having an original Temple Scroll or some other document of great significance to Israel, it could mean big trouble for Freemantle. Maybe I had been right the first time. I had to do something and do it quickly.

She seemed to be reading my mind. "So what are you going to do?"

I tried to sound casual. "I think I need to go back out to Dayr Al Nimrun and find out what's going on."

"But didn't Selmar tell you not to come back?"

"Not exactly. He just told me to conduct future dealings through Adar Al Malik."

"How soon are you going?"

"As soon as I drop you off at the Rockefeller."

Miriam fell silent once more.

I stole a glance at her and saw that her eyes were closed, as if praying or grieving or both.

I reached across and patted her arm. "Don't worry. I'll be careful."

"Yeah," she said softly. But she didn't sound convinced.

After that, Miriam conducted herself like a real trouper. She insisted I not leave the Rockefeller without a couple of sandwiches and a brief hug. But her eyes said it all. Blue diamonds. Bright springs of joy. Deep pools of sorrow.

It made a difference. I drove away feeling as if I really did owe it to somebody to take care. I felt needed, as if there was something to come back for.

Then I thought of Someone Else I owed, Someone who had bought me with a price. I, who would rescue others, had myself been ransomed.

I was His; I was not to love my life so much as to fear death. And I wasn't going to kid myself. A return trip to Dayr Al Nimrun could be a one-way ticket.

On the now-familiar roads toward Selmar's mountaintop enclave, I was haunted by regret that Kamlo wasn't with me to share the risks, to share the adventure, and to bolster my courage—and by the inescapable notion that I was being followed.

I guessed the latter was probably only my paranoia, like a little boy's in the dark. I just didn't want to give away the location of the secret repository of the missing scrolls, although, considering Selmar's attitude toward me, it was probably a little late to worry about that.

I gave enough credence to my apprehension to slow down a few times and to wait an extra few moments at several intersections, just to see what might show up in my rearview mirror. But I couldn't pick up a pattern. It always seemed to be a different vehicle or nothing at all. I resisted the idea of pulling over or driving a diversionary route to shake any tail I might have.

Once I thought I saw a rearview image of a little red car resembling the lipstick-colored Mazda that Miriam drove. But I reminded myself that she was miles away, safe back in Jerusalem, minding her own business.

I refused to give in to imagination or paranoia. Why should I worry about a bloodhound when I was about to walk into the den of a lion?

I wasn't sure what I was going to do once I got there, other than try to take my case directly to Selmar. When I thought of my big friend Kamlo, locked up, and of the thug who had smashed his father's camera, the anger still burned. This was a case of righteous indignation akin to overturning the moneychangers' tables.

I felt like roaring into Dayr Al Nimrun, knocking down the door, lifting Nadi by the shirtfront, and demanding the release of my friend and of Freemantle. And if I got really brave, I might even call Mrs. Cray, roust her out of bed, and insist that she cough up more money for the scrolls.

However, by the time I crested the last rise to Dayr Al Nimrun, a different feeling began to grow upon me. I couldn't quite put my finger on it, but it was rather the opposite of the feeling I'd had of being followed. This was more a sense of emptiness and desolation.

It was hard to see why I felt that way. The blockhouse

appeared deserted, but that was no different from before. Maybe it was the utter stillness. It was just, as they say in the Westerns, too quiet out there.

The walled estate gleamed in the early afternoon sun. As before, the gate stood open. This time, however, I had none of the feeling of being in the crosshairs of someone's rifle scope as I drove onto the grounds.

I parked the Toyota close to the building, halfway between the garage and the main entrance. I was hedging my bet. In my imagination I pictured a daring Hollywood-style rescue, Kamlo and Freemantle and I trying to outrace the bad guys on foot. There was no way of knowing in advance through which door we could make our escape.

My more immediate problem was not breaking out of the place but getting in. In my heart I still wasn't convinced there was anybody home.

The sun was warm on the back of my neck. There was a vague hothouse smell on the air, and I noticed that halfway between the first cedars and the building proper were several grape arbors. Past them grew some small palms and graceful ferns, all tastefully arranged in terraced beds. That Selmar Hajabeel. What a man of culture and refinement.

I walked directly to the main door and rang the bell. Happily, there was no guessing about its functionality. I could hear the muffled blatting of a buzzer somewhere inside. Unhappily, there was no answering stir from within.

Mostly out of habit, I gave the door a few good blams with the side of my fist and began looking around for I didn't know what. This was more than a little odd.

Just the other day, there were at least enough people at Dayr Al Nimrun to get up a good game of volleyball. And that was not counting people I might not have seen. Where were they today?

Still hearing nothing, I hied over to the big garage bay door and blammed on it three times. That produced a deep booming that couldn't be missed. Unless he was working the impact wrench, any grease monkey would have to hear it. The response was the same as before. Nothing.

As a long shot, I grabbed the lip of the bottom edge of the door and gave it a pull that threatened to dislocate a few of my vertebrae. No dimes. It too was locked.

The eerie feeling that had been nibbling at me was now overwhelming. I couldn't believe that no one was home. Still, another part of me was convinced beyond question. It had become a matter not of *if* but *why*. I wasn't leaving without getting to the bottom of this.

I went on past the garage area and circled back around to the rear of the building. There I found what I thought I could use to make something happen. Behind the garage wing was a stack of firewood. I grabbed one of the smaller pieces and went looking for a first-floor window.

I found a back door that I guessed was to the kitchen, but the thing was solid metal like the security doors in high-crime areas. There was no glass in it, nor was there any nearby window.

I was about to despair of finding any point of vulnerability when I spied a cellar window. This was almost too good to be true. The thing looked flimsy enough to be a pushover. It occurred to me that the lack of vulnerabilities such as picture windows or doors with glass probably had more to do with the fact that this had been an old monastery than any specific concerns about security.

Three good pokes with my log, and I had enough glass out of the way to get my hand in there and work the catch open. I carefully swept the window ledge clear of any remaining glass shards, then began lowering myself feet first through the opening, which was none too generous. It was an experience guaranteed to make one grateful for not being claustrophobic.

I thought my feet would never reach the ground. Finally, about the time I was thinking about backing off in favor of another approach, I touched down. Glass fragments snapped, crackled, and popped under my feet. And then came a thought that froze me in my tracks: I was in total darkness, and I had no real idea what was to my right or my left.

Why had it been so easy to break in? Did they have another security device? Maybe one with sharp teeth and a waggly tail?

*At their marvelous stations are spirits,
many-colored like the work of a weaver,
splendid engraved figures. In the midst
of a glorious appearance of scarlet, colors of the most holy spiritual light, they
hold to their holy station before the
King, spirits of pure colors in the midst
of an appearance of whiteness.*
—Songs for the Holocaust of the
Sabbath (4Q405) 23ii

21

Suddenly I became a tree, fixed and immovable, with roots
going halfway to Singapore. I had no phobias that I knew of,
but this total darkness came pretty close. It was a darkness that
had power to change shape into any deadly thing my imagination
could concoct. For all I knew, I could be two steps away from a
junkyard dog or a leg-hold trap.

I took a few deep breaths and made an effort to rein in my
imagination and my racing pulse. Then I noticed that the darkness was not total. It had just looked that way in contrast to the
small rectangle of light behind me where I'd punched out the
glass. As my eyes adjusted, I saw a thin horizontal line of light
across the way, near what should be the ceiling.

I moved tentatively toward the light. Once, I tripped over
something that felt and sounded like a heavy iron chain, but I
quickly regained my balance and came to the bottom of a set of
stairs, as I had hoped.

I climbed gingerly to the top and found a door handle. It
turned, but the door would not give. There was, however, enough
play in it to convince me there was no deadbolt. I threw myself
against the door—not too hard, lest the rebound send me tum-

bling back down the stairs. It helped to have a railing to steady myself after the impact.

There was a satisfying crunch.

I tried it again and felt wood wrenching partly loose. On the third heave I lurched out into the kitchen. As I had suspected, the door had been secured with only a hook-and-eye latch. The only thing I'd really damaged was a bit of the door-frame molding around the eyelet.

Here, the sense of desolation descended upon me in spades and trumps. But it was nothing I could immediately put my finger on.

The kitchen certainly suggested habitation. A few dishes still sat in the sink and half a pot of dark stuff in the coffee maker. As I moved out into the hall where I had last seen Selmar leaning against a doorway, I felt as if I'd come aboard one of those ghost ships with the crew mysteriously missing.

Still, I walked on eggshells as I traced my way down the hall to the wicker room, the place with the green marble floor, where I had awakened after being clobbered. The vibes in this place were enough to keep me on edge with or without its bizarre cast of characters. I almost expected Nadi or Selmar or that other ruffian to pop out of the shadows around the next corner. But what appeared was a whole lot of nothing.

I revisited Selmar's posh office. There was the landing-strip desk, the mounted menagerie of endangered species, the conference table where Freemantle and I had talked scrolls, the wet bar, and the glass sliders leading to the pool. I let myself out onto the pool deck. This time there was no one around, least of all bathing beauties.

I whiffed chlorine on the air. I bent down and felt the water. It was definitely heated. I could hear the filter pumping too. It was as if Selmar and his gang had just pulled up stakes and fled without bothering to wash the dishes or cancel the paper or feed the cat.

I went back inside and decided to sit and think about it. Selmar's desk looked like a good place. I sat down and put my feet up, just like Selmar. It was a comfortable chair. I began to think this might be a good place to start a study center for Dead

Sea Scrolls, when something began gnawing at me from the inside out. It wouldn't go away, but it wouldn't come any closer either.

I got up and began pacing. What was this troubling sensation that wouldn't show itself? It was like a forgotten familiar melody that becomes more elusive the harder you try to nail it down.

Increasingly frustrated, I decided to forget it and get busy. There were plenty of other rooms to check out. Maybe by some chance the scrolls would still be here. I was convinced that the same could not be said for Kamlo and Freemantle.

I set out down the hall, back toward the wicker room. But now the eerie nagging totally engulfed me in the dense silence. It was an intense solitude. There was nothing here but the echo of my own footsteps and the sound of my own breathing, magnified in my ears.

And then it all clicked. I was back in the wilderness, only this time I was awake. Incredibly, this was my dream scene from last night, when I had found myself in a place of echoing footsteps and total emptiness. I didn't know what to do but keep putting one foot in front of the other. I'd never walked into one of my own dreams before. Unfortunately, I hadn't been shown how it would all come out.

Just as I came to the wicker room, I noticed something different. The door onto the hall was closed.

I hadn't shut it.

I was tempted to flee but knew there was no point in running. I would have to face whatever it was. Just as in the dream, I was alone with the pounding of my heart and the sound of my own breathing. Yet not alone. I had assurance of God's provision. I believed the dream meant that if I wanted to set captives free and get those scrolls, I should go for it.

Praying silently, I opened the door slowly and quietly onto the familiar wicker room. I was ambushed by a fusillade of blue diamonds.

"Miriam!"

She sat on the same chair I'd once occupied with a splitting headache.

I went to her, realizing too late that her grim-faced unresponsiveness was all wrong. I only realized why when a man behind me spoke my name in a familiar voice.

I whirled. It was a familiar figure too, tallish and erect in a military way. Zeev Nahat. But it was a different Zeev Nahat from the one I knew. This was more like his malevolent twin.

This Zeev Nahat had on a different hat, literally. It was the kind of dark felt fedora that, with a smaller brim, would have looked smart in the financial district. But with the larger brim at this angle, almost over the eyes, it was more like something from the Purple Gang or Murder, Inc. This Zeev Nahat was smoking, the cigarette sticking out the side of his mouth in the manner of Humphrey Bogart.

Most significant, this Zeev Nahat was aiming a pistol at my chest.

"Colonel Nahat," I said, mostly to keep my mouth from drying up. "What brings you clear out here?"

He took a step toward me. "Just do not move, my friend. In fact, I would appreciate your putting your hands in the air. You know, just like in the movies."

I put up my hands, and he began patting me down. I assumed this meant he wasn't going to shoot me. Otherwise, why worry about whether I was armed? It occurred to me that Nahat might be looking for something else. But what? Scrolls? Not likely I could hide something like that on my person.

Miriam, with downcast eyes, just sat on the wicker chair.

"You OK, Miriam?" I asked, whether Nahat liked it or not.

"I'm so sorry." Her voice sounded miserable. "Please forgive me, Jim."

It took me a second. "For what?"

But she didn't have to answer. I was pretty sure what she meant. I had been right the first time about that little red Mazda in my rearview mirror.

"So, Colonel Nahat," I ventured, "you let Miriam lead you to me. But how did you get inside this place?"

"Less talk, please," said Nahat, who was finishing his pat down.

I tried again. "Through the basement window?"

Somehow I didn't think so.

Nahat ignored the question. "Now we are going to search this place, you and I, from top to bottom."

"Let Miriam go," I insisted.

The business end of the pistol looked me in the eye.

"We search first," said Nahat, "talk second."

For the next two hours we went through every room in the place, including eight bedrooms, two of which I assumed must have held Kamlo and Freemantle. They were the ones with dead-bolts on the outside. I knew it wasn't the one with the jacuzzi and the big-screen TV. We spent the most time in that room, but Nahat's "we search" was more than a little exaggerated.

I pulled up the carpet. I pulled down the ceiling tiles. I lifted the mattress off the box springs. I took the top off the toilet tank. I pried up the squeaky floorboard for a peek inside. I lowered the window shades to make sure nothing was rolled up inside.

He held the gun.

Miriam hung nearby, arms crossed, staring at her shoes.

After more than an hour and forty-five minutes of that, I finally had had it.

"Look, Nahat," I said, letting him hear my anger. "If you're looking for Dead Sea Scrolls, they're obviously not here. They must be with Selmar Hajabeel or Kamlo or Dr. Freemantle or one of Selmar's henchmen, wherever these people have gone."

He surprised me by actually responding. "Forget Dr. Freemantle."

Something bothered me by the way he said it. "Why?"

There was a faint sigh. "Freemantle is dead."

I glanced at Miriam, who looked horrified. My thoughts raced.

"He was found early this morning, floating in the Dead Sea. Ironic, is it not?"

The image of this gentle beanpole of a man with the curly hair and the soft British voice was still fresh in my mind. I remembered his quirky mannerisms and his plucky subterfuges to placate Selmar while clueing me in on the Dayr Al Nimrun scrolls. I could still picture his scratching his face with crossed fingers.

I winced at the thought of the bullet or knife that ended all this and wondered if he had met death quickly with eyes wide open or slowly in torment and terror. Most of all, I wondered with a wave of guilt if our tête à tête had caused his undoing. Would he have lived if I had done something differently?

I felt grieved for Mme Catherine, regardless of whether they had been in cahoots in some kind of fame-and-fortune scheme. I still believed her affection and concern for him were genuine. But I also remembered a wife back in England who was going to have a hard time understanding all of this.

Then I thought of Kamlo. He faced exactly the same dangers, and my shock began turning to anger and fear.

"Look, Nahat. Why don't you either shoot me or put away that gun? I'm not planning on running, and I'm tired of playing games. I assure you I want to get to the bottom of this thing as much as you do."

Nahat looked at the pistol as if wondering how it had gotten into his hand. With a shrug, he made it disappear somewhere inside his sport coat. I guessed it could reappear just as quickly.

"That is just as well," he said. "We were about to go outside anyway."

He ordered me to drive his car, a late-model black Honda Accord that was parked between Kamlo's jalopy and the main entrance. Nahat sat in back beside Miriam, where he could best control both of us.

Something told me that Selmar Hajabeel's front door had presented no problem for Nahat. I thought I smelled government agent all over this. That would explain a lot—the coincidences, the chance meetings, the tailings, and now this encounter. But why? What would be the Israeli government's interest?

Not likely that I was going to worm it out of Nahat. I couldn't even get him to tell me where we were going.

"Just drive," he said in a tone that sounded as if it had a gun in it. "I shall tell you where to turn."

He sure did. I might as well have been a conscriptee in Colonel Nahat's one-man army. When we got to the bottom of the hill, I slowed down to turn left at Kamlo's sign-that-did-not-exist onto the road toward Jerusalem.

"No turn," he ordered. "Straight on."

It felt oddly unnerving to pass up that turn. This was a deeper descent into the unknown. I had no idea what lay ahead, and what's more, I didn't want to know. I wanted to go back to Jerusalem, back to the Belvoir, back to the Rockefeller, back to civilization. I wanted to run off with a girl such as Miriam and settle down, maybe have a family.

Instead, we were apparently heading out into the wilderness. The landscape was quickly flattening out into scrub and rock fields. All it needed was a few circling buzzards to make the picture complete.

Wild thoughts began popping up randomly as I drove ever deeper into the *arabah*. I thought of swerving into a tree on the passenger side before Nahat could draw his gun—and immediately dismissed that. I wasn't about to attempt that kind of thing with Miriam in the car, even if I thought it would work. Besides, I really did want to find out how this would all come out. It might be too late for Freemantle, but I prayed Kamlo was OK, wherever he was.

"Your partner, this Kamlo Mattar . . ." The laconic Nahat startled me by speaking—and also by what he said, as if he'd been reading my mind. "Do you know where he might go?"

I shook my head. I had wondered what he knew about Kamlo. Apparently he'd been doing his homework.

"He was a captive at Dayr Al Nimrun. If they moved him somewhere—Beirut, Timbuktu—I'd have no idea."

"But if he escaped captivity?"

"Then I assume he would return to Jerusalem. To me. So if you're trying to find Kamlo, we just missed our turn."

"Jerusalem is the first place they would look. If he were being pursued, this is the direction he would have to travel."

The man spoke with such certainty that it was hard to doubt it.

"If not?" I asked.

"Then kiss him good-bye. He could now be a captive in Jordan."

"Like a vampire at dawn, Selmar Hajabeel returns to his native soil?"

I stole a glance over my shoulder at Nahat. He wasn't smiling.

I tried smoking out some information through the back door. "So what's the government's interest in Selmar Hajabeel?"

He didn't bite. "Who said anything about the government?"

"Come on, Nahat," I insisted. "You and I both know it wasn't archaeology that kept bringing you to Ehud's restaurant when Miriam and I just happened to be there."

"What was it for *you?*" he retorted. "Biology?"

I heard a little snort of disgust directly behind me from Miriam.

I felt my neck and ears burning with the first flush of anger. But I kept my hands on the wheel, the car on the road, and my temper largely in check. I decided the safest tack was to change the subject. Two could play this game.

"Selmar told me he had nothing to fear from the government. Dayr Al Nimrun is Palestinian self-rule territory. And maybe he'd also spread around a lot of baksheesh to the right folks. So—go sit on your hat, Israel. This is a Jew-free zone."

I stole another glance backward and saw Nahat's icy blue eyes turn to fire. When he next spoke, it was in a quieter voice through a tight jaw.

"I could tell you a thing or two, Dr. Harper. But you would not like it."

I was getting an unsettling feeling. "And why would that be, Colonel Nahat?"

"Because afterward you would have to die."

That shut me up. I couldn't tell if he was serious, angry, or just toying with me, but I didn't want to find out. While I tried to think of another approach, the colonel surprised me by speaking again.

"Let us just say, Dr. Harper, that these assertions about self-rule are laughably overstated, especially when it comes to matters of national security."

National security.

"Did Selmar Hajabeel admit possessing Dead Sea Scrolls?"

Nahat's question invited reading between the lines. I suddenly realized that he only *acted* as if he knew everything. There was a big difference. I was loath to help him out too much by answering.

Then it struck me. That made us even. I was shooting in the dark too. Maybe we could trade.

I could feel his eyes on me.

"Yes," I conceded. "You might say that. But what would that have to do with national security?"

"That would depend on what kind of scrolls. Did you see any actual documents?"

"No, but I was led to believe that one of them might be the kind of thing we discussed days ago in your office."

Nahat was silent for a long moment before muttering, "That was just what we were afraid of."

"So by national security you mean the status quo of the Temple Mount?"

Nahat said nothing.

I persisted. "Which might be upset by the discovery of an ancient document encouraging the radical element to upset the Muslim apple cart and set a cornerstone for the Third Temple?"

"Selmar Hajabeel had been under investigation for some time for his freelance merchandising tactics, but it was not known that he was also trafficking in scrolls until you started sticking your nose into it."

"And you just hung back, waiting to see what I would come up with."

"Perhaps we gave you too much credit."

"What would have happened if I had succeeded in obtaining the scrolls?"

"What do you you mean, 'What would have happened?'"

"Would I have ended up at the bottom of a cliff with a broken rope, like the Austrian and the Swiss?" Then I added, "Sorry, Miriam."

Nahat snorted. "We were not responsible for those unfortunate accidents."

"Who was? Selmar's people?"

"Perhaps. We have reason to believe that is how he came into possession of the scrolls."

I didn't know whether to believe him. I knew that, in his business, truth was just another commodity to be adapted to fit the circumstances. He had already shown his true colors more than once in that regard.

We cruised along in silence. Without my fully realizing it while we were talking, we had entered a more fertile plain. There were date palms and figs—even oaks like those back in Pennsylvania—and many trees I couldn't identify. I suspected that we were nearing a habitable region, perhaps were even near irrigation.

As we began another mild descent, I could see out over a somewhat lower plain, part of which appeared to be cultivated fields. In fact, I briefly glimpsed a dot of color that I imagined must be a tractor or other agricultural machine.

But then it appeared that Nahat had spied something else. "Up ahead," he said. "Pull over."

I looked to our right and saw what he had just seen. Parked off the road at the intersection of a country lane was a car I instantly recognized—or thought I did. It seemed too coincidental to be the same little sporty runabout from Selmar's stable. But how many white, thirty-year-old Mustang convertibles in mint condition could there be in the neighborhood? Had this perhaps been Kamlo's escape vehicle from Dayr Al Nimrun?

I pulled off the road, right behind the Mustang, and cut the engine.

"The keys," he snapped.

I plopped them into his outstretched hand. He wasn't about to risk our driving off without him.

The colonel was out in a heartbeat, and so was his pistol.

I followed a few paces back, motioning to Miriam to stay put. I told myself this gun business was silly, but I wondered what Nahat thought we might be facing. All kinds of thoughts filled my head as I approached the car, mostly unthinkable things like pictures I'd seen of drive-by shootings with bodies in the backseat. I said another silent prayer for my good friend Kamlo.

I heaved a big sigh of relief when I looked in the window and saw no bodies and no blood.

Nahat turned to me with a curious expression, as if he had seen something in my face.

"Do you recognize this automobile, Dr. Harper?"

"Yes. This appears to be one of Selmar Hajabeel's vehicles. He has a whole fleet of collector cars."

Nahat nodded, not taking his eyes from my face. "Yes. I saw them."

"Did you see a white Mustang in that garage?"

"No, I did not."

"This must be it."

Before I could say another word, Nahat had his pistol holstered and was beating it back to the Honda. He wasn't going anywhere till I got behind the wheel, but I didn't want to tarry here either.

Before I turned the key in the ignition, Nahat surprised me with another question. "Is this Kamlo the type of person who might attempt a daring escape in a borrowed car?"

"Oh, there's no doubt in my mind. I just hate to think what might have happened to him."

Nahat gave me a quizzical look. "I would not worry so much."

That stumped me. "Why not?"

He pointed just past the Mustang to what I had recognized only as an ancient, gnarled oak that might have been there since the Exodus. On second glance, I saw a hand-made sign nailed to it. *Kibbutz Lador*, it said in Hebrew.

"OK," I granted, starting the engine. "Kibbutz Lador must be down that road. What about it?"

"Very simple. If I were Mr. Kamlo Mattar, I would want to ditch this conspicuous American muscle car to elude my pursuers as soon as possible. But I would not do that until I could arrange alternative transportation. Hitching a ride on a truck heading kibbutzward would be such a wonderful opportunity, would it not?"

"Sure," I agreed, nodding vigorously.

I felt much better already, just thinking of Kamlo riding to safety in a truckload of melons or cucumbers.

As for me, shaking and trembling seize me and all my bones are broken; my heart dissolves like wax before fire and my knees are like water pouring down a steep place.
—Thanksgiving Hymns (1QH) IV 7

22

Sure enough, the bumpy country lane had a little farm town at the end of it. There was even a tall, gunmetal-gray grain silo that could have been imported from Iowa and a few red-brick smokestacks that might have been at home in Buffalo or Gary.

But when we actually pulled through the gate of Kibbutz Lador, the resemblances to Heartland, U.S.A., ended.

Except for a freckle-faced adolescent boy at the gatehouse, Kibbutz Lador appeared to be a ghost town. There were cattle in the distant fields and even a few horses around a nearby red barn, but not another human was in sight. A bag of mail stood inside the gate, unattended.

Miriam gave voice to my thoughts. "Where is everybody?"

I pulled into what looked to be the main parking lot a little farther onto the grounds. I got out and strolled a few yards to a broad plaza that spun off footpaths in a half dozen different directions. Some led to buildings I could see in the distance. Others meandered off to no visible destination except possibly the barns and fields.

This place should have been teeming with people—farmhands, nurserymen, mechanics, teachers—going about their appointed rounds. Instead, all about me were the sounds of silence. I was once again the wilderness dream traveler, in the throes of déjà vu, immersed in the echo of my own footsteps and the sound of my own breathing, magnified in my ears.

I glanced back and saw Miriam leaning against the Honda, arms folded, patiently surveying the eerie environs. She looked as if she had recovered from her self-recrimination enough to be a factor in this mission.

Nahat walked over to the shack. I saw him flash some kind of wallet ID, and the teenager waved us on through.

We got back in the car, and Nahat directed me on a wind-shield tour of the place. We circled the barns and factory build-ings, where there were still no signs of kibbutzniks at work, though this was the middle of the day. Then we motored around the parking lots of several buildings that looked like dormitories. They too appeared deserted. This was truly strange.

"Let's go back and ask that kid what's going on," I sug-gested.

Nahat hesitated, then nodded. I was grateful that he agreed, rather than dragging us through private living quarters where people might not appreciate the intrusion.

The curly-haired teenager, who said his name was Ari, was sitting in the shack by the main gate, apparently watching televi-sion. He smiled again and answered Nahat's question with one word. *"Sicha."*

My limited modern Hebrew vocabulary suggested he was referring to some kind of meeting.

When Nahat asked where, the young man hitched his thumb over his shoulder and said something that could have meant "Gymnasium."

"But, of course, nonmembers may not attend," he added with another smile.

"Of course," Nahat agreed, minus the smile.

"Who is it you want to see?"

"The director."

He motioned us into the shack. "Teicher. You can see him here."

When we were inside, he pointed to the TV. On the screen, a portly bald man with a salt-and-pepper beard was answering

218

questions from an audience of people in work clothes. I gathered from the discussion that there were some security concerns, possibly stemming from a shooting incident.

And then I realized that what we were seeing was a closed-circuit video of the actual kibbutz *sicha* in real time. That was why everybody was off the streets and off the job.

After a minute of this, Nahat was off to the races. "What is this shooting?"

"We had a couple of visitors this morning," Ari said, as if he relished telling the story. "Both Arabs. The first one hitched a ride into the kibbutz on one of our trucks, saying he was in fear for his life. He said that criminal Selmar Hajabeel was trying to kill him."

"Was his name Kamlo?" I asked. "Is he all right?"

"I do not know what his name was. And yes, he is all right—the last I saw him."

"Did he have documents in his possession?" Nahat asked.

Ari looked mildly surprised. "Yes. He seemed to think that was why Selmar wanted to kill him—for those papers."

Nahat kept pressing. "What about this other Arab—the one that was shot?"

"This person—a real wild man—got here maybe ten minutes after the first man. He forced his way into the kibbutz, threatening us for hiding a criminal, and then he pulled a gun. That is when he was shot."

"Who shot him?" Nahat demanded.

Ari reached into a box on the floor and pulled out a nasty-looking Uzi.

"I had the honor," said the youth. "Kill or be killed. That is the way it goes."

Nahat and I exchanged glances. Mine was veiled astonishment. I wasn't sure what his was, unless it was curiosity as to my reaction.

Miriam hung back by the door, looking increasingly uncomfortable.

"Where is the body?" Nahat asked.

Ari turned and pointed to a plaque on the wall. It was like one of those signs in a campground with the different sites numbered, even to a yellow arrow and "You are here" in Hebrew. He was indicating a smaller building just this side of the dormitory housing.

"He is in a cooler in the rear of the infirmary."

"All right," said Nahat, then turned to me. "Let us go."

"Wait," said Ari. "It is not permitted for you to go in there."

Nahat swung around to face the teenager, close enough to read lips. "You want we should have you prosecuted for manslaughter?"

The young man paled and said after a hard swallow, "Never mind. I see nothing. Just please be quick."

We didn't waste any time. I certainly had no desire for prolonged corpse viewing. We drove to the infirmary and parked by the front door.

Miriam gave me an imploring look. "I'll—I'll wait out here."

I glanced at Nahat, who gave it a moment's thought, then nodded. "Just give me the keys."

I handed them over, noting our changing relationship. Nahat was no longer watching us like a bird of prey, but he wasn't ready to risk the loss of his wheels. Little did he know that bailing out of this adventure was probably the last thing Miriam would do.

No one appeared to be in the building just then. Even the sick people must have been in the *sicha*.

Past the front desk was a short hallway with examining rooms on either side. A back room was stocked with medicines, miscellaneous supplies, and cleaning materials. At the end of this room was a door. No doubt this was where they kept the perishables—and the perished.

Nahat stopped in his tracks. It was locked.

"Wait here," he directed.

I didn't know where he went, but in less than a minute there was a low electric buzz. I grabbed the door handle and pulled. It opened. I walked in. I could hear Nahat returning behind me. It was a good forty degrees cooler inside and quite dark. My fingers found a light switch by the door and gave it a flip.

On the far side of the room, up against the wall, was a gurney covered with a sheet over something about the right size and shape for a body. While I pondered that, Nahat went up and pulled back the cover.

Even from where I stood, there was no mistaking the puce-colored running suit, the snakeskin cowboy boots, the gold neck chains, the familiar pockmarked face, and the iridescent blue sunglasses. The running suit was badly messed up where his chest had absorbed flying lead.

Nahat was looking at me.

"*Tio Piña,*" I muttered.

"Who?"

"Uncle Pineapple. Nadi is his real name. Selmar's big hurt. Not the only one, but his main man. I could understand someone having to kill him. And he's probably Freemantle's killer."

I wasn't entirely prepared for what Nahat did next. With clinical nonchalance, the Israeli began patting down the body.

I viewed this corpse through the prism of two emotions—relief that a killer was out of commission and sorrow that this man's mother had lost a son so violently, his soul passing into a Christless eternity.

"We must search his car," Nahat said when he was done, having found nothing. "Then we can go."

But I wasn't ready to leave. "We have to find Kamlo."

At the car, Miriam asked no questions, and I offered no details about our impromptu inquest. We returned to the shack, where Ari was still watching TV. The *sicha* apparently was still going on hot and heavy.

"Where is the dead man's car?" Nahat demanded.

The young man was no longer smiling. Maybe he was getting tired of this game, especially knowing that we didn't necessarily consider killing Arabs heroic.

"He did not have a car."

Nahat frowned menacingly. "Then how did he get here—by magic carpet?"

"No, sir. He had a motorcycle."

Suddenly I remembered the first time we had seen Nadi at Dayr Al Nimrun, greeting us at the entrance like an Arab Hell's Angel.

221

"He's telling the truth, Nahat. The guy was a biker."

Nahat's frown stayed in place. "Then where is this motorcycle?"

Our host looked a little sheepish. "The other Arab took it."

"Yes—the first man," I hurriedly interjected. "What became of him?"

"And the documents," added Nahat. "Where are they now?"

Ari looked bewildered. "You see, it is like this. After the shooting, Teicher demanded to see these papers. I have no idea what they were, but they must have been very important because he had them sent on to another kibbutz where there are experts in such things."

I was almost beside myself. "But the other man—"

"The other man was quite upset about having these papers taken, and he—when no one was looking, he jumped on the motorcycle and drove off."

My heart felt a little lighter. At least Kamlo was probably alive.

But Nahat was still anxious. "Where is this other kibbutz?"

Ari blinked naively. "You mean where the papers were sent?"

"Yes! Yes! Where the papers were sent."

I thought Nahat might strangle the boy. He mopped his brow with a handkerchief.

"Oh, they were sent to that ultraorthodox kibbutz just this side of Nablus—Har Habbayit Qannim."

The handkerchief froze. After a moment Nahat let his hand pass down across his face and away. Now he had an expression that I'm sure was intended to be a friendly smile but which fit his face about as well as a pair of Nikes on a mackerel.

"Oh, yes," he said in a syrupy voice. "That is wonderful. At least we know that these documents will be in good hands."

"Yes," Ari agreed, his own smile returning.

I knew something was up, and I didn't believe for a second that Nahat thought this was peachy keen.

Now he was ready to go. "Thank you very much, young man. You have been most helpful."

We waved farewell, and I wasted no time getting the Honda out the gate. Nahat told me to retrace our route down the country lane, then head out the opposite direction on the main road toward Nablus. It was Har Habbayit Qannim or bust.

As I took one last look at Kibbutz Lador, I felt a sadness for the world's fallenness that could produce in someone so ingenuous as Ari such a casual attitude toward killing. And then I recalled something that had helped me regain the eternal perspective in times past. It was the inspired counsel of a missionary wife. Seeing the expression on her husband's face when no one turned out to greet them in port on their Stateside furlough, the woman said, "Don't grieve. Remember, we're not really home yet."

Had I been disappointed with God? I needed to be disappointed with life in this world and to be longing for my heavenly home—the kingdom that cannot be shaken.

Just then, though, I needed to know what Nahat was up to. "What was all of that sweetness and light back there with young Ari?"

For once, he sounded edgy. "I want that youngster to make the most innocuous report possible of our visit. I want them to think we are dropping it. We may have a chance, since I do not think he wants to admit he let us view the body."

"I especially didn't believe the part about those scrolls being in good hands. What is Har Habbayit Qannim?"

"You are a biblical scholar. You tell me."

I had something of an idea. "Well, literally the name means 'the Temple Mount Zealots.' But that's a rather unusual name for a kibbutz."

"It is a rather unusual kibbutz."

"How so?"

"You shall have opportunity to see for yourself. Let me just say that there could hardly be a worse place for a document such as you described to end up. In national security terms, this could be the big one."

"OK. Just what do you intend to do about it?"

I may have pressed too far, for he growled, "That is my business, my friend."

"Sure, but you're making us accomplices in it."

"Listen, American hero. It is only right that you help undo this terrible thing that you have started."

I couldn't help asking a question whose answer I might not want to hear. "And if I don't?"

There was a pause before Nahat spoke low and darkly. "I will not hesitate to use any means necessary."

By the time that sank in, I had nothing further to say.

Either they were making the days shorter, or I had lost track of time. Daylight already was fading by the time we reached Highway 60, heading north. I mentioned the need for food, and Miriam murmured something about freshening up.

Nahat gave us no argument. Just a few more miles down the road, he directed me to a turnoff into a small Palestinian village with a decent delicatessen.

They didn't exactly roll out the red carpet for us, but it was not unpleasant. We were able to purchase at a reasonable price some falafel, some lamb *schwarmin,* and some strong black coffee that went down as if it could keep us awake until a week from Sunday.

Nahat used a pay phone on the premises. I didn't bother to ask—I knew he wouldn't tell me—but I assumed he was getting directions to our zealot kibbutz.

I was beginning to wonder where we would spend the night. But I didn't spend much time on it. That was the least of my worries. I knew Kamlo wouldn't let those scrolls get away that easily, especially after all we had been through to get them. But did he know how to find this nest of zealots? Unlike Nahat, he couldn't just drop a shekel in a pay phone and get some secret agent to give him directions. Nor, like me, did he have an escort insuring the correct turns and right moves with the implied threat of gunplay.

And if Kamlo did find the place, how did he expect to recover the goods? I could appreciate some of Nahat's concern. I somehow doubted that these zealot characters would hand over the documents to some Arab on a motorcycle who claimed they

224

were his. I had total faith in Kamlo's determination, but I also knew this could land him in big trouble.

What would they do to him? What would I find when we got there? What could I do to help him? If these zealots were people of faith, would that necessarily keep them from violence? The sad fact, well-known to skeptics of every stripe, was that religious fervor had too often been the cause of more bloodshed than most faiths would like to admit.

These were some of the thoughts and worries that rattled around in my head as I drove on in silence. It made me wonder what was going through Nahat's mind. Perhaps it was occurring to him that this would not be a cakewalk for him either. Except for that pistol inside his jacket, he was just as outnumbered as Kamlo.

And then I realized that wasn't entirely true. He had me. And Miriam. For whatever that was worth. So then, what were the odds? Four versus four hundred?

Night had fallen by the time we reached the kibbutz. We'd taken one wrong turn, which cost us another half hour to unravel. Fortunately, it was the last turn before the kibbutz, and we quickly realized our mistake when we began seeing signs for Mount Gerizim. I had thought it was odd that we should have been steadily climbing those last few miles.

Now we were the Rough Riders again, except that this time it was with Nahat instead of Kamlo. This dirt-and-rock country road was not the nice *derekh* of Kibbutz Lador, level from the flattening of truck traffic and heavy agricultural equipment. It was for sure that the suspension and shock absorbers of Nahat's vehicle took the abuse much better than Kamlo's beater. Only half our teeth rattled out of our heads.

As the gate to Har Habbayit Qannim loomed ahead under the glare of a mercury vapor lamp, I suddenly realized we were arriving without a crucial element—a plan. I doubted that the direct approach we'd taken at Kibbutz Lador was really going to fly here, especially considering the lateness of the hour.

When I pulled the Honda off the road and took it out of gear, Nahat looked at me in mild alarm.

"Look, Nahat. What if these kibbutzniks don't want us poking around here? What if they have somebody a little tougher at the front gate than our friend Ari?"

Nahat gave me a measured look. "I think your friend Nadi found Ari tough enough."

"But you know what I mean."

Nahat nodded faintly. "What do you propose?"

"Let me take the lead here. I'm not a spook from Mossad or Shin Beth or some place. I've got writer's credentials. I can probably talk my way in, whereas you would have to shoot your way in, and I don't think you have enough bullets."

He spoke again after a moment. "Fair enough. Then I shall try to stay in the background. I cannot pose as your assistant, in that I have no camera."

I drove on, wondering if it was a lucky guess or if he actually knew the role Kamlo had played at Dayr Al Nimrun, and, if so, how?

The entrance was reminiscent of Kibbutz Lador—a wide-open gate in a chain-link fence, flanked by a shack that I hoped contained no trigger-happy teenagers with Uzis.

It didn't.

In fact, it contained no one at all. Just as before, I pulled the car off to the side.

"Wait here," I told Nahat and Miriam. "I'll see if anybody's home."

As I stood there under the stars, gazing and wondering, I caught myself changing roles. I had come a long way from taking orders at gunpoint to orchestrating our next move. The unsettling part was the realization that at some juncture our purposes—mine and Nahat's—were bound to collide. So far, our pursuit of the scrolls was proceeding on twin tracks. True, my goals included finding Kamlo. But sooner or later, it was going to come down to the scrolls. And only one of us was going to walk away with the prize.

I knew I had to give the edge to the man with the gun. But what was I supposed to do? Wait for an opportunity to break a bottle over the guy's head? Somehow that didn't square with my image as a biblical scholar. Not to mention the fact that it would be ethically questionable.

"And so, Rev. Dr. Harper, how did you manage to acquire those famous holy scrolls?" the press would ask.

"It was your basic smash and grab," I would explain. "All for God and country, of course."

More likely, I realized, was a preemptive strike from my counterpart. I was the one who needed to be looking out for my noggin. It was a prospect I didn't want to contemplate. I wasn't at all sure I believed the agent's denials of involvement in the deaths of the cave climbers.

I also had Miriam to worry about. But at least, as a potential witness, she might be a restraining influence on Nahat. I told myself not to start worrying—yet.

I strolled back to the car to tell them to sit tight while I explored a little further. There had to be somebody here. I couldn't believe this kibbutz was empty as well. This stuff was starting to give me a complex.

"Nahat," I said, opening the door—and then stopped.

The car was empty too. I froze for several long seconds, listening to the sound of nothing.

"Nahat?" I said again into the darkness, but not too loud.

"Miriam?"

Now my arms and legs were covered with goose bumps in the cool night air. My senses were as heightened as a cat's listening for the breathing of a mouse. I was afraid to move and shatter the stillness with the explosive crunch of gravel under my feet.

It was happening again. I was once more the wilderness dream traveler, immobilized by the echo of my own footsteps and the sound of my own breathing, magnified in my ears.

The priest who offers the holocaust shall receive the skin of the burnt offering which he has offered. You shall offer the lamb in the evening with the same grain-offering as in the morning and with the corresponding drink-offering as an offering by fire, a soothing odor to YHWH.
—The Temple Scroll (11QT) XIII

23

Abruptly the silent night was rent by a piercing sound like that of a trumpet blast, though without the metallic sharpness. I dismissed the first thing that came to mind—a shofar. This had to be my imagination getting carried away with itself. Maybe this was just a fire drill, and that's what had become of everybody.

And then the blasts came twice more, sounding each time more like what my sensibilities said couldn't be. I started to move toward the sound—it seemed to be coming from some distance beyond the camp to my left—then realized that I had little evidence that the kibbutz was actually deserted. I turned away from the sound and toward a row of shadowy buildings, which could have been cabins or other living quarters.

Then I stopped again. I didn't really want to start a laborious search of the camp, nor did I want to lose my sense of direction toward that sound. I felt if I didn't stray too far off course, I could trace my way right to it. Inspiration told me to do something bold.

"Is anybody home?" I hollered toward the stars and the cabins and the shadows and the suggestions of shapes in the distance.

I was anxious for Miriam and Kamlo, apprehensive about

this Nahat character, and mystified by this strange, wilderness dream place. Just a minute ago, my voice would have split the night. But since the blare of the horn, it sounded small and ineffectual to my ears, swallowed in the darkness without echo.

I tried once more, even louder. *"Can anybody hear me?"*

This should have been enough to raise some kind of alarm—or curiosity, at least. So when there were no sounds of approaching footsteps and the only answer was a louder silence, I began walking tentatively toward the source of the horn blast.

I immediately regretted not having a flashlight, but my feet found a path that led away from the buildings into a shadowy copse. I was threatened momentarily with disorientation until I spotted the soft glow of a patch of luminescent yellow paint on a tree.

I moved cautiously toward the glowing spot and found myself on a footpath through the woods that had been worn nice and flat, with little chance of my tripping over an exposed root and stumbling into a thornbush or briar patch. Not only that, but by the time I reached the glowing spot I spied another just like it a distance down the path. No doubt this pattern would continue, I deduced.

It did.

After a while, the terrain began to rise, and the trees began to thin out. I was running out of luminescent yellow patches to follow, but a different glow in the distance served as a beacon, though to what I had no idea.

As the vista cleared, I could tell that the amber brightness was uphill. That made it easier to track, but it was certainly going to be harder to make a sneak approach, a lot harder to see than to be seen. That was always the way with the city on a hill—the advantage lay heavily with the defenders.

Now I could hear voices coming from the vicinity of the glow, which now was taking on every appearance of firelight. The voices came in rhythmic unison as if in some choral mode. And then as my ears grew attuned to what they were hearing and my feet drew me ever nearer, I thought I could discern a singular male voice setting the antiphonal pace.

But before I could make too much of that, the responsive

229

vocals abated. I was beginning to see long shadows, the kind cast by people against firelight at ground level. Unfortunately, I was probably now close enough to be seen myself. My advantage was that my eyes were looking from darkness toward light, while anyone spotting me would have to do the reverse with constricted pupils. I was glad I was wearing dark clothing—gray Dockers and navy pullover.

A crowd was assembled about the firelight. I slowed until I could find some cover, which I finally located just at the crest of the hill in the form of a rock pile. It was a little too close to the action, but you have to take what's available. If I was going to be caught, this was the most likely juncture. I tucked my head down and scampered for it.

I lunged into the lee of the rocks like a runner diving to beat a pick-off throw at first base. I lay there a minute on my belly, regaining my breath. A moment later I was relieved to hear the singular male voice once again, in normal tones that indicated nothing amiss. The words were now almost distinct enough to make out.

I got up on my knees and peered over the top of the sheltering rocks. As my eyes adjusted to the flickering illumination, I could see that its source was a fiery mass of wood upon a huge stone altar, in addition to numerous hand-held torches.

Before I could get a good look at what appeared to be scores of white-robed men, my attention was drawn to the far side of the altar, where a priest wearing a richly embroidered vestment gestured with a flash of metal in his hand. Another man crouched at his side, holding something white.

Now I could hear the priest's Hebrew words clearly enough so that I didn't have to guess what he was saying.

"Look down from Thy holy habitation, from heaven, and bless Thy people Israel and the ground which Thou hast given us, a land flowing with milk and honey, as Thou didst swear to our fathers."

Even more clearly came the congregational response: "Blessed be the name of the glory of His kingdom forever!"

At this, the crouching man placed the white object into position as if making a presentation. It was what I should have guessed in the first place—a lamb. No doubt a perfect lamb, one without spot or defect.

I cringed at the thought of what was sure to happen next.

At least, these seemed to be practiced hands, and it didn't take long. The snowy windpipe was quickly slit, and a gilded bowl was rushed beneath to catch the crimson flood. It was as if I could see the life literally draining out of this poor lamb, and something in my heart ached for it.

Then the priest began to intone, "'For the life of the flesh is in the blood, and I have given it to you on the altar to make atonement for your souls; for it is the blood by reason of the life that makes atonement.'"

The words echoed sickly in my ears, and my knees felt wobbly. I let my clammy forehead rest a moment against the reassuringly cool solidity of the rock. The whole lurid tableau was starting to swim before my eyes.

Risking another look, I saw the priest dip his hand into the golden bowl and sprinkle its liquid contents, black in the stark firelight, against the base of the altar. Where it spattered, the inky fluid skidded down in multiple tracks.

"The life of the flesh is in the blood . . ."

I couldn't seem to get my breath. This couldn't be. The Jews no longer practiced animal sacrifice, though I had heard of a tribe of present-day descendants of the ancient Samaritans who were rumored to do so. Why was this happening? It defied reason and added to my panicky sense of unreality.

Then the lamb, each pair of legs bound together, was hoisted onto the altar, and the priest moved in, wielding a larger knife this time. With a flourish the butchering began.

"The life of the flesh is in the blood . . ."

I was afraid I was going to be sick. Casting caution to the wind, I tried to stand up and turn away from the spectacle, but my knees had other ideas. The last thing I remember was thinking that I should try to keep my head from hitting a looming rock.

I couldn't have been out too long. At least, I didn't think so. All I knew in my muddled condition was that I was now being jounced along, head down, in the fireman's carry by some strong male who smelled mildly of perspiration and wood smoke.

I had apparently been in this posture long enough that the stress on my left hip and left shoulder was beginning to graduate from discomfort to ache. I fancied a time or two that I could see the ground in the darkness, but that only increased my vertigo, so I shut my eyes again.

My handler finally had me where he wanted me—a building of some sort. He stopped long enough to open a door, and then there was light.

Abruptly a woman spoke. "What have we here, Tuvya?"

"An interloper, Hulda," said my handler in a husky voice as he eased me down onto a padded table.

As soon as I whiffed the distinctive aroma of isopropyl alcohol, I guessed *infirmary*. I decided to leave my eyes shut for now, just to hear what might be said about me.

"Another one?" said the woman.

"We found him like this, unconscious on the ground at the high place during the holocaust."

Holocaust. Literally, "burnt offering." I took that to mean the evening sacrifice. But again, such things were not supposed to occur these days. Or so I had learned to think.

"So? Let us see."

I wondered what the woman named Hulda intended to do in order to see, but I didn't have to wonder long. I heard a little crackling as of the seal of a medicine ampule being broken, and the next moment I was inhaling ammonia fumes. I worked my head back and forth to evade the noxious smell, and my eyes snapped open.

"Ah!" she said. "Perhaps our patient can assist in his own examination."

This Hulda was a middle-aged woman with a strong, inquisitive face, no makeup, and more than a few gray streaks in her pulled-back black hair. It was a face that bespoke little ego and probably even less truck with nonsense.

"Where does it hurt?" she asked.

I pointed to the side of my head. "Here. A little. I think I hit it on a rock."

Hulda's voice sounded away from me. "He has been searched for weapons?"

The man named Tuvya must have nodded, for I heard nothing.

"All right, then," said the woman, drawing near again. "Let us have a look. And just remember that Tuvya over there has a gun."

She parted the hair above my left ear and peered and poked.

I winced a bit, but it wasn't too bad.

Hulda gave a dismissive little snort. *"Pah,* a little hoopoe egg."

I guessed that was the local variant of goose egg.

She next tested my pupil dilation with a little examination light that temporarily blinded me.

"Any blurred vision? Nausea? Loss of memory? Problems balancing?"

"No. I haven't had a chance to stand up and find out, but I'm OK, I think."

"Good. In that case, can you remember who you are and what you were doing up at the high place?"

"Sure. My name is Jim Harper. I'm a researcher and writer. Right now I'm looking for a friend named Kamlo and some documents that belong to us." I decided not to mention Miriam at this point.

The man and the woman traded glances that might have been significant. Or they could have been simply dumbfounded, but I didn't think so.

"And just what kind of documents might these be?"

"Ancient manuscripts, possibly Dead Sea Scrolls vintage. Is my friend Kamlo here?"

"What proof do you have that these manuscripts are yours?"

I realized that I had no proof, no receipt for Mrs. Cray's $17,500, no nothing. But I was saved by the man's interruption.

"These are matters that should be saved for Rebbe, Hulda."

It was my turn to interrupt. "Is he your leader? I need to speak with him immediately."

The woman looked skeptical. "Immediately? I do not think so. Morning will be time enough, after you have had a good night's sleep and some chicken soup, maybe."

She turned away to get something from a tray.

When she turned back around, I saw it was a syringe. My defenses sprang to red alert. I would have been off the table if the man named Tuvya had not pushed me down with a strong hand.

The next thing I knew, both his strong hands had me pinned against the padded gurney. I pushed back in a brief but futile attempt to break loose. I probably could have put up some better kind of fight, but my brain was working well enough to know that the outcome was already assured by the pistol I now saw riding on his hip.

I almost didn't feel the stick in my right upper arm until it was all over. But that was not my greatest worry. Somebody had to know about Nahat.

"If I don't get to see your Rebbe immediately, I predict big problems for him and this kibbutz."

"Oh?" said Hulda with the tone of a humoring mama. "What is it you would tell Rebbe?"

"There is another man here, a dangerous man."

"Another intruder like yourself?"

"Yes."

Tuvya was relaxing his grip on my arms and actually helping me to sit up. But it required more effort than I expected. Tuvya certainly had been in no danger from me. And now my head was feeling a little woozy.

The woman looked mildly interested. "Dangerous? In what way?"

"He is armed, for one thing. Also, he will stop at nothing to get those manuscripts."

Tuvya helped me slide off the table to my feet. I could barely feel the floor, and my knees didn't quite seem to know what to do. Holding onto the table helped.

Hulda was speaking. "And how did you get here, Mr. . . . uh . . . Carter?"

"That's Harper. I came here in a carter . . . I mean a car."

"All right. And how did that dangerous man get here?"

"The . . . uh . . . same car."

"I see," she said triumphantly. "Perhaps he would tell us that *you* were the dangerous man."

"But I can explain. I—"

"Tell it to the Rebbe."

"That's exactly what I'm trying to do."

She turned a scorching glare upon me. *"In the morning! Now, good night."*

With that, I felt myself being propelled toward the door by a steely grip under my left armpit. This Tuvya fellow was a pretty big guy. My feet barely touched the ground as we left the building and crossed a gravel path toward another structure. I stumbled once as the wooziness began to rob me of coordination. But my strong-handed escort kept me on the straight and narrow.

By the time we reached the other building, I didn't much care if it was full of snakes and spiders, as long as it had a bed. In fact, I wouldn't have been picky about the bed as long as the place had a floor that wasn't on fire or under water. I needed some rack time, with or without the rack.

The door required a key. While Tuvya fished it out, I decided to take a little rest by sitting down on the ground.

But Tuvya wasn't having any of it. "None of that," he snapped, jerking me to my feet.

The next thing I knew, he'd snapped on a light and I was being marched down a shadowy hall in what could have been a rundown hotel toward a room at the other end. Another lock and another key, and we were inside.

"We have some company for you, Moshe," Tuvya announced on the threshold.

Dimly I saw a large figure, reclining on a cot, turn his head toward us and into shadow. Until that moment his face had been lit by the shifting lights of a small-screen television on which appeared the ubiquitous Phil Silvers.

And then I heard the man's voice, deep and disapproving. "I certainly hope he does not smoke. This is a no-smoking area, you know, Tuvya."

"Not to worry," Tuvya assured him. "Mr. Carter here is ready for a good night's sleep. I am sure he will be no bother."

"Carter," echoed the big man.

But it was too late. The door was shut. The tumblers turned in the lock. Tuvya was gone.

I practically fell into the other bed, not even bothering to pull the covers back or take off my shoes.

Before I could shed consciousness, my roommate spoke again. "Mr. Carter, I would like to say some things to you about peace in the Middle East."

I was almost gone, and this was not computing. "What?"

"Middle East peace, I say. There is nothing more urgent."

"Yes, there is. I'm doing it. Good night."

If the High Priest is to minister to YHWH, whoever has been ordained to put on the vestments in place of his father shall offer a bull for all the people and another for the priests. He shall offer the one for the priests first. The elders of the priests shall lay their hands on its head and after them the High Priest and all the priests.

—The Temple Scroll (11QT) XV, XVI

24

I woke up with something like the plagues of Egypt in my mouth and a Goliath of a headache. How I wished for a toothbrush and some aspirin. I tried moving and discovered that easier said than done. I must not have changed position in the night, and now I was like a fly trying to break out of amber. Each limb and each joint seemed to have been frozen in place.

It took a moment to recollect just where I was.

In fact, it took a glance at my rather large roommate to jog my memories of the night before. He had piercing brown eyes, a lion's mane of bushy gray hair, and a flowing white beard that might have been at home on the chin of a desert prophet.

"Good morning, Mr. Carter," said the man in an officious tone. "They shall bring your manna in a few minutes."

"Uh . . . do they serve home fries with that?"

"And then I shall tell you about Middle East peace."

It was too early for this. "That's an oxymoron, if I ever heard one," I muttered.

My roommate sounded somewhat alarmed. "What is that you say?"

"I say Middle East peace is a contradiction in terms," I said loud enough to be heard in the next room. "At least until the Prince of Peace comes."

"Mr. Carter," said the man, as if fixing to get to his long-awaited point, "I do not care what you say. Nor do I care what Anwar Sadat or anyone else says. Trading land for peace is wrong. Peace will not come until the children of Israel possess all of the land given to them by God. It is written."

Now the light bulb was going on. "Wait just a minute. You are confused. The name is not Carter; it's Harper. And I have never been president of the United States. I'm not even very good with a hammer and nails."

The man stood up to his full height with a prophetic finger in the air. "And when the Lord your God shall deliver them before you and you shall defeat them, then you shall utterly destroy them. You shall make no covenant with them and show no favor to them."

The light bulb was becoming an arc light. "What did he say your name was?"

"Moses."

"Moses what?"

"Just Moses."

"OK. Never mind."

I shut up.

All I wanted to do was get cleaned up, change clothes, feel halfway human again, and resume my mission, not get into political arguments with a lunatic. Well, that wasn't all. I also wanted to see the Rebbe, find Kamlo, and liberate the Dead Sea Scrolls. I wanted very much *not* to find Nahat.

But above all else, I had to know about Miriam. Where was she? Was she safe? What might she be doing at this moment? I had to get out of this place for more than one reason.

I looked around the room. Not much was there beside two beds, one dresser, a table, two chairs, and Moses' TV. In a far corner was a door I assumed led to the bathroom.

My thoughts returned to my sidekick.

"Say, Moses. Have you seen a man named Kamlo here?"

"Yes. He was in this room just yesterday."

My pulse quickened. "What became of him?"

238

His scowl returned. "I asked for his removal. He was not serious about Middle East peace. I think he was crazy."

"Where did he go? What became of him?"

Moses shrugged. "They probably took him down the hall. What does it matter?"

Down the hall? I went immediately to the outside door and began banging on it vigorously.

"*Kamlo! Kamlo!*" I cried. "Are you here? Can you hear me?"

Just then the door opened. I stepped back to see a boy of thirteen or fourteen enter with a tray containing two bowls.

Moses quickly relieved him of the bowls and set them on the table.

Momentarily I wondered what would stop someone from banging this boy over the head and forcing one's way out the door.

The boy turned to me. "There is no need to awaken Kamlo. He is eating his breakfast too. When you are finished, Tuvya will take you to see the Rebbe."

I was silently rejoicing. "Kamlo too?"

"Yes."

And then the boy was gone.

Tuvya. That probably explained why the boy wasn't particularly afraid of me. Big Tuvya and his pistol were here.

I ate in a hurry. It tasted something like cream of wheat but different. The blueberries were good. I would have wished for some coffee, but I had more urgent things in mind.

I hoped Kamlo was all right. Somehow, as I thought of a Rough Riders' reunion, my confidence began to soar. The good guys' odds were looking better all the time.

It also didn't hurt that I finally had some food in my stomach. I've always been impressed by just how much good a normal blood sugar level will do for one's outlook.

No sooner had I finished scraping the bowl than a key turned in the lock and the boy was there again. As the door opened wider, I saw that was not all. Behind him stood Tuvya and someone else.

"Come with us, Mr. Carter," said Tuvya in his rumbling voice.

I was out the door. We were off to see the Rebbe.

"Wait, Tuvya!" Moses hollered before the door closed. "This Mr. Carter. He too is not serious about Middle East peace."

"Few are," Tuvya agreed, then shut the door.

I stopped dead. The "someone else" with Tuvya and the boy was my old *compañero*.

"Kamlo!" I fairly shouted.

He was grinning his famous grin. "Boss."

I almost couldn't think of what to say. "Where have you been?"

"Just down the hall. I had to move. Mr. Moses did not appreciate my attempts to get him to see the Palestinian perspective."

"I would think not."

"He is worse than the *Likkud.*"

I chuckled. "I guess it only figures."

"How is that?"

"I wouldn't expect lunatics in Israel to believe they're Jesus Christ, the way they do in America."

We were exiting this low-rent establishment. Kamlo was flanked by Tuvya, and I was flanked by the youngster. I nodded at the boy and addressed Kamlo in English.

"You suppose they figure I'm easy?"

Kamlo chuckled this time. "Maybe he knows karate."

Tuvya shot Kamlo a dirty look, which told me what I wanted to know: English was not necessarily a safe harbor.

In that expression I got my first good look at this sizable man who had carried me on his back. It was a rough-hewn face with a straight black beard, curly black hair, and expressive, dark brown eyes. The total effect was candor without artifice.

It was almost eight o'clock, and now, finally, I was seeing the farmhands, nurserymen, mechanics, and teachers I expected to see on a kibbutz, short-stepping to their appointed rounds with the tools of their trade in their hands and sleep in their eyes. It was a delicious morning of cool air, bright sunshine, and long shadows that seemed to conceal a thousand new secrets, to unfold as the day unwound.

We must have been crossing the same gravel concourse

where I had stumbled the night before from the infirmary to the place I'd spent the night. Whatever it was—the guest house, the jail, the mental asylum. It seemed we were heading away from all of the buildings and out toward the fields.

Even with two extra pairs of ears with us, I couldn't wait to hear what had happened in those final hours at Dayr Al Nimrun. These were not things that the Rebbe necessarily needed to hear, and I assumed they would not mean much to our companions, especially in English.

I tried to be casual. "Do you know what happened to Freemantle?"

Kamlo looked at me with large eyes. "What do you mean?"

"You haven't heard?"

Kamlo shook his head. "He is . . . dead?"

"His body was found in the Dead Sea."

Kamlo was silent for a long moment before speaking. "I was afraid of that."

"So he was alive when you left Dayr Al Nimrun."

"I know he was. He helped me to escape with two manuscripts. I thought he made it so everything pointed at me."

"They must have figured it out. How did he help you?"

"There was a telephone in my room—a house phone, you would say. The kind where you cannot dial outside."

"Yes. I saw these phones—and a lot of other things."

Kamlo, not knowing of my return to Dayr Al Nimrun and my forced labor there, looked surprised. But he continued. "Dr. Freemantle had some freedom. I had none. He would call me on the telephone and tell me things."

Now I was surprised. "That could have been a problem right there, if someone heard the ring and decided to listen in. What things did he tell you?"

"It was a silent ring—with a red light. There was an Arab scholar who was supposed to come. Dr. Freemantle was afraid of that. I think he felt he had run out of time to do something."

I nodded. "Sure. Selmar probably would have found out that he'd been lying about what those documents really were."

"I know only that Selmar was having second thoughts

about selling them. Dr. Freemantle also believed Selmar feared some kind of government investigation."

I nodded again. "Despite Selmar Hajabeel's tough talk about self-rule, he's not immune to the laws of the land regarding things like smuggling and organized crime. But if he was having second thoughts about selling the manuscripts, why would he have to detain you any longer? You were simply the surety for him to get his price from us."

Kamlo shrugged. "For all I know, he may have been planning to let me go, but it surely would not have been with any scrolls. I do not think Dr. Freemantle wanted to miss a chance to get some of these out to the world."

I was still troubled by something. "But if he could get the scrolls out of there and get you out of there, why couldn't he save himself?"

Kamlo shook his head slowly. "That I do not know, Boss. It did not seem that he considered himself in much danger. He had enough freedom that he could have left the same way I did."

"Please finish telling me about that."

"Dr. Freemantle told me to wait for a key. That night, somebody slid a key under my door. I estimate it was Dr. Freemantle. Then he called and told me where I could find the two manuscripts in a locked room. This key worked both on my door and on the room down the hall."

"OK. But how did you manage to drive out of there in Selmar's white Mustang?"

Kamlo chuckled. "That was the easy part—if you can get up early enough while everybody is still asleep. The keys all hang on pegboard in that garage. It was a piece of pie."

"That's cake, Kamlo."

Kamlo's familiar mangled lingo reminded me of how much I appreciated having him back. I would have to find a way of telling him so.

Up ahead loomed a large pavilion decked with brown asphalt shingles. Tuvya pointed at the structure and said something about the Rebbe.

As we approached, I could see row after row of white-shirted youths about the age of our younger escort, arrayed on plank

242

seating inside. There must have been a hundred of them.

Tuvya motioned for us to find seats in the back row. It was a lecture, and the instructor was a large man I guessed to be in his fifties, dressed in white shirt and khaki pants and with a magisterial bearing. His face was weathered like the Judean wilderness and fringed with a goatlike beard. His voice was strong, his manner supremely confident.

On a floor-to-ceiling easel behind him was a large diagram with an exploded rendering of an ox or steer, labeled with Hebrew equivalents for the cuts of meat—shank, round, rump, flank, loin, chuck.

Then it clicked. This Rebbe had been the officiating priest at last night's evening holocaust. The Rebbe was a butcher?

But as I tuned in to his lecture, I realized that the chart was supposed to be some physical representation of religious principles. He was making points of distinction among types of offerings that involved the manner of disposal of the meat, blood, and innards.

"In the first type of sin offering," he was saying, "the sacrifice is not eaten. The fat, kidneys, and covering of the liver are burned on the altar, and the rest is burned outside the camp. The blood is sprinkled before the inner curtain of the Holy of Holies.

"In the second type, the organs are burned on the altar, but the meat may be eaten in a holy place by the priest and his male relatives. The blood is applied to the horns of the altar and poured out at its base."

Here the big man put on thick reading glasses to consult some notes on the podium. Then he glanced at his watch.

"And so, novitiates, to review, we have the three basic types —sin offering, burnt offering, peace offering. Tell me now how we think of these ceremonially. They stand for expiation, consecration, and what?"

"Communion!" at least ninety-nine of the hundred youths called out in unison.

The Rebbe nodded solemnly, closed a book on the podium, and raised both hands, palms out, over his flock, as if in blessing. "'You will chase your enemies and they will fall before you by the sword; five of you will chase a hundred, and a hundred of you will chase ten thousand, and your enemies will fall before you by the sword. So I will turn toward you and make you fruitful and multiply you, and I will confirm My covenant with you.' You are dismissed."

As if a silent bell had rung, the youths began filing out of the pavilion quietly but nonetheless cheerfully.

Tuvya rose, and we took that as our cue. The four of us began moving toward the front while the exiting youths paid us little mind.

At the podium, the Rebbe was pocketing his eyeglasses and collecting his papers. Just as he looked up, Tuvya spoke.

"Rebbe, these are the men who claim they own the documents sent here from Kibbutz Lador."

The Rebbe's eyes flashed, and his eyebrows arched in either disbelief or astonishment. "Is that so? Are they here to collect the rent?"

I had to speak up. "Rebbe, that's not totally accurate. A client I represent owns an interest in the scrolls by virtue of having deposited a five-figure sum of money toward their purchase. We were simply trying to complete the purchase."

The Rebbe looked skeptical. "From whom?"

I cringed. "From Selmar Hajabeel."

"*Selmar Hajabeel!*" he thundered. "It is as they said. Then they are contraband!"

"Only Selmar Hajabeel knows their true provenance," I replied evenly. "Unfortunately, his whereabouts are currently unknown."

"And so, how did they get to Kibbutz Lador?"

I hoped my face didn't show my embarrassment as my mouth tried to form words that wouldn't come.

Kamlo jumped in. "I swiped them from Selmar and escaped with them."

"Oh?" said the Rebbe in even greater astonishment and to my even greater embarrassment.

"They killed a man there, a criminal, who tried to steal them back."

The Rebbe looked at both of us. "And the two of you are working on this . . . transaction . . . together?"

We both nodded, Kamlo more enthusiastically than myself. I felt as if we had just crashed and burned. I would have to speak to Kamlo about letting me do the talking in the future.

But to my surprise a thin smile came to the Rebbe's face. "Perhaps we should talk about this. Come."

Tuvya seemed as surprised as anyone. The boy looked at him, and Tuvya shrugged in bewilderment. They trailed us at a generous distance as we followed the Rebbe back out into the open spaces.

The Rebbe took big strides, and we had to double-time it to catch up.

When we did, the big man turned to me and said, "My name is Adoniram Cohen. I am the spiritual leader of Har Habbayit Qannim. What is yours?"

"I'm Dr. C. James Harper, and I'm a writer and researcher in the field of biblical archaeology and ancient languages."

Kamlo spoke up. "And I am Kamlo Mattar, a sinner saved by grace."

The Rebbe did a quizzical double take. "Both Christians?"

"Yes," we chimed together.

"I am a former pastor," I added.

"Then I should explain a few things to you, and perhaps you shall understand."

"Rebbe," I countered, "there is something *you* need to understand."

"And what is that?"

"There is someone else here looking for the documents, and he is armed."

"You have told Tuvya this?"

"Yes."

"Then it is in God's hands. We have no reason to fear one man. We also have a few guns of our own."

I was debating whether to tell him about Zeev Nahat's being a government agent when a flatbed truck wheeled up beside us and a smudgy-faced young man asked the Rebbe if he wanted a lift.

The Rebbe nodded and got into the seat with the driver while we climbed onto the rear bed with Tuvya and the boy. We hung on for dear life as we bumped and rattled our way toward the distant barns.

The most remarkable sight en route was a tidy, little white clapboard farmhouse nestled among a stand of cedars that would not have been out of place in rural Wisconsin.

Tuvya saw me eyeing the place. "That is the Rebbe's home. He is a lover of livestock."

But we were going to the barns. I couldn't figure why.

We piled off the truck and caught up to the Rebbe on the way to a one-story red barn with a corrugated metal roof. Once he entered the barn, he appeared to lose track of the world of Homo sapiens. I couldn't figure whether this Adoniram Cohen was oblivious to us, was putting on a performance, or was just plain eccentric.

The Rebbe unlatched a rude gate into a series of pens and stalls bathed in shadows. By the time my eyes began to adjust to the severe darkness, we were moving toward the bright sunlit fields beyond. Judging by the sounds and smells in these stables, there were some tenants at this very moment. To my untrained nose, they seemed more bovine than horsey.

Tuvya and the boy closed the gate behind us as the Rebbe proceeded out the other side onto the beaten track of an expansive board-fenced corral.

My concentration was broken by the Rebbe himself.

"Stay right there," he commanded.

I only thought he had forgotten us. I watched as the big man strode purposefully toward the center of the corral. It was then that I spied a reddish brown spot against the fence on the other side.

A shrill, piercing whistle gave me a start. I looked and saw that it was the Rebbe with his little fingers stuck into the corners of his mouth.

The brown spot grew larger and larger until it became a full-grown cow of an odd russet hue. But by the way it gamboled and trotted across the field, I judged it to be barely mature.

The Rebbe dug something out of his pocket and offered it to the animal on his upturned palm, the way I was taught as a boy to feed the ponies without getting bitten. Cohen scrubbed between the creature's ears while it ate. He appeared to be talking to it. Then it was gone, kicking up its heels, tossing its head, and shrinking once again to a distant ruddy spot near the far fence.

The Rebbe seemed a different man when he returned. His previously grim face was relaxed and open as of one treasuring a secret love.

"All right," I said pointedly. "What was that all about?"

Cohen looked at me as if for the first time in his life.

"Have you ever heard of the red heifer?" he asked.

Justice and justice alone shall you pursue that you may live and come to inherit the land that I give you to inherit for all days. The man who accepts bribes and twists just judgment shall be put to death. You shall not fear to execute him.

—The Temple Scroll (11QT) LI

25

I watched the Rebbe's calmly passionate brown eyes watching me, measuring my responses. Of course, I'd heard of the red heifer. I just never thought I'd see one in real life.

I nodded mutely. I knew more than I was willing to let on, but I didn't want to short-circuit the Rebbe's expansive mood and miss a unique opportunity.

He glanced at his watch again. "If you will join me for morning tea, I will make all things plain to you and perhaps propose a solution for your dilemma."

How could I refuse? "Thank you, Rebbe."

We began ambling toward the farmhouse, Tuvya and the boy still in tow. A pensive silence seemed to grip us as my thoughts and questions churned.

Surely this was not what it appeared. I had heard the rumors but never gave them much credence. The temple sacrifices had been in abeyance for the better part of two thousand years. Theoretically, the red heifer could change all that. The ashes of this mysterious beast, described in the book of Numbers, supposedly could be used to consecrate a new generation of priests and reinstitute the sacrificial system if the temple were ever rebuilt.

But who on earth would be qualified to consecrate the consecrators? Not to mention the fact that the blood of Christ had rendered all of this obsolete.

We entered at the side door of the farmhouse, which entered upon a kitchen where a plump woman about the Rebbe's age, with gray hair in a bun and calm, patient eyes, was working with steaming liquids and jars at the sink, apparently canning some produce.

"Tea?" asked the woman expectantly.

The Rebbe nodded, murmured something, and led us into a small dining area. The room was dominated by a large trestle-footed table covered with an elaborately crocheted tablecloth, the obvious product of many hours of labor by loving hands. Against one wall was a credenza holding a small menorah, several framed pictures, apparently of children and grandchildren, and a few assorted knickknacks.

"Please be seated," said the Rebbe.

As we did so, I noted that Tuvya and his young sidekick were lingering back in the kitchen. The woman I assumed to be Mrs. Cohen came with a tray of steaming cups and several bagels. For the tea to be ready this quickly, it must have been a regular mid-morning ritual in the Cohen household.

I'd been ready for coffee a long time ago, but this would do. The only thing lacking now in my morning was a warm shower, but I doubted that the Cohen hospitality extended quite that far. In fact, I had no doubt that even this present courtesy had its price. As we took our first sips, I wondered what the Rebbe's agenda was.

"It is no doubt providential that the red heifer is here," began the Rebbe in his professorial tone, "and that the scrolls are here—and that you are here as well. Where are you two gentlemen from?"

I traded glances with Kamlo, and he spoke first. "I live in Jerusalem, but Sebastiya is my hometown."

"Ah, ancient Samaria, capital of the old Northern Kingdom. Then you are almost back in your old neighborhood here. Have you ever been to Mount Gerizim?"

"Only as a child."

"Mount Gerizim is half the reason we have located our kibbutz here. It is amazing. Archaeologists are unearthing the remains of the Samaritan temple, which was constructed to be an exact replica of the temple in Jerusalem. While we cannot excavate our own Temple Mount because of the Muslims, there is very much to be learned here. And you, Mr. Carter?"

"That's Harper, Rebbe. I'm from Pennsylvania. I teach at Williamson University."

"Pennsylvania," the Rebbe repeated thoughtfully, as if intrigued by the sound of the name. "Our red heifer was imported from a special herd in Oklahoma."

I could only guess that the Rebbe had the two places pegged as next door to each other. I had no intention of disabusing him. I wanted to hear more.

After a bite of bagel and a sip of tea, the Rebbe continued. "We are called the 'Temple Mount Zealots' because we believe in rebuilding the temple and reinstituting the full temple sacrifices. Centuries ago, the land came under blood guilt through rebellion and idolatry, and the way to God has been closed since the temple was destroyed. We intend to restore full relations with the Lord our God. We intend to reopen that way."

I didn't want to say it, but I felt compelled. "Rebbe, the way already has been opened by Jesus Christ, who gave Himself as a permanent sacrifice that need never be repeated."

The Rebbe nodded eagerly. "I believe that may well be the case—for Christians. Evangelical Christianity has been a good friend to Israel and religious Jews. We respect your ways and expect only the same in return. Some of these things are a mystery. As a student of the Bible, have you ever considered the truly unique aspect of the red heifer?"

I drew a blank. "What aspect?"

"What gender is the heifer?"

"Female. While all of the other sacrifices are males."

"Without spot or defect."

"And why is that, Rebbe?"

He shrugged modestly. "Again, I say some of these things are a mystery. But consider this: All of the things that make a person ritually unclean—corruption, disease, discharges, and all **forms** of Levitical defilement—eventually trace back to the ultimate defilement, death. Ironically, the sacrificial system itself would produce ritual defilement because it involves the taking of life."

I nodded. "I suppose that's why the priests themselves must be cleansed with the ashes from the *female*—representing new life."

The Rebbe beamed. It was a gratified smile that lit up his entire face and straightened out the seams so completely that I imagined I was seeing the way he had looked as a young man.

"Very good. Very good, indeed. I think you are ready for the rest of this. Please come with me."

Kamlo and I looked at each other as the Rebbe got up from the table. This man was full of surprises. The only thing we could do was follow.

He brought us back into the kitchen, past Mrs. Cohen still canning at the sink, and to a door adjacent to the side entrance, where one might expect to find basement stairs.

We indeed found what I expected.

"Watch your step," said the Rebbe over his shoulder as he began his descent.

Over my shoulder I saw that the boy and Tuvya apparently were remaining behind.

It seemed fairly ordinary, as basements go. A single light bulb in a ceramic fixture illuminated a utility area with water heater, clothes washer, and dryer. Through a narrow doorway I saw a larger area under the main house with a Ping-Pong table and a workbench cluttered with tools and wood scraps. But I didn't think he had brought us down here to show us his new birdhouse.

The far wall of this area, I judged, should have been an outside wall, except that it had another door in it—with two locks. I wondered if he was taking us back outside, but when he opened the door with two keys from a belt chain, all was dark.

"Careful," the Rebbe said, flipping a switch that showed we were about to go down another flight.

This had just ceased being your normal basement. This descent was at least twice the depth of the first. And at the bottom we still weren't anywhere.

Now we were entering a tunnel that, judging from the light at the far end, led away from the house at least the length of a football field. I judged that it would bring us to somewhere in the vicinity of the barns.

We had to walk partly stooped, because the tunnel was only about five feet high, and that got old very quickly. But at last we reached the lighted area, where we could stand—and then some.

The place was cavernous. In fact, it looked quite like a natural underground cave. I didn't know what to make of it at first. It appeared to be something like a trophy room, walls lined with case after glass case of mysterious metal objects and paraphernalia.

The illumination was coming from a six-foot-high menorah in the middle of the room, which appeared to be burning real fuel with smoke and flame. As we stopped to take it in, I heard a gentle purr that could have been an exhaust fan somewhere overhead.

Our host flipped a switch, and soft fluorescent lights came on along the cases, erasing some of the shadows.

I turned to the Rebbe. "With all of this down here, your kitchen must be a very busy place for foot traffic."

"There is another entrance."

He obviously was not volunteering the rest of that information, but I guessed I was probably right about the barns. I could see a shut door in the opposite wall. The other way in must be through one of those structures aboveground. Actually, more was the wonder that he would show us this much. There had to be a reason.

Kamlo was gliding along the glass cases, peering inside. "What is all this?"

The Rebbe seemed content to let us guess for a while. "Local ware. We have some artisans on this kibbutz as well as a foundry."

I was intrigued by the giant menorah and was beginning to form a notion about all of this. I walked up to the overgrown candlestick holder and ran my fingers over its surface. It appeared to be cast bronze.

"If these are the furnishings for the future temple," I asked, "where's the gold?"

In the flickering menorah light, the Rebbe's face looked less benign, even a bit sinister.

"Do you have any concept of how much it would cost to do what you suggest?"

"Probably not," I conceded.

"When the time comes, this project will have to be underwritten by the nation of Israel. I am told this piece alone could cost as much as ten million dollars."

"Ouch."

"But at least we have the castings. We have studied every available record and have reconstructed ninety-three of the various vessels, bowls, firepans, and other implements used in the temple service. And now we have some even better information."

I hoped he didn't mean what I thought he meant.

"What is this thing?" asked Kamlo, putting an index finger against one of the glass cases.

The Rebbe went over and opened the cabinet. He brought out a strangely shaped silver vessel that looked like an inverted oil can with handles on the sides and a pointed bottom.

"This is the *mizrak*. It is used to catch the blood from the sacrifice and remove it to the altar."

Kamlo frowned. "Why the pointed bottom? Would that not cause spillage?"

"If you cannot set the vessel down, there is *less* chance to spill. It guarantees that you finish the sacrifice swiftly."

I was personally intrigued by an entire case of bone-handled knives in sundry sizes and shapes, from straight little daggerlike instruments—that I could picture being inserted into a vulnerable neck—to big, curved-blade jobs that looked as if they could hack a lot of flesh from a carcass. The workmanship of the gleaming instruments was as fine as I had ever seen.

"And this," I could hear the Rebbe telling Kamlo, "is called the *psakhter*. It is used to scoop ashes from the burnt offering."

I tore myself away from the knives and tried to put some meaning to it all. By the time I had taken in the long-handled turning forks shaped like Neptune's trident, various incense burners, and the priestly garments, vestments, ephods, and other paraphernalia—pots, shovels, bowls, dishes, basins, censers, and lampstands—my eyes were beginning to glaze over.

That's when I saw, over one of the cases, a photograph of the white-shirted teenagers. I recognized the location. It had been taken at the pavilion. The students were arrayed in three rows with the shortest in the front and tallest in the rear, like a class photo.

Then I saw another photo much like it a few feet away, except that in this case the subjects were grown men, ranging from my age to the Rebbe's and possibly older.

The Rebbe cleared his throat. "What you see is the very future of the theocracy. We have one hundred and forty *kohan-im*—men, like myself, who can trace their lineage back to one of the priestly clans of Aaron—plus scores of Levites. So we have the priests, the Levites, the red heifer. What else is needed?"

"Someone to consecrate the priests?" I asked.

"Correct again." I could hear the Rebbe's genuine pleasure. "That is why the boys. We have nearly one hundred boys who are potentially qualified to perform that kind of service."

"But what makes them so special?"

"These are young men who have lived their entire lives in a special environment away from the city. They have been protected from everything that defiles. Even their living quarters are built on rocks over hollow spaces so as to avoid inadvertent corruption from an unknown grave transmitted through the earth."

I couldn't let that pass either. "What provision have you made for the things that proceed from the mouth?"

For once, the Rebbe looked at a loss. "Please explain."

"What proceeds out of the mouth defiles the man. These are the sinful thoughts and words that overflow from the heart."

The confused look changed to one of irritation. "This is your Jesus again, I gather. Please, let us not mix apples and oranges here. We have more serious business to discuss."

That gave me something to think about while the Rebbe began fishing something out of his pants pocket. I had to marvel at the man's sense of the theatrical. I also had to admit that it worked; he had my full attention.

I watched his every move as he went to the lockbox drawer of a metal base cabinet and inserted a small silver key from the belt chain. His hands, quick like an artist's, had the drawer open in an instant, and out came a large, dark cloth drawstring bag.

"The scrolls!" Kamlo cried.

"Now," said the Rebbe, establishing eye contact with both of us, "do you remember what I said upstairs about providence?"

But I couldn't keep eye contact with this man. My eyes kept going to the drawstring bag like a sea lion to a fish. I did recall specifically what he had said upstairs, because it had struck me so pointedly at the time. I had wanted to ask him then what it meant.

"You said there were three things that were providential," I ventured. "That the red heifer was here. That the scrolls were here. And that we—Kamlo and I—were now here. I understand the first two, but why do you say the third?"

The Rebbe hefted the bag by its string and watched it dangle for a moment. "Come. That should be obvious. So we can talk about this ownership interest you say your client has and what we might be able to do to transfer it to Har Habbayit Qannim. They really do not belong anywhere else, you know."

"Listen, Rebbe," I said, licking my dry lips and feeling opportunity slipping through my fingers. "Your friends at Kibbutz Lador did not have rightful possession of these documents when they passed them on to you. They took them from Kamlo here—"

"Yes, while they were protecting him from another man—a criminal perhaps—who also claimed they belonged to *him*. But do you not see? These priceless texts should not be the property of collectors or scholars or thieves. They belong to the people who are going to bring the new temple to fulfillment."

"Namely, you?" I challenged.

The sarcasm was not lost on Cohen. "I understand your frustration. That is why I would propose to compensate your client for every penny invested. And, by the way, do you have some documentation of your claim?"

I didn't, and I believed he knew it. I was beginning to see that beneath this smooth exterior beat a heart of solid flint. It was a treacherous combination. This wasn't the kind of person who finished last.

"I don't need documentation," I asserted coldly.

"Oh? Why is that?"

"Because I have no intention of making any deals, especially of the sellout variety."

"Dr. Carter, I am afraid that your own position to bargain is not just weak; it is nonexistent."

"The name's Harper. So you're telling me that what you can't get legitimately you'll just appropriate?"

"Now, listen to me—"

"No, *you* listen. Forget my client's interest. The asking price for those scrolls was at least a million dollars, not seventeen thousand five hundred. You're not suggesting that you're prepared to cough up that kind of money, are you?"

"The scrolls are holy books," the Rebbe sputtered. "Nobody has the right—"

"So holy books are all right to steal? What about the defilement from that kind of sin? Or do you just slit the throat of another innocent lamb?"

I knew I'd gone a little far, but I wasn't prepared for the reddened face and the bulging eyes that stared back at me murderously. For a moment I thought he was going to maybe break out the knives from the glass case or just break my neck with his bare hands.

But the next moment he sighed tensely, ran a hand nervously through his thin hair, and then softened. "Come on," he said gently. "This is no way to talk business. Let us go back upstairs and do it the civilized way by the teapot."

I felt a little of my own anger abating. "All right."

What choice did I have? I certainly wasn't going to stay down there in that cavern.

The Rebbe flipped out the artificial lights, and we started walking back, lost in the silence of our own thoughts, retracing our steps through the long tunnel to the house.

I realized the Rebbe was right about one thing: my bargaining position was about as thin as a politician's promise. I had no receipt. I had no weapon. And I had no cards in my hand except the spot card of moral suasion, and that one was already in play to limited avail.

I noticed that the Rebbe, just ahead of me, had brought the drawstring bag with him. Maybe I would at least get to lay eyes on the scrolls just once, even if the first time was also the last.

"Rebbe?" I called.

"Yes?"

"Have you had a chance to read these scrolls yet?"

"Only a very little. They must be handled very carefully, you know."

"That is true."

Walking stooped over through a tunnel in single file was not the easiest way to hold a conversation, but I was highly motivated by a gnawing curiosity.

"What did you find?" I persisted.

"How is that?"

"What do the scrolls say? What is their subject matter—their content?"

"Oh. The one is a very valuable document. It may answer many of the things about the construction of the temple that are not found in *Dibre Hayyamim*. Needless to say, this could be very helpful to us."

I felt an eruption of goose bumps. *Dibre Hayyamim*. The books of Chronicles—literally, "events of the days." Now perhaps Yigael Yadin's notion of a far older, archetypal Temple Scroll was no longer just a theory. Still, it was almost beyond belief that such an ancient document could survive that many centuries.

Despite the tensions between us, I wanted to know what the Rebbe thought about this. "You certainly don't think this could be a document from the time of David, do you?"

I could not see the Rebbe's expression, but I could imagine his shrugging.

"I am no biblical scholar, but it would not have to be that old. It could be a copy of the same vintage as the other scrolls, while its text is older by a thousand years, yes."

"That," I said pointedly, "I would very much like to see."

The Rebbe sounded conciliatory. "I do not see why not. We may need some help from the professionals in interpreting the text and certainly for dating it."

I shut up. I didn't feel like telling him again that we weren't

257

selling. Let him get his own accelerator mass spectrometer.

We exited the tunnel and mounted the steps to the Rebbe's basement proper. By the water heater, the Rebbe turned to me, and I could see the fire in his eyes.

"This could change the course of history," he breathed with unvarnished zeal and clenched fist. "If we can pinpoint the correct spot on the Temple Mount to set the cornerstone, there will be no turning back. The work will begin, even if the Dome of the Rock must crumble to dust."

With this, the fist made a sickening smack into the flat of a hand as of a wrecking ball slamming into Kubbat es-Sakhra. I shuddered. The air was rank with obsession. This was a man who would stop at nothing.

I hastened to counter his intensity. "Do you think the Muslims—or even your own government—will stand for that?"

"Let them try to stop us. If Jews die for this, the government of men will fall. Then divided Israel will rise up as one man to claim its destiny. This is something that I and every last man and boy of Har Habbayit Qannim would gladly give our lives to accomplish."

"That could begin a very great bloodbath."

The Rebbe's features finally softened, and he shook his head slowly. "In my heart I do not believe so. When the time is right, it may be done without the firing of a shot. Remember, when Joshua led the Israelites into the Promised Land, the Lord did not stop up the Jordan River until the priests actually set foot in the water. The obedience comes first."

"Yes," I agreed, "but Joshua's priests were carrying the Ark of the Covenant."

At this, the Rebbe actually smiled, almost mischievously. "Perhaps the Ark shall be there waiting for us this time, under the Temple Mount."

He turned and began leading the way upstairs to the kitchen.

Nothing—not even the Rebbe's maddening answers for everything—could dampen my excitement and my eagerness to get these scrolls out of their bag and to feast on them with my own eyes. It would be the culmination of all my work these past weeks in Israel.

But when we finally emerged, blinking, into the bright kitchen daylight, I immediately sensed something amiss. Water was running in the sink, but no one was there. Mrs. Cohen was nowhere to be seen. We walked slowly into the dining room. The first thing I saw was Mrs. Cohen sitting at the table with eyes downcast.

The second thing I saw was Tuvya, along with the boy, standing in the corner with his hands on his head and an empty holster on his hip.

The third thing I saw was a man holding Tuvya in this position with two pistols, one of them apparently Tuvya's own. And then with a sick feeling, I saw who it was.

Zeev Nahat. Of course.

If a prophet or a dreamer appears among you and presents you with a sign or portent, even if the sign or the portent comes true, when he says, "Let us go and worship other gods whom you have not known!" do not listen to the words of that prophet or that dreamer.
—The Temple Scroll (11QT) LIV

26

We were frozen in place, the Rebbe, Kamlo, and myself. Now the picture was almost complete. But where was Miriam? I was relieved to see that she was not Nahat's hostage. Yet, I didn't know if that was good or bad.

Then Zeev Nahat, taking his eyes momentarily from Tuvya, saw Kamlo and me. A small smile visited his face.

"Dr. Harper," he said appreciatively. "Thank you for creating such a nice diversion and leading me right to the target."

"Believe me, Colonel Nahat," I assured him, "that was anything but my intention."

I was on the verge of demanding Miriam's whereabouts, but something told me to leave it alone.

Nahat ignored me. "Now, I would like every one of you to join Mrs. Cohen by taking a seat with both hands flat out on the table and keeping them there. First, take the Rebbe's bag, Dr. Harper, please."

The Rebbe complied, handing me the drawstring bag and giving me a dark, accusing look.

"Now, remove the contents, please, Dr. Harper."

This was all wrong. It was the thing I most desired to do, but not like this. As my fingers slowly stretched out the mouth of the bag, my personal clock slowed in that eerie, protracted way that is supposed to occur to drowning men and gunshot victims when an entire lifetime plays out in a few moments before their eyes. All senses were heightened in the tense stillness.

I recalled the Rebbe's remarks about the providential circumstances of the red heifer, the scrolls, and Kamlo and myself coming to a nexus here at Kibbutz Har Habbayit Qannim—and his belief that providence also would part the waters for him to march in and take the Temple Mount without a shot. *When the time is right,* he had said.

And I remembered the almost scary providential circumstances surrounding the previous two major scroll acquisitions upon Israeli statehood and the unification of the Old City.

I tipped the bag into the light and leaned forward to see the twin rolls of ancient leather within. My heartbeat quickened.

Providential circumstances? So what was providential about this? Maybe the time was not right. Maybe I was like one of Shakespeare's untimely born, doomed always to be in the right place at the wrong time. I felt as if I had come halfway around the world, combed the deserts of the Middle East, argued with scholars, and dodged terrorist bombs and media smears just to pull the trigger and see a flag pop out that said, "BANG."

Speaking of guns, Nahat apparently was losing patience. He began waving one of his at me.

"Open it up, Dr. Harper."

I pulled out one of the scrolls and removed the silk sleeve that someone had crafted for it. And then I felt the coolness of the smooth leather of the scroll itself sliding in my fingers. The goose bumps were back. I wasn't sure whether I'd have felt any greater sense of historic destiny if I'd just set foot on the moon.

I silently asked forgiveness for improper handling. Ordinarily, I would want to use surgical gloves. At the least, I would wash my hands to avoid getting damaging body oils on the priceless ancient scrolls. I knew better than to ask Nahat if I could go to the kitchen. But I recalled the pictures I had seen of fingerprints that had etched their way into glass bottles over a period of centuries and shuddered to think what the same thing would do to soft hide.

Holding my breath, I untied the string that had been wrapped around the scroll several times. Once I had it off, I wondered why anyone had bothered. The centuries had baked themselves into the turns of this scroll so that keeping it together was the least of one's worries.

I was much more concerned about getting it apart. The hide still retained some suppleness, but it was nearly impossible for me to breathe and unroll it at the same time. I kept fearing that I would go too fast, hit a brittle section, and damage the precious document.

But at last I had the first column of writing exposed, and my breathing returned. Just as in the books and archive photos, I finally beheld the elegant, flowing Hebrew script, majestic and mystical, nearly as crisp and clear as the day some scribe had penned it so many centuries ago.

My mind nearly balked at the enormity of it. This was a document that, but for chance and circumstance, Christ Himself could have stood and read in the synagogue at Capernaum or Bethsaida! Or the temple in Jerusalem. And I was holding it in my own twentieth-century hands. I felt very small and unworthy.

"Read," Nahat commanded.

I could hardly believe my ears, but my eyes told me I had better respond. One of the pistols was still looking my way. He knew I could read Hebrew as fluently as English. I took a deep breath, cleared my throat, collected my wits, and took the plunge.

"This is the word that came to Nathan the prophet from the Lord in the sixth month of the seventh year of David's reign over all Israel. 'Go and tell my servant David, "This is what the Lord, the God of Israel, says: 'I have cut off all your enemies and have made you a great name. Nevertheless, you shall not build a house for My name because you are a man of war and have shed blood. Your son Solomon shall build My house and My courts according to the plan that I will show you, and your house and your kingdom shall endure forever through him.'"' So I, David, began to fast and to pray and earnestly to seek the Lord's face, that He might show me the plan for His house and

His courts. And the Lord revealed to me all the details of the pattern for the porch of the temple, its buildings, storehouses, upper rooms, inner rooms, the room for the mercy seat, the surrounding rooms, the storehouses, the weight of gold for all utensils for every kind of service, the weight of gold for the golden lampstands and their lamps—"

"Stop! That will do."

I was startled to hear Zeev Nahat's voice over mine. I had been so absorbed in what I was reading that I'd nearly forgotten my audience.

The words were even more amazing than the scroll itself. Could this really be the more ancient text that Yigael Yadin had speculated about when he named the later manuscript the "Temple Scroll"? I didn't want to stop reading. I didn't want to put it down. When Nahat's voice broke my concentration, I lost my grip on the scroll's end, and it flapped back together like a window shade.

Mrs. Cohen visibly started in her chair as if someone had fired a gun.

"Dr. Harper," said Nahat, "now I would like to hear your interpretation of what you just read."

I resisted the temptation to say something flippant. Even I knew that wasn't a good policy toward unpredictable men with guns. Whatever he was up to, I had to play it straight.

"This appears to be the fulfillment of that verse in First Chronicles chapter twenty-eight, when David said the Lord gave him all the details for the construction of the temple and its implements."

The colonel did not respond directly but said, "Rebbe Cohen, what is your interpretation?"

I saw brief uncertainty in the Rebbe's eyes. His clenched jaw suggested angry defiance, but I could see some wavering with this unexpected questioning, as if Cohen thought there was still a chance to change the outcome of this unfortunate development.

The Rebbe cleared his throat and spoke with a tight voice. "I am no Bible scholar, but this I know something about. I think Dr. Harper is on the right track. But if you look in the chapter before, you will find a book of writings mentioned by name that has been lost to us—*Dibre Hayyamim Lamelekh Dawid.* Perhaps this is that book."

That rang a bell. The Chronicles of King David—in which the nation was supposed to be counted in the sinful census that brought a judgment of pestilence upon Israel. And so the census number was left unrecorded, and the name of the book, recording many other events of the kingdom, survived as little more than a footnote in the Old Testament.

"If that were the case," said Nahat, "and it were to contain all of the vital information for the temple, what would you do with such information?"

The Rebbe's chin jutted out defiantly once more. "We would build it."

Nahat's voice grew sharper. "Correction. You would *try* to build it. But instead of building anything, you would succeed only in destroying something—namely the nation of Israel—because it would start a civil war that no one could stop. And that is why these scrolls must not be allowed to be used in that manner."

The Rebbe leaped to his feet.

Nahat's pistol followed his chin as if connected by an invisible strand.

"So," the Rebbe demanded in a shrill voice, "you intend to wrest the scrolls from us by force, like a common criminal or terrorist?"

"I am claiming them for the State of Israel. Hand them over, please, Dr. Harper." He stuck the extra pistol into his belt.

I began calmly replacing the silk sleeve on the scroll, preparatory to placing it back in the bag. This action only intensified my regret that I would not get to view the other scroll at all. Reluctantly I handed the bag to Nahat.

The Rebbe was now livid. "You will never make it out of this kibbutz!"

"Is that so?" said the colonel, tucking the bag under his arm in order to fish something out of his pocket. "Then you should know that I will not hesitate to do what I have to do, even if it means the loss of a priceless document."

With that, he pulled out a device slightly larger than a

cigarette lighter. He flipped something on the contrivance, which emitted a long blue flame with the intensity of a plumber's torch. I shuddered at the unthinkable. Surely not even Zeev Nahat would dare torch something as precious as ancient scrolls.

Would he?

"You Philistine!" the Rebbe shrieked, lunging out from the table and knocking over his chair.

Mrs. Cohen put her hand to her mouth and closed her eyes.

Fortunately for all of us, Tuvya wrapped his arms around the big man, stopping him in his tracks.

"Let me go!" the Rebbe hollered, trying unsuccessfully to shake off his captor. "For this, I am not afraid to die!"

But Tuvya did not let go.

Nahat pocketed his torch, straightened, and gave every impression of preparing to make his exit.

"And one more thing, Rebbe," he said with an edge. "I require your pledge of safe passage out of here, or you will lose more than these documents."

The defiance in the Rebbe's demeanor appeared to be turning to bitterness. "Exactly what are you threatening us with now, Philistine?"

"You know very well, Rebbe, that this kibbutz is living on borrowed time here in the West Bank. If I were you, I would try to keep the lowest possible profile. My sincere advice to you is not to do anything to antagonize the government, or you will wake up one morning to find yourself being handed an eviction notice by men in army uniforms. I guarantee it. Come to think of it, what a quaint Palestinian village this could make."

"Nobody is moving us!" the Rebbe sputtered, but it sounded unconvincing.

"Maybe you would enjoy trying your rabble rousing inside an army prison. But I would not recommend it."

For a long moment I felt like a puny mortal between two Titans—the Old Covenant versus the New World Order. Man trying to save himself through the blood of bulls and goats versus man's attempt to achieve a godless, earthly Zion. Both absolutely committed to their own belief systems. Both absolutely doomed to failure.

I could see Tuvya's grip relax as the fight seemed to go out of the Rebbe.

The older man said nothing, but he dropped his gaze in apparent defeat.

I felt a twinge of sorrow—for the Rebbe and for Kamlo and myself. If we represented the New Covenant in this scenario, why did we seem to be without recourse? Perhaps we were still paying the price of living in a fallen world until the Redeemer comes from Zion, but that didn't make it much easier to accept.

I even felt some pity for Nahat, who was picking up all the marbles. I recalled what the Rebbe had said about falling governments and realized that people such as the colonel and his bosses always lived on the razor's edge, desperate to avoid the plunge into the chaos below on either side. Yet, the only cards they had to play were the ones they were dealt, and they were rarely winning hands. I certainly wouldn't want the responsibility for something like trying to keep Arabs and Jews out of each other's face on the Temple Mount.

At last the Rebbe spoke in a defeated tone. "Tuvya, I want you personally to escort Colonel Nahat from the premises and make certain that he leaves unmolested."

"Better yet," said Nahat, plunking down a set of keys on the table, "why don't you just have my car brought up here?"

The Rebbe glared at him, then nodded.

Tuvya picked up the keys and handed them to the boy with a word of instruction nearly inaudible to the rest of us. The boy dashed out of the room, into the kitchen, and out the side door.

The next five or six minutes seemed to last forever as the five of us stared past each other, scrupulously avoiding eye contact and being forced to think about the things that shouldn't be and what might have been. I suppressed a nervous urge to clear my throat, not wanting to break the silence and draw attention to myself.

It was then, in the tense, pin-drop stillness, that I heard the tiny metallic workings of the clock upon the credenza. It was one of those shiny brass wedding clocks in a bell jar with a mechanism that rotated first this way, then that. It transported me back across an ocean to a home in Dallas, where I had nervously cooled my heels not so long ago.

I recalled how time becomes an excruciating thing when it's measured out in the ticks of an antique clock in a strange house. Alien sounds flit across the threshold of hearing—a wooden creak, an electric hum, a chattering pipe, a muffled cough—setting the nerves on edge, teasing the imagination.

At last came the sound of a distant engine, at first like the questionable product of wishful thinking and then, unmistakably, followed by the distinctive crunching of tires on gravel. A moment later came the *thunk* of a car door, and then the boy was coming back in.

Nahat looked first at me, then Kamlo. "Come with me, please, Dr. Harper, Mr. Mattar."

I shook my head. "Not before I find out the answers to two questions."

Nahat blinked. "Just two?"

I nodded mutely, wondering for a moment if this was the way people got shot.

But he apparently wasn't ready to plug me—yet. "Speak," he growled.

It was hard to maintain my concentration while sighting down his gun from the wrong end, but I swallowed the great knot of panic in my throat and gave it a try.

"I want to know what's become of Miriam and what you intend to do with us."

Nahat scowled. "Unfortunately, I know the answer to neither of your questions at this time."

My brain cramped on that one. That was not what I'd wanted to hear.

There was an awkward silence as I took a last look around. Tuvya was patting the Rebbe on the shoulder, and the Rebbe squeezed his wife's hand.

"This," the Rebbe said with an air of fatalism to no one in particular, "reminds me of a verse in the book of Esther."

"It does?" I heard myself say without thinking.

"Perhaps 'deliverance will arise for the Jews from another place.'"

"'And,'" I finished for him, "'you and your father's house will perish.'"

"At least we tried," said the Rebbe. "No one can take that away."

When our eyes met, I felt as if I were looking into twin brown pools of infinite sadness. I would never forget that look. It was the look of Christless eternity.

But Nahat's patience was at its end.

"March, friends," he commanded.

That meant us—Kamlo and myself. We were headed out the door and onto the road again. The Rough Riders plus one.

I had no idea whether this would be a journey to freedom or to ruin. What's more, in the scheme of things—the rising and falling of the kingdoms of the world—it hardly seemed to matter much now. The pool of despair seemed a decent place to drown.

I was in the driver's seat of the Honda once again, numbly clutching the wheel, dumbly driving where I was told.

Beside me, Kamlo stared straight ahead with a blank expression.

But Nahat, behind us, the man with the gun and the government portfolio, was really the one in the driver's seat. Under the present uneasy circumstances, silence reigned.

My brain was replaying an old tape, the one that featured Nahat's demanding that I undo the terrible thing I had started and threatening to enforce his demand by "any means necessary." The good news—for him—was that he now had the scrolls. The bad news—for Kamlo and myself—was that we were the ones whose loose lips could spoil his party. Perhaps we were about to find out just how far Colonel Nahat would go to prevent that.

We were not far down the road, retracing our route from Kibbutz Lador, when he broke the silence.

"Dr. Harper, I believe I am prepared to answer your questions now."

I hadn't really believed he was napping, as my surreptitious peeks in the rearview mirror had seemed to bear out. His eyes had only been closed in further scheming, as I'd suspected.

"Speak," I replied.

"I have decided to return the two of you to Dayr Al Nimrun. There you shall retrieve Mr. Mattar's vehicle and proceed with your affairs, and I shall proceed with mine."

This was too simple. There had to be more.

"And?"

"And what?"

"Aren't you going to threaten us or something?"

In the mirror I could see Nahat shaking his head slowly.

"No threats. If you or Mr. Mattar try to do anything that would endanger Israel's national security, we shall know it instantly. And you shall both find yourselves outside the country very quickly. That is a fact, not a threat. Did you really think I was going to shoot you and dump your bodies?"

"Not really," I asserted.

I didn't tell him the only reason I didn't think so was because our little secret was also shared by the Rebbe and all the folks at Har Habbayit Qannim. I knew he didn't have enough bullets for all of that.

"But what about the other question?" I persisted.

"Ms. Boynton? I think you will find her safely back in Jerusalem. At first, I did not know what had become of her. She disappeared right after we got out of the car. Upon further reflection, I think there is no other explanation."

This man was aggravating.

"Other than what?"

My thoughts raced. If Miriam had gotten away from Nahat by simply fleeing into the night, she had taken quite a chance. I was sure he would have preferred keeping her as leverage against me, but he had managed OK with just his wits and a couple of pistols. That's pretty good leverage any time.

Tiredly, as if addressing a slow child, Nahat said, "Start with the premise that no one else seems to have seen her. Couple that with the fact that in the middle of the night I heard a vehicle leaving the grounds in a hurry. I knew which vehicle by its very distinctive engine sound, and this morning I saw that the vehicle in question was indeed gone from the kibbutz. Q.E.D."

I lapsed into silence, hoping he was right. I knew better

than to press further, which would only get me more riddles or stonewall silence. By now I knew my Zeev Nahat.

When we reached Highway 60 headed south, my stomach started complaining of running on empty. I looked at my watch and realized the morning was gone. I had heard professional athletes talk about "muscle memory"; I figured I had stomach memory.

Then I remembered the turnoff to the little Palestinian village where Nahat and I had found coffee and victuals the first time. He made no objection to a return visit, but he insisted that I stay in the car with him while Kamlo got a carryout order for the three of us. I guessed he wasn't ready to trust us too far yet.

The falafel and *schwarmin* were as tasty as I remembered them and the coffee just as hearty. Nahat, perhaps tired of sitting, ate his outside, leaning against the car. That allowed Kamlo and me the luxury of some small private conversation.

"What are your plans," Kamlo asked, disregarding everything Emily Post said about talking with your mouth full, "once we get back to Jerusalem?"

Swallowing suddenly got just a bit harder. "I think I'm going to get a long rope and start exploring the caves around Qumran."

Kamlo didn't know whether to take me seriously or not. "Is that not the way Miss Boynton's friend was killed?"

"Right. But then I wouldn't have to explain to her aunt what happened to her seventeen thousand five hundred dollars."

Kamlo rolled his eyes sympathetically. "I see. You are basically a failure."

I looked at him, not knowing whether to laugh or cry. "Yeah, Kamlo. You got that right."

Kamlo did a pretty good job of making the rest of his food disappear, but somehow mine had lost its savor. I left the last of it uneaten in the bag on my lap.

We were beginning the familiar ascent toward the mountaintop enclave of Dayr Al Nimrun when Nahat ordered me to stop the car. We were almost beneath the Sign That Did Not Exist.

"End of the line, gentlemen," he announced, opening his door.

Kamlo and I exchanged puzzled glances as Nahat then opened the driver's door and waited for us to get out. As soon as we did so, he slid in behind the wheel, gave a little nod and a wave, and drove off.

I stared after him in disbelief. After a second, I noticed that Kamlo was staring likewise.

I watched the Honda shrinking to a speck in the distance until the idea finally penetrated my thick skull. "He really did it, the rascal," I exclaimed. "He expects us to hike the rest of the way up to Selmar's crib."

Kamlo sounded unimpressed with my powers of observation. "That seems to be true, Boss. But why?"

"I guess he really doesn't trust us. He's giving himself at least an hour's head start back to Jerusalem. He took care not to dump us out so far that we couldn't make it on foot, but it's got to be another three or four miles to Dayr Al Nimrun. And all uphill. Clever."

"I think he may be worried about Miss Boynton," Kamlo suggested. "What do you think she might be doing back in Jerusalem?"

It was certainly a thought. "If I know Miriam, she's raising a ruckus with Dr. Starlander and the Editorial Committee. And if Nahat knows Miriam as well as I think he does, he has good reason to worry. He has a security problem on his hands there."

And then an idea that had been lurking in the recesses of my mind began to emerge from the shadows.

"Come on, Kamlo," I said with new resolve, if not new energy. "Let's go."

He gave me a questioning look. "OK, Boss. You have something up your shirt?"

"That's sleeve. Let's just say that perhaps Zeev Nahat and Randy Plunkett haven't had the last word in this whole affair."

It certainly gave me something to think about the rest of the way uphill to Dayr Al Nimrun.

My eyes are closed by the spectacle of evil, and my ears by the crying of blood. My heart is dismayed by the mischievous design, for Satan is manifest in their evil inclination. All the foundations of my edifice totter and my bones are pulled out of joint; my bowels heave like a ship in a violent tempest and my heart is utterly distressed.
—Thanksgiving Hymns (1QH) 10
VII

27

It must have been an hour later when we finally trudged through the familiar security gate, winded and surly. I was almost too tired to lift my arm and look at my watch.

The former monastery still appeared deserted. Like two boys at a haunted house, we wasted no time in sliding through the basement window and dashing up the steps despite our fatigue. Adrenaline will do that.

We made a beeline through the wicker room, down the hall, and past the other painfully familiar scenery into the cavernous garage, where the battered blue Toyota sat waiting like an old friend.

Intellectually, I knew that He who is in me is greater than he who is in the world, but at that point my spiritual antennae were on red alert. Silly or not, I didn't really breathe easily until Kamlo had us back out the gate and trucking down the long hill that had so tuckered us out just an hour before on foot.

I picked up the car phone and prayed that Nahat was right about Miriam's getaway. I was afraid to find out that the Israeli was wrong, but I had to know.

"Miriam Boynton?" they would say in my nightmare scenario. "I am sorry, sir. Haven't you heard about the terrible acci-

272

dent?" Or, "We haven't seen her. Nobody knows where she is."

It took me a minute to get through the museum bureaucracy, but they put the call through normally, which was a good sign. At last, to my unbounded relief, I was hearing the familiar dulcet tones of my favorite public information officer.

"Jim!" she said with a hint of desperation. "Is everything OK?"

"Sure. Everything except the mission. But I should ask *you* the same thing. You had me concerned."

There was a brief pause at her end. "Worried, you mean? Now maybe you know what it feels like."

She was right, of course.

"I'm sorry, Miriam. But if you hadn't followed me out to Dayr Al Nimrun—"

"And, Jim, *I'm* sorry about that. But I'm just not going to stay home with my knitting anymore and wait for the authorities to invite me to come identify the body of the man I love."

I gulped. Talk about tough love. "Remind me not to argue with you. But how did you get away from the kibbutz? Nahat thinks you stole a car in the middle of the night."

"I did nothing of the sort." Her voice was indignant.

"No?"

"No. It was a motorcycle."

I was floored. "A motorcycle? You rode a *motorcycle?*"

"They had one just hanging around in the parking lot, so I sort of commandeered it."

I snapped my fingers. "So that's what Nahat meant when he said the engine had a 'distinctive' sound. It was no doubt the only motorcycle on the kibbutz. I didn't know you knew how to ride one."

"Hans taught me. Last night I was highly motivated, shall we say, to make it work."

"You're unbelievable," I told her.

"It was out of fear, not bravery, I assure you."

"Did you know whose motorcycle that was?"

"Yeah," she said morosely. "I thought about that all the way back—that dead guy, Nadi? Well, at least he didn't need it anymore."

273

"But what about your car? I can tell you it didn't make me feel good to see it there. I was worried."

"I'm getting it back. A couple of maintainance guys from the museum are picking it up for me. But tell me about the . . . uh . . . items you were trying to recover. The *mission*, as you called it. What happened?"

I didn't want to get into that on a car phone. "Without going into detail here, Miriam, let's say that the man who's been following us around now has possession of your aunt's material."

There was another pause while that sank in. "Oh. I see. What about Kamlo?"

I told her, then said, "Listen, Miriam. Our mutual friend has about an hour's head start on us. It may still be possible to do something if we can get Dr. Starlander to intervene. Have you spoken with him?"

Miriam sounded exasperated. "I tried, Jim, but Dr. Starlander's got his hands full. You have to understand that the Rockefeller has been thrown into quite a tizzy over Dr. Freemantle's death."

"I bet. How is Mme Catherine taking it?"

"I don't really know. She hasn't been back, although someone in Dr. Starlander's office may have been in touch with her to process her leave of absence."

"How is the rest of the staff taking it?"

"Pretty shaken up, as you might imagine. Randy Plunkett is buzzing around—probably trying to make it look like the Editorial Committee did in Freemantle—but nobody's talking to him."

"I can imagine."

"But the worst thing is the lawsuit."

"Lawsuit?"

"Mrs. Freemantle over in England has filed a multimillion-dollar wrongful death suit against the Israel Antiquities Committee, the Rockefeller Museum, and the members of the Editorial Committee."

"That quickly?"

"I think there had been some expectation of this kind of outcome for Dr. Freemantle for some time. People are shocked

274

but not terribly surprised, if you know what I mean. What are you doing? Are you on your way in to the Rockefeller?"

"Yes. I'm going to talk to Starlander if I have to kidnap him."

"Jim? Please be careful. Please."

"Yeah, sweetheart," I said, remembering she liked that. "I think we're out of the woods. But thanks for caring."

It wasn't just something to say. I really meant it. But the part about being out of the woods—I wasn't quite so sure.

It was balm to the aching soul to see Miriam again and to feel the press of her soft hand in mine. Too bad I had to spoil the salutary effect on my outlook by adding a large dose of Merrick Starlander.

The way his secretary, an older, sharp-eyed woman with a fierce stare, barked at me when I breezed past her to his office and threw the door open, she must have thought I was having fun.

I wasn't. Fun would have been forcing my attention on somebody who appreciated it—such as Miriam Boynton and her blue diamonds. This, on the other hand, was work.

The old man looked up from the telephone, said a few more words, then hung up.

"Just what is the meaning of this, Dr. Harper?" he demanded.

Before I could answer, his secretary burst in behind me in a huff.

"Sorry for this intrusion, Dr. Starlander," she snapped. "Shall I call security?"

"Yes!" I cried. "By all means, call security. Call them immediately. Tell them this institution has been penetrated by a spy—and the editor-in-chief sitting here is a willing accomplice."

In the stunned silence, the words hung in the air, reverberating with their stinging accusation. Not that I really knew for a fact that Starlander was implicated in Nahat's intrigues, but it would be hard to believe in his total ignorance. I was just a guy whacking the hornet's nest with a stick to get something started. It also served to turn the tables on their bureaucratic threats.

"Never mind, Hanna," said Starlander. "Dr. Harper here is just a little beside himself. I can handle this, thank you. That will be all."

Hanna didn't look so sure as she edged out the door, but she had her orders.

"Now," said Starlander, "if you can please get a grip on yourself, my good man, just what seems to be the matter? Have a seat, if you please."

I was beginning to think Starlander was being a little too nice, as if maybe he had a pretty good idea what was the matter and knew he'd better be careful.

"I prefer to stand," I said, pacing slowly. "It's about a member of this Editorial Committee who is working as a double agent."

Starlander did a tolerable job of looking shocked. "Surely you jest, Dr. Harper. Otherwise, that is a jolly serious accusation you are making. I hope you are prepared to document it."

I aimed a thumb at my chest. "I myself am an eyewitness. More Dead Sea Scrolls have come to light, Dr. Starlander. I have seen them with my own eyes. I was forced at gunpoint to assist this man in stealing four of these ancient documents—including one that appears to be your famous Temple Scroll archetype."

With that, Starlander's face assumed odd new shapes as he burst into laughter, lusty peals that assailed my ears like amplified taunts.

I felt my neck and ears reddening.

He removed his glasses and wiped his eyes. "Ah, me. Sorry, Dr. Harper. It's just that I haven't heard anything so rich since Randall Plunkett's journalistic fictions."

I reminded myself that I was under scriptural injunction to show older men the respect due a father. I would have preferred to have the rest of this conversation while holding this fellow by the front of his shirt and shaking him.

"Do you deny that you have a government agent on the Editorial Committee as a working member?"

Starlander put his glasses back on a bit too casually. "Couldn't you be a little more original than to accuse a former army officer of being a government mole?"

"That's very interesting, Dr. Starlander. I hadn't yet told you who it was. Did you just tip your hand?"

His expression darkened. "Just what do you mean by that?"

"Could it be that all of this supposed anti-Semitism and

276

supersessionism has been nothing more than a pretense to mask your committee's relationship with the spies?"

I was mostly shooting in the dark, but he didn't have to know that.

Starlander wasn't intimidated. "Oh, come off it, man. Any fool would know you couldn't be talking about anyone but Colonel Nahat. Has he been bothering you? Would you like me to speak to him?"

"That's exactly what needs to happen, but not on my behalf. You need to exert your authority for the protection of these newly found Qumran scrolls. Colonel Nahat has threatened to destroy these priceless documents if anyone attempts to interfere with him."

I had hoped that the research scholar in him would recoil in horror at such a suggestion. But I was disappointed.

A look of bored amusement visited his face. "Maybe you should give Mr. Plunkett a call. He might go for a yarn like that."

"Listen," I growled, preparing to forget all my biblical injunctions and lay him out.

"No, you listen," said Starlander with surprising forcefulness. "I understand you've been under some stress, Dr. Harper. I would suggest you get some rest. Perhaps it would be a good idea to see a doctor. We have a specialist who—"

"Look, I'll tell you about stress. If you let Zeev Nahat get away with this, I will make it my business to see that the Rockefeller becomes the media capital of the world. Have you ever seen a disaster scene crawling with reporters in a feeding frenzy? This will make Randy Plunkett and *Ground Zero* look like a wiener roast."

Starlander got to his feet, pointing a finger at me. "I shall not be threatened in my own office. Dr. Harper, there's the door. I suggest you use it. Now."

But he probably didn't expect me to use it quite so vigorously. Its shutting sounded like a thunderclap behind me.

Back in my own office, Miriam took one look at my face and cringed. "Uh-oh," she said. "It didn't go well, did it?"

I shook my head. "Please do me a favor. Call Jerry Simon at

the *Herald* and see if he can meet me somewhere. Tell him I'm ready to give him that big story."

She hesitated. "Uh . . . Jim, we are under orders from legal counsel to say nothing about any of these matters to anyone, especially the press."

"Well, I'm under no such orders. I'm no employee of the Editorial Committee or the Rockefeller."

"But—"

"Am I named in the lawsuit? Am I being represented by your lawyers?"

"No. But you certainly can't bring a reporter here. And I don't think I ought to be arranging anything off premises either, if that's what you're thinking."

"Fine. Just give me the number for the *Herald*. I'll call them myself."

Jerry Simon was having a busy day on the national desk. He sounded glad to hear from me, especially when I dropped some heavy hints about the nature of the information I had for him. But he was also in the middle of some story about water, Israel, and the West Bank.

It seemed water rights were a sticking point with the Palestinians, since fully a third of Israel's potable water came from an aquifer underlying West Bank territory. It all came down, as Moses would say, to how serious they all were about Middle East peace. In Moses' case, I doubted that he would give an Arab a cup of water if he were on fire.

We agreed to meet in a small park just a couple blocks from the *Herald* building in the New City section of Jerusalem. It reminded me of Central Park without the street crime but with a similar scary undertone of potential ethnic conflict. There were pigeons and park benches and old men with newspapers and young women with dogs.

"I do not like this," Kamlo said when he saw it.

"Why?" I thought it was a reasonable question.

Kamlo shrugged as if he didn't need a reason.

I tried again. "Do you see something that bothers you?"

"I am just thinking about some things."

278

"What kinds of things?"

"What if Colonel Nahat is still using surveillance on you? Telephone and car phone conversations, for example, are easily intercepted."

"I almost hope that's the case," I asserted. "I want him to know that he can't get away with this. The truth will come out."

We were strolling along a bike path a few minutes before my appointment with Simon.

Kamlo looked at me incredulously. "For Nahat," said my friend, "the solution would be a no-brainer."

I nodded approval. "Excellent use of American colloquialism. You mean eliminate me?"

Now he nodded. "Exactly."

He had a point. I was the one person who could cause Nahat a problem. I didn't really believe the colonel would do me any harm, but I had to wonder just what he *would* do. It was not reasonable to assume he'd do nothing.

"But what else?" I asked. "Is there something about this meeting that bothers you?"

"Maybe. Why does this Jerry Simon not want to meet you in the *Herald* building? I could understand why *you* might not want to be seen there. It is the reverse that I do not understand."

"What are you driving at?"

"Is it possible that he does not really want to do a story on this?"

I shook my head. "I wouldn't know why. He's been pestering me about this stuff from the start. Maybe it is just a courtesy to me—to protect my identity."

"Maybe." Kamlo sounded unconvinced.

I looked at my watch. "It's time for him to be here. I think the fountain is just the other side of that little playground."

Simon had said to meet him at the fountain, where we could sit on one of the benches and talk. I would spill my guts about the scrolls and how a member of the Editorial Committee was a government spy and had confiscated ancient holy texts that belonged to mankind. The truth would come out, and justice would be done. Eventually. It was an Israeli journalist who had, not long ago, ignited a firestorm by reporting long-suppressed facts about the Israeli killing of Egyptian prisoners of war.

As we rounded the little playground and caught sight of the fountain, I thought of the fierce exchange Nahat had had with the Rebbe and wondered if I were really up to this. A "civil war that no one could stop" was how Nahat had described the potential fallout of the Temple Scroll. The destruction of Israel, he'd also said. If true, was I prepared to take that upon myself?

It was a little late for second-guessing and second thoughts. I saw a man resembling Jerry Simon at a distance, taking his seat on a bench. We passed a mama with a pram and two preschoolers crawling around a sandbox. On past the park benches was the only other person in this part of the park, a man heading our direction in a dark business suit with dark glasses and a briefcase.

The closer we got to the benches, the surer I was that it was Jerry Simon sitting there.

About the time it appeared he had spotted us, Kamlo grabbed my arm and pulled me back. "Wait," he breathed. "There is something not right about this."

I stopped in my tracks. "What's not right?"

"That I am not sure."

I am not a good judge of distance, but I would say we were less than a hundred feet away at this point. Playing it cool, Jerry did nothing to acknowledge that he had seen us. I was sure he wouldn't do so until I sat down beside him while Kamlo played lookout. Maybe Jerry had seen too many American movies.

But then I got the same feeling that Kamlo had.

The man in the dark suit passed the park benches and stopped, ostensibly to light a cigarette. It was only a moment, and then he resumed his onward trek at an accelerated pace.

Suddenly my heart almost stopped. The man had left his briefcase in front of the bench next to Jerry's.

Jerry didn't see it. He was watching us.

"*Jerry!*" I shouted, breaking toward him.

"No!" Kamlo hollered behind me.

Something yanked me from behind and spun me around. Then something else flattened me. I was on the ground. I couldn't hear. I couldn't see. I couldn't breathe.

And time ceased to exist.

All the nations have seen Thy glory;
Thou who hast sanctified Thyself in the
midst of Thy people Israel. They brought
their offering to Thy great Name, silver
and gold and precious stones together
with all the treasures of their lands, that
they might glorify Thy people, and Zion
Thy holy city, and the House of Thy
majesty.
—The Words of the Heavenly Lights
(4Q504 IV)

28

Iawoke to the sound of a crying baby and a woman calling my name.

"Jim!" the woman was calling. "Can you hear me? Can you answer me?"

Answering was not an option. I couldn't breathe, and I couldn't see. My entire body felt like a leg that had fallen asleep, and my head was spinning. This was more than mere fright. It was the choking, gut-wrenching panic of the near-death experience.

Something terrible had happened, and I didn't know what it was. Everything was confused. My ears were ringing.

The woman was imploring someone to help her. Then I realized she was speaking to me. But how could *I* help? I was trapped on my stomach under some heavy object.

The crying baby somehow had become two wails.

Miriam. I knew there was a woman named Miriam who ought to belong to that voice, who was something in my life, if only I could remember what that meant.

I was hearing other voices and footsteps farther away. I tried moving and felt the weight shifting on top of me.

"That's it," said a woman in a lower vocal register than Miriam, possibly with an accent. "More."

Had I imagined Miriam's voice? I tried rolling over and pushing at the same time against the weight. I could feel the results of her labors as the object began sliding off me. It felt like a body.

I got to my knees, my heart in my throat. I saw the woman with the little children from the playground—a woman about Miriam's age but darker and larger-boned and wearing a blue polka-dot babushka. It was her baby in the pram that was crying. It was then that I realized that the other wail was that of an approaching siren.

But where was Miriam? How could I have imagined she was there? Suddenly I wanted her like my next breath.

My battered senses began to piece things together. The man. The briefcase. Jerry Simon. Bombs were so quick. There was no chance. But then, what terrorist or assassin would be interested in a slow explosion . . .

Such muddled thoughts as these were wallowing through my head when I turned to view the object that had pinned me. It was Kamlo.

Kamlo!

Then I saw his face, eyes shut in either unconsciousness or death. I tried to go to him, but the woman put a hand against my chest.

"Stay back," she said with authority. "I am a nurse." She turned back to my partner, opening his shirt at the collar.

I wobbled to my feet and almost passed out.

A warm hand clasped my shoulder, and a soft arm went around my waist, steadying me.

"Miriam!" I cried, turning to find her face, grim but still lovely as in my dreams.

So I hadn't been imagining things, despite the confusion. Two wails, one baby. Two women's voices, one Miriam.

Kamlo was on his side, and I could see his back. His clothes were in tatters and scorched. With a wave of grief, I realized that my *compañero* had shielded me from the blast. For all I knew, he had given his life. I couldn't accept it.

And what about Jerry? Unsteadily, I turned toward the park bench, half of me not wanting to see what I expected to find.

It was worse than I'd expected. What was left didn't look much like Jerry Simon. It didn't look much like anyone. I had to turn away.

In a sickening flash I knew this was the gruesome reality of too many places in the world—Bosnia, Belfast, Beirut—up close and personal. I didn't know whether I was going to throw up or pass out. I had already done the latter. It appeared I was going to do the former. I had just enough time to turn my back on everyone and do it mostly in private.

Now, on top of everything else, I was feeling turned inside out. My knees were wobbly and non-weight-bearing all over again.

Then I heard the huskier voice of the woman who claimed to be a nurse. "He is alive!" she declared. Her fingers were pressed to Kamlo's neck.

My relief was boundless. I prayed he'd hold on until that siren arrived.

Fortunately, we didn't have long to wait. But by the time the ambulance came blowing onto the scene, a small crowd had gathered.

With an effort, I got myself up off one knee and back onto my feet again. My mouth tasted nasty, and I considered dipping my head into the fountain for a swallow. Amazingly, I saw movement on the ground when I turned back to Kamlo.

I hustled over to him as well as my rickety legs would allow. "Kamlo!" I cried, bending down and extending a hand.

He was trying to get up. The nurse/mama had one elbow. I took the other, and we helped him to his feet just as the paramedics joined us.

They wanted to put him on a stretcher, but the nurse pointed out the burns on his back, and they switched to helping him walk. Just as the paramedics began to cart him off toward the ambulance, he looked over at me and managed a small smile.

"Boss," he croaked. "We must stop meeting like this."

I nodded and bit back tears. I remembered the little girl we had saved from the bombed-out building that day that now seemed so long ago. This time, in a perfect world, the picture in

283

the paper should be of an Arab-Christian hero, the man who risked his own life to save mine.

They got rid of me pretty quickly at the hospital after checking my pupils and for other possible signs of a concussion—all negative. It reminded me of being in Hulda's clinic at the Rebbe's kibbutz.

I'd dodged the bullet yet again. Except for some residual stress and a case of shaky hands, I was pretty much good as new. Counting the bombing where I'd met Kamlo, this made my third close scrape. If a cat had nine lives, I wondered how many a biblical scholar had.

Kamlo, of course, they kept there as an inpatient. His back was going to need some attention but nothing, they said, that should keep him in the hospital more than a couple of days. And certainly nothing life-threatening.

Miriam drove me back to the Belvoir in relative silence. We were both a little wrung out. I stared out the window, and my mind wandered onto strange ground. I remembered a time not long ago when she had totally sworn off men with hazardous lifestyles. Now she was showing up uninvited at mountaintop fortresses and clandestine park rendezvous. This wasn't something I felt I should be encouraging.

Unexpectedly, she broke the silence. "How well did you know Jerry Simon?"

"Not all that well. I guess I'd feel the same way about seeing anybody get blown up though. It's . . . horrible. Disturbing, to put it mildly."

"Is that all?"

There was something about her question that suggested she was beginning to know me all too well. When something was eating me now, she could spot it.

"Miriam," I said quietly, "I do have a concern."

She glanced at me without speaking, as if to acknowledge I had her attention.

"Why did you follow me to the park?"

Her voice sounded small and distant. "You mean without your permission?"

"That's not the issue."

"Then what *is* the issue?"

"I don't want you getting that directly into harm's way."

"Then you understand my feelings about your daredevil escapades."

"Yes," I conceded, "I do understand your feelings, but—"

"But give me a break. This was supposed to be a *walk in the park*. Literally, for Pete's sake."

"No, Miriam, this stopped being fun and games a long time ago. It's become a very deadly game, and I can't allow you to risk yourself this way."

"Listen, Jim." Her voice was patient but firm. "I believe in the doctrine of submissiveness—in marriage. Short of that, I'm going to continue to do what I feel I have to do."

"You mean if I want to do the protective-guy thing, I have to marry you?"

She allowed herself a small chuckle. "Either way, I think you're stuck with me. 'Whither thou goest' and all that."

I groaned. "You could at least get the right book."

She shot me a puzzled look. "What book?"

"Esther. You're quoting Ruth. I'm the Esther guy, remember? Just ask Dr. Starlander."

The next morning I got to the Rockefeller about an hour behind Miriam. Even after something close to twelve hours of sleep, I still awoke with a vicious headache. But Miriam, looking dapper and fresh in a crisp blue-and-white print dress, was a sight for a sore head.

The second thing I wanted to see was the newspaper. Like most Americans, I almost couldn't believe that any of yesterday had really happened until I read it in the newspaper or saw it on TV. I asked to see the *Herald*. Since that was Jerry's paper, it was a pretty good bet they'd have a story.

Miriam shook her head. "You won't find the real story on this in the *Herald*."

I had no idea what she was talking about. "What do you mean, 'the real story'?"

She gave me a curious look. "It looks like Jerry Simon was a government agent."

I couldn't believe it. "Jerry Simon—CIA? No."

"Not CIA." Miriam pressed a button on the intercom and asked someone named Naomi to bring in a copy of *Ma'ariv*.

"And a cup of coffee!" I cried.

While we waited, she explained. "I've checked, and most of the news reports treat this incident as a random act of terrorism. One death is not real big news here. The only difference for the *Herald* was that it also had a quote from the publisher mourning the loss of a valued employee."

I nodded. It was sad but too true. "Maybe there have just been too many decades of this kind of thing to raise much excitement."

The door swung open, and in came the young curly-haired woman I assumed was Naomi. She smiled and handed the newspaper to Miriam, who introduced her to me. I was glad to meet her, happy to receive the coffee, and apprehensive about the strange tidings. What Miriam had told me was disturbing, but I had to know the truth.

I took the paper and started reading. It became clear very quickly why no one else carried this account. It was an enterprise story of unnamed sources and tenuous connections. It also had the ring of truth.

It said government sources were divided over how to respond to this terrorist attack because they did not believe it to be a random act. Some were pushing for a punitive raid against a terrorist camp in southern Lebanon. Yet others were not willing to acknowledge the true nature of the initial provocation by responding.

It all depended on the nature of Simon's relationship to the government. If he had been a full-fledged operative, there could be embarrassing questions to be answered about the extent of the government's infiltration of the news media.

Kamlo and I were mentioned only indirectly, and then not even by name, as apparently innocent bystanders unrelated to any of this cloak-and-dagger business. It made me wonder how an enterprising reporter could overlook such an obvious connection. Probably this enterprising reporter was in reality just another spoon fed journalist with a convenient source. It almost made me want to call up the *Ma'ariv* just to set the record straight and lay the same cards on the table that I would have done for Jerry, rest his soul.

Emphasis on almost. I was ready to quit playing this news source game. When people started dying for unknown reasons, it was time to start holding your cards a little closer to your chest. But I wasn't ready to believe that Nahat or anybody else in the government had had Simon eliminated because of me and what I knew about the scrolls.

"What do you think?" Miriam asked as I folded the paper.

I sighed deeply. "I think I just heard my mother calling me."

"Do you think the story is true?"

I scratched my head and put the paper down. "Well, I still don't know about Zeev Nahat's involvement in any of this, but it does shed some light on Kamlo's concern."

"What was that?"

"He was suspicious about Jerry's arranging to meet me off site. In that light, his being a government agent fits. As an informant or operative or whatever, he would be naturally eager to pump me about the scrolls, but as a newspaperman there was no way he could do the real story about Elliot Freemantle, Selmar Hajabeel, and his fellow agent Zeev Nahat. Nor could he afford to be seen with me inside the *Herald* offices on this non-story."

Miriam nodded slowly. "OK. But what *do* you think about Zeev Nahat?"

I bit my lip and looked at the ceiling for an answer. "As much as I dislike Nahat, I just can't quite bring myself to believe that he would have anything to do with that briefcase bomb. Jerry probably did have other enemies. But we can't rule Nahat out."

"No," she agreed. "We can't."

"Has he shown up to work?"

Miriam shook her head. "No. He's 'out in the field,' as they say." She looked puzzled for a long moment.

I finally asked, "What's going through that steel-trap mind of yours?"

She frowned. "I was just wondering. How much would you have told Jerry Simon?"

"Well, I wouldn't have told him the whole story about the Temple Scroll. I would have told him about Colonel Nahat stealing ancient documents at gunpoint from Adoniram Cohen, but I would have identified them only as previously unrecovered Dead Sea Scrolls. I saw only a small portion of one of them myself."

"Jerry Simon would have had no way to determine that for himself?"

I shook my head. "Only two people had the full picture—Dr. Freemantle and the Rebbe. Freemantle is dead, and I don't think Jerry would have been able to get much out of the Rebbe if he had tried."

Miriam looked thoughtful. "Tell me more about the Rebbe. I had to leave, as you recall, before I had the pleasure."

"Sure. Adoniram Cohen and the Temple Mount Zealots have assembled almost everything they need to reinstitute the temple sacrifices. I saw it—the red heifer, replicas of temple implements, and a hundred lads who are ceremonially undefiled. All they lack are more exact details, such as precise dimensions and the location for the cornerstone for actual construction. From a small section I read of one scroll, it appeared to contain that missing information—whether you want to call it the real Temple Scroll or the Chronicles of King David."

Miriam's eyes grew saucerlike. "That could start some big trouble. I can understand why Nahat would be concerned, if he's what you say he is."

I nodded, then had another thought. "Have you seen Starlander since I talked to him?"

She gave a little snort. "Just a little while ago. I asked to see him first thing this morning. He got pretty huffy and defensive, even red in the face toward the end."

"Toward the end of what?"

"Of his tirade, accusing me of seeing spies under every bed. He was adamant that this kind of scurrilous rumor was attached to Colonel Nahat simply because of his military background and that it was a disservice to a man who had devoted a lifetime to his country."

"You sound a bit skeptical. What does your gut tell you?"

She looked as if that was a new concept. "My gut? My gut tells me he was lying through his teeth—or maybe denying something he knew in his heart to be true."

I chuckled softly.

"What's funny?"

"Just thinking about the irony of my trying to blow the whistle on a government agent to another government agent! I can afford to laugh now that I know Kamlo is going to be all right. It's Mrs. Cray I'm worried about."

Miriam looked worried for me. "What are you going to tell her?"

"That's a good question. No, that's a *great* question. Do you have any suggestions? I could use some answers."

"Can't you just tell her what happened?"

"What? That I almost had the scrolls, but a secret agent stole them, and that I almost got blown up trying to get them back? Why don't I just tell her my dog ate them?"

"You don't have a dog."

"I'll tell her *your* dog ate them."

"I don't have a dog either."

"Get one. We'll name him Zeev."

"Seriously, shouldn't we let her know what happened so she can cancel payment on that check?"

"That's a nice thought," I agreed, "but I have to believe that baby's been cashed out days ago, considering the nature of the animal we're dealing with. If not, I'd rather first try asking Big Al to hand it back."

"Jim, I got the distinct impression they didn't want to see us back there again."

I nodded. "I wouldn't try it without somebody like Kamlo with me, which is out of the question under the circumstances."

"Which brings us back to Aunt Dot."

"Maybe," I conceded, "but if you recall the time difference between Jerusalem and Dallas, that gives us almost an entire business day to come up with a Plan B."

Miriam shook her head despairingly. "In that case, I would suggest prayer—lots of prayer."

"Sounds like a good idea to me."

And so we prayed, right there in our office in the Rockefeller. We prayed for Kamlo's speedy recovery. We prayed for justice in regard to Mrs. Cray's $17,500 in earnest money. We had started to pray for the return of the scrolls to their rightful owner when two remarkable things happened.

The first was my growing uncertainty about just who the rightful owner really was. It was a no-brainer, as Kamlo would say, to discount Selmar Hajabeel and Zeev Nahat. But why, in fact, should ownership go to Mrs. Cray any more than to the Rebbe or the Israeli government? That prompted us to begin praying that God's will would be done in the matter, not ours, no matter the outcome. It changed our perspective.

The second remarkable thing was a voice on the inter-com—probably that of Naomi—interrupting our prayers to inform us that we had a visitor. It was a Mr. Mattar, she said.

The only Mattar I knew was Kamlo, which couldn't be.

"He is on his way up," Naomi said.

Further praying was impossible with this strange thing headed our way. We were still exchanging puzzled looks when there was a knock at the door. Before we could loosen our tongues, it opened, and a big head poked through.

"Kamlo!" I cried in delight at this impossibility. "What are you doing here?"

He smiled shyly. "Getting on with my job, Boss."

"I mean, you're supposed to be in the hospital."

He looked as if he was going to shrug but thought better of it. "The hospital is a bad place to be. It is full of sick people, just lying around."

"Kamlo, I don't know if I can go along with this. Did you just sneak out of there?"

He looked almost offended. "Sneak? I should say not. I checked myself out. They had me sign a paper that said it is not their fault if I die."

"Sure, a waiver for discharge against medical advice. They know what they're talking about, Kamlo. If you develop compli-cations, your recovery can take much longer than it would have otherwise."

He pulled out a folded sheet of paper from his shirt pocket. "I have a prescription for antibiotics, and there are doctors who can change dressings. I am no pastry."

Miriam looked bewildered.

I smiled with secret knowledge. "I think he means cream puff, Miriam."

"Or patsy?" she suggested, catching the spirit of Kamlo-speak.

Kamlo looked impatient. "Where to, Boss? I am reporting for duty."

"Well," I said, reluctantly concluding that I might as well get on with it, "how do you feel about a trip to Bethlehem?"

Kamlo's eyes lit up. "That would be fine. Al Malik? I believe he owes us some money, does he not?"

"Yes, but no rough stuff. He's an old man, and you're a cripple."

Kamlo winked at Miriam. "Not quite, Boss. Like the bear, I am most dangerous when injured."

I groaned. "That's exactly what I'm afraid of."

His wisdom will reach all the peoples,
and he will know the secrets of all the
living. And all their designs against him
will come to nothing, and (his) rule
over all the living will be great. His
designs will succeed for he is the Elect of
God. His birth and the breath of his
spirit . . . and his designs shall be forever.
—Horoscope of the Messiah
    (4QMessAr)

29

Kamlo and I piled into the famous BBT—battered blue Toyota—and drove first to Miriam's place to pick up Nadi's motorcycle. Kamlo didn't have to say why he wanted the two-wheeler. All I had to do was watch him leaning forward in the car seat to know. On a motorcycle you don't have a seat rubbing against your raw back. And now, through unfortunate but providential circumstances, we had such a vehicle at our disposal.

Miriam had offered to accompany us, but I held firm. We were not only uninvited at Al Malik's, but we were plainly unwelcome. Big Al had made clear that our business was completed. This was a long shot at best. I meant it when I said I couldn't allow her to subject herself to risk, and I hoped she respected my wishes.

I turned on the radio to get something else into my head besides defeatism on this all-too-familiar trek to Bethlehem. I knew the route so well now that I didn't have to concentrate on it. My mind was free to wander among all the thickets and weeds and underbrush that grow up along the roadside of one's life journey.

One station was playing some languorous symphonic music full of a kind of modernistic abstraction of despair. Another aired some annoying Israeli pop that sounded like obnoxious leftovers from the disco era. Finally, there was smarmy Eastern jazz that reminded me too much of the hamster fights at Big Al's opium den.

I snapped off the radio and faced the silence. Especially in my current frame of mind, it was all noise anyway—one of the world's many ways of tuning out pain and loneliness and turning out hollow men.

I could feel my anxieties rising to the surface, where they needed to be dealt with. Was this whole Dead Sea Scrolls fiasco going to be the next in my growing collection of disappointments with God? I knew that was the wrong perspective. There had to be some purpose in all of this. If it wasn't yet time for someone like the Rebbe to rebuild the temple, maybe it also wasn't yet time for someone like me to find the Chronicles of David or the Temple Scroll.

But, I reminded myself, there had been *four* scrolls. Why couldn't Providence have allowed me at least to recover one of them? Even if two of them were copies. And I didn't even know what the fourth one was.

Maybe my plans just didn't match God's. In that case, what was He up to? What was I supposed to learn? Was all of this just random chaos in a world with Murphy's Law running rampant? Or would all of these frustrations and confusions make sense somewhere down the road?

I tried to reason out what other value this mission might have for me and those in my life. And I kept coming back to one thing and one thing only: *Miriam.*

I didn't really want to be single. Things had just turned out that way. I hadn't let too many people inside my perimeter, the inner circle of my defenses. In college, one young woman had scaled the wall and taken me hopelessly captive for a season before setting me free again far too soon, minus my heart. The pain of that loss was so intense that I had kept the door firmly shut ever since.

But now that I *wanted* to throw the door open for blue-eyed Miriam, it didn't seem to want to budge. Time had corroded the hinges and corrupted the lock. Who could turn this key?

I was virtually at the end of the line. If I blew this golden opportunity and had to confess to the loss of the $17,500, it was a foregone conclusion that Mrs. Cray would never hold still for any more wild scroll chases. In that case, I would soon be heading back across the Atlantic, perhaps never to see Miriam again. I wasn't ready for that. But what *was* I ready for? Proposing marriage? That was a scary thought, though not entirely unappealing.

And at that moment I found myself almost driving off the road. A wave of longing for this woman rolled over me so powerfully that I nearly stopped and turned the car around. The prospect of leaving her behind tore at me so forcefully that I might as well have contemplated giving up breathing.

She had become part of me, and I knew something of the sort had happened to her too. I would have had to be blind not to see her glow when I called her "sweetheart"—or see the haunted look in her eyes each time she watched me leave for what might be the last time. And now that time might really be at hand. Unless . . .

Maybe Miriam and those blue diamonds were the treasure I had come here to find. Maybe I didn't have to leave the Holy Land empty-handed. If I didn't bring home the treasure I had been sent to recover, perhaps I would obtain a treasure of another sort. Either way, it appeared I was about to find out.

At last we rounded the final corner and headed down Al Malik's street. Inexplicably, it felt all wrong, but I couldn't say why. It was like that intangible feel of wrongness back in the park where Jerry had met his end, but without the sense of impending disaster. It was more like being in the wrong place at the wrong time. I had never expected to be back here, and we certainly were not expected back by our former hosts.

I felt like a character in one of those old black-and-white *Twilight Zone*s where two travelers innocently stumble into a town harboring some sinister secret that no outsider is supposed to share. If only these things were just my imagination. Unfortunately, they had been proving to be all too real. I would be glad to be done with all of this intrigue.

At the end of the block, Kamlo, who was several hundred feet ahead of me, pulled in about where I remembered Big Al's house to be. But he stopped the motorcycle at the street end of the drive and parked it. I wondered why he didn't just pull on in. When I got farther down the street, I saw why.

The house was no longer there. Like an empty tooth socket, a vacant lot stared back at us.

I parked on the street and walked toward Kamlo. There were none of our usual feathered friends to flap and squawk their raucous greetings. There was no dark-haired window-peeper tugging at the front curtain to check us out. No goateed nephew with kaffiyeh and sneakers to open the door for us.

I stood and stared at the vacant lot, dumbstruck and aghast at the craters of destruction that seemed to follow me around. Mrs. Cray collected Hummel and Hepplewhite. I collected craters, holes where things disappeared. It was not a positive trend for someone whose mission was to *find* things.

To all appearances, no one else was on the street—not even any of the ubiquitous tykes with toy guns who played war the way other kids played baseball and soccer. But I knew we were hardly alone. I had the feeling that we were being watched through the folds of other front-window curtains. A tingling sensation on the back of the neck made me hope none of this staring was being done through a rifle scope.

I stood beside Kamlo, letting my eyes roam across the vacant lot that had once been a house, scanning for clues.

There were a few obvious ones, all tied to the same simple fact. It was easy to see that this had not been the result of an explosion or natural cataclysm. Neat piles of stones at the far end of the property spoke clearly of a systematic, if not orderly, dismantling of the structure. And the tire treads of heavy equipment could be discerned in the perforated soil and traced in fainter patterns of thin, dried mud down the drive and onto the street.

Kamlo was no longer standing beside me. He had intercepted an old man walking down the street, who had escaped my attention until he was almost upon us. Kamlo engaged him in some animated conversation.

Then, with an impatient wave of his hand, the old man was gone, his small figure diminishing in the distance.

"So," I prompted Kamlo when he returned, "was this another case of Israeli government urban renewal?"

Kamlo shook his head. "No. CIA."

"*CIA!*"

He nodded. "So they say. Have you not heard that everything here is either the result of the Jews or the CIA?"

"Yes, but the last I heard, the CIA didn't run bulldozers through people's homes."

"Of course not. But perhaps that is more palatable than accepting the obvious."

"OK, smart guy," I challenged, "if it's so obvious to you, tell me what really happened."

Kamlo shrugged. "It is what the Israelis formerly did around here to subversives. Now that it is the Palestinians themselves..."

He waved his hand with a world-weary gesture, as much as to say little ever really changes for the average Joe when victor and vanquished trade places.

I had not forgotten that we were in Palestinian self-rule territory. "But," I objected, "why would the Palestinians want to do such a thing?"

Kamlo had a distant look in his gaze. "I do not pretend to have answers like that. But if one were found to be an Israeli collaborator..."

He let the thought go, but I got the general drift. "I see. It's much easier for people to blame the old CIA bogeyman than to accept betrayal by one of their own."

Kamlo nodded.

"Still," I continued, "I have a real hard time with the idea of Big Al as an Israeli collaborator."

Kamlo shrugged again. "He would not actually have to be a collaborator. Just the appearance would be enough."

Then the light went on. "The Selmar Hajabeel investigation. People like Zeev Nahat show up here, asking questions. People like you and me—"

I broke off with a start. A piece of the puzzle suddenly snapped into place, and it had my face on it. Who, in fact, among the visitors to this place would most closely fit the profile of a

CIA agent? With a shudder, I realized that Kamlo and I could be in grave danger.

"Come on," I said, stiffening. "Let's get out."

The moment we broke for it, shots rang out. Three times. It was impossible to tell how close. Unlike in the movies, there were no whizzing ricochets or other visible evidence.

Kamlo jumped on his motorcycle. I raced toward the Toyota.

Two more shots rang out. This time there was no doubt about their proximity. One whanged into the car in front of me. I slid to a stop. A third bullet hit the Toyota. They were trying to cut me off.

For a moment I froze, reconsidering. I could retreat and flee for the rock piles where Al Malik's house had been. But another slug, digging into the pavement behind me, convinced me that would be suicide.

There was only one thing to do. I said a silent prayer and beat a path, bent over, for the old BBT. More shots hit the car, and I realized they came from streetside. I might just make it from the curb.

I dropped down and opened the passenger door. Keeping my head down, I dove into the car. My heart was trying to hammer its way out of my chest.

I turned the key in the ignition, but I didn't hear the engine. It was drowned out by the explosion of the driver's side window in a shower of glass. I was stung by a swarm of bees down my left side. My left eye felt as though it had caught on fire. While I tried to shake off the burning, I looked round with my good eye.

I heard the roar of a motorcycle and saw Kamlo wheeling around in the street. What was he up to?

Then I spotted the source of the gunfire. From an open front window of a house across the street protruded the barrel of a rifle.

Kamlo apparently had seen it first. In one swift motion, he extracted a pistol from inside his jacket and snapped off three quick rounds as he roared past the house.

The rifle tumbled from the window, landing in a bed of pink flowers.

Kamlo glanced back as I was getting the Toyota into gear. He gave me a forward-ho wave and then stepped on it, making Nadi's hog roar.

There was something warm and sticky in my eye, and it still burned ominously, but I wasted no time following his lead. I slammed the Toyota into a sloppy U-turn and put some pedal to the metal.

Unfortunately, the BBT wasn't going anywhere in a hurry. Something had felt definitely wrong as I was wheeling it around. Now it lumbered and lurched violently instead of sailing off into the sunset. My heart sank. They must have shot out the tires.

I was all but dead in the water. It didn't look as if I was getting out of here in the old BBT. I hoped Kamlo had looked in his rearview mirror and realized I wasn't following.

Then, even more unfortunately, a side door opened in the house of our assailant, and two men piled out, brandishing rifles. Maybe they had figured out that all of the gunfire from our side had come from Kamlo, now gone, and if I had a gun, I would have used it long before now.

For a moment I hoped wildly that these men were merely fleeing the scene after what had happened to their comrade. No such luck. They were quickly headed toward the BBT like men with a mission.

I ducked down as their weapons turned my way, expecting to hear more metallic whanging and bursting glass. Hardly daring to breathe, I prayed for the Lord to take me quickly if this was the end of the line.

Instead, I heard another sound that took me a couple of heartbeats to recognize. It was the roar of an approaching motorcycle. If that was Kamlo, there was still hope. I heard gunfire, but it didn't hit the Toyota.

I took a chance and looked out the blown-out window. My two assailants were turned the other way, shooting at the approaching cycle. My heart almost stopped. It was indeed Kamlo, but this was a kamikaze mission. Against two riflemen, with just a single pistol from a rocky motorcycle seat, he had no chance. Still he came on.

Once again he was risking his life to save me. I couldn't sit still for this.

"*No!*" I hollered through the shattered window.

That was enough to distract the men momentarily.

I killed the engine and opened the driver's door. If I was already a sitting duck in the disabled car, I might not be any worse off on foot.

I heard another crack of gunfire, this time from Kamlo's direction. My distraction helped him to draw first blood. A gunman fell to one knee, apparently hit.

But Kamlo too was now within range. The other gunman stood his ground and cranked off two shots.

I was out the door and onto the street and saw it all. One shot seemingly found its mark. I didn't know whether the hit was Kamlo or the cycle. There were two more shots, and the next thing I knew, the hog was spinning out. Kamlo, pitched from the seat, was rolling across the road like a professional stuntman who knew how to fall.

And then Nadi's cycle burst into a fireball. This time it *was* just like the movies. Maybe one of the bullets had found its mark around the gas tank.

I didn't wait for Kamlo to find his feet—if he could. Right now he was the sitting duck. He had risked his life for me. Now it was my turn.

As soon as the injured gunman raised his rifle toward Kamlo, I rushed him.

The man heard me coming and tried to switch targets. But he was a moment too late. I grabbed for the gun as he took an unsteady step back. I grabbed air, but my shoulder knocked him down.

An instant too late I saw his rifle coming at me in a vicious arc. My swollen left eye had betrayed me. But I sure felt it as the weapon smacked into the back of my head. It was like the briefcase bombing in the park that had made time stand still. But this time I had moved just enough to reduce the impact from a sure knockout to a good stun.

I stood there, blinking with my good eye, tasting something salty, and hearing gunfire down the street. My mind wasn't working. All I knew was that I had to get that rifle. Except that now I was staring down the business end of the barrel.

I ducked just as the thing went off, tearing the air above me.

Back on my knees, I got my first good look at my man—a thin-featured Arab with beady eyes. Spraddled on the ground, he would have looked harmless without the long gun. I could see the growing dark spot on his pants leg where he had taken Kamlo's bullet.

Even unarmed, I should have some odds on my side. Unfortunately, if I failed to crack his skull or tear out his throat, he would soon blow my brains out.

Most of the hand-to-hand combat techniques I'd learned under Uncle Steve came back as if it were yesterday. I dove and managed to get a hand on the rifle barrel. That was a mistake. After all the firing, it was like touching a stove burner. But I forced myself to hang on, despite the pain. If I could ignore fire in my eye, I could ignore it in my hand. As the man tried to wrench his weapon away, I slugged him full force in the head with my right fist.

Something felt wrong in my hand. Now I had fire in both hands. We rolled on the ground, struggling for control of the rifle. Somehow it ended up underneath us, and a knife blade ended up against my throat.

I held his knife hand temporarily at bay with a fevered grip on his forearm. But the man was remarkably strong for all his wiriness. It was a seesaw affair as our trembling arms forced the knife first farther away, then closer. In some strange way beyond explanation, the two of us merged into one entity in a delicately balanced equilibrium.

This state seemed to go on forever. I could feel cold sweat breaking out on my forehead and see the face of my enemy gleaming with its own sheen of sweat. My right arm was beyond exhaustion, but giving in meant instant death.

I tried to shift position to get my left arm free from under me. The effort, however, only won me the bottom position as the Arab managed to roll over on top. His left hand found my throat. I grabbed his hand but couldn't pull it free.

I seemed to be losing my strength, my breath, and my will to resist. I was seeing spots. The weaker I got, the firmer the hand that squeezed off my breath. And the more my breath was shut off, the weaker I got.

My lungs were bursting, and my brain was in a frenzy for oxygen. With a final burst of effort, I writhed desperately, left to right, to try to dislodge my tormentor. My enemy. My . . . killer.

It wasn't working. There was a sound like gravel crunching, and then I was gone.

Once more I was the wilderness dream traveler. I was alone with the echo of my own footsteps and the sound of my own breathing, magnified in my ears. In a twilight world of semiconsciousness I could feel life flowing out of me onto the ground like a stream.

Yet, there was also a growing resistance, as if something was tugging me back. Things became more confused. I was hearing a soft engine sound, punctuated by distant gunfire. Someone was shaking me, ever more insistently, toward wakefulness. A woman I knew was calling my name, almost right in my ear.

"*Jim!* Hold this on your neck!"

My eyes popped open. I seemed to be half under the bumper of a car. I turned weakly onto my side and saw that it was a familiar-looking Mazda, lipstick-red. And its owner, a beautiful woman, was kneeling beside me, trying to get me to sit up and take a towel from her.

"Take it easy," she said. "Lean against the car."

I was weak and dizzy and fell back against the bumper.

Miriam pressed the towel against my neck.

"Hold that right there," she repeated.

I didn't understand what was happening. I was still hearing intermittent gunfire. Where was the man who had almost killed me? How did Miriam get here?

Then I saw the blood. It was all over me. I was sitting in it. My hands were covered with it. The white towel was becoming red with it.

"Quick," she said, grasping my upper arms. "We have to get into the car. We can't stay here."

With a supreme effort, I made it to my feet. I swayed dangerously. I was seeing spots everywhere. I hoped I wouldn't pass out.

Miriam opened the rear door, and I fell in. She ran around to the driver's side. The engine was running.

"Keep your head down," she said. "Kamlo's pinned down. We're going after him."

Keeping my head down was no problem. I couldn't sit up straight if I'd wanted to. It was a struggle just to stay conscious and to keep the towel pressed against my neck.

I could still hear gunfire. It got louder as Miriam wheeled around and stepped on the gas. I heard a couple of whangs like the ones that had hit the BBT.

Feebly, I tried to keep my head from rolling and jerking around. Miriam was pulling some tricky moves behind the wheel.

Then she hit the brakes. Two more whangs slammed into the side of the car.

The driver's-side rear door popped open, and Kamlo piled in, breathing hard. His eyes froze as he saw me.

"Hold tight, Boss," he said softly, patting my shoulder. "We'll get you to the doctor, very soon. Go all the way to the end of this street, Miss Boynton—the way you came—and turn left."

I felt us tearing away, but not before another round whanged into the back of the car. The last thing I remembered was a great feeling of sadness for Miriam's pretty, bright red car, now getting redder on the inside and full of whangs on the outside.

No man shall send to the altar any burnt-offering, or cereal offering, or incense, or wood, by the hand of one smitten with any uncleanness, permitting him thus to defile the altar. For it is written, The sacrifice of the wicked is an abomination, but the prayer of the just is an agreeable offering.
—The Damascus Rule 11:20–21

30

I had once read a book about basic personality types that pegged me pretty well with the "melancholic" disposition—sensitive, creative, but prone to moodiness and even depression—the classic artist temperament. That meant that discouragement was often an issue for me. And now, lying in a hospital bed somewhere in Jerusalem, I found myself holding an invitation to a major pity party.

I had been drifting in and out of consciousness. As much as I needed to sleep, it didn't seem to last more than five minutes before someone in green scrubs or white smock was dragging me kicking and screaming back to wakefulness to inflict upon me yet another indignity. It was always some procedure involving light in my eyes, a needle under my skin, or worse.

But never during all of those punishments did I have strength enough to ask anyone what he was doing to me or why. I wanted to know about my own condition but couldn't quite articulate the desire.

Now that some of my strength seemed to have returned, there was no one around to ask. My memories were a jumble. I seemed to recall that someone had cut my throat, but I wasn't sure why.

Slowly, though, it began coming back. I remembered that Kamlo and I had been trying to get Mrs. Cray's money back when we were ambushed by men with guns. I had barely escaped with my skin, and now I had to admit abject defeat.

This mission was finished, and I had failed. It was all over but the shouting—Mrs. Cray's, that is. As Kamlo had innocently suggested, I was basically a failure. That's when despair began to prey on me like a carrion bird picking my bones.

My left eye was covered with a bandage. With my right I looked around the room for clues and found few, beyond the fact that it could have been a semiprivate hospital room in almost any country. An institutional green curtain divided my area from my roommate's. In the utter stillness I could hear the low sound of rhythmic breathing as of someone asleep just on the other side of the divider.

My left arm was connected to some IV tubing, some of which fed into a blood bag drooping from a pole. With my right hand I tried to feel my throat, but I was doubly thwarted by bandaging on both neck and hand. Under the gauze, my hand felt as if it might even be in a small cast, judging by the stiffness.

Then I noticed a button that had to be the nurse's call light. My fingers seemed to be taped together, but eventually I managed to push it. The effort drained much of my limited strength.

About the time I was deciding that maybe it wasn't really the call light after all, I heard footsteps. A dark-haired, middle-aged nurse with a puffy face and tired eyes came into the room and immediately began checking things such as the IV drip, as if she had been summoned by the equipment rather than the patient.

"Uh . . ." I said, struggling to formulate my question. My throat was tight and raw.

"Are you all right, Father Harper?" she said, without looking at me.

I thought about correcting her but let it pass. "You tell me," I said instead.

She gave me a cursory glance. "I would say you are fine, considering."

"Considering what?"

"Considering what you have been through."

I was quickly tiring of this. "What have I been through?"

She finished checking all my connections and interfaces. "Dr. Ruben can tell you all about it in the morning."

"I want to know now."

Her eyebrows arched. "You want to scare yourself out of a good night's sleep? If you feel that ambitious, maybe you are ready to receive a visitor."

That brightened my outlook considerably. "A young lady?"

She almost smiled. "A very pretty young lady. She has been waiting around for a long time. I shall send her in."

I'd barely blinked, it seemed, and the nurse was gone, replaced by a young woman who was so beautiful it made my eyes water. But what, I wondered, did she see when she looked at me, here on my bed of affliction? A wreck? A failure?

"Hi, hero," Miriam said softly, coming up to the side of the bed.

At first I thought she was teasing. But I couldn't believe she would be so heartless. Then she took my hand and looked at me with an intensity that told me she was dead serious.

In her eyes maybe I *was* a hero. And that was all that mattered.

"Hi, sweetheart," I croaked.

Right then, I did something embarrassing to my male ego. I cried. It started as a miserable little laugh—laughter at my own stupidity, at the absurdities of life, at how things are so rarely what they seem. But the laughter quickly turned to tears—tears of frustration, joy, fatigue, love, and relief all at the same time.

It didn't make a whole lot of sense, but it just kind of poured out of me in a flood, demolishing all my defenses. I felt like a fool.

Miriam looked mildly perplexed.

"Jim, are you all right?"

"I don't know," I admitted between sniffles. "That's part of the problem. I don't know. What do you think?"

She smiled. "Yes, Jim, you're all right—under the circumstances."

"You sound just like that nurse. What circumstances?"

The smile faded. "For someone who had his head half cut off."

I shuddered. "What?"

She squeezed my hand. "Honey, you've got more stitches right now than a Singer sewing machine."

It took a moment for the room to stop swimming. This was *my* head she was talking about.

"How much," she continued, "do you remember?"

"I was trying to fight off the man with the knife. I couldn't breathe, and I was passing out. The last thing I remember is hearing a crunching sound—like gravel. Then I was gone."

"That was me—and my car. It was the only thing I could do. I went into a skid right up to him, but he was intent on cutting you and didn't move. I had to back up again and actually ram him before he would leave. You're fortunate I didn't run over you. I was pretty panicked."

I was amazed—at both her boldness and the fact I hadn't been killed.

"You're the hero, Miriam," I said quietly.

She shook her head emphatically. "I wouldn't agree with that. Neither would Kamlo."

I started. "How *is* Kamlo?"

"Fine. He's right outside in the visitors' lounge. They wouldn't let him come in here. But you should have heard him." She lowered her voice and gave it a pidgin Kamlo accent. "'You tell Dr. Jim he gave me the fighting chance by getting one of those men off of me. One on one, I will win. That is no boast, just fact.'"

I started to laugh but quickly sobered. "What about the other gunman?"

"Kamlo dispatched him. No boast, just fact. But you scared Kamlo when he got into the car—the way you looked. Jim, if you don't believe God was with you, wait till you talk to the doctors."

"Why is that?"

"Dr. Ruben kept saying he'd never seen anything like it— such 'perforations,' I think he called it—in the neck without severing an artery. He said it was as if an invisible hand had pulled

306

the knife back a centimeter each time the blade approached the wrong thing. He couldn't stop talking about it."

This was giving me goose bumps. "Any other injuries?"

She talked as if she had memorized the medical report. "Nothing serious. Contusion to the back of the head. Some lacerations to the left cornea from glass shards. A busted metacarpal in your right hand—"

That registered. "When I hit the man with the knife. I knew I'd done something to my hand."

"And a second-degree burn on the palm of your left hand. What was that from?"

"Holding onto a very hot gun barrel."

She motioned at the blood bag. "And, of course, blood loss. But it's the neck that's got them calling you a very lucky fellow. I told Dr. Ruben it wasn't luck; it was God. He gave me a funny look, but he agreed it was something of a miracle."

I fell silent. I couldn't tell her what I was really thinking. That if God had saved me from the killer's knife, what was the purpose of saving a failure? That at this point I wasn't entirely sure it wouldn't have been better if the knife had found its mark. Under the circumstances, what difference would it have made?

Then I looked at Miriam and thought again. There was something undefinable in her eyes that told me it would have made a big difference to her.

"Come on," she said. "Smile. God loves you, and so do I. So cheer up."

"OK," I said, forcing a small smile.

Her eyes were twinkling. "Isn't there something in the book of Revelation about a man making a miraculous recovery from a neck wound?"

I laughed weakly. "I think that was the head."

"Well," Miriam said in a tone that sounded as if she was thinking about going, "you're probably tired—"

"Who, me?" I didn't want her to go. "Listen, Miriam. How long are they going to keep me here?"

"Dr. Ruben says, barring complications, they ought to have you out in a couple of days."

"A couple of days?" I echoed, dismayed. It sounded like

forever. "I thought there was basically nothing wrong."

"Not *seriously* wrong," she corrected. "There's a difference. I think Dr. Ruben is concerned about building your strength back up. And making sure your head stays attached."

The nurse reappeared in the door and pointedly cleared her throat.

Miriam looked at her watch. "Better go," she said, giving me a soulful look and patting my hand.

Something else needed to be said. "I'm glad you didn't listen to me."

She looked puzzled. "Listen to you about what?"

"About staying home. You know. With your knitting. Otherwise, I wouldn't be here . . . to tell you I love you."

Her eyes filled with tears, and her voice quavered when she spoke. "Love you too, Jim."

And then she was gone. But she had left me with something very important.

A reason to live.

Those were possibly the slowest two days of my life. At first I was afraid to move much—out of fear that I would do something bad, such as pull out my stitches and lose my head. The second day, when they let me get out of bed to go to the bathroom, I kept wanting to hold my head, just in case. But it stayed firmly attached without my help.

Out of boredom, I found myself getting hypnotized by the television that my roommates turned on all the time. I had a different roommate each day, an Israeli Jew and then an Arab. Both were older men and big fans of Phil Silvers and *Hogan's Heroes*.

Nurses and doctors kept checking my neck and saying things to each other in Hebrew they probably thought I couldn't understand. But I did. The gist of it was that I was coming along very nicely, for someone who should have been dead.

It gave me a chance to witness to Dr. Ruben, a young resident who might have been humoring me to get me to talk. But he seemed genuinely interested in our brief religious conversations and said he would think about what I had to say. He peppered me with many questions and finally asked if I minded if he wrote about my case for a medical journal. I said I was used to being an oddity, and he laughed. I didn't tell him I wasn't entirely kidding.

Other than those interludes, there were just hours of putting my brain into TV idle and feeling my limbs go to sleep and my back get stiff. But it gave me time to think about a few things. Such as Miriam Boynton and my reason for living.

And, of course, about Aunt Dot. Dorothea Benson Cray. I needed to give her a call and break the bad news. I wanted to get it over with and get on with life. You can get pretty tired of listening to thoughts like that, mixed up with the wit and wisdom of Sergeant Bilko and Colonel Klink.

By the time they were ready to discharge me, I was ready to boogie—cautiously—out the door. Even if my head fell off.

I tipped the cabby outlandishly, like a man glad and free, and started to bound up the steps to the Rockefeller Museum. I quickly dropped that notion, as my body reminded me that it was a bit soon for that kind of exertion. Tomorrow I might take the steps two at a time; today I would dog it a little.

Miriam had said she would pick me up from the hospital, but I got discharged early, and I wanted to surprise her. I also wanted to talk to her about a few things that had been on my mind. I was feeling pretty good, considering—as they liked to say. I could see out of my left eye now, and, other than a flesh-colored bandage on my neck and a small cast on my hand, I was even looking arguably human again.

I could hear loud voices all the way down the hall as I approached my office, Freemantle's former haunt. It was two women, and I was pretty sure one of them was Miriam. As I got closer, I could tell she was the one talking in a more normal tone. The other woman was the one ringing the rafters.

I paused outside the door just long enough to get the general drift but not so long as to be considered eavesdropping. I knew that angry voice, and I knew I should know its owner. I opened the door.

It was Mme Catherine Lacuneau, red in the face and in a confrontational pose with Miriam, whose eyes flitted to me momentarily from her seat at her desk.

"It is none of your *business* who my friends and associates are!" Mme Catherine railed, emphasizing her point with an upturned, quivering hand.

"That's fine," Miriam replied calmly, "but neither are we under any obligation to release any documents to you even if your status were not under review by the Editorial Committee."

I let the door close loudly behind me.

Mme Catherine, whose back was turned to me, visibly started.

"Excuse me," I said. "Is this a private fight, or can anybody join in?"

Mme Catherine turned a withering gaze upon me. This was a different Catherine Lacuneau from the one I had known. Perhaps I was seeing the real person for the first time.

"Never mind," she snapped. "I was just leaving."

With that, she spun on her heel, clutched a manila file folder to her breast, and exited in what I imagined to be a swirl of fire and brimstone.

Miriam's coolness under fire now dissipated with a deep breath and a long, stressful sigh. She shook her head as if to dislodge a few errant curls. Then she stared at me wide-eyed in an astonished double take.

"What are *you* doing here?"

I smiled at her surprise. "They got tired of me at the hospital and told me to go do something productive instead of taking up bed space."

"Sorry," she said, looking sheepish. "It's not that I'm not glad to see you. It's just—I guess I'm having one of those days. I wasn't expecting you."

"What was that all about just now?"

"You remember when we were checking out phone records for Dr. Freemantle and Mme Catherine?"

"Sure."

She looked sheepish for the second time. "I should have checked my own."

"What do you mean?"

"My phone log had all kinds of calls to one of the places we knew Catherine Lacuneau had been calling. And another one that was quite a surprise."

"Let me guess. London?"

She nodded. "Correct. Gilbert West Literary Agency."

"What was the other one?"

"You'll never guess."

"Surely not Murray's Rare Stamps and Coins in New York."

Miriam shook her head. "Not quite. Mme Catherine may be a lot of things, but she is no stamp collector. Actually, it was London as well."

"OK. I give up."

Miriam assumed a look of righteous indignation. "Randall Plunkett."

My wheels began turning, slowly at first, then faster. "No. Are you sure?"

She nodded. "I'm sure. I called the number, and I got his answering machine. Listen to this." She hit the playback on her own answer phone.

"Hi-o," said a breezy English voice that I recognized instantly. "Randy Plunkett here. So sorry you missed me. Leave your name and number, why don't you, and I'll see about getting back to you. Have a decently adequate day."

"'Have a decently adequate day'?" I repeated, baffled. "What's that supposed to mean?"

Miriam shrugged. "Probably just his chic, supercilious sense of humor. If you have to ask, you obviously don't deserve to know."

"So Mme Catherine was in cahoots with old Tabloid Randy. But how did these calls end up on your extension?"

She nodded at my desk. "Have you ever looked at your phone closely?"

I looked at the instrument sitting on my desk, formerly Dr. Freemantle's. It had four lines, my own plus three others. I had used this phone only a few times and hadn't paid particular attention. But now I could see that one of those lines was 227. Miriam's extension.

"OK," I said. "I can see how it would be possible, considering Mme Catherine's relationship with the former occupant of this office. But how do you know it wasn't Freemantle himself calling those numbers in London?"

"I know this is circumstantial, but bear with me. First of all, many of these are dates when Freemantle was not in the office. Second, Mme Catherine was frequently seen working in this office. Third, this is the only office besides Dr. Starlander's that has my extension on the phone."

"But—"

"But wait," she said, holding up a hand. "There's more. I finally called Gilbert West and had a nice talk with his administrative assistant."

"Oh?"

"Yes. A woman named Ramona. I used the excuse of Dr. Freemantle's death to go straight at it. I explained that we were the late Dr. Freemantle's employer, and we wanted to know if he still had a book deal."

"And—" I prompted impatiently.

"And she said yes, a freelance journalist by the name of Randall Plunkett had agreed to step in and help finish the project with Catherine Lacuneau. The working title is *Deadly Sea Scrolls—The Grim Business of Biblical Scholarship.*"

"Plunkett, eh? And just the kind of sleazy project we'd suspected. Was somebody actually going to publish this tripe?"

"Acropolis Press. It's a done deal, and it's supposed to be out by Christmas."

"When did . . . uh . . . all this develop?"

Miriam smiled. "The phone records turned up yesterday, which is another story. But all the rest of it unrolled this morning. I told Dr. Starlander, and he has had all of Mme Catherine's files and effects impounded, subject to review by the Editorial Committee. That's why she's so upset. It may be a little harder to finish that crummy book without some of those documents."

"How did she find out about it so fast?"

Miriam shrugged. "We knew she was coming in today anyway. But I also suspect that she may have already spoken to Ramona or somebody else at Gilbert West and knew we were snooping around. She's not real happy."

"I could tell. She's beautiful when she's angry."

Miriam rolled her eyes. "So how are you feeling? You look great."

"Thanks. I feel 'decently adequate.'" I looked at my watch. "It's almost twelve. How about lunch?"

She nodded and gathered up her purse. "Where to?"

I moved toward the door. "How about Ehud's?"

"Fine, if not terribly original."

"I'm more into familiar today."

I didn't tell her that, with what I really wanted to discuss with her, I desired the comfort of familiar surroundings.

And in that day the deaf shall hear the words of the scroll, and the eyes of the blind shall see out of their gloom and out of darkness.
—Isaiah 29:18 (author's trans.)

31

At Ehud's I was reasonably relaxed and cool during our salads. I told Miriam about my discussions with Dr. Ruben. She filled me in on Dr. Starlander's new assertiveness, suggesting that I might have shocked him into at least beginning to acknowledge some serious problems on the Editorial Committee.

But knowing what I had to tell her, I found it hard to concentrate on these peripheral things, and my mind wandered. We were starting on our duck soup—more of a chowder—when my palms began to sweat.

Despite the lunch crowd, we had managed to get a fairly isolated table where we could talk. I would have no better opportunity. The time had come. I stifled rising panic with an effort. I couldn't let myself get tongue-tied or let the moment pass.

"Miriam," I began, "after I talk to Mrs. Cray this evening, I'll no doubt be wrapping things up here."

She almost stopped chewing, and her features assumed the kind of guarded look that goes with bad news.

"Yes," she said slowly. "Will you be . . . going back home soon?"

It didn't sound like a notion that pleased her.

"That's right," I agreed. "Not necessarily tomorrow or the next day, but . . . soon."

It looked as if she was swallowing hard. "So . . . is that pretty much it for . . ."

"Us?" I finished the sentence for her.

She nodded faintly.

"No," I said firmly. "It doesn't have to be. I certainly don't want it to be over. Do you?"

She shook her head, more definitely this time.

I had given some thought to this stage of things. "Would you give me your father's phone number?"

She looked stunned. "What?"

"Your father's phone number."

"What—what for?"

"I would like to speak with him about something very important."

"About . . . *us?*"

"Yes," I said, beginning to wonder about her incredulous reaction. "Is that OK?"

The blue diamonds of her eyes lit up spectacularly. "It's . . . very nice. What would you tell him?"

"I would tell him that I am outrageously head over heels about his daughter and that I would like his permission to . . . uh . . ."

Her eyes were dancing in the bright afternoon light streaming through the restaurant window. "To marry her?"

"Well," I stammered, "uh . . . yes, as a matter of fact."

"That's great. But why don't you tell his daughter first?"

And that was one of the things I loved about her. She was honest enough to force me out from behind my low-risk strategies. I didn't think I had blown it yet, but I would have to cut to the chase.

With every ounce of determination I could muster and more than a little perspiration, I forced myself off the diving board. "Miriam, I—"

And then I lost her attention. Her eyes broke from mine, lost their sparkle, and her face fell. I realized I wasn't the cause; it was something across the room. Something moving our way.

Zeev Nahat.

I was instantly full of fury. "Why, that—"

I felt a small foot atop mine, pressing lightly. "Save it," she said.

I couldn't believe this was happening all over again.

Besides that, I had more than a little unfinished business with Colonel Nahat. I thought of Jerry Simon's death and Kamlo's injuries and the Rebbe's misfortunes, not to mention my own wild scrolls chase, and it was hard not to hate. I had to pray silently for the Spirit to take over from the flesh.

"Dr. Harper. Miriam," Nahat said simply with a nod as he arrived at our table. "I'm not interrupting anything, am I?"

Miriam and I looked at each other, and we both laughed the laughter of tension release.

"No, nothing at all, Colonel Nahat," Miriam said mischievously.

I had to look hard for the reaction, but I did detect the briefest double take in his steely blue eyes.

"Sure," I heard myself say carelessly. "Have a seat, Zeev, old buddy."

To my surprise, he did just that, his angular frame slipping easily into a chair and scooting up to the table, on which he placed a package a little smaller than a shoe box. I hadn't originally noticed that he was carrying anything.

"I won't take long," he began. "It is not likely that I will ever see either of you again."

Miriam and I traded glances. I certainly had no idea what this was all about. I just wanted him to get it over with so I could get back to my marriage proposal.

"I am about to embark on an extended foreign service assignment," he continued coolly. "Miriam, I have just tendered my resignation to Dr. Starlander, who has accepted it. Dr. Harper, I just wanted to assure you that I had nothing whatever to do with that bomb that killed your friend Jerry Simon. Such things are totally repugnant to me. I have devoted a lifetime to opposing such things."

I nodded. His assertion seemed genuine, but would I have known if it wasn't?

316

There was more. "I know I can do nothing to keep you from writing about some of the things you have witnessed, nor would I try to. But I know you are an honorable man, and I would only appeal to your sense of discretion in not unduly jeopardizing the lives of others in the things you might make public."

I nodded again. It was something I would have to consider long and hard, especially when Randy Plunkett and Mme Catherine's book came out. No matter how egregious the lies that cried out for correction, I would have to think twice about doing anything that could provoke a Temple Mount conflagration. That was not something I wanted on my conscience.

"No promises, Colonel Nahat," I said respectfully. "But your point is well taken."

"That is all I can ask." Nahat stood up, smiled faintly, and without bidding adieu, turned to go.

"Colonel Nahat," I said. "Your package."

He turned, and all three of us looked at the box. Nahat smiled again.

"That is for you," he said. "A wedding present, perhaps?"

And then he was gone.

I was glad to get back to the subject at hand. "As I was saying—"

"Jim," Miriam interjected. "Aren't you going to open the package?"

I felt as if I were going down for the third time in an empty pool. This was crazy. I was tempted to jump up and shout, *"Will you marry me, already?"*

Instead, I picked up the box and examined it. It was then that I noticed it was a box for a bottle of liquor. Peppermint schnapps. But by its weight, I knew that was not what was within.

I flipped open the end flap and peered inside. And suddenly I was back in the Rebbe's house, reading from the Temple Scroll at gunpoint. Inside was what appeared to be one of the scrolls I had seen at the kibbutz of Har Habbayit Qannim.

I took a quick look around the restaurant, determined that no one was close enough to have any clue, tilted the box, and slid the object out. It had the same sort of cloth sleeve that I had seen before. My heart began racing all over again.

I couldn't believe that Nahat would have turned loose the Temple Scroll while breath remained in his body. Then what was this—the other scroll that had not been examined?

"What is it, Jim?" Miriam asked in a hushed tone.

"Well," I said, sliding off the sleeve and carefully unrolling the first column, "this appears to be your basic Dead Sea Scroll, right here on our stage."

"You're kidding," she breathed. "Which one?"

I was still trying to grasp the notion that it was a gift. "Until I can translate some of it, all I know is what it's *not*. I know it can't be the Temple Scroll because that's government property now."

Now I had it open far enough to begin reading the Hebrew. My skimming eyes hopped across key words like stones in a stream—King Ahasuerus, his 127 provinces from India to Ethiopia, and his wife, Queen Vashti . . .

"Hadassah!" I cried.

"So what is it?" asked Miriam, unimpressed.

"This is . . . unbelievable. It's the last missing biblical book from the corpus of the Dead Sea Scrolls—the book of Esther."

"Let me see," she said, excitedly now.

I turned it around for her to appreciate, flat on the box so none of it would risk contact with the table.

"It's . . . beautiful," she whispered. Then her eyes brightened. "Jim, I just realized—this is a personal vindication for you, isn't it?"

Words wouldn't come. They were stuck in my throat. In bittersweet retrospect, I realized that Freemantle hadn't been taunting me when he referred to a *Hadassah* scroll, despite our professional differences. He realized he'd been wrong, and he was big enough to admit it.

In fact, Freemantle had, in effect, given his life that this great corroborating ancient text of the Word of God might see the light of day. That all by itself made up for a whole flock of Mme Catherines and Tabloid Randys.

"Miriam," I said, my voice cracking, "this is something much bigger. Think about it—the ancient record of the biblical texts is now complete."

318

She shook her head as if in disbelief. "And think about the timing."

She was right. I had thought that my mission was a failure and that I was in serious danger of losing Miriam too. And now, just as the very words of commitment were barely upon my lips, it was all falling into my lap—like the manna from heaven. Mrs. Cray might not be getting her $17,500 back, but she would get this one-of-a-kind scroll text at an incredible price. I had not failed, after all.

"It's God," I asserted. "He has done exceeding abundantly beyond all that we could ask or think."

I reached out my hand toward hers.

With a smile that melted away all of my unbelief, she gave me her warm, soft hand. I was not about to let it go any time soon.

"That's not all," she said. "In case you didn't notice, you really blew me away when you asked for my father's phone number."

I smiled. "Well, yes. What was that all about?"

"I believe in those old values. And something that my mother said long ago has stuck with me over the years."

"What was that?"

"She said that if any man asked me to marry him, to think it over three times. If any man asked my *father*, I should not think twice. He's the one for me."

It was goose-bump time again. I had walked right into this little prophetic fulfillment without realizing it.

"I think your mother was onto something."

"And you can tell my dad," she said, "that his daughter says yes."

It was hard to speak. "I can't believe how much my world has just changed in fifteen minutes."

"That's *our* world now," Miriam corrected. "Say, I have a question."

Her eyes were twinkling, so I was on my guard. "What's that?"

She squeezed my arm affectionately. "You know how married couples have these little nicknames for each other? When we get married, can I call you Chuck?"

"Only if I can call you Dot."

"Well," she said brightly, taking off from that, "I guess calling Aunt Dot tonight won't be such a pain now. What will you tell her?"

Dorothea Benson Cray. She was one of the subjects I had thought so much about on my hospital bed. She and her mansion in Dallas with its antique clock measuring out time on a marble mantel. She and her fortune and her high-handed way of making a grown man feel like a second grader in the principal's office.

I laughed. I wasn't going to mind at all calling her. In fact, I looked forward to it.

"I'll tell you what I'm going to say. I'm going to tell her my name's Jim and not to call me Chuck. Ever again."

Moody Press, a ministry of the Moody Bible Institute,
is designed for education, evangelization, and edification.
If we may assist you in knowing more about Christ
and the Christian life, please write us without obligation:
Moody Press, c/o MLM, Chicago, Illinois 60610.